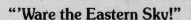

"'Ware the Eastern Sky!"

A dragon plummeted out of the clouds, its huge, batlike wings half-tucked at its sides, serpentine tail trailing arrow-straight behind. It streaked toward the defenders on the Tamisan side of the ford, toward their barricades, siege towers, and rows of upraised pikes. High-pitched screams rose as men caught one brief glimpse of the beast's deep, indigo eyes. Dragonfire obliterated the front ranks.

Keron gasped. Gloroc himself! The Dragon had come inland. . . .

The Schemes of Dragons

*Books by Dave Smeds
from Ace*

THE SORCERY WITHIN
THE SCHEMES OF DRAGONS

THE SCHEMES OF DRAGONS

DAVE SMEDS

ACE BOOKS, NEW YORK

This book is an Ace original,
and has never been previously
published.

THE SCHEMES OF DRAGONS

An Ace Book/published by arrangement with
the author

PRINTING HISTORY
Ace edition/March 1989

ISBN: 0-441-79559-5

Ace Books are published by The Berkley Publishing Group,
200 Madison Avenue, New York, New York 10016.
The name "ACE" and the "A" logo are
trademarks belonging to Charter Communications, Inc.
PRINTED IN THE UNITED STATES OF AMERICA

10 9 8 7 6 5 4 3 2 1

ACKNOWLEDGMENTS

This book would not have been the same without the contributions of the following people.

For material and financial support: Connie Willeford Smeds; Bob Fleming & Cherie Kushner; Alfred, Josephine, Fred, and Paula Smeds.

For commentary on the manuscript: First of all, to the Spellbinders, Inc., one hell of a writers' group—Deborah L.S. Sweitzer, Shirley Johnston, Brian Crist, Bob Fleming, Marian Gibbons, Patricia Albertoni-Stillman, Cherie Kushner, Jonathan Sachs, Walter Sauers, Lucy Buss, Dinene McClure, Ken Macklin, Steve Swenston, Marge Windus, Jon James, Hank Roberts, James D. Hudnall, and James Ellison. And to the others: Connie Willeford Smeds, Becky Priest, Paul Avellar, Jim Musto, Sheri Cohen, Robbyn Fenster, Kathy Payne, Sasha Miller, Joel Fruchtman, Obert Sonsten, Jamie Willeford.

For the cartography, astronomy, and some of the place names: John Gast.

THE CIVILIZED LANDS

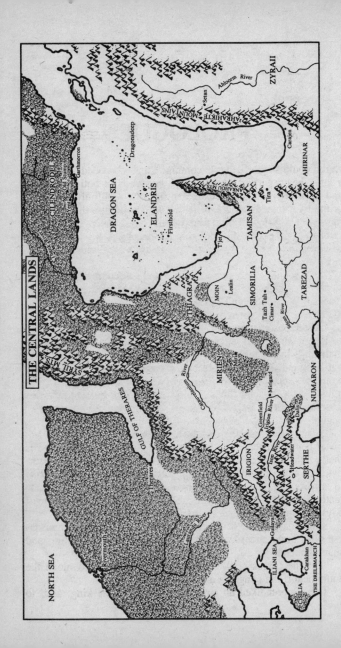

≈ PROLOGUE ≈

Keron could smell the battle coming. Clouds brooded, promising a long, heavy torrent. Below him, the troops of both defending and invading armies stirred like angry ants, with only the width of the river to separate them. *It will be now*, Keron thought. The rains would bring floods, and winter would keep the channel swollen. If the Dragon was going to establish his foothold, it would happen before the storm broke, while his forces could still cross the ford.

"Hail, King of Elandris!" the herald announced as Keron stepped out of his pavilion. Two pikemen automatically fell into place at their sovereign's heels.

"Where is the crown prince?" Keron asked.

"At the observation post," the herald replied.

Keron strode off at a pace that his men had a hard time matching. In his mid-fifties, the king was lean and strong, with not a strand of grey in his hair. *Wizard's blood*, his subjects would whisper. *The years flow slowly for the sons of Alemar.* Yet now there were sharp lines in his face that had been faint traces less than four years earlier, when the Dragon's offensive had begun.

He passed beside the smithies, assailed by the sounds of hot metal being quenched, of hammers, of voices murmuring spells that would bind carbon to iron. On the other side of the path, fletchers were feverishly attaching both new and salvaged points to arrows and complaining about the inferior quality of the feathers they had to work with, their pace still vigorous in spite of days and nights of constant work.

Keron flagged the armorer, a hirsute, barrelchested Tamisanese with arms and face scarred by a lifetime of smelting and shaping metal.

"Let the forges cool. You'll need to be ready to move the equipment if the Dragon's army overruns us."

The armorer fixed an antagonistic gaze on the king, as if to deny the prospect that Tamisan might be overrun. "Aye . . . Your Majesty," he said finally. The pause before the honorific was intentional.

One of his pikemen stiffened, but Keron held up a calming hand. It was not the time to argue over etiquette. The king continued on, past racks of freshly made swords and shields. He recognized a man at a grindstone as one of his own Elandri craftsmen, and nodded. The man lifted the sword he was sharpening in a brief salute, then set it down again into a shower of sparks. Elsewhere among the workers, among the native Tamisanese, Keron was met with glares and narrowed eyes. He could sense their thoughts: *You're the one who brought this doom upon us. The Dragon came to this land on your heels.* Like the armorer, they were not happy about his presence.

Allies bickering among themselves. Small wonder Gloroc's invasions had been so successful.

As he climbed the knoll to the observation post, he spotted his son. Val, young, strapping, and magnificent in his armor, was standing beside Treynaf, Keron's cousin.

"Father," Val called, "we've been expecting you."

Keron clasped his offspring by the forearms, smiled, and turned to scan the view. Down in the valley, the invading army was assuming its formation, readying for the command to plunge into the river. On the near bank, the men of Tamisan were lining up behind their barricades. On the left flank they were reinforced by Keron's army of exiles, on the right by a small contingent sent by the shah of neighboring Simorilia.

Keron was surprised to see Treynaf. His dour relative seldom emerged from his quarters for any reason, as shown by his pasty complexion. As usual, he had the globe of Alemar nestled in his palms, and was staring into it. Curiously, he lifted his gaze every few seconds toward the battlefield, as if comparing the scene in the valley to that within the talisman.

"What do you see, cousin?" Keron asked.

"The sultan has deployed too many men to the flanks," Treynaf replied with surprising certainty. "He has weakened the center."

Keron had only been half-listening. It was a joke among the Elandri refugees, from the common troops to the king himself, that Treynaf only foresaw the obvious. This was not the prince's usual type of prediction.

"That's ridiculous," Val said. "There are plenty of men in the center. The sultan has to place *some* elsewhere. The Dragon's

2

army won't all cross at the ford. They have boats. See for yourself."

There were dozens of dinghies and canoes among the Dragon's entrenchments. As they watched, soldiers carried more to the front.

"Well, Treynaf? What is your answer to that?" Keron asked.

"I see no boats," he replied. He was looking in the crystal ball, not at the river. Keron could smell an acrid, narcotic aroma each time his cousin exhaled. Treynaf was so drugged it was a wonder he could still talk.

"The Dragon is moving quickly," Val said. "I'd say they'll mount the charge within a quarter hour."

Keron scanned the increasingly organized rows on the far bank. "Best get down there. Enret will need you."

One of the pikemen brought Val his mount. "Keep in mind what Treynaf said," Keron added as his son climbed into the saddle.

The young man barely disguised his disdain. "I will," he said respectfully, and snapped the reins.

His countrymen would take heart to see their crown prince riding among them. Keron envied Val that role. As king, Keron could only look down and note how insignificant his band of refugees seemed beside the battalions of fresh, never-defeated Tamisanese. He had barely more than ten thousand men left after the fall of Elandris and the Dragon's subsequent campaigns through Thiagra. Down on the plain the sultan emerged from his pavilion. This was a Tamisanese fight now. Keron was little more than an old navy man driven to dry land.

He ran his fingers along the length of his scepter. He could feel its sorcery, latent, waiting for him to activate it. It was tangible evidence that the Dragon had not won everything. The talismans of Alemar Dragonslayer were still in free Elandri hands. The scepter was with him, the globe with Treynaf, the belt with Val, the amulets and the gauntlets with Alemar and Elenya, and the other, as yet inactivated articles kept by the royal cadre of sorcerers. Gloroc might yet be destroyed, and the wizard's dynasty returned to power.

Keron held on to that thought as tightly as he held the scepter. Perhaps the tide would turn here, in this land that even the Calinin had not been able to conquer.

The Dragon's army was not moving, though it had long been gathered into position. The horde was waiting. For what? Suddenly Treynaf snapped out of his meditation.

3

" 'Ware the eastern sky," he said.

A dragon plummeted out of the clouds, its huge, batlike wings half-tucked at its sides, serpentine tail trailing arrow-straight behind. It streaked toward the defenders on the Tamisan side of the ford, toward their barricades, siege towers, and rows of upraised pikes. High-pitched screams rose as men caught one brief glimpse of the beast's deep, indigo eyes. Dragonfire obliterated the front ranks.

Keron gasped. Gloroc himself! The Dragon had come inland! Away from the sea, the source of his magical power.

The attackers rushed into the river, driving toward the opening the Dragon had created. No one took to the boats. They dropped the craft on the banks and concentrated their manpower into a single phalanx. Treynaf had foreseen correctly. The attack was not spread widely. It would pound the center, where there were not enough defenders to bear the full brunt of it.

The Dragon blasted the barricades. This time some of the sorcerers of Tamisan overcame their shock and managed to erect wards. But the flames they deflected merely struck elsewhere, and at least one ward failed altogether. It was a rare wizard who could fend off a direct bolt of dragonfire. Archers shot their pitiful missiles at the Dragon's hurtling body, but if by some miracle their aim was true, the Dragon's own ward thwarted them.

The Dragon dived three times more, wrecking havoc, though less each time, as a sorcerer here or there remembered the ancient lore that a dragon's powers were weakened by the energies stored in dry land. The magicians called upon the spirits of the soil and their wards began to withstand, bouncing the blazes back up into the air. The Dragon trumpeted his mockery and abandoned the tactic. He had no more than one burst left anyway. He raced toward the knoll, straight for Keron.

Keron anchored the scepter in the earth. A ward spread, covering him, Treynaf, the pikemen, and most of the hilltop. The dragonfire enveloped them, raged for a moment, and withered without harming them. The Dragon seemed unconcerned. He flew back across the river, landing at the rear of his army.

Within moments, he had risen again, clutching something in his great talons. Keron felt a pang of recognition. Gloroc carried his burden over the Tamisanese trenches and dropped it. A curtain of flame leaped around a ward, dancing off it to lick at a siege tower. Oil. The Dragon was employing the tactic that had made his presence against the ships of Elandris so formidable. He

4

could fly high above arrows and other projectiles, dropping fire bombs until the wards of the victims gave out.

He destroyed the cohesiveness of the Tamisanese forces. His phalanx crossed the ford, splitting the defenders down the middle. Unless stopped they would continue straight up the slopes and attain the high ground.

"Sound the retreat," Keron yelled.

Trumpets blared. The sultan, if he survived, would curse him for a coward, but there was no choice. The Elandri troops responded to the signal, and gradually the Tamisanese and Simorilian forces also ceased their panicked scurrying and began to organize themselves, surrendering ground in an orderly fashion. The Dragon's army would win the river crossing, but it would not break Tamisan's back in one stroke.

Gloroc himself was the problem.

But even the Dragon was vulnerable. He was apparently drawing power from the storm clouds, but it could not be nearly as much as he drew from the sea. With him over land, several superb sorcerers working together could spin a trap, perhaps negate the fundamental spells that allowed his massive body to fly. Keron sent for his head magicians. He would gather them on the knoll and use the scepter to protect them during the casting.

Gloroc rose into the clouds, his laughter blanketing the battlefield, and was gone.

Keron felt like an eighty-year-old man. The Dragon had what he wanted: a beachhead for his army. He would let his human minions mop up, risk their lives, expand his empire. He had breached the last country on the coast of the Dragon Sea still free of his domination. Fear and time would finish the job for him.

Treynaf had stood like a statue throughout the battle, even when Gloroc had aimed his breath at the knoll. Now he stirred, spoke, his voice resonant, unclouded, poetic:

"A shadow shall sprout in the Dragon Sea
And grow till it covers the East,
Swallowing the armies that stand in its way;
On wizard's children dragons will feast."

"Spare me your auguries!" Keron bellowed. "I've had enough of your doomcrying."

Treynaf did not flinch. "Those were not my words. The stanza is one of the prophecies of the great seer, Shahera of Acalon, written fifteen centuries ago. It came to me suddenly."

5

"I don't care. Give me something useful. Give me knowledge that will help me fight Gloroc. Otherwise be silent."

"There is something there," Treynaf murmured, as if speaking to himself. "The poem contains a clue."

Keron scoffed. "Perhaps the line about wizard's children? Shall we poison your flesh and feed it to the Dragon?"

"I don't know." Treynaf stroked the globe. "I see a palace beneath the sea. I see a dragon, dead."

That, at least, was moderately cheering. For the thousandth time in his life Keron wished that some member of Alemar the Great's descendants would be born who could use the globe to its potential. He turned from Treynaf and found himself face to face with his herald.

"Summon two messengers," Keron snapped. "They're to carry the news of the battle. One will go to my son and daughter in Cilendrodel. The other goes to Struth."

The herald saluted and ran to do as he was told. On the battlefield the Dragon's men had seen that their momentum was checked. They fell back to reinforce their beachhead. Both sides resigned themselves to a long, bitter engagement.

PART ONE
ELENYA'S VENGEANCE

You let your magic tortoise go,
And look at me, frowning.
Inauspicious.

> —*I Ching*, 27th hexagram, first line

I

The strangers had been tracking him for two days. Toren stilled his breathing and listened again. The forest hummed with its sounds: a firemoth laying eggs underneath a nearby leaf, birds chirping in the heights, beetles rustling through the mulch at his feet. Yet, the frogs were quiet, back along the overgrown path where he had been not long before. By now they should have resumed croaking.

Toren bent down and loosened his moccasins. His legs throbbed from knee to toe. He had run as only a modhiv could run, for two days, foregoing food and sleep. The breeze struck his sweat-drenched clothing and sent chills down every side of his torso. His eyes burned.

He had run enough. It was no longer a case of personal danger. Before him was the stream that marked the borders of his tribe's land. Duty demanded that he protect his people.

He knelt on the muddy bank, pulled three small blocks of pigment from his pouch, wet his brush, and began his deathmask, using the stream's surface as a mirror. He took his time, painting the area under his eyebrows just so, mixing the colors to the exact hue he wanted, recreating the design that his grandfather's grandfather had worn to his grave. Once it had dried, he cast the blocks to the current.

So be it. If the strangers followed him now, someone would die.

He rubbed his feet, ankles, and calves with an ointment and waded into the stream, his passage making almost no sound. He travelled downstream at the same rate as the current, disturbing the silt as little as possible. Within a few minutes, a school of chikchik gathered around his feet, flashing their razor teeth inches from his skin. They smelled the ointment and swam on to find other, perhaps larger, prey.

Toren did not seize the first of the many branches that overhung the water, nor even the tenth. When he saw the one he

8

wanted, he used it to lift himself from the stream, crawled hand over hand toward the trunk, and waited until his feet had dripped dry. He jumped directly from the trunk onto a jumble of rocks and put on his moccasins. By the time he had to step once more on soft ground, he was many yards from the bank.

That would not stop the strangers from finding the trail, not if they had failed to be thrown off by the other, more sophisticated tactics he had used during the past two days. It would, however, give the impression that he was still trying to hide it.

He hurried into Fhali land. After an hour he passed a hoary, old tree where he had cached food ten days earlier, on his way to scout the territory of the Amane. The cache was still there, in a cleft long ago created by lightning. He scooped up the satchel and ran on. Presently, however, he began a wide circle that brought him within sight of the tree again, near the path down which he had originally come.

He hid deep within the brush beside the trail, tortured by the thought of the food he had retrieved. He didn't dare chew; the action of his jaws would dull his hearing. His ancestors encouraged him to have discipline, and he put hunger and the cold weather to the back of his mind. He focused his bloodshot eyes at the trail. Not once had he actually seen—or directly heard—whoever or whatever followed him, but he could sense the danger dogging his heels. There were at least two, possibly three, pursuers.

He took his blowgun from its sheath, selected a dart, and examined the brown smudge at the tip. Satisfied that none of the poison had rubbed off, he slipped it into the barrel.

Toren had never killed a man before. He asked his ancestors to help keep his aim steady and his breath strong.

Finally, Toren heard soft footfalls along the trail. While he remained hidden, a lone man loped past, his eyes on Toren's spoor, and stopped beside the old tree, examining the crevice from which Toren had taken his cache. Toren waited in vain for the appearance of the man's companions. The stranger was another Vanihr, probably a modhiv, tall and lithe like Toren himself, with long blond hair and smooth, golden skin. What tribe Toren could not tell. His bow was strangely shaped. His hair was tied high—behind the head, rather than behind the neck, and bound with a clasp of an unfamiliar metal. He wore a knife far longer than any Toren had ever personally seen, as long as the swords of the men of the Flat. Curiously, his bow was unstrung and tied behind his back. He carried a small net in his hand.

Toren was reassured to see a flesh and blood enemy—a weary-looking one at that. It seemed to him that only a spirit should have been able to track him so far, yet this was obviously a living being, alone and vulnerable.

Toren inserted the end of his blowgun through an opening in the foliage. The distance was not ideal, but he had the element of surprise and his lungs were rested. He aimed and fired. The stranger chose that moment to step away from the tree, turning not to continue along the trail, but to look back in the direction from which he had approached. The dart struck him in the upper arm, rather than the back.

The stranger cried out, flung aside his strange net, and clutched at the dart. Toren faded further into the brush, taking refuge behind a tree, out of arrow danger. He would stay out of sight until the poison took effect.

A spider web seemed to dance in front of his face. Suddenly the world went dark.

Toren felt cold ground beneath his legs, rough bark at his back, and ropes binding his limbs. His skull ached miserably. It was an effort just to open his eyes.

He looked up into the face of an animal.

In another moment, he realized it was a man, but one with hair all over his jaws and chin. Black hair. His skin was nothing like the golden brown of the Vanihr; rather it was pinkish, almost white in places protected from the sun. Even the memories of his ancestors contained no image of such a man. It was several moments before Toren was convinced that he viewed a human.

To the left stood the strange Vanihr he had fought, eating burrost from Toren's cache. One of his arms was in a sling. Beside him was a woman. She at least had no hair on her face, but her complexion was just as pale as the first man's, and her hair a deep brown unknown among Toren's people except in legends. Like the others she wore a loose shirt and full-length trousers tied at the waist and ankles. She carried another of the unusual bows. All three strangers had the haggard look of people who have led a long chase.

"Not feeling well?" the Vanihr asked, between bites. Toren could barely understand his dialect.

"No."

"Good. That was a nasty pin you stuck me with," he said, gesturing at the sling and the poultice of mud and grass over his wound. "I almost didn't find where you kept the antidote in time."

Toren tried to lift a hand to feel his swollen head, but not only were his arms tied to his sides, but his whole upper body was tied to the tree.

"What do you want with me?"

"We need you to kill a dragon."

Toren stared back incredulously.

"It's a long story," the Vanihr admitted. "But we'll have plenty of time to explain. My name is Geim. The lady is Deena. The one who startled you is our leader, Ivayer."

Toren scowled. He was embarrassed to have shown his fright to foreigners. "What is your tribe?" he asked Geim testily.

"I was once of the Ogshiel."

Toren stared. "That is far northeast, at the edge of the Wood."

"Yes. Near the Sha River delta."

"Your people fought the Shagas."

Geim shrugged. "In the past. There have been no Shagas on the lower river in modern times."

"Why have you journeyed so far from your home?"

"For you."

Toren shifted off a rock that was digging into his buttocks. "To get me to kill a dragon."

"You learn quickly."

"I think you have me confused with somebody else."

Geim said something to Ivayer. The latter held out a silver bracelet decorated with blue stones. Identical ones hung on Geim and Deena's wrists. At a word, one of the gems began to glow, throbbing from bright to dull. As the bearded man moved his closer to Toren, the pulsing grew more rapid.

"We used these to find you. When we began our trek, they were as lifeless as an Ijitian's mind. The farther south we came, the more active they grew," Geim stated. Ivayer touched his gem to Toren's ankle. Upon contact, the glow became constant. "There is no doubt. You're the one we want."

Toren shrank back. This was potent sorcery. "Where did you get these talismans?"

"We were given them by our mistress, the god Struth."

In a way, the use of magic soothed Toren's pride. It explained how people unfamiliar to the Wood could have caught him. He could tell from their blank expressions that Geim's companions did not even understand Vanihr languages. But what he was told made no sense.

11

"There are no gods," Toren said.

"Call her something else then, but Struth exists. I've talked to her, felt the wind of her breath. That's more than I can say for my ancestors."

The implication made Toren pause. "Your ancestors do not live inside you?"

"They do in you?"

"Of course. Ever since I came of age."

"The legend is true," Geim murmured. "We've heard it is this way among the southern tribes. Our shamans all died in the wars against the Shagas. There are none left to pass the memories from father to son."

Toren felt shame rising. Not only had he been taken, but it had been done by *cheli*—incomplete beings, subhumans. Better that he had been captured by children.

Geim bit off another piece of the burrost. Toren watched enviously, reminded of his empty stomach. The dried tree serpent was one of his favorite foods. To his surprise, Geim offered him some.

"I do not share food with enemies," Toren snapped.

Geim shrugged, and put the meat back in the satchel. "We're taking you back with us to the temple of Struth. It's in the country of Serthe, on the northern continent. A long walk. Eventually you'll want to eat something."

Toren glared back. "And how are you going to get me there? Drag me?"

"We have a means to gain your cooperation," Geim replied. "Now that you're awake we can proceed." He spoke to Ivayer. Toren could not understand the words, but he felt danger closing in.

Ivayer took off his magic bracelet and set it on the ground near Toren, then inhaled deeply, waved his hands over the talisman, and began uttering soft, rhythmic sentences. The strange poetry probed a place deep inside Toren's skull. He tried to shout in order to drown out Ivayer's voice, but could not. His throat was filled with something. It was crawling upward. Its hard, bulbous contour scraped painfully against his palate. He felt stubby, flat-bottomed legs walk across his tongue. His jaws and lips were pushed open against his will.

Toren panicked. He watched in horror as his totem emerged from his mouth and began walking down his body. When it slid off his thigh to the ground, he could freely observe that which he had seen only once before in all his life, on the day of his manhood ceremony.

His totem was a tortoise. It was blue, translucent, with white, pupilless eyes. It walked sluggishly toward the bracelet. One of the gems—not the same one that had been flashing earlier—was starting to gleam. The tortoise walked straight into the illumination, shrinking, until it vanished within the facets. Ivayer ceased his spellweaving, and exhaled sharply. A droplet of sweat fell from his chin.

"You've taken my ancestors," Toren whispered. He listened in the places of his mind where the familiar voices should be and found silence. The remembrances of past generations, which had seemed so much like his own memories, would no longer come to consciousness. He stared forlornly as Ivayer picked up the bracelet.

"We are sorry it has to be this way," Geim said. "If you had lived in the civilized lands, we might have offered you gold or iron. But we had nothing you value enough to make you leave the Wood, until now."

"You have made me a cheli. It would have been more merciful to kill me."

"The process can be reversed. Your ancestors can be returned to you."

Toren looked up, startled and suspicious. "After I've killed your dragon for you?"

"Before," Geim said. "All we ask is that you come with us to Serthe, and speak to Struth. She'll give your totem back to you. In fact, she's the only one who can. It's easy to put it in the gem, but only a god has sufficient magic to restore it to your body."

Toren stared at his feet. Ivayer spoke.

"Perhaps we should put it another way," Geim translated. Ivayer gestured to Deena, who untied the ropes. Toren winced as a rush of blood returned to his extremities. Ivayer held out the bracelet.

"Take it, return to your shaman. See if he can free your ancestors," Geim said.

"They would cast me out if they knew I had let foreigners defile my totem." Even his son would be compelled to shun him.

"Then it seems to me your choices are suicide, or coming with us, letting Struth restore you, and in time being able to return as a complete man."

Toren found it difficult to care what his alternatives were. That morning he had been a modhiv, one of the best scouts his tribe

13

had. Now he was not even a true Fhali. He could no longer call up the memory of the founder planting the tribe's home tree, only his own meagre recollections of the tree at its present, mighty girth. When he rose, it was almost as if someone else moved his muscles.

Geim seemed to smile. "This is not funny," Toren snapped.

"No," Geim answered quickly. "I was merely thinking of something that Struth said. She assured us that you would be a person with a well-developed sense of self-preservation."

Toren glowered. When Ivayer offered him the bracelet again, he waved it away. He would walk north for now. There did not seem to be any alternative. But that did not mean he had to stop behaving like a modhiv. When they set out, he was in the lead, as if he were the master, not the slave.

<center>~~~ II ~~~</center>

The main street of the hamlet of Old Stump rumbled with the sound of mounted soldiers. Citizens prudently sought the shelter of the buildings, where they peered cautiously from shadowed doorways and curtained windows. A high noon sun washed the community with hard, revealing light, giving the watchers a view more vivid than they would have preferred.

They saw twenty riders seated atop heavy battle oeikani, the thick-necked breed seldom seen in Cilendrodel. The animals' short, knobby antlers had been capped with brass cones, and on their forward feet their cloven hooves had been filed to cleaver-like sharpness, so that they clicked as they crossed the tiles between the hall of the elders and the home of the mayor, the only paved section of roadway in the region. The mayor's wife and daughters heard the clicking and struggled to banish the unwelcome memories summoned to their minds.

The riders were all dressed alike, in chain mail hauberks and bronze greaves. They carried broadswords, dirks, and wooden shields reinforced with copper bands, except that the pair of archers at front and rear had substituted bows and quivers for the shields. But most important for Old Stump's populace, each of the soldiers wore a red and black design on the right breast of

14

their jupons, so that there could be no doubt that they were the Dragon's men.

The second group of ten rode somewhat behind the first, leaving a gap at the center of the procession. The ninth and tenth riders were dragging something in the dust behind them. Owl, the tavernmaster, peering tentatively through the open half of his main doorway, decided the thing must have once been a man.

It was not easy to tell, even after the soldiers had reined up in the center square of the hamlet and lifted their burden up out of the dirt. The body had no eyes, no nose, no genitals. Several fingers and toes bent at impossible angles. His skin was covered with welts, burns, clotted blood, or in some cases was simply missing.

Four of the soldiers dragged the dead man to the center of the square. Until three years earlier the site had been home to Old Stump's great father tree, which antedated the first house. Now there was only a crudely hacked-off trunk, eight feet high, to which the soldiers tied their trophy. When the last knot had been cinched, the patrol leader dismounted and shuffled lazily to the spot.

The latter was stout but muscular, perhaps a bit less than forty years of age. He wore brass knuckles, polished to hot brilliance, and a sash of fine quarn silk. His cheeks bore shallow scars from a childhood bout with the pox. There were those in the hamlet who could remember the year when that sickness had swept through, taking one in ten of the children, and one in twenty of the adults. Others could recall when the man had been taunted by his juvenile peers because he had been afraid to climb the great father tree. Those were the days before Lord Puriel's nearby castle had been fortified as one of the Dragon's outposts, and many of Old Stump's homes taken over in order to quarter the men of the garrison.

The patrol leader pulled his dirk from its sheath and used the tip to carve a pattern in the corpse's abdomen, leaving gouges that seeped a few drops of cold blood. There were not many in the village who could read what was written; even the writer was merely copying it from a design he had memorized an hour earlier. They were characters of the High Speech of the Calinin, and they formed a name: Milec. In ancient days in the kingdom of Aleoth, this had meant fifthborn son of the weaver. It was a common enough name in Cilendrodel, but there was one particular Milec more famous than any other. When certain watchers

15

saw the letters formed, they knew the rumor of his capture had been true.

The carver finished his work and turned away. He found that an old woman was standing in the middle of the street, watching him. She lifted a bony finger at him and shook it.

"May your mother turn in her grave, Claric," she said, strong-voiced in spite of her age.

He laughed. "Aunt Seerie. Where are the menfolk? Afraid to show their faces? They leave old women to render their complaints?"

"This is a good man you have murdered," Seerie continued, as if Claric had not spoken.

"He was a criminal, condemned by Governor Puriel himself," Claric answered hotly. "It isn't murder to execute a rebel."

"And to mutilate him?"

"If he had told us what we wanted to know, he could have saved himself most of that." Claric climbed into his saddle. "The Dragon is not unkind to those who acknowledge his lawful rule."

From oeikaniback, Claric called to the buildings surrounding the square, "Tell the precious prince of Elandris and his whore of a sister that I will see them hanging from this same post one day."

He paused, as if challenging the village to speak, but no reply came. Then he spurred his mount and rode past his aunt in the direction from which he had come, missing her so narrowly that the wind of his passage nearly toppled her. She steadied herself with her walking stick. Half the patrol followed Claric at a gallop.

The ten men remaining, including all the archers, assumed stations around the square, two in the saddle, the rest standing. Seerie gave them a cold stare, which they met with disinterest. They joked as she limped away down the street.

By evening, Old Stump came back to life, in a quiet way. Light glowed from the tavern windows, and the lamp above its sign clearly displayed the name: Silver Eel, called that because of the house specialty, delivered daily by local fishermen. A new squad arrived from the garrison, and several of those who had guarded Milec's body throughout the afternoon gladly whiled away the first of their off-duty hours in the pub room. Houses rattled to the sound of children running and wives cooking. Citizens occasionally appeared on the street, until the curfew drew near.

16

There was even some activity in the square, though no one lingered there. An elderly man, with cataract-tainted eyes stopped and peered at the corpse, but a soldier's half-drawn sword kept him ten paces off. If anyone had any interest in the spectacle that went beyond morbid voyeurism, they hid it. Here in the shadow of one of the Dragon's strongholds it was not prudent to show concern for an enemy of the state. As Owl the tavernmaster put it, "Better him at that post than me."

In the small hours of the morning, a sentry yawned and thought once more of the relief squad due at dawn, and of the night's gambling that he had missed. Motherworld hung overhead, full and oppressive, staving off darkness with a bright orange glow. The shadows of the dead man's eye sockets seemed to hide an accusing stare. The sentry almost wished the rebels would try something, thereby relieving his boredom. But they would not. This was too deep in the Dragon's territory. If it had been otherwise, the guard would have been more numerous. The entire scheme had been staged merely to humor the Dragon's sorcerer.

It came as a shock, then, when the latter burst into the square, nearly drawing fire until the guards recognized his fine silk garb. "Have care!" the wizard shouted. "There is magic being cast."

The swordsmen drew their blades. The archers nocked their arrows and pointed them toward the shadows of adjacent buildings. But all they saw or heard for their trouble was a silk moth fluttering across the avenue toward the light of the tavern.

The sorcerer lowered his arms. "It is over now," he said.

"What was it, Master Omril?" asked the leader of the squad.

Omril stepped forward, rubbing his cheek in a habitual gesture, and sniffed the air at various points within the square. Eventually he strode up to the body of Milec. Even before he spoke, some of the sentries saw what he had discovered.

"The name is gone," Omril said.

Where Claric had carved Milec's name, there was now only smooth skin. One of the sentries made a sign against demons.

"Enough of that," Omril snapped. "It's only a trick." But he knew otherwise. It was a rare enough thing to be able to heal damage so quickly. To be able to do it to a corpse, and at a distance, was a talent beyond even the best of the Dragon's sorcerers.

One of the archers suddenly spun on the balls of his feet, pointing his weapon toward the middle of the street. An old woman bundled in a shawl was approaching, her shaky steps supported by a cane.

"It's Claric's aunt," one of the swordsmen declared.

"She's out after curfew. Arrest her."

Seerie made no attempt to shake off the hands that clamped on her thin upper arms. "A clumsy trap," she called to Omril. "Did you think the prince would let himself be caught?"

"If he wants the body, he or his men are going to have to stand revealed. Trap or not. If he doesn't come, then Milec will stay until he rots, and that will be a lesson in itself."

"I suspect he'll not rot, however long he stays there."

The sentry made the sign again. Omril felt another sliver of doubt, picturing the corpse's fingers straightening out, its skin becoming pink again. "Are you the rebel's spokesman, then?"

"I am only an old woman, who has lived too long already," Seerie stated. "And so I can speak my mind freely." She started to say something more, but stopped to stare behind them, eyes wide.

They all turned to look at the body. One of the archers gasped. Omril's jaw dropped, and he probed more thoroughly, but to his consternation sensed no magic in the vicinity.

"It has wings!" a swordsman yelled.

The body looked as if it were covered with a horde of huge moths or dragonflies, all fluttering at great speed. As the man watched, the ropes fell away, and Milec began to rise upward. Both archers fired. Omril saw at least one shaft strike home in the dead man's thigh, then the body was airborne. It shrank to a silhouette against the globe of Motherworld, and was gone westward, toward deep forest.

Seerie laughed.

Omril turned toward her with fury. "He's gone, but we have you. Will you be so smug in the governor's dungeon?"

"I am on Death's door," Seerie said calmly. "I have a cancer. I have no fear."

"You will," Omril promised.

"It is you who should fear, you and Lord Puriel and my nephew Claric. That was no ordinary rebel you killed."

"I have the favor of Gloroc himself," Omril said. "I'm not afraid of your prince."

"It is not the prince you need worry about. It is the princess."

⇝ III ⇜

At Ivayer's gesture, Toren stopped in his tracks. They had reached a bend in the path. Ahead, barely visible through the underbrush, they could see a hayeri nibbling at the leaves of a collberry tree. It was a young animal, sleek with fat—enough meat to last them several days. Toren had wondered when the foreigners would notice it; he had smelled it a dozen paces earlier.

Ivayer gestured to Geim, who drew out his throwing net. The undergrowth, which would have interfered with an arrow, seemed not to worry him. His prey browsed, unaware. Geim threw the net lightly, but once released, it picked up speed, flying over the brush and enveloping the animal's head. The target went down as if struck with a heavy mallet.

Ivayer strode forward at his leisure, finished off the hayeri, and settled down to gut and dress it. Geim, handicapped by his stiff upper arm, assisted as best he could.

Deena, as usual, nocked an arrow and guarded Toren while her companions were occupied. Toren, however, was not thinking of escape. He sat on a bed of ferns to observe the gutting. The men worked with a practiced air.

"Do you always butcher your game yourself?" Toren asked.

Ivayer and Geim both seemed intrigued that Toren had initiated a conversation. "Of course," Geim answered. "How else would we do it?"

"If possible, a modhiv would take it back to the village and let one of the hunters deal with it."

"A modhiv?"

"I am a modhiv," he said disdainfully. "We watch the tribe's enemies, fight the skirmishes, inspect the borders."

Geim nodded slowly. "I see. Among the Ogshiel, warriors and hunters are the same caste." He tapped his gutting knife. "Things change when one has no ancestors to tell the living how things should be."

Toren was shocked. Geim not only was unashamed that he had no totem active inside him, he actually seemed proud of it. He

19

should not even talk to such a heretic. Yet, perversely, questions rushed to his tongue.

"That net—another gift of Struth?" Toren asked. His head still felt swollen. He had originally believed himself to have been knocked out by Deena or Ivayer, until Geim had mentioned that the other two had rendezvoused with him later.

"No," Geim replied. "This was given to me by Ivayer's teacher, a wizard named Obo, when he learned what our mission was to be. You'll meet him. He resides at the temple."

"Is that your home now, too?"

"Yes, of course."

"Why did you come to live so far from your birthplace? Were you banished?" It was hard for Toren to conceive of any other reason why a Vanihr would leave the Wood.

"Not exactly." Toren was not sure what he saw in Geim's expression, amusement or wistfulness. "Let's just say I had to leave in a hurry, and it wasn't wise to return. Still isn't, as far as I know."

Ivayer had neatly skinned the hayeri. Geim laid the hide on the ground as a platter on which to place the meat as it was cut. Toren gazed longingly at the handsome chunks of flesh yielding to the foreign metal. Ivayer noticed and said something to Geim.

"You ought to be truly hungry by now," Geim translated. "If we cook some of this now, will you eat with us?"

"No."

"Suit yourself," Geim said. "Frankly, I wonder why Struth made us go to so much effort to catch you." He held out a crimson hand, palm down. "I see only this kind of blood on your hands, young modhiv. You have never taken a human life. How you'll manage to take that of a dragon is a mystery to me."

Toren frowned and looked away, eyes level.

They finished the butchering, wrapped the meat in its skin, and settled the bundle onto Toren's shoulders. "We'll give you some more time to decide about the food," Geim said. "Ivayer wants to cover some ground while the weather's good."

By early afternoon, the clouds thickened and turned black. Thunder rumbled off the low hills to the north. Small animals darted by, their concern for shelter superseding their fear of humans. Not far ahead they saw a huge, flat boulder straddling two others, forming a natural pavilion.

"We'll make that our camp," Geim told Toren, after Ivayer had given the directive in the northern tongue.

Toren smelled the shift in the air and knew that the deluge was already falling. They could see a curtain of rain obscuring the opposite side of the valley. They arrived under the shadow of the rocks just as the first droplets struck. The full torrent soon followed, pasting dead leaves and humus to the ground, driving the shrews out of hiding, and turning every low place into a puddle or stream.

They found a colony of snakes tucked in the cleft at the base of one of the boulders, and dispatched them with swords. A pair of hawks watched cautiously from a shelf just under the overhanging rock. Otherwise the arch seemed designed for the four travellers. The floor was flat, and well protected even when the rain was driven slantwise by gusts of wind. A firepit had been constructed at the center, and wood had already been gathered and stored where it would stay dry. Ivayer dug in the ashes and found nothing but cold char. The only recent spoor around the hearthstones belonged to various species of animals.

"A modhiv camp," Toren explained. "Used by wanderers. This territory belongs to no tribe." It was used primarily by the Fhali. Toren himself had slept here on occasion.

Ivayer nodded with satisfaction once Geim had translated. Since the torrent would prevent anyone from spotting their smoke, they built a fire and took advantage of the opportunity to cook the hayeri meat.

Toren sat with his back against one of the boulders, disturbed by a gnawing tick of apprehension. It was the storm. Though the lightning had passed, and they had found an excellent place to wait out the sky's fury, he knew that afterward there would be mud. Soft ground made it difficult to hide tracks.

Eventually he managed to doze, though it was fitful. He dreamed of playing with his son, and it made him lonely. He waited in vain for the voices of his ancestors. The scent of food drove him awake.

Deena was holding out a strip of roast hayeri. "*Lom,*" she said.

Toren shook his head firmly.

Rather than withdraw her offering, she pointed at the sections of the animal still cooking. "*Lom,*" she repeated.

This time he understood. "Meat," he said in Vanihr.

She mimicked him easily. Both languages used only one syllable for the word. Next she pointed to the knife with which she held the morsel, and said, "*Kolich.*"

In response he gave her the general term for bladed weapons, rather than one of the array of specific names a modhiv might use.

She nodded, and used the knife to cut the meat in half. *"Kolich zebret lom."*

"Knife cuts meat," he translated. As Deena began chewing one half, she held out the other to him. *"Um lom,"* she said emphatically.

He took the strip.

If she felt triumphant, she disguised it with a modest smile. Toren forced himself to be dignified—chewing slowly, taking small bites, as if he were not at all hungry. The truth was that the first taste made his need much worse; until that moment his body had been reconciled to its continued lack. In what seemed like seconds he was swallowing the final bit.

She made no move to get more. Instead she gave him water, taught him her word for that, the verb for drinking, and then another ten words.

"Toren *um lom*," he said finally in exasperation.

She smiled and cut another strip hot off the spit. While it cooled she taught him a little more, corrected his pronunciation, and eventually rewarded him with the meat. He endured it by reminding himself that his shrunken stomach would only accept small portions anyway. She had by far the greatest impudence of any female he had ever encountered. She dressed in warrior clothing, carried weapons, and treated him as if she were his equal, perhaps even his superior. He wondered how he could subject himself to her behavior, but on a less conscious level, he appreciated the attention. It filled the hollow space left by his ancestors' absence with human companionship.

The rain slowed to steady, moderate precipitation, wet but no longer violent. Geim and Ivayer consumed their fill of the roast and began drying most of the remainder of the hayeri into jerky —as well as could be done in the limited time they had—by hanging strips high above the fire. While it cooked, Geim joined Deena and Toren.

"Yriha gam habet," Toren told him. Deena chuckled.

"I'm afraid I didn't understand that," Geim replied. "Deena has been teaching you the language of her homeland. All I've ever learned of it are the greetings and swear words."

Toren hesitated. Just how many peoples were there in this place to which he was being taken? "I said—I think—that your legs are hairy."

Geim smiled at the joke. Like all Vanihr, his only prominent

22

body hair was that in his armpits and around his pubic area. Deena had hairier legs than he.

Once Geim had seated himself, Deena spoke to him. Toren tried to understand a word or two, and found that he could not. But that was to be expected. They would be conversing in their mutual tongue. Listening closely, he was pleased to be able to catch the different flavor of the sentences.

Geim seemed thoughtful at what Deena had said. Presently he told Toren, "She would like to know what is considered the primary duty of a modhiv."

"To protect the tribe from its enemies."

"That's what I told her. She wonders if you will understand, then, our motives for kidnapping you."

Toren stared into the flames. His captors mystified him. They were cheli, yet they seemed honorable—they had not abused him more than necessary even though he had tried to kill one of them. The thing that struck him most, however, was that it was now clear to him that the three of them represented different tribes—different races—and yet were united in their effort.

"The dragon threatens you all?" Toren asked.

"Yes," Geim said firmly. "In all honesty, I believe that if Struth's plan fails, eventually the Wood itself will feel the weight of Gloroc's rule."

Toren searched Geim's face thoroughly, but could see no trace of guile, despite the incredible claim he had made. He glanced at Deena, and saw the same sincerity. "I don't understand," he said finally, "but tell her I will be thinking about it."

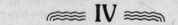 IV

Elenya sprinkled the seeds of sweet herbs over the grave and raked them under the newly-turned soil. Alemar handed her the water bucket, from which she took three handfuls in studied precision and cast them in droplets over her planting. Finally she lowered the sprig, its length thick with the tiny flowers that, after a season, would decorate the entire mound. Their fragrance rose through the heavy foliage toward the sunlight.

Milec the rebel had found his resting place.

On Elenya's left hand the gauntlet twitched, humming like a

wasp caught in a bottle, its jewels casting off sudden, multicolored sparks. She stared at the grave, saying nothing.

Alemar turned to face the solemn assembly. His gauntlet, while silent, throbbed with a glow no less vivid than the display from his sister's. "Let's leave her alone," he said, waving everyone toward the shelter of a massive broadleaf tree. His twin made no acknowledgment of their leaving.

Alemar found a grassy spot and sat against the tree's trunk. He rubbed the puffy edges of his eyelids. He had never before tried to heal a dead man's flesh, and he doubted he ever would again.

Wynneth came to him holding a ewer and a gold cup. He caught the smell and wrinkled his nose.

"No, no, no," she said firmly. "You know you need it."

She filled the cup and handed it to him. He drank it quickly, wincing at the vile taste. It was his own concoction, and would mitigate the enervation brought on by such strong sorcery.

"Thank you," he said, a trifle insincerely.

"You would have forgotten it altogether," she scolded. "I'll not have a husband looking like an old man."

"Look who's calling whom old," he said. "You've got over a year on me."

She smiled and filled the cup again.

Even his wife's camaraderie could not banish the funereal gloom. They had lost both a good friend and a capable ally. Milec's father had been the lord of the province of Yent, one of the original victims of the Dragon's sudden takeover of Cilendrodel. The son had been among the first to join Alemar's small band, and he had proved to be not only a staunch fighter but an invaluable liaison between the rebels and the displaced royalty of the nation.

Alemar glanced at one of the lookouts half-hidden in the brush. The governor's patrols were combing the area around Old Stump in hopes of catching the rebel prince and princess. Though the rythni watched as well, the two dozen men and six women of the party kept their bows strung and their sword hilts unbound. Inevitably Alemar's gaze fell on his sister's back. He could see dirt from the gravedigging caught in her long black hair.

"It did me good these past months, to see her with Milec," he told Wynneth. "I would catch her smiling for no reason at all. Meeting him was one of the few joys she's had since we returned from the desert."

"I know," Wynneth said gently. "Don't dwell on it. You can't bring him back."

24

He sighed, and put an arm around her. "I just wanted Elenya to experience what I've found."

Wynneth nestled her head in the crook of his neck. "I wanted that for her, too, my love. Do you think she would have found it with Milec?"

"What do you mean?"

Wynneth kept her eyes down, as if she regretted bringing up the subject at that time. "I mean that they were good for each other, and they were infatuated, but I don't think Elenya would have married him. She's waiting for someone. I don't know who. An ideal maybe, not a living man at all. Someone she can respect as well as love."

Alemar plucked a wildflower from the ground. "Yes. You're right."

Wynneth closed the lid on the ewer and set it in the grass. A streamer of sunlight momentarily peeked through a gap in the canopy of leaves and lit her short, brown hair. Even in her mid-twenties, she still had a baby face. Some people were shocked to discover the strength behind it.

"Where will we go next?"

Alemar shrugged. "Toward Garthmorron, I think. There's more uninhabited land out that way. We might find the space to breathe."

"And then?"

"What are you getting at?"

"We've played cat and mouse with the Dragon for three years, waiting on Struth before we take the offensive."

"Yes. But now the end is in sight."

"In six months or a year. We may not have that much time. It was well known how important a member of our band Milec was. If Puriel could lay hands on him, the common people will conclude that all of us will be taken. The price on your head and Elenya's is fifty amath pearls each. Even the most loyal to the cause could be tempted by that. If they believe the Dragon will win in the end anyway, they may feel there is nothing to lose. Unless we make a bold move, the revolt will be snuffed out."

"I'm afraid that is true," Alemar conceded.

"I know you and Elenya have been discussing the matter. What have you decided?"

"Nothing. I wish I could be more like her sometimes," he said, gesturing toward his twin. "She knows her way and follows it without hesitation. I forever debate which road I will take. Are you so eager for the fight?"

25

"No," she stated firmly. "But Puriel must die."

He blinked, startled. Gradually he nodded. "Yes, unfortunately that much is clear. What I am not certain of is how horribly he must die."

It was Wynneth's turn to be startled.

"Vendetta is a serious thing," Alemar said. "I learned that much in my years in the desert. I worry that when I am done, the people will look at me with just as much fear as they reserve now for the Dragon."

He reached out with is left hand—the one without the gauntlet—and gently stroked his wife's abdomen, feeling for the life growing inside it. "What sort of legacy will I leave this child?"

She rested her hands on top of his.

Finally he said, "Tonight, when we're well away from Old Stump, I'll confer with the rythni. I'll need their help."

The murmurs of the camp were indistinct behind him, as Alemar sat at the pool's edge, waiting. Serpent Moon was full, its white and blue reflection dancing on the water, the image's purity soiled by the glow of Motherworld, hidden somewhere behind the canopy of leaves. An iridescent gleam of tiny wings appeared over the stream. A moment later the rythni had settled on the moss-covered boulder beside him.

"*Heeoo, Hiephora-bani*," he said, quietly so as not to overwhelm her sensitive ears. She was not quite ten inches tall, slender and smooth almost to the point of androgyny, face wreathed in abundant dark blue tresses. Like all rythni, she went unclothed, but unlike most, she wore a fine gold chain around her neck.

"Greetings, Prince Alemar," answered Hiephora, her rendering of the High Speech as smooth as if it were her mother tongue. Her voice was tiny, barely able to be heard above the hum of nearby insects or of frogs calling from the stream. "You have committed Milec to his gods?"

"Yes, we have," Alemar stated solemnly.

"Our bard has already made a song about last night. It is called 'The Hero with a Hundred Wings.' May I teach it to you to pass on to your minstrel?"

"Yes, I would like that. But first, tell me how it went with your elders."

Hiephora perched cross-legged on the moss. "They're much like your own elders, I would imagine, only more so because of the centuries they have lived. To hear them talk, you would think

26

I made my women kill a man, instead of rescuing the body of one from unkind hands. No matter. Am I not a queen? I left them to argue among themselves."

"How is the casualty?"

"The arrow only grazed her. She'll be fine. The elders had a fit about that, of course."

Alemar hesitated.

"I see a troubled conscience," Hiephora said. "Tell me what burdens you so."

"What if I *were* to ask you to kill?"

She looked as if she had been stabbed. "That would be another matter."

"Your people would not wield the blows. But their actions would result in the death of others."

"I see. I feared this, when they took Milec. I understand the human need for revenge."

"If it were vengeance alone, I would bide my time, run away as I have for the past three years. Certainly I would deal with it without troubling you. This, I'm afraid, is a case of self-preservation."

The moon and planet glow created deep shadows under the rythni's eyebrows, which made her expression seem doubly serious. "As for myself, there is no question. Gloroc is a great evil, and his governor a reflection of him. However, I cannot order my subjects to follow me, though many of them will. This defies tradition enough that my elders may well rouse out of their bowers in order to discipline me. We might soon both be rebels."

"Then you must not do it," Alemar said quickly.

"I made my decision to be part of your destiny years ago," Hiephora answered softly, "the day I tipped over your mother's cup of amethery. Do what you must do, prince, and I will be there."

He paused, as if to protest, but she held up her hand. Finally he sighed and touched his fingertip to her palm. "So be it," he said.

Music drifted through the forest of Cilendrodel, past the many watchful, tiny eyes. Wynneth waited by the fire, while Alemar sat with Solint the Minstrel, playing in unison "The Hero with a Hundred Wings" on lute and cittern. By now the musician had caught the tune and Alemar had to concentrate to match him. It did Wynneth good to see her husband apparently absorbed with the song.

Presently she glanced up, and saw a small, manlike form flit across a path of half-night sky. At the same time, she became aware that someone had joined her.

"Wondering when they'll talk to you?" Elenya asked.

Wynneth made room for her sister-in-law. "I would be surprised if they ever did."

The firelight splashed over Elenya's face. There were no tears on her cheeks. "They might. You're like him," she said, gesturing toward her brother. "The same gentle soul. They can see that."

"Alemar tells me they used to talk to you."

"When we were children," Elenya said pensively. "I even learned a little of their language. But it ended when I reached puberty, and it never did compare to the rapport Alemar had with them. To be truthful, I didn't mind; I was too busy becoming a woman, or a fencer, or a princess."

Wynneth stared fixedly at Elenya. Her husband's sister had been completely silent on the journey from the grave site to this camp. Even now, her preoccupation was obvious from the pattern of her speech and the ominous warbling of the great wizard's amulet at her throat. Wynneth rubbed her belly nervously.

Elenya noticed the motion, and said, "Alemar told me last night you're pregnant."

"True," Wynneth said, and self-consciously took her hand away. "As a matter of fact, it was he who told me. He knew what had happened within hours of conception."

"Where will you go for the birth?"

"I don't know yet. Somewhere north, away from the coast."

Elenya stretched her gauntlet closer to the fire, letting the flames reflect on the polished metal. "Do you know, I have never even considered the thought of having a child?"

Wynneth waited several moments before speaking. "I know," she said finally.

"What will it be, a boy or a girl?" Elenya added after an equally long pause.

"A boy."

"Good. That's good."

A son of the Blood, Wynneth thought. And, now that Keron had been declared monarch of Elandris, in the absence of a capable leader among the survivors of the late King Pranter's more immediate family, the child might one day be a contender for the throne. That was assuming that the Dragon's possession of the kingdom could be ended, and the dynasty of Alemar Dragon-slayer restored.

The women's conversation died out, and did not resume again that night. The music became a lullaby. Wynneth stirred from a doze to find that Alemar had left the minstrel's side. He leaned over, kissed her on the lips, then helped his sister to her feet.

As their gauntlets touched, they crackled with static. For a moment, Wynneth saw not her husband and sister-in-law, two people whom she knew and understood well, but two frightening, powerful beings. They stood face to face, short, lean, dark-haired magicians, descendants of perhaps the most powerful sorcerer ever to have lived. They turned together, walking away from the camp to confer, using the wordless method permitted by their amulets, leaving Wynneth to her all too normal humanity. Her thoughts turned to the child inside her. Would he one day frighten her as much?

 V

The dungeon reeked. Seerie smelled stale urine, mildewed wood, dank stone, and rats. Occasionally there would be a scuffing of feet or a muffled groan from one of the cells across the corridor, but Seerie made no attempt to communicate. Damp straw and dirt sent rivers of cold into her bony rump. She guessed she had been there for at least twelve hours, uncertain because she had dozed some time after the jailor had shoved a plate of unappetizing gruel under her door. The vermin had eaten it.

The pain was back, dull and throbbing, low in her abdomen. She accepted it along with the other discomforts. Soon enough there would be release from all of them.

A new sound dragged her out of her feverish reverie. Heavy boots reverberated on the wooden slats of the walkway. The glimmer of lanterns filtered through the bars of the peephole.

Keys rattled in the lock. The door swung outward. Seerie blinked her eyes, trying to adjust to the illumination. A lumbering silhouette took two steps into the chamber, while the jailor waited in the corridor.

"Aunt Seerie, the Dragon's magician has summoned you!"

Claric held the lantern high, casting garish streaks of light and shadow across his face. His gold tooth gleamed.

"The captain of the guard is now an errand boy," Seerie observed.

"Mind your tongue, old woman. I'm here for the pleasure of it."

"Obviously. You haven't changed, only grown worse with a lord who indulges your vices." She met his glare squarely, in spite of the distance he loomed above her.

"I might show you your place, Auntie, but Omril wants you intact, and I've no need to lift a finger to you. You're half a corpse already. What's the good of your fancy healer prince if he can't cure one old woman?"

"I will be glad to die, rather than live knowing I have kin like you," she said calmly.

He poked her sharply toward the door. She winced, but masked the reaction immediately, and started to walk. The jailor led the way through the maze of cells. Claric pressed uncomfortably close behind her. She had trouble keeping her balance on the slats. She reminded herself that they were easier to negotiate than the naked floor of mud, and carried on stoically, knowing that the less she seemed to suffer, the less Claric would like it.

The stairs were much worse. Before she had climbed to the servants' level, her right knee began to wobble ominously. She began to gasp. The jailor returned to his station, leaving Claric to nudge her backside the whole trip up to the lord's level. A guard smirked at her as she was hustled along a hallway. She marched on, determined not to stumble, though they had taken her cane when they had arrested her. At least the way was level now.

To her dismay, Claric directed her toward another flight of stairs. She began to climb them, depending almost entirely on her left leg. She crumpled on the fifth step.

Claric cursed, but rather than exhort her to get up, he slung her over his shoulder like a sack of flour and continued on. The Dragon's mage must be in a hurry, Seerie decided. She wanted to jab her elbow into her nephew's kidneys, but she was too exhausted to bother. She hung limp, nose full of the odor of sweaty leather.

They passed a narrow window, and she could see that they were ascending the northwest tower of the stronghold. Outside the sunset was mirrored in the water of Rock Lake. It was a view much too beautiful for the likes of Lord Puriel.

At the end of the stairs Claric rapped on a heavy door. They heard the wizard's command to enter, and, obeying it, found him contemplating the same scenery. His quarters filled the top of the tower. Along every wall were cabinets and shelves filled with books, scrolls, and vials of various powders and liquids. Pigeons cooed in a small coop. At the center of the room was a broad, finely polished table, on which stood a single scroll, weighted down by a pair of exquisite sculptures of dragons.

Claric dropped Seerie ignominiously on the floor, bruising her weak knee. She forced herself not to cry out.

"Leave us," the wizard told Claric.

Claric did so, without a word. Seerie made a note of it. Claric only gave this sort of silent obedience to someone he feared. Yet Omril had lived in Cilendrodel scarcely more than a fortnight.

Seerie did not bother to glance up as Omril walked slowly toward her. She could see his deceptively young face reflected in the gleaming marble floor.

"You are well thought of in Old Stump," Omril said, evincing none of the anger he had displayed in the town. "That is, according to the reports I've collected today."

Seerie's eyebrows rose in spite of herself. "You asked about *me*?"

"How else am I supposed to learn anything?"

Seerie did not know what she had expected when summoned to the magician's presence, but it was not this. "Come, sit down," he said, shocking her even more.

"What do you want with me?" she said, finally facing him. It was hard to do. His pale eyes left her feeling as if she were naked. She sank uncertainly into his cushioned chair.

"Why, knowledge, of course. You are the rebel's spokesman."

"I told you before, I am only an old woman."

Omril shrugged. "I speak metaphorically. Sometimes important facts hide in the most trivial of places." He gestured at the open scroll on the table. "Take this, for example. I found it in the library of this castle. It's considered the definitive work on the rythni, thin as it is. Yesterday I would have considered it a work of fiction. An hour ago I read that their females are winged during their reproductive years. Now I understand how Milec's body was spirited away."

Omril lifted one of the paperweights and allowed the scroll to close. "This prince and his sister are a danger to my master. My mission is to learn as much as I can about them. You'll tell me all you know."

"No. I won't."

31

"You'll resist, of course," the wizard said judiciously. "But it won't do you any good. Have you heard of dragon-touching?"

Seerie sank deeper into the chair.

"The human version is far weaker than that of a dragon, as one might expect, but Gloroc is an excellent tutor. It takes special training to be able to thwart the technique. Regrettably Milec had such training. You, I perceive, have none. It's best you don't struggle. It will save me from leaving permanent damage."

He uttered a word in a language Seerie did not recognize, and suddenly bands of silk sprung from the rear of the chair and bound her. Within a beat of her heart she was rendered immobile. Omril placed the bar against the door, moved a stool next to her, and took her hand. His grip was frighteningly gentle.

"Look at me," he said.

She did not want to obey. She kept her face turned. But she could not resist one quick, apprehensive glance. For the barest instant, her eyes met his. That was all it took.

Two soldiers of the garrison left the house, laughing at an obscene joke, and headed toward the Silver Eel. Seerie stood in the shade of the tree across the lane, stifling her rage. The soldiers had occupied the house for only two months, yet already the shrubbery she had so carefully cultivated had died. The men had carved their marks in the door frame. A pile of refuse had grown under the front window.

She had moved into that house as a bride. With her husband dead, her home had been the greatest comfort of her elder years. Now she had only a room in her sister's small residence. According to the new regime, old women did not deserve houses of their own when men of the garrison could make use of them.

She glared at the departing figures, most especially at the Dragon's insignia on their shoulders, and hobbled off to a part of the hamlet where she would not have to view what used to be.

The pain in her gut flared again. She groaned and tried to stretch out completely, hugging the bedcovers to her neck to ward off another sudden chill, but her abdominal muscles would not relax. She hardly noticed that her sister had entered the room, nor that she had brought someone with her.

He came forward into the candle glow. He was short, lean, black-haired, and wore a green cape. His right hand was enclosed in a jewel-encrusted mail gauntlet. . . .

Seerie felt a tug at her mind, halting the flow of the memory.

Over and over she saw the gauntlet, just as she had that night: *The metal seemed to be gold. Tiny gems were placed at regular intervals across its surface, as well as a large, brilliant stone on the base knuckle of each finger. Each of the larger jewels shone with a different color. It was not the candle light they reflected; the illumination came from within them. At the sight of such a talisman, Seerie knew the identity of her visitor.*

"Lilara," she murmured to her sister. "How did you . . . ?"

"I didn't bring him," Lilara said. "He just appeared at the door."

"I heard of your condition," Alemar explained. "I've come to see what I can do."

Seerie swallowed. Dared she hope? Before she could speak, he took her hand in his bare palm, closed his eyes. His expression grew blacker. He sighed and looked at her with compassion.

"It is your time," he said solemnly. "I cannot stop the progress of this disease. Your body wishes to die."

She looked down and nodded. She had feared it. In a way, it relieved her to be told the certainty of it.

"However," he added, "there is something I can offer." He withdrew a flask from his pouch, pulled the stopper, and tipped the spout to her lips. She took a small amount. It tasted like wine, lacking the bite of fermented fruit, but mimicking the rapid, suffusing warmth of alcohol. It had hardly reached her stomach before she felt her belly begin to unclench. Not only was the pain fading, but she could think more clearly than any time for the past week.

"One sip per day will ease your suffering, yet leave your mind unclouded." He gave the flask to Lilara. "That contains as much as you are going to need, I'm afraid."

"How can I thank you?" she asked.

"Drink my medicine," was all he said.

When she saw the twenty riders dragging their grisly burden down the center of Old Stump, Seerie knew she had borne as much as she could. "I'm going to follow them," she told her sister.

Lilara waved her pudgy hands in alarm. "What will you do?" she cried as Seerie reached for her cane.

"I will speak my mind," Seerie answered, and opened the door. The procession was well ahead of her; but she knew their destination. Lilara begged her to come back, but did not herself emerge from the house. Seerie turned a deaf ear. She would

33

*confront the nephew who had driven his mother, her youngest
sister, to an early passing; she would speak against the governor
who had ousted her from her home; she would proclaim the no-
bility of the prince who had eased her pain. She would do what
others, with something to lose, feared to do.*

Seerie came gradually to consciousness. The memories lingered like vivid dreams, detailed, but unreal. The incidents no
longer felt like personal history; they struck her as moments from
someone else's life.

Two men were talking. She opened her eyes and found that
she was still in the chair, but the bindings had disappeared. Several candles and a pair of lamps lit the wizard's room, brightening
what Motherworld provided through the windows. The air was
cooler. She knew then that far more time had passed during the
dragon-touching than she had perceived.

She glanced up into the gaunt visage of Lord Puriel, governor
of central Cilendrodel.

"That's all?" he asked Omril. He glared at Seerie, tugging
absently at his slate grey beard.

"She is strong-willed," the magician stated, brushing a piece
of lint from his fine attire, "but she hadn't the skills to keep me
from seeing what I wished. She is what she claims, only a dying
old woman, angry at the change in her fortunes."

Seerie felt color rise in her cheeks. She felt raped, exposed,
tossed aside. All her noble plans of the previous day had resulted
only in giving the conjuror information about the prince's gauntlet.

"She's worthless to us, then," the governor said, as if in echo
of her thoughts. "She can rot in the dungeon with the other trai-
tors."

"I suggest not, my lord."

"Eh?"

"She will be dead in less than a fortnight, even if we give her
your lady's chambers and feed her sweetmeats off silver platters."

"All for the best, then," Puriel said.

"I mean that it is pointless to keep her. She can do us no harm
outside. If she dies while incarcerated, some of the populace may
conclude that we fear old dames so much that we murder them.
She would become a martyr."

Puriel scowled and twisted one of his many rings back and

forth on his finger. "I see. Very well, then, we'll let her go. Not that I care what the rabble believe."

"My lord is wise," Omril said, with what seemed to be honest deference.

Seerie was not fooled. Puriel did not deserve such a capable ally. Seerie feared for the rebel twins. The Dragon had sent one of his best after them.

There was only one small way in which she could be of help. The idea made her heart race. If only. . .

Whether by fate or conscious intent, her wish was granted. She was dead before Puriel could summon the guard to escort her out of the castle.

≋ VI ≋

The sunlight had barely begun to filter through the trees when Toren and his captors broke camp. The rain had quit early the evening before, but its effects were still omnipresent. The leaves sparkled, heavy with moisture; the ground squished beneath the travellers' feet; and a chorus of frogs was loudly celebrating its good fortune.

Toren stared at the crumbling ash of their fire. The ring of hearthstones was the last evidence of Fhali presence he would be likely to see. His grandfather had placed some of those stones, though the memory was now lost with the totem. He whispered the ritual words spoken when taking leave of the dead, and turned his back to his tribe's land.

He walked for four days like a drugged man, taking no interest in his surroundings. Deena taught him a few words of her language each time they camped, but he memorized the lessons with some distant part of himself. He did not care which forks of the trail they took. Each morning when he was roused, he would already be longing for the night, when his weariness would pull him quickly off to sleep.

What would his son be thinking? He was due back at his village. As the days passed, would Rhi assume that he had been killed? Surely, after a month, he would.

Rhi would have to be adopted by his uncle, or his grandfather, and plan to receive their totem in place of Toren's. Toren wished there were a way to tell his son that he would be back in time. It would be many years before Rhi's manhood ceremony. Surely he would be back by then.

The voices of his ancestors sent no comforting words.

On the morning of the fourth day, something intruded into his fugue like a woodpecker battering at a weather-hardened tree. He stopped.

Geim barely avoided bumping into him. "What is it?"

Toren shook the dust out of his head. "I don't know," he said, but even as he spoke he felt a familiar, ethereal tug. In the past he had always interpreted the sensation as the speech of his ancestors. The signal pulled him past Ivayer, down the trail to a large boulder.

The top of the stone was flat. Bones had been placed there.

Toren pointed. Ivayer picked one up. It was a human ulna. There were also a few ribs, a section of a tibia, and several other smaller fragments difficult to identify. Each showed indentations left by filed teeth. The hair on the nape of Toren's neck began to rise.

"It's a border marker. We are entering the territory of the Amane," Toren told Geim.

"Amane? The cannibals?"

"Yes. I have a bad feeling."

Geim frowned, and translated Toren's comments. Ivayer ran a finger along the gnawed surface of the bone he held and answered in slow, thoughtful tones.

"How far is it around the Amane nation?" Geim asked.

Toren pointed east, then west. "Their range stretches all the way to the coast, and all the way to the Flat."

Ivayer seemed displeased with the news. Eventually he tossed down the bone and jerked his thumb at the trail. Geim translated his comments.

"We came through on the way south. In fact, it was near here that we first spotted your tracks."

"You were lucky," Toren responded. "By this time they may have discovered traces of your earlier visit. They will be more vigilant."

"Nevertheless, there doesn't seem to be a way around them. We will go on."

"Then give me my blowgun back so that I can give an accounting of myself before I am eaten."

Much to his surprise, Ivayer granted the request, though they

36

made him place his pouch of darts on the rear of his belt, where it was in plain view of Geim and Deena. The latter, as usual, kept a nocked arrow in her bow.

Ivayer led the way. Toren kept his weapon in his hands. He drummed his nails against the hard reed tube. The premonition refused to fade.

The forest, contrary to his mood, was bright and fresh. Birds twittered through the branches, gathering material for nests. The moist humus and the recently washed leaves gave off a thick, fecund aroma. As they passed through occasional clearings, Achird's rays beat pleasantly on their shoulders, mitigating the late winter chill. The scene should have had a cheering effect.

Half a day's hike past the border marker, the sensation of danger suddenly overwhelmed Toren. He pitched forward into the mud. An arrow whistled over his head.

Ahead, Ivayer screamed, dropping to his knees, struck by another arrow squarely in the center of his chest. Toren rolled into the brush. He saw Geim dive for cover. Deena, however, stood her ground, her bowstring drawn back as far as she could pull, feathers at her chin, searching the brush. She fired. Someone screamed. Deena bolted for the protection of a fallen log. An arrow caught her in the forearm, just as she ducked out of sight.

Toren turned back to Ivayer. His face was a rictus of pain. He clutched the shaft in his heart. He had a few seconds at most to live. Yet, to Toren's amazement, he sloughed the bracelet off his wrist and threw it to the modhiv.

As Ivayer collapsed, the woods filled with the sound of charging men, at least two coming down the trail, and others through the foliage at either side. "Run!" Geim shouted. As he called out, an arrow grazed his upper arm, ironically the one Toren had wounded days before.

Before the archer could reload, Toren sprinted down the trail toward Geim's postion.

An arrow hummed past his side and ricochetted off a small rock.

Toren cursed. The latest missile had come from a new direction. An archer in a tree was cutting off their retreat.

Geim launched his net. It snared the archer. The man gave one spasmodic jerk and fell to a hard impact beside the trail.

From the original direction, four Amane warriors burst into view, bearing spears and shields.

Toren fired his blowgun. The dart caught in the thick hide of a shield. There was no time to reload. Toren jumped behind the log where Deena had taken refuge. Geim was already there. He had finally had time to pull his bow from behind his back and draw an arrow from his quiver.

The Amane lifted their shields and kept coming. Geim drew back and released. The arrow raced completely through the shield and sank deep in the lead warrior's body. The Amane staggered, jaws agape. The second Amane collided with the first.

Deena's wound made it impossible to use her sword. She drew it and shoved the hilt toward Toren. Geim eliminated the third Amane as he had the first, then the fight became too close for archery. Toren brandished the sword and the fourth man, perhaps daunted by the worsening odds, halted his charge. Neither he nor Toren would commit to a thrust or a throw. In the meantime, the second Amane recovered his footing.

Geim drew his sword. It was an almost instantaneous motion; one moment his hand was empty, the next it held the blade. "Out of the way!" Toren barely managed to comply. Geim waded in, slashing. Both Amane stepped back, shields out. But the thick leather and wood were not equipped to thwart a steel edge. The first two cuts opened huge rents in the shield of one warrior, the next drove through that of the other man and sliced his arm.

The Amane reevaluated their postion, turned, and ran away.

Geim tensed as if to rush after them, but Toren yanked him sideways. An arrow flew by. The remaining archer was still vigilant.

"Come on," Toren said. "The Amane like to patrol in bands of eleven. That means there are four we haven't seen yet."

Geim sheathed his sword, picked up his bow, and they retreated, keeping behind cover. On the way Geim recovered his magic net from the fallen archer's body. When they were sure they were out of the surviving bowman's line of fire, they straightened up and quickened their pace.

The entire ambush had taken about two minutes. Toren's head spun, thinking of all that had happened in that time. He scarcely noticed that he was loading a dart in his blowgun, but because of it he was the person most prepared when they rounded a massive tree and found themselves face to face with another pair of Amane.

The cannibals seemed equally surprised by the encounter. Toren aimed his weapon and blew with all the force his lungs possessed. His dart disappeared to the feathers in the gut of the closest man. The second one reacted instantly, driving toward

Toren with his spear. Toren twisted, but it was not sufficient.

Geim drew his sword and cut downward in a single motion. The blade clipped off the spear head. The blunt shaft slammed into Toren's abdomen, knocking the air out of him. He and the Amane fell together to the ground. He stared straight into his enemy's glare, smelled the breath erupting between filed teeth. Geim followed through. The glare went dim. Deena pulled off the spasming body while Geim dealt with the man Toren had wounded.

Toren sat up. His upper abdomen throbbed. The spear haft had torn his skin open, badly bruising the muscles beneath. Finally he was able to inhale.

Geim kneeled down beside him. "Are you all right?"

"I will be shortly," Toren wheezed. "I am lucky you know how to use that sword so well."

Geim shook his head. "I am an amateur compared to the men who instructed me. I started too late in life."

Toren's attention was sucked in by the last feeble, waning movements of the Amane he had shot. Geim had wielded the deathblow, but poison so near the heart had guaranteed loss of life. A dose of antidote would not have worked in time. Toren had killed a man.

They heard no indication of pursuit, so Geim allowed Toren a few moments to recover, and went to Deena. She, due to their previous haste, still carried the arrow in her forearm. The shaft had travelled completely through so that it jutted out the far side. Geim broke off the point and drew it out. She bit her lip, tears welling, but made no outcry. Geim bound both entry and exit wounds.

That done, he picked up the discarded obsidian tip and examined it, frowning.

"The Amane do not use poison," Toren commented. "They believe it taints the meat."

Geim nodded, and tossed the point away. Deena said something emphatic to him. He glanced at the cut on his arm and grunted. Though superficial, because of his exertions during the battles it was bleeding badly. At Deena's insistence, they delayed even longer while Toren bound it.

They were ready to go. Geim glanced doubtfully to the right and left. "This time, you choose," he told Toren.

Toren picked a direction at random, and they set out.

≈≈ VII ≈≈

Bats glided low over the lake, scooping up their minute prey. Occasionally, one would flit past Toren's vantage point, twittering, only to be lost in the modest light of Serpent Moon and Urthey. Though dusk was barely over, it was the darkest part of the night. Toren readjusted his stance on the rocks and noted with satisfaction the activity on the shore. In the past half hour several hayeri, a troop of forest monkeys, and finally a moon cat had come to drink at the lake's edge, obscuring the traces left by the passage of Toren, Geim, and Deena. It was only the last of many tactics the humans had used to conceal their spoor in the hours since the fight with the Amane.

Toren turned his back to the lake and climbed down the outcropping to join his companions. "I think we're safe for the moment," he told Geim.

The northern Vanihr's arm remained limp in his lap. The wound had opened sporadically throughout their run. Deena also had lost a significant quantity of blood. Toren had been forced to wait for them more than once.

"No premonitions?" Geim asked.

"Not since soon after we left. Perhaps the other Amane didn't find the battle site right away; perhaps they felt they had lost too many men."

Geim nodded. He was being especially quiet. At first Toren believed it to be the pain in his arm or fatigue, but the alert glare of his pupils belied it. The northerner stared toward the direction of the ambush, stiff-jawed.

Toren knew of one other reason why they had not been followed, but he did not say it loud. Geim thought of it anyway.

"We should have plunged one of your darts into Ivayer's body. The poison might have prevented the cannibals from molesting it."

"There wasn't time," Toren said. He realized the fact was not much consolation. "They will sooner eat their own dead," he added quickly. "They believe their totems are made stronger when they consume the flesh of family members." That did not

40

mean that the tribe would refuse to eat Ivayer, but Toren avoided that point.

"There were five of us when we set out from the temple," Geim said morosely. "We lost one to a forest stalker, and another to an infection. Now Deena and I are the only ones left."

Toren was surprised that he could feel sympathy for persons who had captured him and stolen his totem. He lifted the bracelet. "He did not think of himself at the last. Instead, he saved my ancestors."

"Of course."

"Because I am valuable to you?"

Geim sighed. "Believe what you like." He shifted gingerly, taking special care not to jar his arm. Toren marvelled that he had managed to wield a bow and a sword despite the wound and the lingering effects of the blowgun poison. "I don't know how I'm going to tell Obo that he has lost his apprentice. He had high hopes for Ivayer. He regretted having to send him on this quest. Said he's seen too many people dear to him sent off to distant lands."

Toren remembered Obo as the individual who had made the magic net. It was unclear how he fit into the scheme with Struth, but Toren realized that Geim was speaking not so much to his listener as to himself, and let the conversation lapse.

Toren raised a blowgun dart up to the moons' light. During their flight, he had continually pictured the Amane he had shot. He had always imagined that his first kill would be different. With all the memories of his ancestors, some of whom had been modhiv, available to his call, he had "seen" what it was like to slay someone. Though some of the images were not pleasant, he had thought himself inured. A warrior was required to kill. He had done so honorably, in self-defense, swift to the mark. It was proper vengeance for all the Fhali who had gone to the cooking pots. Yet it bothered him. There were no internal voices to reassure him; there was no hero's welcome as he carried the news to his village. There was only a dead man.

The night breeze, seasoned with the scent of the lake and its reeds, was cool. It gave him goose flesh. They did not dare light a fire. He rose and paced.

Deena had gathered the bows and had tried to unstring them. Her injury had prevented it. Toren finally noticed and lifted the smaller weapon out of her limp fingers.

"Bow," he said.

"*Mennich*," she replied.

41

He began to unstring it. And grunted. It took far more effort than he anticipated. Once the tension was gone, the bow actually bent in the opposite direction. It was not simply wood, but a composite of wood and bone, bound together with sinew. He examined it for several minutes, noting the fundamentals of its construction. When he picked up Geim's bow, rather than unstringing it, he selected an arrow.

The northerners stiffened as he armed himself, but neither tried to interfere. Toren drew back the shaft and aimed at a rotting log twenty paces away.

The arrow impacted with a hard, lethal cough, drilling deeply into the wood.

The firing power was at least double that of a Vanihr bow. Yet, Toren was certain his shot was considerably weaker than what Geim had been able to effect earlier that day.

"Hold the string, not the arrow," Geim said. Toren did not understand what he meant, so Geim showed him. Instead of pinching the nock in order to pull back, he placed a finger on either side of it and pulled the string directly.

Toren tried the method. Thanks to the unaccustomed grip his shot flew slightly to the side, but it punctured the log so deeply that the pile came out the other side. He was unable to dig either arrow out of the log in one piece, though he salvaged the metal. He ceased experimenting before he used up any more of their precious supply.

He pictured Geim's shots penetrating completely through the hide shields of the Amane, and his steel sword severing a spear haft in one blow.

"Does everyone have bows like this on the northern continent?" he asked Geim.

"They're known everywhere outside Vanihr lands."

Toren pursed his lips. It was no longer so bizarre a thought to imagine a dragon and his army sweeping over the Wood. He pointed to the bow and the sword. "Will you teach me how to use these weapons as we go north?"

Geim seemed to read the sentence for all its implications. "Yes," he said firmly. "I'll teach you anything you ask, if it's within my ability."

"Good." An image came to Toren's mind: his son and father, greeting him with pride as he returned from far-off lands, bearing knowledge that would profit the tribe. For the first time, he did not feel like a total captive.

He unstrung the bow and set it aside. It was time to eat; he had not carried the hayeri jerky this far, on the run, to see it go to waste.

For once, Deena did not offer any language lessons. It was halfway through the meal before she spoke at all. Geim translated.

"You knew ahead of time that the Amane were going to attack. How?"

"I always know when danger is near. It's an ability I've had since I was a boy."

"Does anyone else in your tribe have this talent?"

"Not as far as I know."

"Didn't you wonder about it?"

"I asked my shaman about it once, when I was interested in becoming his apprentice. He said it was a minor gift, good for a scout."

"And you believed him?"

He stared Deena straight in the eyes. "Yes. Of course," he replied, but the question clung to his mind long after the meal was over. When he went to sleep, it was still there.

As usual, he dreamed of home.

Beside Toren were all the other modhiv candidates of the Fhali, twenty youths arranged in a long line, each one standing straight as a spear, trying not to reveal their intimidation. Olaxl, the high master, paced in front of them, his aging eyes alert and still able to stare down the bravest of his pupils. Who would he chose?

The old man stopped in front of the tallest of the group, a muscular boy with heavy-lidded eyes.

"Borei," the high master said.

The candidate stepped briskly into the sparring circle. Toren felt his pulse quicken. Borei was fast. His strikes left bruises.

"Toren."

The student next to him let out an audible sigh of sympathy. Toren's feet tingled as he crossed the packed earth. He kept his glance on Borei, his opponent, avoiding Olaxl's stare. He dared not show weakness to the high master. Olaxl had the sole power to determine who would be made a modhiv and who would be dropped as a candidate. To lose his respect was to suddenly join the ranks of the hunters. Toren was close to his coming of age; it was past the time to begin an apprenticeship in one of the other specialized castes, such as the healers or artisans, and far too late to study to be a shaman, as he had once fantasized. Caste choice had to be made before he received his totem. It had to be based on his own abilities, without help from the memories of ancestors. If he failed now to become a warrior, a hunter was all that would be left, a role of no distinction. His father and brothers were hunters.

This match might be like any other. Or it might be the one that Olaxl used to make his decision. A candidate would never know until after the fact.

"Begin," the high master commanded.

Toren knew he had to move first. He circled, kicking to Borei's ribs. Borei blocked, kicked back, and Toren fended off the leg by pressing his foot into the other's knee. Borei used the spin to swivel around and kick with the other leg. The technique caught Toren neatly on the navel, a perfect impact, landing solidly but not penetrating, letting Toren know he'd been hit, yet not leaving damage—ideal control.

Toren blinked. He felt but did not see a strike to his ribs. Another whisked by his cheek. He backed up. Borei closed the distance immediately. He felt the wind of a blow in his ear lobe, the firmness of a foot landing in his gut, an open hand pressing on his shoulder.

Then Borei was on the ground, gasping for breath, and Toren's wrist was smarting from the pain of an ill-prepared strike to Borei's midsection.

"Stop!" the high master called.

Olaxl did not glance at Toren, who remained at stiff attention in his starting place. Instead, the elderly modhiv bent down and gripped Borei underneath the arms and pulled him to his knees, stretching out his chest to counteract the cramping of his diaphragm. Within a few moments Borei was able to inhale. Olaxl allowed him to regain his composure, then gently ordered him back to his place in the line. All eyes turned to Toren.

Goose pimples crawled up the young candidate's spine. If he had made a small error, the high master would have chastised him privately, but this was to be in front of all the others.

Olaxl said calmly, "You thought Borei was going too fast, that he would lose control and injure you. So, in your fear, you injured him." The high master glanced down the line of candidates, letting them know the message was for them, too. "We must never forget that, though we train in killing arts, the partners we work with are members of our own tribe. Do not be so mistrusting, Toren. The ability to know one's allies is just as important as to recognize one's enemies."

And it was over, as if the incident had not occurred. The others would remember it as just another lecture. Not so for Toren. It was the only one of Olaxl's lessons he ever ignored. He had *known*, without question, that Borei's next blow would have hurt him.

"Wake up."

Toren was alert instantaneously. Geim squatted nearby. The constellations above said that it was midnight.

"Your watch," Geim said.

Toren had scarcely climbed out of his bedroll before the other Vanihr settled down to sleep, leaving him alone with the night. Toren thought it ironic how quickly roles had reversed. The previous night, he had been under guard. Now he was the guard.

Deena snored lightly a few paces away. She looked like a child curled up in her blanket. She was small compared to most Vanihr women. A lock of her impossibly brown hair had fallen in front of her nostrils. Toren lifted it away before it woke her.

He keened his senses. No danger in the air. Amane territory might surround them, but they were safe. He was certain of it. He had never before had quite such faith in himself. For many years he had disregarded his own abilities, laying his trust in the accumulated wisdom of his ancestors.

His shaman had lied to him.

He could not keep pace with all his thoughts. The world was changing. He was still displeased to have to make the journey north, but the tracts of forest ahead no longer seemed so daunting. While his ancestors slept, he would be awake and learning.

≈≈ VIII ≈≈

The forest reverberated with birdsong. The fragrance of honeysuckle clung to the breeze. The glade reminded Elenya of the one where she had often hidden as a little girl, a short way inland from Garthmorron Hold, away from the roads, where the foliage locked out the revealing light of the sun and the shadebrush grew so thick that a child could avoid an adult with ease. Her nostalgia was appropriate; Garthmorron was only a few leagues away.

Behind her the other rebels went quietly about their activities.

Wynneth groomed a oeikani; Solint the Minstrel repaired his doe-skin jerkin; Dushin and Iregg, having served on the night watch, were catching up on sleep. Elenya guarded the trail.

It was a harder task than usual. Over the past year, at times such as this, Milec would have been with her, perhaps taking advantage of a few hours out of sight of the other members of the band. She idly plucked her bowstring. Seven days he had been dead and buried. Now the flight from Old Stump was behind them and she had time to think about peaceful moments gone by.

Hoofbeats.

She nocked an arrow and pointed it at the path. In due course a lone rider emerged between the boles of the giant trees, thread-ing carefully along a way meant for deer, not their larger cousins, the oeikani. Elenya let him continue well into range.

"Well met, Sir Enns," she called.

The rider flinched, and stopped his mount. He stared toward the foliage where she knelt. His glance continued to wander, searching the shadows for some sign of her. Eventually he gave up.

"Well met, princess," he said. "I see you are not wearing white."

"Not today. How went your mission?"

"We've food for a week. It should be ready to fetch almost immediately."

"Good. You'll find Alemar by the spring."

Enns nodded and continued into the camp. Elenya set her arrow on the ground, but kept an eye toward the trail in case Enns had been followed.

After about half an hour, Alemar joined her.

"Two people need to go back with Enns to bring the supplies. Care to go?"

His expression was far too innocent. "Are you thinking I need something to occupy my mind?" she asked.

Alemar managed a guilty smile. "Enns suggested it this morn-ing. Wynneth and I both thought it was a good idea."

She shrugged. "I suppose it is. I'll go."

"Good," Alemar said, appearing relieved. "Dushin's awake. He'll be the third. If you leave now you can be back well before sundown."

They each took two animals, one for riding, one as a pack beast. Their destination was a silk farm out on the extreme edges of the settled area surrounding the community of Eruth. The

46

farmer was sympathetic to the rebel cause, though, like most of Cilendrodel's populace, he did not make his loyalties public. Once or twice a year he would accept rebel funds and purchase foodstuffs and other supplies for Alemar and Elenya's band, leaving them in his barn to be picked up while he and his family were absent. The scheme was deliberately designed to leave as little direct contact as possible between him and the outlaws.

Elenya rode at the back, though she knew this region as well as any of the party, having been raised in the vicinity. She avoided conversation, though she liked both her companions well enough. They had shared a great many trials. Dushin had joined the band two years earlier, after a price was set on his head for having slain the Dragon's soldiers that he had caught raping his niece. Enns, a member of the Cilendri royalty dispossessed by the Dragon's occupation, had known the twins before they left for the Eastern Deserts, and ever since their return had accompanied them in their relentless flight back and forth across Cilendrodel. They did not seem to begrudge her her contemplation.

Enns led them along a twisting, almost invisible track, designed to circumvent roads, though those were not common in this sector of the province. Finally Elenya began to smell the peculiar odor so common to this part of Cilendrodel. Abruptly they left the wild timberlands behind and entered a grove of silk trees, so called because their fragrant leaves were fed to the worms that spun the famous quarn silk. They could see nubs and indentations on the branches where some leaves had been recently harvested.

Elenya felt the watchful gaze of the rythni vanish. The little folk chose not to suffer the discomfort they always felt upon entering an area where the hand of man had disrupted the nurturant energies found in native woodland.

They emerged from the trees into the grounds of the silk farmer's residence. There was a modest house, a stable, and a long shed for the cages of worms. The buildings were nestled in the shade of several massive silk trees, away from the sunlight that would reduce the worms' rate of production. As arranged, no one was home.

They dismounted. Elenya slid her rapier out of its sheath, and the men drew their swords. They circled the buildings on foot, checking the perimeter for signs of armed men lurking in ambush, but the only foot and hoof prints were the expected ones along the narrow lane leading toward Eruth.

They met at the front of the stable. Dushin lifted the bar and opened the doors while Elenya and Enns stood guard. They saw sacks of food piled on the packed dirt between the pens of milk goats and the empty oeikani stalls.

Satisfied, they headed back to fetch their pack animals, sheathing their weapons as they walked. Elenya noticed out of the corner of her eye that Enns's blade seemed very bright, almost as if it were brand new. She forgot about it in her struggle to drag her obstinate oeikani to the stable doors.

They began loading their beasts, each taking responsibility for their own to ensure that each burden would be properly secured. Elenya hooked her fourth bit of cargo into place and reentered the stable. She passed Dushin on his way out, sack of millet over his shoulder; Enns was standing by his oeikani.

Suddenly a small shape fluttered out of the hay loft and sped by Elenya. "Princess! Beware!" it cried.

Elenya heard sounds of rapid movement from the goat pens, the stalls, and the hay loft. She ducked.

She was fast enough to avoid the noose of one lasso, but not the other. It settled around her shoulders and yanked her off her feet. She landed on the sacks, tumbling. As she rolled she brought up one of her demonblades and sawed through the rope that was pulling her. The hemp parted with a snap.

Five quick glances told her the situation: in a goat pen the man who had lassoed her was dropping the severed piece and reaching for a weapon; in a oeikani stall the other rope thrower had already drawn a saber; above in the hay loft a third man was preparing to drop on top of her; at the entrance a fourth man was standing, bloody sword in hand, over the prone, gasping figure of Dushin, whom he had just stabbed from behind; and out near the oeikani, Enns was waiting, doing nothing.

Suddenly she knew how Enns had possessed the money for a new sword. Suddenly she knew just how Puriel's men had known where to ambush Milec.

"Traitor!" she screamed.

The man in the loft jumped, but she was not there. She bounded toward a clear space, flinging her demonblade, fatally stabbing him in midair. She threw her other demonblade at the man in the pens, pulled out her rapier, and charged the man from the stall.

"I told you she was fast!" Enns shouted.

Elenya would show them just how quick she was. The gauntlet blazed. She felt the sorcery course though the muscles of her

48

hands, her hips; her ankles. The talisman made her as fast as a person could be.

Her current opponent was the only one heavily armored. They had sacrificed protection for stealth and mobility. She needed him out of the way quickly. It took four thrusts to mortally wound him, leaving her barely enough time to meet the man rushing in from the door.

As Elenya engaged him, she saw over his shoulder that Enns was mounting his oeikani, not content with the worsening odds. Her rage made her even faster. The soldier came in thrusting. She parried and drove her point in through a seam under his arm. He winced and jabbed again. She sidestepped, blade high, and spotted an opening.

Her weapon was abruptly yanked from her grip. She jumped backwards, caught by surprise. The man from the goat pens had apparently blocked her demonblade throw, or his armor vest had saved him. He was moving in, a mace in one hand, in the other the whip with which he had disarmed her. He lashed at her again, striking her cheek such a blow that her head rang.

Her plight went from bad to worse. The dying man on the ground grabbed her legs, making her lose her balance. The man with whom she had been fencing drove forward. She feared she was lost.

The rythni swooped out of nowhere and beat its wings in the swordsman's face.

Elenya twisted out of the path of the thrust, and, though her legs were still trapped, she managed to fall backward, further out of danger. She kicked. The man on the ground, weakened by blood loss, could not maintain his grip. As she rolled free, she saw that she had landed beside her tackler's discarded saber. In an eyeblink it was hers.

The tip of the lash pinked one of her ears, but she swung in time to sever the last two feet of whip. The wielder blinked in awe at her swift reaction, but like a veteran, did not let it delay his immediate follow-up. She was already out of range, however, on her feet, rushing the swordsman. The rythni had disappeared.

She went high, a dangerous strategy for a fencer. She skewered him in the eye. Though doomed, he began slashing wildly. The first swing nearly cut her belt off of her, but did not touch her skin. She danced out of the arc of the rest.

The whip missed her head so narrowly that the end captured a few strands of hair and ripped them from her scalp. Once again, she spun and trimmed the length.

If her adversary was daunted by the rapid disposal of his companions, he did not reveal it. He flicked his lash and, once again, snatched her weapon out of her grip.

She blinked. The man was good. She was caught off guard by someone who could—at least with that particular weapon—match her exaggerated speed. It left her unprepared for his charge.

Her mind was clear. She knew that if she tried to dive out of the way, or jump for a weapon, she would not make it. So she stepped in.

His mace struck a glancing blow on her biceps, numbing her entire arm. But her mailed fist landed squarely under his nose, caving in the front of his face, the magic reinforcing her punch. He went down like a steer struck by a slaughterhouse mallet.

His momentum carried him into her, knocking her down. She had to pause to regain her breath, then she untangled herself and bolted for the exit, grabbing Dushin's sword from his corpse as she passed. She ignored her mount; she could never catch the traitor on oeikaniback. Her augmented legs were the only hope.

Enns had a good lead. She had lost too much time with the ambushers. She pumped her legs as fast as they would go, until the boles of the trees on either side of the lane began to blur. The jewel above the knuckle of her left middle finger began to throb. She drank more deeply of its power.

He would not get away. She would not let him get away now.

After almost a mile, the lane ended, spilling her out onto the main road. Enns was galloping toward Eruth, visible only as a blur at the head of a streamer of dust.

She ran until her feet ached from the force of the inhumanly rapid impacts and relaunches. She smelled the sweat of the oeikani. The ruins of an old building slipped past on her right, the first indication that the village was near.

Her side was beginning to cramp. She heard the oeikani's labored but regular breathing. It was running at its limit, but it was still fresh. It was meant for this kind of a race, and she, in spite of sorcerous assistance, was not.

Her face was stung by dirt kicked up by the oeikani's hooves. The tail of the animal waved before her eyes, just out of reach. Enns turned. A look of horror filled his face. He began to lash his mount.

Elenya forced herself to one ultimate burst of speed. She readied Dushin's sword. She had the chance for one, and only one, slash at the back of the oeikani's knee.

She collapsed as she swung, the roadway scraping flesh from her face. But the pain there, and in her biceps, and in her side, seemed faint and inconsequential against the scream of the oeikani. She lifted her head just in time to see the hamstrung animal slide to a wrenching, tumbling halt. Its rider was flung heels over head.

She could not inhale fast enough. Spots flickered in front of her vision. She spat grit. Only sheer will kept her from fainting. She forced herself to a kneeling position, bracing her upper body with her good arm. Her weapon lay in the dust not far away, but she left it, unable to do anything but pant. The jewel on her gauntlet had gone dead. That arm, the one struck by the mace, felt like an anchor.

Enns groaned and picked himself up from the road. He stared about, befuddled, eyes drawn first to the thrashing of his crippled animal, then to his torn sleeves, and finally to Elenya. He staggered back, but the half-focused quality left his gaze. He steadied himself and drew his sword.

The graceful way he freed the blade from its scabbard proved that the tumble had not stolen his ability to fence. She crawled to her sword, clasped it, and waited for him on her knees, still doubled over from the pain in her diaphragm.

When he realized how stricken she was, and the mildness of his own injuries, he laughed. He advanced immediately, though with caution, steel first.

He opened with three quick thrusts. She managed to parry them, and when he paused, she threw dirt in his face. He cursed and backed off, instinctively parrying her feeble jab. He stopped after three steps and shook the grit off his eyelashes. She slowly rose to her feet.

Standing took more effort than she had to spare. She got her blade up in time to contact his, but not well enough to deflect his thrust. She stopped the point by catching it with her left palm. As the weapon met the ward around the gauntlet, jagged splinters of electricity snaked out in several directions. She stumbled under the weight of the blow. He winced at the vibrations running down the sword and retreated.

On the next attack he abandoned broad, telegraphed movements in favor of subtle techniques. Elenya parried one thrust with her sword guard, another with her armored hand, and tried to force her enervated body to obey her, tried to shake the effects of the mace blow from her left arm. She licked a trickle of blood, a result of her fall, off her lip. Even if she had been fresh, his

51

swordplay would have been difficult to deal with. Like her, Enns had been taught by Troy, Cilendrodel's best fencing instructor, and he had been an apt pupil.

Enns grinned savagely. "Not so fast anymore, are you, princess?" The sarcasm he put on the title explained a great deal.

She blew a sweat-drenched strand of hair away from her lips. She was finally able to inhale through her nostrils, though she still exhaled through her mouth. She felt a little less dizzy.

"I can deal with a lowly duke's nephew, especially one who uses blood money to buy a sword," she said.

He bared his teeth. "I was always better than any royal bastard."

She nodded. The old adolescent jealousy, which she had thought long buried, had been reawakened by the temptation of the reward for her capture or death.

He pressed. The Ezenean Offense. She blocked the first move, was late with the second, had to step back. He smiled, both of them seeing in that split instant that she would never be in time to stop the third. His jab drove into her right breast.

The pain nearly blacked her out. Yet she wrapped her gauntlet around his sword, preventing him from pulling it out, keeping him within range. She sliced him across his throat.

An expression of disbelief crossed his features. Together they sagged to their knees. Enns was dying more quickly than she; her steel had severed an artery in his neck. He let go of his sword hilt and fell face forward in the dust, writhing.

Elenya kept the steel in her body as motionless as she could manage, which, thanks to her shuddering limbs, was not as still as she would have liked. The tip had gone in deep, all the way to her scapula. She waited on the edge of consciousness, winded yet not daring to breathe deeply. She tasted blood at the back of her tongue. She suppressed an urge to cough. She had to avoid going into shock. She had a chance.

Enns's thrashing nearly knocked her over. She ignored it, focusing every last iota of concentration on the amulet at her throat. Her brother was only a few leagues away; if he was not preoccupied with a task, he might hear her summons.

Five seconds. Ten. Then the wordless voice that she had known for so many years called out, and in one brief image she communicated her need.

The familiar tingle of magic rose up along her spine and flared in a hot corona around her wound. She gingerly drew the sword out. Blood trickled briefly, slowed, and congealed. Then, far too soon, the sorcery ended. She gasped. The puncture remained, barely knit, as if it were a day old. She heard a psychic cry.

Alemar. Pain not her own flared briefly in her mind, and was gone. Her brother had lost consciousness.

What had happened? She swayed, eyes drawn to the nearly still body of Enns. The hemorrhaging of his throat was creating a broad stain in the roadway. "What have you done to my brother?" she choked.

The wounded oeikani was mewling. She had not wished to harm the animal. She wanted to put it out of its misery, but it might struggle, and if it jostled her too much it might tear open her wound.

She had another use for her blade. She pointed Enns's face toward the sky, and with great deliberateness etched two characters in the skin of his forehead. "For Milec," it read in the ideograms of the High Speech.

Finally the tears came, and with them the sore throat, the heat in the cheeks. She wept until the droplets fell from her bruised chin and created small specks of mud in the roadway. She would have sobbed had not the instinct of self-preservation told her not to put stress on her lungs. She had not allowed her grief to surface all week, but now she had no reserves left to keep it in. She cried for the first man to brush that special spot inside her since her days in the desert.

"For Milec," she murmured bitterly. Her mourning was all the more intense for the knowledge that he had loved her far more deeply than she could ever have loved him.

Tiny eyes stared at her. A rythni waited, half-hidden in the grass at the road's edge.

She had no doubt it was the same one who had warned her of the ambush. She beckoned, but the little creature stayed back, wary of the scent of battle, blood, and death. Almost any other rythni would have shied away from the scene altogether, but Elenya knew this was a special individual. She had proved that by flying in the face of the swordsman, breaking her race's strict taboo against taking part in violence. She was trembling, frightened by what she had seen and done. This was no queen, able to fend off the censure of her elders.

The creak of old wagon wheels warned Elenya that someone was coming around the bend. She staggered to her feet and managed to hide herself within the woods before the vehicle appeared. She continued across a shallow creek and into a patch of ferns where she was not likely to be seen once she lay down. The rythni followed, flitting like a butterfly from perch to perch.

Elenya needed the tiny being. Her wounds had taken so much out of her that she had to set the amulet, as well as the gauntlet, at her side. The talismans would draw energy from her that she needed in order to heal. She could not summon her brother with sorcery, even assuming he was well. She waved to the rythni, which finally gathered courage and came near.

"Bring help," Elenya whispered.

The rythni sped away. Elenya sighed, made herself as comfortable as she could, resting her head on the cold earth. Within seconds she had faded into unconsciousness.

IX

Wynneth was standing next to Alemar when he suddenly stiffened. His eyes glazed. She caught him as his knees buckled. His weight dragged her toward the ground.

"Tregay! Iregg!" she called toward the nearest pair of rebels. "Help me!"

The men sped to her and lowered Alemar to the forest loam. She bent over him, heart pounding, and waved her hand in front of his face. His gaze penetrated her palm, past her face, toward some distant vista. She had seen him don the same expression one week earlier, when he had healed Milec's dead flesh.

"He's casting a spell," she said. A tingle of anxiety stood the hair on her arms on end. Why would he need to work such potent magic without prior notice? His amulet coughed, green illumination blazing through his shirt as if it were gauze. She covered her eyes.

"Elenya," he murmured.

Elenya—in need of healing? "Saddle your oeikani," Wynneth told the group that had collected. "Something's gone wrong at the silk farm." Three men dashed away.

Alemar screamed and clutched his temples. His body arched until everything but his head and feet left the ground. Wynneth gasped. Her husband collapsed, eyes closed, breath rapid and staccato.

She raced through her memories of the instructions he had given her of what to do should something like this ever occur. "Get me a moist cloth," she told Iregg, as she stretched out Alemar's bent legs and draped his hands across his chest. She seized several ferns and fashioned a crude pillow, which she tucked behind his head. Iregg scampered back from the spring, holding out a dripping scarf.

Wynneth draped the fabric over Alemar's nose and mouth. The vigor of his inhalation sucked it partway down his throat. She yanked it free, spread it open again, and held it taut. What next? After moisture for the lungs—yes! Cover the ears, cover the eyes, do anything to block out the outside world, give him less to deal with.

Tregay held the wet scarf while she unwrapped her sash from her waist. The rebel raised Alemar's head and Wynneth coiled the silk around, covering the prince's eyes and ears five layers deep. Finally only the top of his pate peeked out. Tendrils of glossy black hair rose of their own accord, like thin, angry snakes. Tiny pops of lightning zigzagged from strand to strand.

A tear ran down the length of her nose and hung suspended from the tip. She soaked it up with her sleeve. The static from his hair stung her hand, but she left her palm against his forehead. No fever. Instead, a breath of frost scooted up the bones of her arm to her chest. She shivered.

"Blankets!" she snapped. One of the camp women—Wynneth was too distracted to notice who—abruptly unravelled the three she had been cradling. Wynneth cast them over her husband.

His breathing steadied. Tregay was able, at last, to lift his hand away from the scarf. The cloth hung stiffly, like a tent, most of the moisture gone. Wynneth ordered another to be dipped in the spring.

Alemar's teeth chattered. Wynneth nearly called for more blankets, but the shaking eased almost immediately. As she placed the new damp cloth over his lower face, the tightness left the corners of his mouth. The muscles in his neck settled back, leaving smooth, relaxed contours. He moaned, and seemed to sink into a normal sleep.

"Crumbly logs, bitter sawdust, and poison bark mushrooms," she murmured—an old curse, suitable for mothers who did not wish to use stronger terms in front of their children. It relieved her tension better than true profanity.

She sighed and looked about. She counted five missing men, off to the silk farm. She prayed that they would bring back bearable news.

* * *

Alemar was still slumbering fitfully when a cloud of rythni abruptly swarmed out of the forest canopy and circled just above him. Wynneth blinked and fell back, startled by their agitated swirl of motion. The other rebels, who had earlier retreated a dozen or so paces away to give a worried wife some privacy, cried out and pointed. In spite of the little people's frequent presence, the humans rarely spotted them, much less viewed them so plainly as now.

The rythni warbled forlornly at the sight of the stricken prince. One slim individual settled on his upper chest, reached under the damp cloth, and tugged his beard. Wynneth recognized Hiephora by the fine gold chain around her neck.

"He's not sleeping. He collapsed," Wynneth said, remembering to lower her voice.

"He must wake up. His sister needs him," the queen answered stridently. Wynneth caught her breath. The rythni had actually spoken to her. That only confirmed the gravity of the situation.

"What do you mean? Do you know what happened?"

"Betrayal," Hiephora trilled mournfully. As she spoke, a second rythni lit clumsily on Alemar's body. The newcomer staggered, wings drooping. Her tiny, boyish chest pulsated visibly, like that of a frightened bird. Her panting was so loud Wynneth could actually hear it. "Cyfee here saw it happen."

Cyfee, when she had recaptured some of her wind, blurted, "She was attacked in the place where the men make worms spin fiber for them. She *stopped* them all, but she is near death. Alemar must come." Wynneth perceived that "stopped" was as close as the little creature could come to the word "killed."

"What happened to Enns and Dushin?"

The rythni wrung her hands. "Dead. Enns was the traitor."

Wood spirits preserve us, Wynneth thought. "Where is Elenya now? Still at the silk farm?"

"No. Hidden. I can lead you there."

Wynneth knelt down and shook Alemar. His head flopped limply from side to side. From his instructions she knew not to force him awake. Yet if the rythni spoke the truth, the men who had ridden to the farm would not find the princess.

Wynneth made up her mind. "Load Alemar onto a travois," she told a pair of rebels. "He has to travel immediately." She turned back to the exhausted rythni. "Lead us."

Alemar woke to the sound of tree limbs dragging through the humus, uprooting the rotting leaves and twigs. His body bounced

56

and pitched, held fast by padded bonds. He opened his eyes and saw a oeikani's rump. The knot of hair at the end of its tail swished just above his head. Behind him another oeikani followed in the hoofprints of the first. Wynneth gazed down from the saddle, saw that he was conscious, and called for the party to halt.

She and Tregay untied her husband. The latter eased slowly off the travois, letting them support him. His knees and spine gradually remembered how to hold him upright. His eyeballs seemed to bounce loosely back and forth, as if too small for their sockets. Each time they struck his skull, pain careened away from the impact point, darted to the back of his head, and blazed a trail into his neck.

"Elenya..." he murmured. Memories of his sister's mental plea flooded back. Sword deep in her breast. Enns dying beside her. Had he healed her? Yes, he had tried. Before he had blacked out, he had sealed the wound as she drew the blade out. But then?

He coughed, dislodging a foul mouthful of phlegm. He had felt unwell after healings, but never this devastated. The effects of healing Milec's corpse still debilitated him. The severity of his sister's wound and her distance from him had strained him beyond his limit. He needed rest.

But not now. The job was unfinished. "Where are we?" he asked.

"We're approaching the main road east of Eruth. Cyfee is leading us to Elenya."

"Cyfee?" he glanced up. With a flutter of wings, fast as a hummingbird, the rythni darted into the air above the path ahead, chirped, and sped down it. Still groggy, he belatedly recognized the note as the rythni word for haste.

"Can you ride?" Wynneth asked.

"I'll try," he said. Tregay and Iregg lifted him into a saddle. He drooped forward, hands full of mane, letting the animal set the pace.

By the time they reached the road, he was sitting upright, though he wished he were not so high. When he swayed, the ground seemed as though it were racing up to meet him.

They spilled out onto the beaten dirt track. Barely wide enough for three oeikani abreast, the route served as the main link between the sparse settlements of the Garthmorron area. They rode faster, no longer hampered by the obstacles of native forest. Suddenly Hiephora zoomed out of the foliage and landed on Alemar's shoulder.

"Men come. Hide."

Alemar repeated the command. The rythni had given sufficient warning. The rebels peered out from thick cover, hands on the broad noses of their mounts to signal the beasts to be completely silent. Three stout woodsmen, one middle-aged, the other two just out of adolescence, rumbled by on a creaking wagon. A body lay on the planks of the flat bed behind their seat.

"Enns," Wynneth whispered.

Alemar spotted the word carved into the corpse's forehead. His teeth settled against each other so hard it aggravated his headache. The wagon rattled out of sight.

He sighed. Let the Dragon's scouts make of that what they would. Of more immediate concern was the knowledge that once the men reached the village, a search party would gather and set out. How much farther? He sent an inquiry via his amulet, and received no response. Elenya was not wearing hers. Or she was dead.

"Let's go," he said anxiously.

Cyfee lit on a tall frond of bracken. Elenya lay supine, nearly invisible beneath the emerald fern canopy. Alemar knelt down, waving the others back. Hiephora landed on his shoulder; he did not notice her. A light bluish pallor clung to his sister's face. Her chest did not rise and fall.

"No!" he cried. He reached behind her neck and lifted her into a sitting position. She coughed.

Alive! His hands shook so badly she nearly slipped from his grasp. Then he went cold. Bright red blood trickled over the edge of Elenya's lip. A few specks ejected by the cough dotted the front of her doeskin tunic.

She was bleeding inside.

Immediately he lay her back down, and shouted at the rebels surrounding him, "Stay back. Her wound has hemorrhaged. I must have no distractions."

He summoned the power. It coursed feebly out his fingers. Not enough. He needed time. But she was dying. If he did not save her now, this very hour, he could not save her at all. He must try to do what he had failed to do from a distance.

"Hold me," he told Wynneth. Without the need for explanation, she sat down behind him and enveloped him, arms circling his torso, an arrangement that would keep him steady, come what may. He took Elenya's hands inside his own, his bare one on top, the one with the gauntlet beneath.

The gauntlet crackled. The talisman itself could not help him; its design prevented that. It merely reflected the intensity of the energies he summoned. He took one deep breath—

And he was inside. The power hummed, drawn from some last, unsuspected reserve. How much he did not know, and he did not waste time speculating.

He sped along the track of the sword gash, bolstering the repair he had begun hours before. Flesh rejoined flesh. Blood seeped from dozens of tiny ruptures. He sealed the holes, but the pooled blood remained in her lung and in the interstices of her chest cavity.

A jolt. Pain. He gritted his teeth and and focussed on the blood. Red mist flowed out of Elenya's nose and mouth. Her lung emptied. She groaned as Alemar purged the last of the internal pools. He inspected carefully to be certain he had found all sources of the bleeding.

Scars next. He began to weave the flesh more tightly still, speeding nature's work. Lung and bone first, then muscle and connective tissue. Simultaneously, he stimulated her marrow to produce replacement blood.

His stomach heaved. He choked. The sorcery evaporated. In agony, against his will, he let go of his sister.

A great blackness welled around him, threatening to swallow him. He sagged back against Wynneth. He yanked off his gauntlet and amulet, so that they would not suck vital life force from him. He had not healed Elenya thoroughly, but though he strived, he failed to summon even one more drop of magic. He had not been on Retreat since his days in the desert, had never had an opportunity to fully restore his powers, and at last whatever reservoir he had tapped during those years had been drained.

But Elenya was out of danger. That was the important thing. He fought off demons of sleep. They needed a place to recuperate—a few days of refuge away even from their comrades.

They were near Garthmorron.

"My grandfather," Alemar murmured to Wynneth, his voice slurred by exhaustion. "Find him. The rythni will help. Take me there. Take Elenya there. Send the others away." He fainted before he finished the final word.

Elenya awoke. She lay on a firm straw tick, covered with warm blankets. Wood smoke tickled her nose, and embers popped and crackled nearby. Every sense told her she was safe. She opened her eyes and saw that she was within a woodcutter's one-room cottage.

Her demonblades and rapier, as well as her gauntlet and amulet, waited on a stool within easy reach. Her clothes, laundered, the tears patched, hung on the nearest wall. Fresh bread and cheese lay on the table, with a flagon of wine. Broth steamed in the hearth.

Examining her breast, she touched a well-healed scar. She flexed her biceps, and found it stiff but unbruised. A glance in the small mirror beside the bed showed that the abrasions on her face were reduced to flesh-colored areas on her otherwise tan features.

In spite of this, she felt absolutely awful.

She tried to control her dizziness as she dragged herself out from under the covers. She noted, gratefully, that the chamber pot had been put close by. She hung on to the bed frame while she used it. By the time she replaced the lid she felt immensely better.

She tried to stand, but even pulling on the bed with her arms only got her to a stooped-over, bent-knee position. She coughed. The taste in the back of her mouth could have dissolved steel. She stayed there, legs shuddering.

"Here, now, what do you think you're doing?"

A man's figure stood framed in the doorway, features obscured by the brilliant daylight behind him. She recognized the voice. "Grandfather," she whimpered. "Help me get back in bed."

Cosufier Elb-Aratule picked his daughter's daughter up by the small of her back and the rear of her knees, lifted her into a sitting position, and propped up her spine with a pillow. He was still as strong as ever, though a bit grey and weathered.

"Alemar said you're to remain in bed until he returns," he said as he pulled the blankets over her legs. "You're not out of danger yet." He patted her hair. She realized from the scent and the unmatted texture that he must have washed and combed it for her while she slept.

"How long has it been?"

"Three days."

"That's . . ."

"Your lung hemorrhaged," Cosufier said gravely. "He almost didn't save you."

"I'm not sure he has yet," she said, stifling another wave of nausea.

Cosufier did not smile at her attempt at humor. He waved at the hearth. "He had me make a soup—herbs and things. I don't think you're going to like drinking it."

She did not answer. For one thing, her throat ached when she talked, but mainly she knew that she would probably say something flippant, and she had seen her grandfather in this mood before. Her rump had never stung so badly as the time, at age eleven, when she had antagonized him at the wrong moment.

"How's Alemar?" she asked.

She was not certain, but she thought she saw a flicker of distress on her grandfather's face. "He's better than you are, though he's only been up since last night. He'd be here except that he's gone to rendezvous with a messenger from your father."

She tried to remember the last few minutes before she had lost consciousness, but everything after she had killed Enns was murky.

"Is there news?"

"That's what Alemar has gone to learn," Cosufier said, pouring a small bowlful of broth and holding it out to Elenya.

She wrinkled her nose. "Smells like oeikani piss."

"That's the main ingredient."

She nearly lost her grip on the bowl.

"I didn't concoct the recipe," her grandfather said indifferently. "I just followed the instructions. He said if it was good enough for Shigmur, it was good enough for you."

She rolled the broth around in a disconsolate manner, and waited for it to cool. Her grandfather seemed unduly cross. She ran a finger over the pattern etched on the porcelain.

"This was one of Mother's," she said.

"Yes. I keep a few things here. It's one of the huts I used to use as a gamekeeper."

"We're on the Garthmorron estate, then?"

"Deep inside it, yes."

"Is that wise?"

"It's territory known only to me and my former assistants. And I don't stay in one place long. Where better to hide than familiar ground?"

"You've seen the manor recently, then?"

He nodded, pressing his lips together. "No change. The Dragon's appointee is still in residence. He's let most of the servants be. Hoping, no doubt, a stray word will lead to me, or to you and Alemar."

"Have you heard from Lord Dran?"

"He's making the best of his retirement in Aleoth, though I know it hurts him to the quick to face the thought of dying away from Garthmorron. Seven generations of his family are buried in this soil. He had already picked out his tree."

Nearly as many generations of their own family had found their rest in these woods, Elenya knew. And now Cosufier was a fugitive here.

"I'm sorry, Grandfather."

The old man shrugged as he threw another log on the fire. "Don't be stupid. If I'm going to blame you for Dragon's actions I might as well blame Alemar Dragonslayer for killing Gloroc's parents in the first place. Yet if he hadn't, Elandris would never have been built, and Cilendrodel would never have been colonized, and Garthmorron would never have existed. You didn't have any choice about the Dragon hating you."

His words came out with an odd, bittersweet undertone. He was not telling her something. "Grandfather? What's wrong?"

He kept his eyes on the fire. "You should have let him go."

"Who? Enns?"

"Yes."

"Grandfather! He tried to kill me! He's responsible for Milec's death!"

"Yes," he answered wistfully. "Alemar and Wynneth pieced it together, with help from the rythni. He deserved to die. But you took a great risk. You almost died, almost lost the gauntlet. There would have been time for revenge later, under more favorable circumstances."

"He was *mine*," she stated.

"And you got him," Cosufier replied. "It was just luck that your brother found you, instead of one of the patrols Puriel sent to comb the woods around Eruth."

The back of her throat ached. Why was he being so sharply critical? It was not his nature. "He might have escaped, gone to the Dragon. What would you have had me do?"

He glanced downward. "Forgive me. You're right. You had no choice," he said quickly, as if sorry he had broached the subject.

"There's something more, isn't there? Tell me."

Cosufier sighed. "I am an old fool. I was going to let you rest, not say a word."

"What *is* it?"

He looked up with haunted eyes. "It's gone. It took too much to heal you. Alemar's power is spent."

Her skin turned to ice. She finally remembered the anguished scream she had heard via the amulet, back at Enns's death site. "But . . . if he goes on Retreat?" she asked plaintively.

"We can hope for the best. But tell me, when will he be able to do that?"

Her hands fumbled at the cup. "I don't know," she said. Even if he were to try, would the Dragon allow him the chance to leave the outside world behind?

Cosufier exhaled loudly and stepped to the door. "Maybe on some fine day when Gloroc's skull is decorating the mantle in Garthmorron Hall and you've put up your sword to make babies." The undertone of accusation had left his voice; all that remained was melancholy.

The snap of a twig under his foot echoed between her ears for long moments afterward. She shivered and drew the blanket up tightly over herself. All at once she raised the bowl and drained the contents in one long, searing swallow.

Or maybe when it rains in the eret-Zyrail, she thought bitterly.

〜〜 XI 〜〜

The tree rose high above the delta. The men in the platform at the top commanded an unparalleled view of the estuaries, islands, bogs, and channels of the lower reaches of the River Sha. Here the land ceased to hide beneath an impenetrable cloak of leaves, giving way to long stretches of reeds, mud banks, and numerous riverside villages of bamboo and thatch, the buildings often perched on stilts. The lookout tree rose from the midst of one of these communities.

Toren stared wide-eyed at the broad waterway. His gaze kept arching toward the horizon.

"It's the end of the Wood," he whispered.

"Yes," Geim said. Behind them lay league upon league of deep forest, a dozen hostile tribes, and long days and nights of travel. The temperate weather of the far South had surrendered to the hot climate of his boyhood. He inhaled deeply the aroma of the delta, and pointed at the lookout platform. "That's an Ogshiel tradition. The Shagas sometimes used to attack from the air."

Geim had called a halt when the platform had come into view. Now he waved them forward, out from under the trees. There was no infiltrating or detouring around the Ogshiel nation the way they had the other Vanihr lands of their route. Their destination lay at the mouth of the delta, across countless fingers of the Sha. The only way to travel that spiderweb of channels was by boat; a man did not swim this section of the river unless he wanted to be eaten.

As Geim, Toren, and Deena strode along a wide path through a field of domesticated pomegranate bushes, a horn blast sounded up on the platform. Soon eight warriors loped into sight, spears ready.

Geim raised his hand. "The river runs clear today."

The leader of the troop scanned them carefully, pausing on Deena's alien features, and noting Geim's sword. Toren, hair tied up high like Geim, elicited only a brief examination.

"May it be clear tomorrow," the man replied.

"I am Han of Three Forks Village," Geim said genially, waving upriver. "We caught our canoe on a snag and it is no longer riverworthy. We would like to hire a boat to take us to Talitha." He gestured at Deena. "We are escorting the lady to her home."

The villager evaluated the story. The law of the land forbade Ijitians or other foreigners to travel freely on the Vanihr side of the river, but it was quite common for the Ogshiel to hire out their rafts and canoes to merchants and others engaged in travel up and down the length of the Sha. Finally he nodded.

"Afterward will you need to be taken upstream to your canoe?" he asked.

"No. We'll be spending a few days in the city," Geim said smoothly.

The villager grunted. "It's too late in the day to set out. Sleep over and this evening I will find someone who wants the task. What do you offer?"

Geim jiggled a small pouch. "Market tokens."

The sentries surrounded the visitors and led them into the village.

In the early twilight, Geim sat on the stoop of the guest hut, watching several women bathe near the village wharf, inside a sturdy barricade that protected them from river predators. Deena raised the door cloth and emerged from the portal. She followed his gaze.

"Your entire race is blessed," she murmured, as one golden-skinned beauty scrubbed another's back. "Even the old ones are trim and smooth."

"Vanihr do not get old. The gods made us handsome by stealing years from our lives." He had at other times mentioned to her how middle-aged members of his tribe tended to die suddenly from disease or organ failure, rather than slowly wind down to senility and decrepitude. The eldest of the women in the bathing pool was probably in her early forties.

"'The Flowers of the Wood,'" she quoted. "So that's what that means."

He did not comment. One of the girls was striding from the river, teeth white and captivating as she smiled at a companion. She was wringing out her waistlength yellow hair, the rivulet trickling over high, scarcely matured breasts.

"Geim? Is something wrong?"

Eventually he lowered his glance to his toes. "I was remembering someone."

She sat down on the step with him, dangling her feet toward the earth. Geim could see high water marks on the pillar next to her calves. "Do you think the villagers believed you?" she asked.

Geim was glad to change the subject. "Yes. As long as Toren doesn't open his mouth and let his accent give them the idea he's a scout for an inland tribe, we should have no trouble." At that moment, the southern Vanihr was dozing in the main room of the hut. It seemed odd to Geim to think of finally sleeping on something other than bare ground.

"He's changed," Deena said. "Sometimes I think he's almost grateful that we took his totem." She rubbed the puffy track on her forearm where the Amane arrow had emerged.

"I can't imagine what life would be like, with an active totem inside oneself. As a boy I worshipped my ancestors, of course, but the technique for keeping their spirits alive has been lost to the northern tribes for so long most say it never existed."

"We would never have made it through the wilderness without his help. I wish we had a proper reward to offer him."

"Yes." Geim paused to watch the village girl slip on her loin-cloth. "I do, too."

A series of hailing shouts shifted their attention downstream. A raft had appeared, two sturdy Vanihr youths driving it with long poles. Their load included baskets of merchandise, a pair of milk does, and coils of rope, enough weight to make their work hard in spite of the lazy current. As the newcomers pulled up to the wharf, Geim and Deena could see sweat dripping from their arms and chins. The villagers hurried out to evaluate the quality of the cargo before the light failed.

Eventually the village chief left the unloading of the raft and approached the guest hut. "These two have just come from Port Ogshi. They'll be taking goods down to Talitha tomorrow. They have room for passengers."

Geim managed not to jump with alarm when Port Ogshi was mentioned. He thanked the man and went down to the jetty to bargain, resigning himself to a night of little sleep.

Geim saw a giant river mong glide past the raft, its dorsal fin knifing the surface. One of the boys lifted his pole out of the way so as not to lose it. The raft rocked in the creature's wake. Geim recalled childhood encounters with the monsters and realized the memories had not become exaggerated over time.

Excitement over, the boys returned to poling, Geim to his contemplation of the Sha, and Deena and Toren to their language lessons. She pointed to a heron as it flew past, called its name, and Toren repeated it. During the past few weeks his vocabulary and understanding of her tongue had grown far beyond the little Geim had mastered. It was ironic. Now any two of them could talk with each other, but only by leaving the third party out of the conversation.

Mostly, it had been Geim who had been excluded. Toren and Deena had developed a camaraderie of which he had no part. It was a modest, shy sort of thing. He was not sure they were aware of it yet.

As the morning wore on, he began to recognize the curves of the river. Shortly before noon they came within sight of a huge village: Port Ogshi, the capital of the nation, his birthplace.

The boys immediately began navigating toward one of the wharfs. Geim's heart rate began to speed up.

"Picking up cargo?" he asked, deliberately keeping his tone conversational.

"Yes," the youngster replied, his foot on one of the few baskets of goods that they had loaded upriver. The raft could hold ten times the weight they now carried. "Our brother is waiting for us here." He spoke proudly, obviously still young enough that it made him feel important that he and his junior sibling had been allowed to pilot the raft all by themselves.

"Going to stay long?"

"Long enough to take on our cargo," the boy said as if Geim were a fool.

"Of course," Geim said, and maintained a stony silence as the juveniles tied up, climbed the bank, and disappeared down the broad avenue between a pair of large bamboo and wicker warehouses. Nearby other traders were arriving or leaving. A fishmonger was hawking his wares at the end of the pier.

"Should we wait with the raft?" Deena asked.

"Yes," Geim said, rather quickly. "We don't want to disembark here."

As he thought further, he had her sit down behind the small pile of goods already aboard, to draw less attention to her complexion and hair color. He himself kept his face toward the river as much as possible, turning only when he heard the boys' footsteps rattling along the bamboo of the wharf. A man Geim's own age walked beside them, regaling them with descriptions of the excellent haggling he had done while they had been gone.

"So these are the passengers—" the man began, stepping onto the raft and stopping two paces in front of Geim.

The man's jaw dropped.

Every bit of moisture left Geim's mouth. "My friends and I would like to thank you for the transportation," he said hoarsely.

"Is it truly you?" the man asked.

Geim chuckled nervously. "I'm afraid so."

"My great grandfather's ass!" The man pointed to the far end of the raft. "Stay out of view. I'll get us loaded as fast as I can." He jerked a thumb at his shocked little brothers. "Let's move!"

The boys jumped. The three of them took the raft to the next pier and began shuttling a stack of merchandise aboard, assisted by Toren. The boys struggled with baskets and chests that would ordinarily be handled by a pair of the porters who could be found lolling on the banks or helping other merchants. The fewer of the village adults who got a look at Geim the better, however. The process took almost an hour, an excruciatingly long wait.

"I appreciate this, Feirl," Geim told the raft owner as soon as they were under way.

"What in your mother's name brought you back here?" Feirl demanded.

"I would have avoided it if it had been practical," Geim said. "I take it that things haven't changed."

"Ophob is still the chief, if that's what you mean. And he'd still have your balls if he saw you."

Geim laughed. "Of that I'm certain," he said emphatically. "And Ysmet?"

"She'd have more than that," Feirl said ominously. "She brought one of the worst bride prices a high chief's eldest daughter ever had to settle for. She's married to Derest, the warehouse owner."

"Ah," Geim murmured wistfully. "Is she unhappy, then?"

"Content enough, I think. A boatload of brats. But I guarantee you she's never forgotten how much better she might have done."

At the mention of children Geim's eyes brightened. "The baby?"

"A girl. Pretty and bright. You'd have been proud of her." Feirl gave the pole a listless shove. "Died at three of the pox."

Something stung Geim down in the gut. On the shore a pack of toddlers bolted from a children's house, engaged in an excited follow-the-leader race while several mothers supervised. He sighed.

Suddenly self-conscious, he turned. Toren shifted uneasily from foot to foot. Geim felt his face flush, grateful that Deena could not understand the words. "Fifteen years ago I was fool enough to get the chief's daughter pregnant," he said. Toren had the tact to merely shrug. Geim turned back and watched the village slide from view.

Geim's mood remained black as the raft wended its way through one tributary after another, past islands, more villages, and foul-smelling backwaters. Finally they emerged into the main course of the Sha. Many of the craft they passed carried Ijitians as often as Vanihr. Geim caught Toren staring at their pale complexions.

The southerner was rubbing his upper lip and frowning. Geim followed his line of sight, and saw that the tiller man of the nearest boat had a mustache. "Like Ivayer," Toren said presently.

"Get used to it," Geim said. "On the northern continent all men have hairy faces. It's only here in Ijitia that some of them

68

shave. In imitation of our race, I suppose." He did not bother warning Toren that there would be those who would consider him effeminate for being unable to grow a beard. The southerner would encounter that sort of thing soon enough.

The river traffic thickened. A canoe nearly collided with them. One of Feirl's brothers rapped it with his pole, nearly provoking a fight. In another half hour the first buildings rose above the treeline.

Geim recalled the thrill he'd experienced the first time he saw Talitha. The city sprawled across the outermost large island of the delta, its southern edge devoted to the docks and markets where the Vanihr traded. The city itself belonged to the Ijitians. The people of the Wood, distrusting of large scale communities that reminded them of the Shagas, left the rule to others by preference, though their merchant's guild wielded considerable influence. The Ijitians, in deference to their neighbors, used chiefly wood and mud for building materials, avoiding the stone and crystal favored by the serpent men. To the young Geim it had been awe-inspiring. To his jaded older eyes, Talitha seemed shabby, small, and odoriferous, nothing compared to the principalities of the Calinin Empire.

The raft bumped the pier. Feirl and his brothers tied it fast. The water clopped and sprayed between the craft and the pylon, salty from the rising tide. Geim handed each of the boys a market token, the closest thing to money that Vanihr used. At Feirl's suggestion they rushed off to bargain for something of their fancy in the marketplace.

Geim handed the elder brother the rest of the payment and clasped his hand. "It's been good seeing you again."

"The same," Feirl replied. "I'm glad that life in the north has not ruined you yet." He stole a furtive glance at Deena and Toren. "Though it brings you to journey with odd companions. He's a southerner, true?"

Geim nodded. "A Fhali."

Feirl's eyes widened. "They live almost to the Firelands, so I'm told."

"That's true."

Feirl shook his head. "Leave it to you to lead a colorful life."

"It has been that," Geim admitted.

"Good luck."

They could use it, Geim mused. He bade farewell and they set off into the city.

• • •

Geim noticed that Toren glanced constantly left, right, up, and down as they ambled past the vendors. The first time the southerner saw a woman with red hair he was so distracted he nearly bumped into a wagon. As they continued, the Vanihr faces became fewer and farther between, until some of the people they passed began to openly stare at them. They had now entered the Ijitian section. Vanihr normally stayed in the south quarter. Few, in fact, actually lived in the city; even the dedicated merchants were glad to be able to retreat to the forest. Crowded environments left the race too vulnerable to plague.

"I'm hungry," Toren said. "When are we going to eat?"

"When we get to the northern continent," Geim replied.

"I can't wait that long."

"Don't worry," Geim said.

They turned a corner and stopped. Down the avenue loomed the largest building they had yet seen. Chipped blocks of ancient stone rose three stories high, fronted by marble columns. Along the rim of the façade, a row of broken, eroded statues arched over the square like carrion vultures. Toren gazed in fascination at the vaguely manlike figures, from their long reptilian snouts to their broad, leathery wings: Shagas.

"They built this temple," Geim explained, glancing uneasily at the images of his people's historical foes. The works of art made it easy to understand why the race was known as the lesser dragons. "It's the only one of their structures left in Talitha."

"Why was it not torn down?" Toren asked.

"There was a ward around it for a century after the Ogshiel sacked the city. By the time it faded, the new settlement had surrounded it, and the Ijitians left it as a relic of the victory."

Geim led them forward. One of several guards glared at them as they crossed in front of the broad stone steps and continued down the street. Geim strode up to a nondescript door on the far side of a nearby building and rapped.

The cover of a peephole opened, revealing a tiny square of darkness. No greeting.

"There is a shadow over the Dragon Sea," Geim murmured.

They heard the sound of a heavy bar being dragged aside. The door abruptly opened. A small, portly Ijitian waved them hurriedly within.

They found themselves in a wine cellar. Rows of oak casks stretched into the murk, the air heavy with the aroma of fermentation, dank stone, and spilled wine. The Ijitian swiftly replaced the bar.

"Taking a long trip?" he asked Geim meaningfully.

"Yes. News from the north?"

"Tamisan has capitulated."

Geim frowned. It was hardly unexpected, though he had hoped for another season or two.

Their host produced three tapers and handed one to each of them, lighting them from his lamp. He led the way down a treacherously slick walkway between the barrels. They came to a stairway and descended past five landings to a small room lined with racks of bottled red wines. He pressed a subtly hidden latch and rolled back one of the racks, revealing a cobweb-hung corridor.

"Safe journey," the man said.

Geim waved the others after him. He nearly bumped his head on the corridor's ceiling, and frequently had to pull spider makings out of his hair. Rats skittered out of their path, the rustle of their tiny feet reverberating down the passageway. The air smelled stale.

After three turns and several hundred paces, the tunnel opened out into a broad, low chamber. The walls and the floor were thickly covered in Shaga hieroglyphics. Toren glanced nervously at the symbols his candle flame revealed.

"I don't like this place," he said.

"We won't be lingering," Geim said, setting his taper in a holder on the floor. Toren and Deena, at his instructions, did likewise. The feeble glow scarcely reached the limits of the room.

"We're under the temple, aren't we?" Toren stated.

"Yes." Geim had pulled a small, round lens of crystal from a pouch. He exhaled on it, and held it forward. "Cover your eyes."

The room erupted in daylight.

Toren leaped back. Half the underground chamber was gone. In its place was a view of grassy, rolling hills. Immediately in the foreground was a cairn of earth and weathered rock that suggested the ruins of an ancient edifice. The land seemed uninhabited.

"No trees," Toren gasped.

"There are a few just on the other side of that knoll," Geim said, pointing. "Come. I'll show you."

Toren hesitated. "After you."

Geim shook his head. "No. The bearer of this goes last," he said, holding up the lens. He gestured to Deena.

She smiled at Toren and stepped across the line between the

chamber and the pastoral landscape. As she crossed, a burst of static electricity darted over her body. Then she was on the other side, beckoning to him.

Toren swallowed and jumped across. Geim grinned at his startled expression, then followed.

The humid air of the delta was replaced by the pollen-rich atmosphere of open countryside in early spring. Geim turned back to the wide window behind them. Their sunlit vantage made it impossible to distinguish features of the room they had left. The only things he could make out were the flames of the candles.

He wiped the lens clean and put it away. The portal closed. The view in that direction now showed only green hills, blue sky, and grazing sheep.

"Now, let's get some of that food you were wanting," Geim said.

〰 XII 〰

As Toren, Geim, and Deena emerged from the portal, they were watched.

The watcher's name was Hadradril. He was a wizard of the Ril, one of the elite cadre of magicians that studied under the Dragon himself—currently the lowest ranked of them, but that was no insult. The youth glowing from his lean, almost gaunt features was natural, not the result of longevity spells. That he had come so far so soon proved his ambition, ruthlessness, and talent.

From his vantage behind a berry bramble two hills away, he made out only the simplest physical details of the new arrivals. The sun flashed off the blond heads of the two tall ones. They carried themselves like men despite lack of beards. The short one with the brown hair walked like a female.

On another level, he sensed a great many facts. The last man to emerge possessed minor magical abilities, enough to activate the talisman that opened the portal, and wield simple magical weapons, of which he carried at least one. The woman had essentially no gift, though like her companions she wore a talisman of pursuit, calibrated for her use—which meant that she had been in contact with a major sorcerer.

The other man interested him most of all. His aura blazed with green, snakelike filaments of energy, at least as potent as those Hadradril had seen emanating from his fellow Ril wizards. But the filaments coiled in wild, unchannelled patterns. Only a fraction of his power had been disciplined and brought under his control. He should have been put into training as a child; now, in adulthood, he might never be able to organize and tap his abilities.

This was the quarry Hadradril had waited weeks to snare, the prize that Gloroc had sent him to find. While most of the other high magicians stayed safe in Elandris, hoping to win the Dragon's favor by keeping close and constantly in view, Hadradril had ventured into the territory of the enemy, and now had the means of quick promotion at hand.

The newcomers closed the portal and set off down the hill. Hadradril let them go. The sun shone brightly. The grassy countryside, though vibrant with the green of springtime and beautiful to behold, provided few places to set up an ambush. He would be patient. He raised his talisman of pursuit. The necklace's gem pulsed with a steady, blue glow. He would not lose track of his prey.

When the strangers had disappeared toward the nearest town, Hadradril brought his oeikani out of concealment, mounted, and followed at a leisurely pace.

Toren gazed about, numb. First the city, now this. His hunger crawled into some hidden niche of his body and was forgotten, obscured by the unease of walking on land that he considered barren. The country rolled and spread to the horizon like the Flat, home of the Alahihr, the Vanihr's most hated enemies, who dared to cut trees down to plant their crops. He had seen the Flat once, but that had been from the safety of the forest. Here trees, when they occurred, stood alone in a sea of nibbled grass, while livestock dung decomposed in their shade. It was even worse when they reached the first of the cultivated fields.

"What's wrong?" Deena asked.

"This ground," he said, pointing to the upturned soil. "They grow food in it?"

"Of course."

He was in a land of sinners. Deena pressed him to say more, but he kept silent. He decided he lacked the words in her language to explain why ground crops were evil.

Deena spoke to Geim, who seemed to grasp the problem.

73

"This land is not barren because the folk cleared it," he told Toren. "It has been this way as long as they can remember. They grow food because the earth provides very little otherwise. Is that a sin?"

"Men should not live without trees. They will go mad."

"On the contrary," Geim said even-handedly, "most people in the north find this type of landscape soothing."

Toren did not believe that. "What is the name of this place?"

"We are in the nation of Irigion."

"How much farther north is Serthe?"

Geim paused. "Serthe is southwest of here. The portal dropped us in the center of the continent."

Toren felt his home sail farther over the horizon.

The farms became more frequent as they left the slightly rolling terrain and entered a broad valley. Fences rose around the pastures. Homesteads appeared. A shepherd boy watched them from a haystack, a horn hanging at his side—a dark-haired boy, with a pale complexion like that of Deena or the Ijitians Toren had seen in Talitha. Now it was Toren whose skin color did not belong, as the stare of the boy proved.

They stopped to watch a farmer open a floodgate to let water flow down a shallow canal toward his orchard. The orchard astounded Toren even more than the plowed fields. Trees, deliberately placed in rows, instead of allowed to sprout at random as nature intended. Even when they grew honest food, they did it sacrilegiously.

As the sun grew swollen and red in the west, they reached the edge of a small village. Two armed men met them at the perimeter.

"Your business?" the taller one asked. They startled Toren by using Deena's language.

"We were told to ask for Mayor Korv," Deena replied. "And to show him this." She held out a copper coin. Toren briefly glimpsed the engraved image—a frog.

The sentry took the coin. His eyebrows raised. "I will fetch him. You can wait at the inn. Vodd will take you there."

"Our thanks, Goodman."

The first man strode away. Toren, Geim, and Deena followed Vodd toward the hamlet's only two-story structure. The town bustled, full of laborers done with their day's work in the fields, or wives gossiping before preparation of the evening meal. Toren could not keep up with the new sights—people in skirts, men with beards, walls of clay brick, oeikani much larger than those of the Wood. The citizens blinked and pointed at the golden skins of the Vanihr. They made less of a fuss about the hair, though villagers who were blond tended toward darker, honey tones, rather than the brilliant yellow of the southern race. Toren could not help but notice that an unusual number of the inhabitants carried weapons.

He picked up snatches of conversations—twice he heard "faces like boys" murmured behind his and Geim's backs—but for the most part the chatter blended into a chaotic buzz. Some of the people spoke the language that Geim and Deena shared, which, other than the familiar sound, completely washed over him.

"What is this place?" Toren asked Deena.

"The village is called Greenfield. Struth has an arrangement with the local officials—they keep watch on the portal exit, and provide hospitality for those who come through, in exchange for gold and certain gifts of sorcery."

"Why are so many of them armed?"

"Greenfield is near the border of Mirien, my homeland," she said wistfully. "Many of the people living here are refugees from the Dragon's invasion. They are wary of further incursions." That explained the presence of two languages.

A pretty tavern girl greeted them inside the inn. "Visitors for the mayor," Vodd announced.

"Then they'll want to sit in his booth," she replied, and showed them to an alcove. Toren chose the seat against the far wall, behind the table, grateful to slip out of conspicuous view.

"We'll get you some new clothes soon," Deena said. "It will make you feel a little less out of place."

"I like what I'm wearing now," Toren said.

The front door opened, letting in Vodd's companion and a stout elder in a well-tailored shirt and kilt. The latter joined them in the alcove.

He lay Deena's coin on the polished wood. "I'm Mayor Korv. How may I serve the emissaries of Struth?"

"Food, a night's lodging, and a few supplies for the road," Deena answered. "We'll leave for the temple in the morning."

"A modest request," Korv declared. "I'll tend to the first right now." He beckoned the serving girl. "You've just come from Talitha?" he asked when she was gone.

"Yes."

"Then you'll want news."

"Yes. How go the Dragon's conquests?" Deena asked.

The mayor's face clouded. "You've heard that he took Tamisan?"

"Yes."

"His main force is now moving slowly into Simorilia." He tugged his kinky, disarrayed beard. "We seem to be safe here for the moment. I hope it lasts."

"It won't," Deena said.

Toren had to listen attentively to be able to follow the dialogue. His command of the tongue still wavered, and Korv spoke with a different accent than Deena. He gave up, which was just as well because the conversation soon shifted into the other language, which the mayor seemed equally comfortable speaking. Geim asked him several questions.

The girl brought bowls of stew. The rising steam smote Toren with the sharp, bitter aroma of unknown spices. He guessed that the meat came from the small, woolly grazing animals he had seen earlier that day. The vegetables looked like some sort of roots or tubers.

"Are these grown in open fields?" he asked Deena, poking at a vegetable with a two-tined fork.

"Yes," she answered. "That one is called *nioc*. It's very good."

He glanced at Geim. His fellow Vanihr was shovelling his portion down with gusto. Toren did not know what to do. Every bit of the recipe offended the religious laws of his people. Even the meat came from livestock raised on treeless land. Yet he had to eat something sooner or later.

Geim nudged him. "You're not going to start this nonsense again, are you?"

Toren scowled, and took a bite.

"You see?" Deena said encouragingly. "When I was a child my mother fed us *nioc* every day. She taught me how to prepare it a dozen different ways."

He grimaced as he swallowed. "That must be why you are so pale."

"Try the mutton, then. These spices are delicious."

"I'd really prefer some snake," Toren said, but he relented and began eating everything. It filled his belly with a soothing heat, and it did curb his hunger. However, he could not muster the enthusiasm Geim and Deena were displaying.

Half an hour later, his stomach suddenly spasmed. The mayor quickly directed him toward the rear door. He staggered away and, once free of the shame of observation, he lost the meal.

I will never eat sinner's food again, he vowed.

When he did not return immediately, Geim came to find him. Toren was leaning against the outhouse, letting the cool twilight air calm the fierce heat in his neck and cheeks.

"You don't look like much of a dragon killer," Geim said.

"I'm not," Toren said stiffly.

"Don't be embarrassed. Strange food often does this. You'll adjust."

"Did it ever happen to you?"

"Of course. My first meals in three different ports. But that was when I was younger. Now I can eat anything."

"Then I look forward to my old age," Toren quipped.

"Come back inside," Geim suggested. "Perhaps if you ate bread only..."

"I'm not hungry anymore," Toren said, but he followed Geim inside, no longer nauseated. The tavern girl tried unsuccessfully to suppress a sympathetic grin as he passed. He blushed. His throat stung. He still felt queasy. A warrior should not have to feel so miserable in front of women.

Korv reassured him, and tore off a quarter loaf of pale brown bread. More sin, but what did it matter? Toren nibbled at it. He found it much lighter than the dense cakes of his homeland, and though the flour tasted of field grains rather than seeds and nuts, it went down easily. He supplemented it with ale, a light, pleasant brew, the first thing he had genuinely liked all evening. It cut the sour film at the back of his mouth.

A small, tousled head suddenly appeared over the table's edge. A young boy stared at Toren and Geim with bright, wide eyes.

The mayor chuckled and patted the child on the head. "My grandson, Pell. I apologize. He's never seen Vanihr before."

Toren's gaze lingered on his awed observer. "I have a boy your age," he told him, suddenly guilty. He had not thought of Rhi all day.

Made bold by the comment, Pell blurted, "Is it true that in your country, you sleep hanging from trees?"

Toren smiled. "Sometimes." But clearly the boy had the wrong idea. How to explain? He turned to Geim. "Do they have a word for *immei*?"

Geim told Deena the term. She translated it for Pell.

"Oh," Pell said, crestfallen. "Hammocks. We have those."

Toren could not face such disappointment. "One of my uncles

77

was stolen from one by a mooncat when he was a baby," he added.

"Really?" Pell gasped. "Did he die?"

"No. Mooncats sometimes catch prey and don't make the kill until they get hungry. My grandfather found him in time."

Pell produced a dozen eager questions about mooncats almost before he took another breath. Toren patiently answered them, assisted by Deena when his vocabulary fell short. A pair of intrigued adult patrons shifted nearer the table. The topic evolved to other points. By the time the second pitcher of ale was empty, Toren felt a little less out of place.

He breathed thanks that his ancestors could not see him now.

Toren endured Deena's appraisal of his new clothing. He had chosen a peasant shirt, vest, and winter trousers, though, as she quickly informed him, in the warming weather the folk of Irigion would be shifting to kilts. He had also picked muted, neutral colors, though local fashion favored brighter tones.

"It will do," she muttered, obviously dissatisfied, but unwilling to argue further. Geim had arrived with the oeikani.

The animals shuffled near the entrance to the inn. Three bore saddles, the fourth complained about its heavy load of fresh supplies. Toren caught their scent on the late morning breeze. He wrinkled his nose.

Deena stepped forward and stroked her beast's nose. The creature did not seem to mind.

"These things are truly tame?" he asked.

"Yes. The doe you'll be riding is especially well behaved."

Deer were meant for hunting, not transportation, Toren believed. No matter how big the species. He examined his from its long, flowing mane to the tuft of hair at the end of its whiplike tail, and down to its cloven hooves.

Geim showed him how to mount.

"Just hold on to the saddle horn," Geim said. "The oeikani will do the rest. You'll get used to it in no time. How does it feel?"

Toren felt much too high, but he was a modhiv. "Fine," he said too quickly.

Geim chuckled, mounted, and lashed Toren's reins to the back of his saddle. Deena took the pack animal's reins.

Mayor Korv came to bid them farewell. They thanked him for his hospitality, and he in turn complimented them on a good evening of tales of distant lands. His final words were more subdued. .

"There was a visitor at the portal earlier this month. He was only seen once, but I thought you should know. There's not much reason for a stranger to pass by the cairn by chance."

"What did he look like?" Deena asked.

"Tall and gaunt. Dark clothing. The shepherd only saw him briefly, from a distance."

Toren felt the beginning of an itch somewhere between his ears.

They began riding. Toren clenched the horn and tried to let his body roll with the oeikani's motion, as he had been instructed. Though the animals strode at a leisurely pace, they reached the outskirts of the town amazingly fast. It was, Toren had to admit, a convenient way to cover distance without taking a single pace.

Little Pell ran to the edge of the village and waved them on their way.

The road climbed into foothills. Pastures evolved into fields of wild grass and brambles. The trees thickened. Toren had not known this type of tree in the wood—oaks, Deena called them. The modhiv sighed as the boughs interlaced overhead, offering surcease from the afternoon sun; the shade made him feel at home. Oak wasp larvae hopped inside their tiny egg cases, bouncing across the forest floor in their struggle to escape; their birthing noise often resembled the babbling of a brook or loud whispers of raindrops striking brittle, fallen leaves.

The pleasantness of his surroundings made the itch in his head all the more noticeable.

"We're in danger," Toren said.

Geim and Deena reined up. "As with the cannibals?" the northern Vanihr asked.

"Yes. We should go another way."

Geim gestured toward the right. There was no road there, but the brush and trees left plenty of passage for the oeikani. "How about that way?"

"Perhaps. I won't know until we try it."

Hadradril frowned. His prey had left the road. He abandoned the ambush point he had selected, climbed back onto his oeikani, and parallelled the detour.

• • •

"No good," Toren said. He stared about. The trees here stood widely spaced, the ground free of brush as if a fire had come a few years before to clear the undergrowth. The sensation of danger pulsed only faintly, but it was growing stronger once again.

"You're certain?" Geim asked.

"Yes."

"I don't know what to do," Geim muttered. "I doubt Mayor Korv would have men to spare as an escort, and we must go on."

"Perhaps we could go back to Talitha for a few days," Toren said, aware that he sounded overly eager.

Geim shook his head. "No, you don't understand. Portals only go one way. To return to Talitha, we'd have to travel by ship, as Deena, Ivayer, and I did when we came south in search of you."

Toren was not sure which bothered him more, the premonition, or the realization that his home was now inconceivably far away.

"Let's go back to the road," Geim said. "If you still sense a problem, we'll go back to Greenfield for the night."

Hadradril's expression blackened. The pulse in his talisman of pursuit slowed and weakened. They had turned away again. Twice could not be chance.

The quarry had enough control over his power to sense a threat. Yet, surely, such an undisciplined talent could be thwarted. The wizard pulled a thin cape from his saddle bags, and draped it over himself. He pulled a blanket of the same material out and covered his oeikani's withers. He whispered the words of activation.

A simple spell, but it would mask his presence. His prey would have to consciously know what to do to circumvent it. Hadradril headed back to his original ambush point.

The itch faded as Toren and his companions approached the road, then vanished altogether. He frowned. He did not trust the sudden way it had stopped. It seemed too convenient.

Yet, perhaps they had fooled whoever threatened them, and were now out of danger. When they reached the road, Geim decided they should continue in their original direction. Toren reluctantly agreed. The day waned; they could not remain indecisive.

The route grew rougher, the ruts of spring rains not yet worn down in this rarely travelled region. In one place a tree had fallen over part of the road. Cover abounded on either side—too much. Toren keened his extra sense, and felt nothing.

Late in the afternoon, as they rose over a small hillock, he assembled his blowgun and laid it across his thighs.

At the base of the hillock, the feeling came on him like fire. He twisted.

An arrow grazed his side.

Only then could he sense how magic had been foiling his ability. Out of a thicket emerged a gaunt figure in embroidered silk riding gear, bow in hand, a plain grey cloak on his shoulders.

Geim threw his net. It raced straight toward Hadradril. The wizard barely had time to drop his bow before he was felled.

Toren, Deena, and Geim jumped out of their saddles, the latter drawing his sword as he dropped. Toren moved to approach the thicket from the left, Geim from the right, while Deena took the reins of the oeikani.

The men made it four or five steps. Then, no matter how hard they struggled, their feet would not leave the road. They were anchored. Toren noticed that the dust on which they stood was strangely colored.

"Just a little trick I learned in my apprentice days," the wizard said blithely, and stood up. He twirled the net in front of him. "Now this is a clever toy. I should make one of my own some time."

Despite his banter, the wizard could not conceal his spellcasting from Toren. A waver in the air led from Hadradril to the colored dust. Not only did Toren's feet refuse to budge, but his limbs grew leaden and useless. Deena, who had been trying to reach the bow in her saddle, lowered her arm. Geim's sword point dropped. Toren's hand, which had been reaching toward the pouch of darts on his belt, stopped.

Hadradril picked up his bow and nocked a fresh arrow. He chuckled. "That's better," he said, and aimed at the modhiv.

He drew back the bowstring with tortoiselike slowness. Toren frowned at the snail's pace of the wizard's movements, then the light of realization dawned. The immobilization spell consumed nearly all the sorcerer's power and concentration. Hadradril could not afford to devote much attention to his physical movements.

The filament of energy binding Toren's arms resembled a rope. And if he disturbed the knot—right *there*—just so. . . .

Suddenly the paralysis disappeared. He loaded a dart, lifted his blowgun, and fired.

The missile struck Hadradril in the chest. He cried out, released the arrow, clutched his chest, dropped the bow. The shaft came at Toren too fast for him to dodge it, but the wizard's aim had been skewed just enough. The point sliced the edge of one of his sleeves and continued past.

"Quick!" Geim shouted. "Get him!"

Geim charged forward and slashed at Hadradril's neck. The sword stopped a finger's breadth away from the skin. Sparks scattered in every direction. Undaunted, Geim continued to hack.

For Toren's eyes, the ward radiated angry, red, resistant tones. He considered trying to negate it, but had no idea how. Deena shoved a sword into his hand. Geim had the right idea—beat at the barrier with all their might. Keep Hadradril occupied, and the poison would do the rest.

Toren had never used a sword, but there was no need for finesse. He chopped at the wizard's legs, while Geim swung at the upper body. Deena, armed with a knife, stood poised to assist, should there be room for her.

Hadradril staggered. He tugged the dart from his chest, but the pain only intensified. He had underestimated his victim. His life eeked away.

Take him with me, was his foremost thought. But it was all he could do to maintain the ward. The venom spread, dulling his senses. He knew no sorcery to counteract it. Hands trembling, he reached back to his quiver, bent down and retrieved his bow. One of the blades had nearly cut through the ward. He winced. He had to be careful, move very slowly.

He drew back the arrow, pointed it at the adept, and let go. Thanks to his sluggish movement, the target anticipated him and simply stepped out of the way.

He withdrew another arrow. The result was the same.

Hadradril moaned. His only consolation was that the other sorcerers of the Ril would not see him fall. He shuddered, knees threatening to buckle. His chest burned. Spots flickered in front of his eyes.

Dying. Only one chance, one remote chance, to fulfill his mission. Once he dropped the ward, he could cast the spell in an instant.

Each impact sent numbing tingles up the sword. The weapon threatened to fall out of Toren's grip. Tiny, brief fires flickered in the twigs at their feet, ignited by the sparks.

Hadradril emitted a weak, strangled cry, perhaps a word. The ward disintegrated with a sudden snap of wind.

Geim chopped off the wizard's head.

Toren set down his sword, suddenly very weary. The head rolled to a stop. The body crumpled to the ground. Geim wiped the sweat from his forehead and stepped back. "You're good with that blowgun," he told Toren.

They heard an odd hissing. Geim stared in outrage as his sword began to sizzle and dissolve. Likewise, smoke rose from the mulch near both parts of the wizard's neck, and from Toren's vest, which had been splattered during the decapitation.

"Take it off!" Deena shouted at Toren. The modhiv was already moving. He threw the vest off just before the fabric burned through.

"The bastard!" Geim growled. "He put a spell on his blood. This was my best blade." He shook it, wiped it on the corpse's clothing, but the metal still bubbled. The fine polished edges warped into ragged, rusted contours.

A foul odor rose from the discarded piece of clothing. Toren watched it being destroyed with a pensive stare.

"Oh, well," Deena said. "You didn't like that vest, anyway."

Regrettably the acid blood was having no effect on the sorcerer's own flesh, though the necklace that had been around his neck fumed and decomposed.

Toren caught his breath. He pointed out the necklace, lying in the twigs near the head. Geim lifted it up with the tip of his afflicted sword. It possessed a single blue gem. Evidently it was still able to draw a small amount of energy from the dead man, because it pulsed with faint but rapid flashes. Geim scowled, and held the jewel closer to Toren.

The flashes sped up, until they were nearly a constant glow. When Geim removed the gem from Toren's immediate vicinity, the flashes slowed down.

"Like Ivayer's bracelet," Toren said.

"A talisman of pursuit," Geim said. "This was no random attack. He was looking for you."

≈ XIII ≈

Alemar dreamed of the Eastern Deserts. He wandered a phantom landscape of scoured, eroded channels, searching for water, and found only barren sand and ossified layers of salt. The voice of his teacher, Gast, echoed from stratified, sun-bleached cliffsides, warning him that he had let his flasks run low, that unless he filled them soon, he would perish of thirst. But though he investigated every spring and river bed, his throat remained parched. The oases had been drained.

He awoke with a foul, bilious aftertaste at the back of his throat. His head swam, unable to still the chaotic remnants of his dreams. With extreme effort, he focussed on the walls of his grandfather's cottage: tightly knit logs, mortared with clay. A griddle sizzled as Wynneth dropped a bit of pork fat onto it. She sorted through a clutch of brush hen's eggs. Cosufier snored in the upper bunk.

No desert here. But a gnawing emptiness ate away at his insides, like the thirst of the night's visions. He wiped a feverish sudor from his upper lip.

Wynneth handed him a cup of water. He sipped gratefully. She tenderly brushed his cheek, her glance drawing his. He shook his head. She nodded.

There was no need for talk. She understood the loss he felt. She knew that he would tell her as soon as there was a change. In the meantime, she would nurture him. Of all the people he had known, she was the one who knew when to draw him out, and when to leave him to his private thoughts. It was why he had married her, when he could have had a lady of greater beauty, higher station, or more vivaciousness. They were twinned in ways that he and his sister were not.

"Breakfast will be ready soon," she said. She kissed him and returned to the task.

He groaned as he sat up. "Where's Elenya?"

"Outside."

The jays screeched, fighting in the treetops, knocking loose the dew. The drops beat out a cadence against the leaves and the ground as they fell. Alemar stepped onto the porch, head still leaden and painful. He peered through the thinning mist. Elenya was practicing her swordcraft near a flat stump fifty paces away.

She had placed a pumpkin on the stump as a target. The rind showed only one tiny hole, barely wider than the thickness of her rapier. He watched her thrust again and again. Once, the fruit wobbled a little under the impact. She steadied it, frowned, and examined the tip of her blade. She had not missed the mark. Alemar decided that she must have thrust deeper, penetrating fresh tissue. She adjusted her stance and resumed her practice.

After another fifty thrusts—and probably a hundred before he had begun to watch—she shifted her rapier to the other hand for the second half of the routine.

In her mid-twenties, Elenya had never moved more efficiently, more confidently, more powerfully. She made no superfluous body movements. Her eyes remained fixed on the pumpkin, her head did not bob. The tension gathered in her ankles and calves. She sprang suddenly, transferring the force straight up to her wrist. The rapier seemed more like an arrow in flight than a blade in hand. When she stopped, it was utter: for a moment she would be a statue, every bit of strength and coordination under complete control.

Alemar counted one hundred fifty jabs. She sheathed her rapier, rotated the pumpkin, and drew both her demonblades. She had begun wearing two from the moment they had left the Eastern Deserts. That, and her frequent choice of white garments, were the obvious reminders that she remembered what it was to be a *hai-Zyraii*, though she seldom spoke of it.

She threw one knife forehand, the other backhand. They lodged side by side. When she pulled them from the rind and assumed her stance again, Alemar decided she meant to continue drilling.

"That's enough," he called. "You're supposed to be recuperating."

She gave no sign of being startled, but Alemar knew she had been oblivious to his presence until he spoke. He left the porch to join her. She wiped off her steel and tucked it away.

"Too long without exercise," she explained. "I couldn't stay asleep. I was going to stop soon."

"Of course you were."

"I'm slow," she said, rubbing the hand where the gauntlet should have been, still keeping her face averted. "It feels like I'm moving through syrup."

Alemar knew she was simply making conversation. She practiced at least once a week without the gauntlet, just so she did not become dependent on magical speed. "You're the most difficult patient I've ever treated," he said sternly. "It's still quite possible to strain your system and develop a fever. Come in and have breakfast. We'll talk." He had returned so late the previous night that they had not had time to confer about what had happened since the ambush.

"I'm not hungry yet."

He tapped her ribs. His fingers encountered firm, unyielding muscle. "Training is one thing. Endangering your health is another. You need some fat."

"I'll borrow some from my brain."

Alemar kept his fingers against her, trying to probe with his powers, trying to see within to judge the speed and degree of her recovery. He saw only a dark veil, heard only echoes of a hollow place inside himself. He shook. He tried to stifle it, but his knees kept wobbling. His hand quivered against her side.

"Please," he said, stricken. "I need for you to look after your body. I can't do it for you anymore."

She looked up suddenly. Tears welled in her eyes. Dried tracks of old weeping led down her cheeks. She'd been crying during her weapons practice. "I know. I'm so sorry," she squeaked, almost too hoarse to get the words out.

They embraced. The feel of her chin against the crook of his neck, the moisture of her tears on his skin, gave him a kind of solace entirely different from that which he received from Wynneth, though just as necessary. Elenya knew what it meant to be a child of the Blood, a rebel chased league upon league, year upon year, by an enemy who might live another five millennia. Despite their occasional bickering, and even though they were both so battered by circumstances that all they wanted to do was crawl into a crevice and abandon the world, they could not stop their concern or understanding for one another.

"I'll rest, I'll eat, I'll be good," she murmured. "I just need to practice."

"I know," he said. He wished he had something to occupy him the same way, a way to use the conflict to hone his talents, instead of draining them. They walked hand in hand back to the cottage.

"Where did you bury Dushin?" she asked as they crossed the threshold. As soon as they entered, Wynneth cracked blue, speckled eggs over the griddle. Cosufier, awake now, huddled in a fur near the fire, looking closer to his age than usual. The air smelled homey and revitalizing.

"We managed to send the body to his relatives in Yent," Alemar replied.

"And the attackers?"

"We dumped them in a ravine," Wynneth said, more matter-of-factly than Alemar could have managed. She had no problem being cold to anyone who threatened her loved ones. For that matter, it had been she and other members of the rebel band who had taken care of the details while Alemar was occupied first with Elenya's healing, and then with his own exhaustion. "We retrieved the food from the silk farm, and tried to eliminate any trace of your visit."

"We had more time than we expected," Alemar added. "Apparently Enns was not working with Puriel's men. He set up the ambush himself."

"That must be why there were only four. And why they were poorly armored," Elenya said reflectively.

"Yes," her brother answered. "I doubt Puriel knows about the ambush even now. Otherwise guards would be all over the silk farm."

Wynneth nodded. "Still, the place is not safe to use again. We don't know just who Enns contacted."

Alemar shook his head. "When Milec was captured, I suspected treachery. I never suspected Enns was the cause."

"The seed was planted a long time ago," Elenya murmured. "You remember back when we were still posing as Lord Dran's bastards, Enns would complain that we received more attention than we deserved?"

A few flickers of memory came back to Alemar, but he shoved them away. "Enough about *him*," he snapped.

Elenya stared, as if trying to read his mind, but their amulets were lying on the stool. Alemar almost gave in and fetched them. He and his sister had recovered enough energy by now to restore the jewels to their necks, though they would have to leave the gauntlets off for several more days. But he was not ready to open his thoughts so completely. When he let go of his anger, it would not be in the presence of loved ones.

As if sensing his need for distance, Elenya turned to Cosufier. "Grandfather, didn't you say that Puriel's patrols were searching near Eruth? Why would that be if Enns isn't the cause?"

"It was two days before the soldiers came," Alemar interjected. "After I had cast the healing spell."

"The Dragon's magician..." both the women said simultaneously.

"Yes. That was strong magic. Omril must have detected it and sent troops to the site where I performed it. We needn't worry. This cottage is leagues away, and there isn't enough psychic residue to lead them here. The rythni will warn us of men heading in this direction."

"Speaking of rythni..." Elenya said.

"The one who fetched me was named Cyfee," Alemar said. "She is a protégée of Queen Hiephora."

Elenya described Cyfee's actions at the silk farm.

Alemar frowned. "That's extraordinary. Rythni have an aversion to human dwellings. You were lucky she was with you, and not another."

"Thank her for me."

"I already have, though I didn't know until now just how much I had to thank her for. For her sake we'd best not let any other rythni know that she committed an act of violence."

Elenya sat down on the bed, near the stool where the talismans lay. "Done. Now tell me the news from the south."

Alemar frowned. "Tamisan has capitulated. The Dragon broke the sultan at Tira."

"And Father?"

"He is in Simorilia. The shah has given his army refuge outside Tazh Tah. There are signs that Gloroc may wait a season to expand westward. The battle at Tira apparently cost him dearly, even though he won."

"Val?"

"Safe. As is Enret."

"How does Father feel about the defeat?"

That had been one of Alemar's first questions to the emissary. "He realizes that he had no real chance of holding Tamisan, not with winter over, and Gloroc so firmly rooted in Mirien. He had hoped Tira would hold out longer, though. That's the city that thwarted the Calinin's best general, back before the days of Alemar Dragonslayer. But Gloroc took to the field again, and the shah's men couldn't hold the walls."

"Was it like before? During a heavy storm?"

"No. There wasn't a cloud in the sky. The Dragon was nearly struck down by Father's magicians."

"Strange," Elenya said. "Gloroc's always been more cautious

88

than that. He could have stayed safe in Elandris and let his army do it the hard way. He has plenty of time."

"Tira was a major hurdle. He must have felt it worth the risk to take it quickly."

"Why?"

Alemar shrugged. "Perhaps he's in a hurry. Perhaps he's worried about us—about the talismans."

"The Dragon, afraid of us, what a pleasant fantasy," Elenya said dryly. "Have you heard the one about the demon who was afraid of the mouse?"

"There was that strange prophecy of Treynaf's last winter," Alemar said. "A dragon dead in a palace beneath the sea. I'm afraid Gloroc suspects the plans we've made with Struth. Don't you think it's significant that he replaced Puriel's former sorcerer with a wizard of the Ril? Omril is said to be an apprentice of the Dragon himself."

"Any word from Struth?"

"The party had not yet returned from the Wood at the time the message was sent."

Elenya picked up her amulet and dangled it from her fingers. "I find it ironic that Gloroc might be worried about our plans. To be frank, I'll believe Struth's man can succeed only after it's done."

All at once everyone in the room paused in shock. The amulet, now that it was touching Elenya's flesh, awakened. It blazed with the deep green tones that warned of magic being cast nearby.

Alemar spun toward the window. A pigeon sat on a nearby branch, observing them. Abruptly it took flight.

"Grandfather!" Alemar shouted.

Cosufier grabbed his bow and quiver, his speed belying his age. He rushed to the porch, the others at his heels. He dumped the arrows out for easy access and strung the bow. He drew back and aimed. The arrow flew long and straight, as his always did, but fell far short of the mark. The pigeon disappeared over the treetops toward the west.

Cosufier cursed.

"No matter," Alemar said ruefully. "Omril's already seen us. Even if we'd killed it, we could not have undone the damage. I'm sorry, Grandfather. We've ruined one of your sanctuaries."

The old man waved away the apology. "There are others. Let's get moving. The wizard's troops will soon be on their way."

Alemar had misjudged Omril. Given three days and the fact

that Elenya, the subject of the magic, had not moved, the wizard did have the power to detect the lingering traces of the healing spell. The tension inside him reached a crescendo. They could not even have a momentary respite. The Dragon would hound them until they dropped. The time had come. If he could no longer be a healer, he would be a warrior.

Someone would pay.

≈≈≈ XIV ≈≈≈

Omril stood on the balcony of his tower, scanning the clouds to the east. A tiny speck appeared, grew, and resolved into the shape of a pigeon. Omril held up his hand. The bird landed on his glove.

"There, there, Swiftwing," the wizard murmured, stroking his servant's neck. He could feel her staccato pulse against his finger. She was barely able to keep her grip. Omril cupped her gently in his palms, comforted her as he stepped into his chambers, and returned her to her coop.

"Your eyes told me a great deal," he said, double checking to be sure the bird and her three siblings had adequate feed and water. He had worked Swiftwing close to her limit, both physically and in terms of the amount of magic she could channel. Still, even her death would have been worth the result.

The rebels had been gone by the time Swiftwing had guided Puriel's quarter cohort of guards to the cottage, but Omril was content. He had flushed them from cover. It was only a matter of time until he did it again. Sooner or later he would trap them. He regretted only that he could not have heard as well as seen the rebels' conversation. However, sending one's eyesight to distant locales was one thing, sending one's ears at the same time was another. Swiftwing had done what she could. The Dragon would be pleased with the news.

Omril unrolled a tiny scroll and dipped his pen. In clear, precise glyphs, he wrote: *I have seen the talismans of Setan*. He closed the scroll, held it under a dripping candle, pressed his signet ring to the hardening wax, and attached the message to the leg of Swiftwing's brother Windborne. He released the bird and watched as it flew south toward Elandris.

~~~ XV ~~~

Above the pass, the snowy peaks sparkled with alpenglow. "Isn't it beautiful?" Deena asked.

Toren kept drawing breath, but the thin mountain air refused to fill his chest. The sun beat fiercely, drying and cracking his lips, but declined to warm the atmosphere. His thighs ached murderously. He vowed silently never to come near a saddle once the journey was over.

They lingered at the crest of the pass. To the right and left rose steep slopes, cloaked in white. Behind them lay the range that separated Irigion from Serthe. Hard leagues. The rough terrain had lamed their pack oeikani, forcing them to transfer its load to the wizard's captured animal. Geim kept saying that they were lucky. The thaw had begun ahead of time, opening the pass early in the season. Even now thick banks of snow were heaped beside the trail in shady spots, eroded and ugly. The oeikani trod on cold mud.

"It is not the place for a Vanihr," he replied. The Wood was a lowland. To him, snow was a light dust on the ground every second or third winter that melted in hours, or at most a few days. He glanced at the peaks; no trees grew that high. He gestured at Geim, who was in the lead, staring at the timbered slopes below them as if searching for something. "I don't know how he has stood it, years without a home, travelling through lands like these."

"Why don't you ask him?" Deena asked.

The elegance of the suggestion hit him by surprise. He took her advice.

When Geim heard the question, he sighed. "It is better now. I serve Struth. Before that, when I simply wandered..." He shrugged, and in the gesture Toren suddenly knew a great deal about the course of Geim's adult life.

"It's good to live *for* something," Geim concluded. Then, changing the subject, he pointed toward what he had discovered.

Far below, they saw the spur of a river valley. Where it opened out onto the plain, the sun sparkled on glass and white-washed structures.

"The city of Headwater," Geim said. "Our destination."

• • •

They continued to descend for two days, passing several riders and small caravans heading the other way—not, according to Geim, as many as there should have been. The reports from the war had made merchants wary. Then they stood before the city gates.

The older part of Headwater was tucked into a gorge where the Slip River spilled out of the mountains in a phantasmagorical waterfall. Bridges, many of them elaborate, ancient constructions, spanned the stream, connecting the two halves of the community. Downstream the houses and shops fanned out onto the valley floor, most of them contained by the fifth and outermost of the city walls, though new buildings poked up outside the gates.

"We are now inside the old boundaries of the Calinin Empire," Geim said as they made their way down the streets. "In fact, Serthe is still part of the commonwealth, tied by treaty to Xais. Headwater was one of the ten great cities of the empire. Alemar Dragonslayer was born here."

The commentary washed right over Toren. The concept of a dozen large, civilized nations and an equal number of protectorates, all under one centralized government for a period of centuries, staggered him. The only times Vanihr tribes had united were for the campaigns against the Shagas and the Alahihr, and these alliances had lasted only for the duration of raids and sorties. The lands of the Fhali, which had seemed so vast, now seemed like a tiny hunting range.

They passed beggars in rags; guardsmen in fine, polished armor; merchants in loose, wraparound robes; and hordes of vendors. Blacksmith shops belched smoke, bakeries taunted them with the aroma of fresh loaves being drawn from the oven, jugglers and musicians provided entertainment in the larger squares and plazas. By comparison, Talitha had been only a sleepy river town. Few people stared at Toren and Geim now. Their appearance seemed mild compared to the bright orange braids and immense breasts of the Cotani slave girls washing clothes at the public fountains, or to the short, stocky dark men—"Drelbs," Geim called them—pushing their wheelbarrows down an alley. They even saw another Vanihr, partaking of wine and cheese in an open-air cafe.

At length they came to a less crowded, cleaner section of the city, where they boarded their oeikani in a stable. They continued down a street lined with great edifices of marble and granite. Toren heard chants filter out of one temple, and through the portal of another saw men kneel and touch their foreheads to the tiles while a eunuch beat on a large brass gong.

"A god for every persuasion," Geim said dryly. "They have one thing in common. They all require plentiful offerings to appease them."

"Even Struth?"

"Especially Struth."

Even as he spoke, Geim indicated the stone wall they were approaching. It towered twenty feet high, surrounding grounds more extensive than any they had seen thus far. Brawny sentries patrolled the top, and more stood in the archway beside a set of imposing doors, looking fierce but otherwise ignoring everyone. The doors hung wide open, and through the gap, in and out, flowed a small but constant stream of supplicants. Geim, Deena, and Toren filtered inside.

They passed through a foyer and came to a spacious amphitheater. Several dozen people, perhaps as many as a hundred, were queued at the far side, in front of a gigantic statue of a frog. The chiselled image rose so tall that the crest of its head was even with the top of the walls, framed by the open sky above.

"The Oracle of Struth, the Frog God," Deena whispered to Toren.

Immediately in front of the statue, separating it from the throng, was a broad, rectangular pool. One by one, worshippers approached a tiny dais and cast coins into the water. As they did so, the supplicants asked questions, some of which Deena translated for Toren. A farmer asked if the danger of frost had ended. A merchant wanted to know if the price of iron would drop soon. A middle-aged matron asked what her new son-in-law should do to prosper in his trade. None were answered. But when a small boy demanded, rather insistently, to know if he would travel to faraway places when he was older, a reply came.

"Yes."

The deep voice made Toren jump. The meaning penetrated far more directly than any common sound could. It seemed to come from the head of the stone frog, yet at the same time, it came from all directions. There was no need for translation. A murmur ran through the crowd, and the boy, grinning with self-importance, stepped down from the dais and headed for the exit.

The supplicants came from all walks of life, from nobles in embroidered finery to beggars in rags. Toren and his companions did not join the line; they waited near the entrance, observing for the better part of an hour. Toren grew restless, but Geim told him to pay attention, to try to see a pattern to the oracle's actions.

At first, it seemed that there was none. About one in five petitioners was answered, some at length, more often with a simple yes or no, with no direct relationship between the amount of money thrown, or the sophistication of the question, and receipt of an answer. But over time, Toren saw that larger offerings did increase one's chances. And once, something unusual happened.

A man in the livery of a Calinin high family came forward, dropped several gold pieces, and said, "Who is my lord's hidden enemy?"

"*He who sleeps with your lord*," the oracle replied.

The man blanched, then nodded knowingly. Then, as he stepped off the dais, the Frog God spoke again.

"*Bide with me for a time.*"

The man jumped, then both he and the rest of the crowd turned toward a curtained alcove behind the statue. The cloth parted, held by a stunningly beautiful woman. She beckoned the petitioner, who burst into a smile and walked quickly into the passageway. Men left behind licked their lips and watched with envious glances.

"I don't understand," Toren said.

"That man has just been favored with the hospitality of Struth," Geim said. "I'll explain later. It's time we went inside. We'll use a less public route."

They left the way they had come. They continued along the wall and around a corner into an untrafficked alley. Geim stepped up to a small door and rapped four times.

The peephole opened, then the door. A drelb stood there. He greeted Geim and Deena by name, spoke a few words, and made way for them.

"He says I'm to go to the high priestess," Deena told Toren. "You and Geim are to wait in the Wine Room." They continued on. The dwarf remained by the door.

They passed through a small anteroom into a garden of lush trees, vines, and fronds. Deena vanished down one path, while Geim led Toren down another between a series of pools—deep rock grottoes stocked with exotic fish, and shallow ponds spotted with lilies and water grass. Frogs croaked. The garden ended in one large, clear pool of flat tile, in which four women waded, each as lovely as the one in the oracle's hall. They smiled and waved at Geim, who waved back.

The temple itself ascended in many tiers, artfully accented with balconies, stairways, columns, hallways, and patios, trellises of flowering vines, and stained glass windows. It did not fit with the houses of religion elsewhere along the street.

As they walked down a well-lit hallway, panelled in wood and decorated with framed paintings, an elderly woman servant handed Geim a key. She continued on without a word, towels in her hand, heading for the pool as if drying the bathing women had been her sole duty.

Geim unlocked a door near the end of the corridor. They stepped into a small room. The scent of incense and wine greeted them. Fine tapestries lined the walls. Along the side opposite the door sat a row of wine barrels, with a smaller cask on a stand in front. Cushioned divans abutted the two side walls, stacked with abundant, plush pillows. In the center of the room stood a glass table whorled into an intricate statue of an octopus, its out-stretched tentacles providing occasional flat spots on which empty goblets were cradled.

"This is one of the reception rooms," Geim said. "One of the places the lucky supplicant to the oracle might be entertained. Each one has its own decor." He picked up a pair of goblets, went to the small cask, and filled them with an amber wine. A rich, fruity bouquet kissed the air. "I have a very fond memory of this room," he added, turning off the spigot. His eyes sparkled. "The hospitality of the priestesses of Struth is legendary, and they deserve their fame."

"They're prostitutes?"

Geim rolled a tiny mouthful of wine across his tongue. Toren did likewise, and realized for the first time that winemaking was a type of art, and that he was sampling the work of an adept.

"You might call them that. The priestesses provide incentive for certain people to visit the oracle. Struth is a gatherer of infor-mation. The more influential the supplicant—the closer to posi-tions of power—the more likely he is to be invited within the walls. There he enjoys the attentions of a priestess, and she, in turn, encourages him to unburden his heart, tell her his inner worries. It's more than sex. The priestesses are sorceresses. By the time a man has been with one for a few hours, her particular kind of magic makes it difficult for him not to reveal his entire life story. Struth knows more about the inner workings of the empire than any living creature. The crown prince of Serthe him-self is a frequent visitor. But it's wrong to call them whores. They are proud of what they do. They do it for the Frog God— the goddess, as they call her."

Toren massaged the bridge of his nose, trying to absorb all the information. "You were a supplicant once?"

"In a way. I was fortunate enough to have been in Headwater five years ago when Struth decided to learn more about the Vanihr. A man came to me in a tavern and hinted that, should I care to show my brown face and yellow hair in front of the oracle, it might be worth my while. I was certain he was playing a game with me, but after he left, curiosity got the best of me. I came to the temple and found, much to my delight, that the invitation was genuine."

Geim swirled the wine in his goblet. "I have never determined just how Struth knows which petitioners have useful information, and which do not. There is a great deal about her I don't know. She is subtle. Most people in this city have no idea how she selects her guests. They offer her money, and think it is her whim when she ignores them. The few who know the way of it have enjoyed these rooms more than once for the offering of a single copper erron."

"And you?"

"Struth saw that I was a resourceful person, and enlisted me. I have served her in various capacities ever since. When the time came to fetch you, it was obvious that sending a Vanihr would be helpful. I was the logical candidate." He sipped deeply. "I have, in fact, visited some of these rooms in the past few years, but only because a particular priestess took a liking to me. Whenever I have useful information, I render it freely, in consideration of the food, the shelter, the purpose Struth has given me."

"And does that purpose fulfill you?" Toren asked. As he spoke it startled him to realize how much he needed the answer.

Geim scratched his head, drank the last of his wine, and re-filled the goblet. "As I said on the mountain, it is better than wandering. Struth plays the game of life at a level most beings are unaware of. To be part of it is always . . . interesting."

"Do you trust her?"

He frowned. "She protects her own, and she keeps her word. I know she will give you back your totem, as promised."

"When?"

"Probably today. She will probably summon you as soon as Deena finishes her report, and I give mine. No doubt she will return it to you then."

• • •

Toren was on his third goblet when they heard a light, tentative knock on the door. Geim gave permission to enter. It was Deena.

She said something to him. He nodded. "My turn," he said to Toren, and left. Deena stayed.

Toren gestured at the cask, and lifted his goblet, but she declined the offer. She stared at the tiles.

"Is something wrong?" he asked.

"The high priestess can be . . . intimidating." She smoothed out the cuffs of her riding breeches. She refused to meet Toren's eyes. "She sees things whether you want them seen or not."

"You were talking about me?"

"Of course. That was the point. She wanted to know a few details of the journey . . . and she wanted to know what I thought about you."

"What did you tell her?"

"The truth. As I said, she has a way of dragging it out."

"Apparently so do the other priestesses." Toren realized she was embarrassed, so he offered the chance to divert the topic.

"Did Geim tell you about them?"

"Yes."

"High Priestess Janna's methods are not so visceral," she said.

Toren raised his brows. "I didn't mean to imply that they were."

"You didn't. I just wanted to be clear." She raised one delicate eyebrow. "Do you have whores in the Far South?" Disdain tinged her voice when she uttered the term.

"They're rare, but the occupation exists. Geim told me something of your practices as we rode through the mountains. Our customs are more strict, because of our totems."

"How so?"

Toren gladly accepted the opportunity to compare cultures. It reminded him of their evenings of talk on the way through the Wood. "A boy must always know who his father is, in order to know which totem to receive. Married couples do not stray. Those who are not married have more choice, but a woman is not permitted to have more than one partner per month, so that if she conceives, she will know the sire. A woman must be infertile to be a prostitute; if a fertile woman is caught selling her body, she is sterilized."

Deena's eyes widened. "How?"

"I'm told it's not pleasant. Sometimes it is fatal."

She shuddered, poured herself some wine after all, and gulped it.

"I'm sorry," Toren said.

"It's not your fault. I asked you to tell me." She coughed. "What happens to an orphan? Who will pass on the totem?"

"Preferably a grandparent, so that the totem would be almost the same. If I do not return before my son comes of age, that's what will happen. Or if my father is dead by then, one of my brothers will take my place."

"What about the boy's mother?"

"Mothers give totems to daughters, fathers to sons. If a boy has no living male relative, he goes outside the family for adoption. It is better to receive any totem than none. Likewise, it is a great tragedy if a man never passes his on. His life experiences are lost. A man who has only daughters will pay very dearly to adopt a son of a man who has many boys. Fortunate is the man with many sons; not only can he pass on his totem many times, but he can make great bargains. My own father was a lucky one. I am his fourth son. I might have easily been given the totem of my father's friend, for whom I am named, but that Toren finally had a son shortly before I came of age."

"I would have thought that you'd be named after one of your ancestors," Deena said.

"No. It would be too confusing, with all those generations in one's head, some of them with the same names. It happens anyway; no need to worsen it."

Deena toyed pensively with the tip of one of the glass octopus's tentacles. "You think about your son a great deal, don't you?"

"How can I not? I am a Vanihr. My son is my immortality."

There was another knock. Geim stepped in, accompanied by a tall, buxom, high-cheeked priestess in a diaphanous gown. The cloth rustled as she walked, a faint, alluring whisper that drew attention to her supple outlines, and to the hint of nipples pressing against the gauze. Toren smelled magic accentuating her seductiveness, but declined to interfere with the spellweaving. She spoke to him in a mellifluous voice. He did not understand the words.

"This is Yari," Geim translated. "She will take you to the high priestess." When Toren did not respond immediately, Deena jabbed him in the ribs.

He jumped up and followed Yari out, only vaguely aware of Deena's jealous observation.

Yari led him through sumptuous rooms and across an exquisite patio to the rear of the temple complex, his eyes locked on the supple twisting of her waist. It was as if he were being pulled with a tether like a pack beast. It was now easy for him to understand the allure of the priestesses of Struth.

They came to a dome, a pale, marble hemisphere three times the height of a man at the apex, featureless and unadorned, save for a doorway. Yari indicated he should step inside.

The interior was a single chamber containing only two semicircular divans. The latter faced each other, about three paces apart, plush and soft, the off-white upholstery matching the hue of the polished marble floor. A woman sat in one.

It seemed as though he had been transported into the midst of an ocean. Outside, visible through transparent walls, swam a bewildering array of fish. Strands of kelp wafted in the current. Elsewhere a sea turtle peered in. Echoes of waves and high-pitched songs of sea creatures filtered through at an almost subliminal level. The perfection of the illusion was broken only by the rectangle of the entrance.

Yari stopped at the threshold. She smiled and withdrew, closing the door. Once shut, it showed no seams, as if none had ever existed.

Toren turned to the woman on the divan. She rose. The top of her head crested no higher than his upper chest; she must have weighed less than half of what he did. She wore her hair in a neat bun. She wore a jacket, close-fitting leggings, and sandals—a handsome outfit, but not in the least suggestive. Yet, as she reached out a hand to him, she struck him as far more seductive than Yari, though as far as he could tell, she dispensed no sorcery to enhance her charm. The brilliant blue of her jacket, her black hair, and her tan flesh presented a vivid spot of color against the austere background.

"Deena was right. You are handsome. Come. Let me look at you more closely." She used Mirienese, Deena's language.

He walked forward, still marvelling at the ocean outside. "Deena said that?"

"Not in those exact words. But she is . . . impressed." She gestured at the divan opposite her, and sat down. "I am Janna, High Priestess of Struth. I bid you welcome in the name of the goddess."

"It was an invitation I couldn't refuse," Toren said sarcastically.

"Indeed," she said kindly. "Geim and Deena inform me that you understand why we had to abduct you."

"They've told me about the Dragon. I believe them when they say he is a threat—perhaps even to my people. But I have yet to be told precisely why I have the means to help you."

"Really?" she asked. "You haven't discovered new things about yourself in the past weeks?"

"Well, yes," he admitted. "But nothing that would allow me to kill a dragon."

"What you can do with training may surprise you." She held out her palms. "Give me your hands."

After some hesitation he did as she asked. Her eyes bore into him. He felt her presence come . . . closer. "Be at peace," she said, and he relaxed. Soon she disengaged.

"Struth was right. You are an astounding candidate."

"I haven't agreed to help you," Toren reminded her.

"Yes. That is the question. But it needn't be answered now. It is your turn to make requests."

Instantly Toren held up his bracelet. "I want my totem back."

"Of course. For that, we must see Struth."

She stood and walked to the center of the chamber. She held her hand out over the floor, and uttered a single word. With his recently developed senses, he saw a glow of power extend from her palm into the marble.

A square hole opened in the floor, revealing a set of stairs. "Follow me," she said.

They descended a straight flight of over one hundred steps, guided by an eerie cerulean werelight of no apparent source. At the bottom they emerged into a chamber so large that the glow from the tunnel would not reach the far corners of the room. The blackness also hid the ceiling. Toren smelled an essence that he identified as frog. Water dripped loudly; the drops echoed, as if across a vast empty space.

"Mistress, we have come," Janna called.

"*Welcome.*" The word reverberated in Toren's mind. Out of the dim recesses of the cavern there took shape an enormous amphibian. Shortly thereafter the werelight spread outward from the tunnel entrance, and he realized that the statue of the frog in the amphitheater was not, after all, larger than life. Here was its model.

"*I am Struth.*"

Each of her bulging eyes was as wide as Toren was tall. She could have gobbled him up like an insect. She towered above him, awesome and intimidating, her smooth green skin rendered grayish and shadowy by the werelight. Toren found it hard to respond to a being whose very eyeblinks frightened him, but he kept the tremor out of his voice. At last he had before him the proper target of his anger. "I am here to collect something that is owed to me," he said.

"I apologize for my methods. I couldn't afford a refusal. You are the best candidate I have found."

"For what purpose? Why me?" Toren asked.

"Of all the people alive in the world today, your energy pattern most closely matches that of the great wizard, Alemar Dragonslayer. With proper training, you may be able to use his talismans to near their full potential. I speak in particular of the gauntlets that were retrieved from the Eastern Deserts by the great wizard's descendants, Alemar and Elenya of the House of Olendim, which were made specifically to fight the children of Faroc and Triss."

Toren tapped his foot against the stone, skeptical. "You're going to keep my ancestors, then, force me to do your bidding?"

"You have no confidence in us. It is understandable. But I will keep the bargain. Put the bracelet on the floor."

Toren hesitated, then did as he was ordered.

The only movement Struth made was a minute shifting of the pupils of her eyes, yet almost immediately one of the bracelet's gems began to glow. In reverse of the spell cast by Ivayer back in the Wood, Toren's tortoise appeared in a facet of the stone, growing larger and larger until it stood, full-sized, straddling the talisman. Toren, hands trembling, lifted it into his palms. Warm, vibrant, it nuzzled its chin against the base of his thumb.

"As soon as you return to the surface, Janna will restore it to your body."

"And then am I free to go?"

"If you wish."

Toren frowned. It was impossible to read sincerity or guile on the face of a giant frog. "I don't believe you. Without me, your plan is ruined."

"Nearly. We have other candidates, though we have found them lacking. However, if we lose you, we will resort to one of these others and hope for the best. Your role is too critical to fill with an unwilling participant. However, I think I can demonstrate that it would be in your best interests to aid us."

"How?"

"Recall your battle with the wizard. It is proof of a great fear

of mine. When I cast the spell to search for individuals who might be able to use the talismans, I invoked great magic. There was a residue created which other adepts can detect. Gloroc apparently has discovered these traces. He knows the nature of the spell. He is searching both for me and the persons that my spell located. He knows that an extremely high-level, non-human magician is somewhere in this city, and he was able to duplicate the talismans I created to track you and the others. Thanks to his efforts you nearly died. One of the other candidates, whom I had been hiding in a nearby province, was recently murdered. I am now exerting a considerable effort to screen you and them. Thus far, I have succeeded. If you should decide not to aid our effort, you are naturally free to go. But it is a long walk, and if you are not an ally I won't be able to justify the expenditure necessary to protect you from the Dragon's eyes. His wizards will be able to find you. Moreover, if he learns that you are a Vanihr, it will be unlikely for you to hide even from common bounty hunters."

"So you have found a different way to coerce me."

"I realize the choice is not fair, but I can hardly do anything about it now. You have seen a taste of the Dragon's resources. I must use any tool at my disposal to thwart him. However, I can also offer positive incentives."

"Such as?"

"Consider the talents you've discovered in yourself since you left the Wood. If you are anything like the Dragonslayer, you won't be willing to let that potential go to waste. I can teach you how to use your power. In fact, I must, if you are to use the gauntlets."

Toren stroked the shell of his totem pensively.

"As I said, you may leave at any time. If you stay, Janna and I will begin our training of you. By the end of that process, you will have to decide whether to take the gauntlets and kill Gloroc, or leave with our best wishes. Think about it after your totem is restored. That experience will be enough to deal with for the moment." Struth's tone seemed sympathetic as she uttered the last sentence; that worried the modhiv. *"Go with Janna now."*

Toren had more questions, but none of them seemed as urgent as getting his ancestors back. The high priestess tapped him gently on the arm. He followed her up the stairs. His totem murmured anxiously.

≈≈ XVI ≈≈

Two tavern boys, bare to the waist, sweating in the kitchen heat, lifted the roast pig away from the bed of coals and set it on the butcher table, where the head cook prepared to remove the stuffing. A girl hurried through with clean steins for the pub room. Owl the tavernmaster surveyed the activity with a critical eye. "Nearly sundown," he cautioned his workers. In fact, Achird had already dropped behind Cilendrodel's giant trees. The light had not yet dimmed because Motherworld, the Sister, and Urthey were all in the sky. A good night for business, Owl predicted. The lack of darkness would mean more traffic.

"Mind you don't run short like last Sisday," Owl warned the cook.

"Never fear," the man replied, his bald head nearly obscured behind the steam rising from the pig's belly.

"I'll have my dinner in my room," Owl announced, and went upstairs to wait for it.

He was enjoying a pipeful of his favorite tobacco when he heard the knock on his door. A bit early. For once his staff had displayed some efficiency. "Come in."

The man who entered was lithe, short, dark-haired, perhaps twenty-five years old. Though he seemed to bear no weapons, Owl's heart began to race as if a sword had been pointed at it.

"You know me," the stranger said.

"You are Alemar," he said hoarsely. "It's tonight, then?"

"Yes. Are you ready?"

The insides of his cheeks went dry. "Yes. Yes. Though I wish it didn't have to happen here."

"If we could avoid it, we would."

"I know that."

"If you have doubts, I could bind and gag you now and leave you in this room."

Owl felt the weight of the prince's gaze. It was as if he could see right into the tavernmaster, measure every weakness, confirm every true word and every lie. Surely that could not be so. Owl himself did not know precisely which way he would go. All he had ever wanted was to run an honest establishment and keep out

103

of politics. If tonight's scheme failed, he might well be branded a rebel. He would be at the mercy of the Dragon's governor.

Perhaps that was why Alemar had not sent an emissary. It would be the prince's decision, and no other's, whether or not to trust Owl. If the latter proved undeserving of that faith, no vassal could be blamed.

It was the point of no return. Like so many others in the province this night, Owl had to make up his mind whether he was content to continue living under the Dragon's rule or not. He sat up straight, and met the healer's eyes.

"I'll play my role."

"Good. We'll see each other again soon." Alemar left.

Owl exhaled. The prince of Elandris himself! Gods, if Puriel or the captain of his guards learned of the plot, half the Dragon's garrison would descend on the tavern within the hour. He suddenly noticed that he was digging his fingernails into his palms. He stopped before he drew blood.

Owl ate sparingly, an unusual practice for him, and descended to the main room early. The tavern had been open for only a few minutes, but it was already half full. The air was growing thick with the aroma of ale, human beings, lantern smoke, and incense. He noted the presence of townsfolk seldom seen at the Silver Eel, most of them young, strong men. Owl weaved his way through the customers to his table by the front door, where it was his habit to greet incoming patrons and thank departing ones. Old Jom was sitting in the opposite chair, as he did every Serday, with the peg board already on the table.

Owl eased into his seat, realizing that he was sweating, but determined not to show his nervousness. "Bound to be an especially good game tonight, eh?" said Jom.

Owl's eyes widened. He had not realized his friend was also a conspirator. Jom stared back guilelessly. "Your turn to move first, as I recall," he said.

Owl calmed himself and moved a pawn forward two holes. Jom immediately responded with a pawn of his own, forcing Owl to take it. The Duke's Opening. It would be a night of challenging strategy.

To his surprise, the game managed to absorb his attention. The tavern became noisier, the smell of roast pork and fried eel more prominent, and the air hotter. It was only when a half dozen of Puriel's guards arrived with their captain that Owl's concentration was broken.

Claric strode immediately to his usual table at the center of the room and pounded a chair against the floor. "Food, ale, music!" he roared. He had already been drinking; Owl could tell by the slurred syllables. Wood creaked as he sat down. Owl had lost a dozen chairs to the captain's abuse in the three years since the Dragon had annexed Cilendrodel, as well as a table or two and countless plates. Tonight he stifled his normal tick of annoyance, casually capturing one of Jom's pawns with a merchant. Only his partner perceived that he was no longer immersed in the game.

Owl's staff, well trained not to keep guardsmen waiting, bustled platters out of the kitchen. The girls managed to set down the food and guard their rear ends at the same time. In the corner a minstrel began to play.

The music was exceptionally fine, Owl realized, far better than anything his regular bard could manage. The guardsmen, however, did not notice. As soon as the initial tune was over, they called for a popular ballad, one that any musician could play. The stranger obliged, and soon blessed the room with his fine tenor voice. Never had such bawdy lyrics been sung so well, Owl declared to Jom.

The soldiers applauded by stamping their feet. Two of them threw coins into the singer's hat. They soon forgot him, engrossed in their gossip, jokes, and drinking. Scraps of meat and spilled ale fell on Owl's well-scrubbed floor. One of the men carved his initials into the table top. The other patrons could hardly hear themselves talk over the noise. Three years ago Owl would not have tolerated this sort of behavior. He asked rude customers to leave. But since the Dragon's garrison had come, there had been two classes of citizens in Old Stump. Owl had learned that there were worse things than broken chairs, burned tapestries, and being the butt of soldiers' jokes. He had seen what had happened to the mayor when the latter complained too loudly to Lord Puriel of abuses and broken laws.

Owl had lived in Old Stump all of his life. He had a daughter approaching the age when she would soon help him in the pub room. He was not a courageous man. He had played amiable host to Puriel's guards night after night because that was the cost of keeping his livelihood viable. He had no wish to become a rebel, but if lending the Silver Eel for one night would lift the shadow of oppression, he would take the risk.

He drummed his fingernails at the edge of the peg board. Jom had made a move some time ago, yet Owl had not even started to formulate his counterstroke. The air seemed to radiate heat, though the hearth was unlit. The tavernmaster licked dry lips and raised his stein. A lone figure in a cape appeared at the threshold. A white cape. Owl glanced inside the hood and nearly inhaled the brew.

In the corner, the minstrel began a new song. Though he strummed his lute no louder than before, the notes cut like knives through the roar of voices, utensils, and pouring ale. Owl recognized the tune. It had been played a great deal over the past two months. It was called "The Hero with a Hundred Wings."

Suddenly men stood up from tables on every side of Claric's men and drew knives. Owl saw the flash of a needle-thin stiletto, narrow enough to penetrate the interstices of chain mail. Only two of the soldiers saw the steel coming. One blocked the first knife, only to take the second in the heart. The other man spun nimbly out of the circle of attackers and bolted for the door. Elenya raised her rapier out of the folds of her cape and ran him through.

The only survivor was Claric, who gawked, speechless, at the knife in front of his face. A man on either side held down his arms. There was another knife at Owl's throat. He knew it was a ruse, but it nearly stopped his heart just the same.

"What is the meaning of this?" the tavernmaster croaked. "What are you doing?"

Elenya gestured to one of the attackers, who shut the main door. "Our quarrel is not with you, innkeeper. Keep out of the way and you'll be safe."

Elenya was so convincing that Owl had to clench his groin to keep control of his bladder. He hoped his performance measured up. The customers who were not part of the conspiracy had to believe that he had not helped arrange the ambush. He felt ashamed that he had taken the coward's way out—the attackers, most of them townsmen, were now branded as rebels—but it was the only way he could agree to let the Silver Eel be used.

Elenya turned away from Owl, who, now out of the spotlight, sighed deeply. The princess stepped over the body of the man she had killed and faced Claric. The captain of the guard finally found his voice.

"Let me go! The governor will have all your heads for this!"

"I think not," Elenya said calmly.

Alemar emerged from the kitchen. This time, Owl noted, he wore the famous gauntlet on his right hand, just as Elenya wore its mate on her left. His scabbard slapped against his leg. His presence silenced everyone. Owl had heard that the twin children of Keron Olendim were intimidating, but he had dismissed the story as rebel propaganda. Now he knew that only half the truth had been spoken. Though short, the twins seemed to be the tallest people in the room.

"Are you uncomfortable, held down, surrounded by enemies?" Alemar murmured to Claric.

"You don't dare touch me!" Claric shouted.

"I won't," Alemar said. "I'm going to leave you to my sister."

Claric shut up. Owl expected Elenya to smile. She had Milec's torturer in front of her, helpless. But not a muscle moved in her face. Her expression was a blank, everything hidden behind the skin. Yet Claric saw something. He began to squirm, trying to shake off the strong arms that pinned him to the chair.

Elenya pulled out a scarf of white quarn silk and twisted it into a cord. The veins on the backs of her hands bulged. Claric cried out. While his mouth was open, she thrust the cloth between his teeth and gagged him, tying the knot so tightly behind his skull that his lips were pressed to bloodless white contours against his teeth. Other rebels swiftly bound his limbs.

Elenya drew Claric's sword and placed the center of the blade across the palm of her gauntlet. She squeezed. The metal crumpled and, with a snap of her wrist, broke. She tossed the sections on the floor. Her expression still did not change.

Three of the attackers hefted Claric up and carried him out the kitchen exit. Elenya followed.

Alemar scanned every face in the room. He gave off none of the aura of a healer. Something brooded within his stone-cold countenance. But he was not like his sister. The customers faced him without flinching. More than that, Owl realized this was a man he wanted to follow. After the oppression of the Dragon, here was the balm to cover their wounds.

And they had done it. They had surprised Puriel's men in the very shadow of the castle. Underneath his terror, Owl felt a gut-tightening swell of excitement. He was proud that he had finally found the courage, even at a distance, to stand up to the regime that had afflicted him and his neighbors' lives. Before them was the man responsible.

"Tell Lord Puriel that he is next," Alemar said. He and Solint the Minstrel led the others out. For several seconds after they had gone no one moved or spoke.

"Well, who wants to go up to take the news to the castle?" asked Old Jom. There were no volunteers.

• • •

107

Omril was sitting in his sanctum when he felt the flash of magic. It was brief, almost instantaneous, then it was quelled. Had he not been meditating, deliberately searching for such signs, he would have missed it. Before the impressions could fade he lifted a vial and held it tight. He concentrated. It took a full ten minutes, but the liquid changed from clear to deep aqua. He grunted in satisfaction and strolled to the windows.

With the serum to focus his sorcery, he relocated the approximate source of the flash. He was right. The spell was still active. The weaver, or a helper, was using a lesser spell to try to conceal the greater one. Had they not been trying to thwart a wizard of the Ril, the tactic might have worked.

Still, the effort was admirable. The serum, unlike a solid talisman, had been ductile enough to capture the spell's flavor on a moment's notice, but it would not hold the impression more than a few hours. Omril fetched Swiftwing from her coop. Given a bit of luck, he could lead the bird to the exact spot where the magic was being performed before the casters finished their weaving and departed.

Omril frowned. No doubt his prey would want him to use that strategy. It was time-consuming. Furthermore, his attention would be completely absorbed while he looked through Swiftwing's eyes; he would not be awake to the world. He could not, for example, renew the serum. He gazed out at Rock Lake. The spell was being cast somewhere on the far side of the water, only a few leagues away.

He put Swiftwing back on her perch, dressed quickly in his riding garb, and descended into the body of the castle.

The governor's audience hall buzzed with activity. Puriel stood next to his great hearth, in a foul mood, judging by the look on his face. He was yelling at his chamberlain. Omril caught a bit of the tirade and raised an eyebrow.

Puriel turned and glared at the sorcerer. "The captain of my guard has been captured under my very nose," he snapped. "Witnesses say both the rebel leaders were there. Where were your watchful eyes?"

"When did this happen?" Omril asked the chamberlain.

"Two hours after sunset," the man replied.

"I was at supper with you, my lord," Omril told Puriel. "I can't eat and converse and search for spells at the same time. Besides, did they use magic?"

"No," the chamberlain said. "Swords and knives. They ambushed Claric at the Silver Eel. Killed all his men."

"Then I would not have known to look there," Omril said. "But I think I know where they are now." He told them what he had detected. "Give me a cohort of troops. If I go myself, I can lead them to the site in an hour or two."

"Done!" Puriel growled. "I'll not stand for this sort of humiliation. I want those king's bastards on my racks by morning. Claric, too, for making me look like a fool. Mind you don't let them slip away from you again, wizard."

Omril bowed. "As my lord commands." He suppressed a smile. Puriel had little to fear from enemies—if he continued in this fashion he would soon perish of an apoplectic fit.

The soldiers roused in short order, came out of the barracks complaining. Most had just retired for the night. Omril let a pair of lieutenants prod and bellow, while he waited sedately on his oeikani. The men glanced his way, dropped their grievances, and made themselves battle ready. They knew where the real authority lay in this castle.

While he waited, Omril stroked the vial. Eventually one end of the serum darkened nearly to blackness, while the other faded to a sky blue. As long as the wizard pointed in the direction from which the spell was coming, this stayed the case. If he pointed it another way, the liquid returned to a pure aqua. By the time they were ready to leave, he had calibrated the talisman to the degree that he would not have to expend undue attention and energy upon it for the duration of the search.

He led the cohort around the shores of the lake. As expected, the hues of the serum became more intense. For the first time Omril's dispassionate attitude failed him; his body tingled. He felt an acid bite in his stomach, savage and appealing. This might be the night when he finally fulfilled his mission for his dread lord.

On the side of Rock Lake directly opposite Puriel's castle, the road branched. One fork continued along the shore, the other penetrated the forest. Omril halted the troops. The vial was hot in his hand. He beckoned both his lieutenants.

"The magicians are little more than a league from this spot, between the roads," he told them. "You'll each take a third of the men and follow the roads. One league along, cut into the wood. I'll go through the trees from here. We'll catch them in our pincers."

He let the flanking groups ride out of sight, then ordered his own contingent to spread into a wide column. They filtered into the trees, moving as silently as was possible for a large group of

109

men and oeikani. Omril cast a minor spell that would reflect the loudest noises toward the rear. The forest here was relatively open. Woodsmen often visited this land to harvest dead trees or plant new ones to accommodate the needs of Old Stump. They made good time, and seldom had to dismount to squeeze through tight places. Omril felt a tickle in his palm, where he held the vial. Soon it spread. After half a league he put away the talisman altogether. He could now directly sense the camouflage spell.

They were very near. He ordered the soldiers into a half circle.

"Charge!" he commanded.

Swords drawn, arrows nocked, they plunged between the trees. Omril followed close behind, with a small rear guard. They had gone only a few hundred yards before the wizard felt the camouflage spell snap out of existence.

There was no magic being cast ahead at all. The major spell was gone, too—and had been for who knew how long.

In the vanguard, men were shouting. Omril emerged from a thicket and found most of the troops gathered around a tree. They were silhouetted against an odd lavender glow. The sorcerer scowled and rode to the front.

He found Claric tied to the tree. The captain's naked body was covered by thin, luminescent tendrils, making it seem as if he had grown a coat of fine hair. The strands waved like miniature snakes, as if wafted by the breeze, but there was no wind that night. He was giving off enough purplish light to read a scroll by.

"Omril! Get this off of me! It itches like the five demons of Emin."

The wizard scanned the surrounding trees. "Where are the rebels?"

"Long gone," Claric spat. "They left after the bitch did this to me."

The statement confirmed what Omril had suspected. Still, there had to be one magician nearby. The camouflage spell, unlike the one on Claric's body, had to be actively maintained, and that could not be done from a great distance.

"Six men stay here," he ordered. "The rest fan out and search the woods." He was doubtful that they would find anything. He had not, as he had fancied, caught the rebels by surprise. They had deliberately enticed him. They had expected him to detect their magic.

"Ebrett!" Claric shouted to the sergeant standing next to Omril. "Cut me loose."

"No!" Omril snapped. The sergeant jumped. Claric opened his mouth to protest. "The spell on him is a trap. Touch him or the ropes and the demonhair will consume his skin, and yours as well."

"What?!" Claric burst out.

"What did you expect?" Omril asked. "That the princess would simply decorate you and leave you here to brighten the forest? She wanted revenge, no?"

"You're the wizard, undo the spell!"

"I can't. I'd have to unravel each thread one at a time. It would take me a week. You'll be dead before then of thirst. We can't even pass water to you." In actual fact, Omril could probably do the job in two days or less, if he went without sleep. But he had never liked Claric.

Claric looked like he was going to vomit.

"If you'd like, I can have the men shoot you with arrows," Omril offered. "It would be swifter. In another few hours the demonhair will start working its way into your, ahem, openings. If you think it itches now. . . ."

"No, no."

"The alternative is leaving you to rot."

Claric moaned and gave no indication as to which he would prefer. Omril turned his attention to the sounds that had been coming from the trees to the north. Soon one of the lieutenants rode up. The first of the pincer groups had met the main party.

"Did you see anything?" Omril demanded.

"Nothing," the officer replied, so fascinated by Claric's outlandish appearance that he almost forgot to salute.

The wizard turned his back to Claric and the spectators and paced. The rebels had more in mind than revenge on Claric; if that had been the extent of it, Omril would have stood back and admired their handiwork. It was a handsome bit of thaumaturgy, requiring considerable patience, concentration, and discipline. He had not thought the female twin, with her hot-headedness, had the temperament necessary to spin demonhair. It was another facet of his enemies to remember. But they had surely not lured him to the site merely to provide an audience for their victory.

The night was growing distinctly darker. First Urthey had set, then the Sister, then Motherworld. Now only the recently risen Serpent Moon was left to shed light over the countryside. It was still several hours until sunrise. A good time, Omril realized, for a military assault.

And here was he, the single strongest weapon Lord Puriel

had, out in the woods, leaving the fortress defenses short by a full cohort of men.

"Mount your steeds!" he shouted. "We're going back to the castle! Now!"

The soldiers had never seen Omril so agitated. They obeyed him even faster than if he had threatened them. They left their former captain to his fate, ignoring his outraged cries and whimpers, and raced back the way they had come. When they reached Rock Lake, they heard the din of battle echoing off the water. The noise came from the governor's keep.

≈≈≈ XVII ≈≈≈

Hiephora and a dozen of her minor queens, hidden in the trees near Lord Puriel's fortress, watched Omril's cohort of men ride out through the barbican. The little people remained motionless, quiet as the flutter of butterfly wings. It was said that a rythni could stand on a man's shoulder and the man would be unaware of it. The riders crossed the moat, turned down the fork of the road leading along the shore of Rock Lake, and vanished into their own dust. If all went well, the wizard would not realize he had been tricked until it was too late. The rythni waited until the horizon concealed first the light of little Urthey, and, soon after, the bright glow of the Sister. Motherworld hung low in the sky, preparing to follow, displaying only half her face. The shadows grew long and dark.

"Now," Hiephora sang in her lilting, melodic mother tongue. Her queens darted off on gossamer wings, leaving her with her handmaiden, Cyfee. After exchanging a nervous glance they, too, launched into the air.

They circled three times, and in response, the leaves shook and fluttered. Hundreds upon hundreds of rythni women flooded out of the trees, a queen leading each wave. Carrying coils of rope, they sped into the open air above the moat, the twilight obscuring them to human eyes. They staggered their formations so that their flitting shapes would resemble the bats that dwelled among the corbels and rafters of the fortress.

The castle loomed, high and intimidating, full of stone and tile and mortar, emanating none of the sweet, nurturing music of the forest's living wood. Hiephora pierced the structure's sphere of influence and faltered, suddenly weak, pitched from straight flight. Many of her subjects, unable to endure the bitter kiss of the air, turned back, terror-stricken, including one of her queens.

"Courage!" she cried. "It fades!" Already the initial shock was lessening, as with the waters of a pond—cold on impact, but increasingly tolerable as one continued to swim. The edifice would do no permanent harm to her people, as long as they did not linger within it. The queens echoed her words of encouragement.

Two-thirds of her women, though they veered and emitted tiny cries, continued gallantly on.

Hiephora and Cyfee landed on a battlement, slipping into an embrasure in order to hide from the sentries. They commanded a view of the entire landward side of the fortress: the moat below, the desolate swath of land beyond that, the trees in the near distance. The last of those who had been daunted vanished into the foliage. She could not blame them. They had not been present when she had prophesied this battle a quarter century ago; they could not directly feel, as she did, why it was necessary to risk taboo, and aid Alemar and Elenya.

As Motherworld dipped sedately out of sight, reducing the night to as near blackness as Tanagaran ever saw other than on Dark Night, the cadres of rythni took their ropes and began looping the nooses around the merlons of the battlements, draping the free ends into the moat.

It was a dry moat, lined at the bottom with shattered rock and sharpened stakes, designed to thwart war mounts and siege engines, but negotiable by foot soldiers. One by one, men snaked across the swatch of cleared land, darkly clothed, faces smeared with black grease, their weapons tightly bound and padded, to join a handful of scouts who had come earlier. They rappelled down the embankment at preselected locations, crossed the moat, and fanned out to seize the ropes the rythni had just planted. Soon there were dozens of men scaling the stone walls.

The majority of the rythni vanished from the battlements, for violence was imminent, and the emanations from that would be far harsher than the kind they had already endured. Hiephora, Cyfee, and the queens remained, along with a few of the very brave, whispering guidance to the climbers, letting them know the exact position and number of the guards. The fastest scaler was over half way up when one of Puriel's men noticed a rope. He shouted and drew his sword to hack at the noose.

Cyfee cringed as the blade struck stone, casting sparks, biting into the thick, resin-hardened fiber. Hiephora called for her flyers to warn the climbers. By the time the guard's chops severed the line completely, the men had shifted to other ropes. They continued to ascend.

Someone reached the alarm bell. Lantern glow beamed out of the barracks and from the windows of the keep. The fortress awakened.

The guards on the battlements, badly outnumbered, seeing death rising up at them, cut at the ropes with frantic haste. Two climbers did not shift quickly enough and fell, breaking legs on the jagged rock of the moat. A third landed on one of the sharpened stakes. Then the leaders vaulted the top and drew their swords. The courtyard rang with the sound of steel meeting steel. The first dribbles of reinforcements issued out of the buildings.

Hiephora darted toward the barbican, leaving Cyfee to assist with the high battle. Those rythni who could tolerate the psychic onslaught of men dying continued to replace ropes. As she glided, she saw the main mass of the rebel army bolt from the forest onto the roadway.

So many of them! The houses and farms of the region around Old Stump must have completely emptied, the residents rising to the cause of the Elandri prince and princess. Hiephora herself would have doubted it possible to gather so many, had she not foretold it.

She wished that she could determine the outcome of the battle, but the leaves of meditation, as with all oracles, had sung a twisted tale. She knew only what would happen if Gloroc were not stopped. He would rule for five thousand years. The land would be raped, the forests cut down within a few human generations. The rythni as a race would fade into history. Alemar and Elenya might be the only hope. That was why she had tipped over Lerina's cup of amethery twenty-five years earlier, and why she had committed her people this night.

But at the moment, the screams of men and swords tore at her determination, making her want to fly far away.

She propelled herself into the barbican just as the guard released the lever that would lower the portcullis and seal it off from the rest of the castle. His brow furrowed when the iron failed to drop. He strode to the portal, gazing up in perplexity, and cursed. The top of the portcullis had been bound into its bracket by hundreds of tiny, rythni-sized cords. He cast a worried look at the fighting on the battlements, then rolled a barrel under

114

the archway, seized a pike, climbed onto the barrel, and began slashing at the cords with the pike tip.

Hiephora whistled, and dozens of her women appeared from their hiding places. They swarmed around the spindle at the center of the chamber. Their combined weight and the rapid beating of their wings were enough to spin the gears. The drawbridge began to lower, just as the first of the main throng of invaders reached the far side of the moat.

The guard shouted and leaped off the barrel. The rythni melted away to the far corners of the room. The man reversed the spindle's action. Meanwhile, some of Hiephora's minions tipped over the barrel and sent it rolling out the archway.

The last of the sentries on the battlements screamed as they were run through or flung from the heights. Dozens of the invaders were already rushing down the stairs. Not enough soldiers had emerged from the barracks yet to foil them from charging the barbican. The guard hissed and ran for the barrel, replaced it, and hacked at the cords again.

The rythni streaked to the spindle and began lowering the drawbridge.

The guard screamed and flung the pike. The rythni darted away, quick as wasps, avoiding injury. The guard abandoned the portcullis and returned to the spindle—permanently, since he knew that allowing the drawbridge to lower would mean at least ten times as many people to fight.

Hiephora ordered her women into hiding, ready to harass further if necessary. To her dismay, another guard arrived, then a third. The first yelled an explanation and the newcomers attacked the portcullis bindings. The rythni held back, unable to attack the men directly.

The portcullis creaked and began to wobble. Just then four rebels burst into the passageway. The lead man caught a pike in the shoulder. The other three mowed down the pair of guards and surrounded the man at the spindle. The scent of blood sent the rythni streaming out of the chamber. Blessing mother forest that her people's role was ending, Hiephora swiftly followed, closing her ears and refusing to look back. Three more invaders arrived at the barbican as she sped away.

Elenya leaped onto the drawbridge even before it was down, at the head of the first wave of invaders. They raced through the archway and into the great courtyard. A throng of guards poured out of the barracks to meet them.

115

The two sides clashed and blended. Elenya stood out in her white leather armor and greaves, her gauntlet a beacon to the opposition. She wanted it that way. Her preternatural speed made her the invaders' most effective weapon. It was imperative that she and the lead phalanx—all trained fighters in proper gear—break through to the interior of the barracks before their enemies could outfit themselves. Then the great mass of poorly equipped villagers in the rear ranks would have a reasonable chance.

A thick-shouldered mercenary with long, dark hair bore down on her. She twisted around him, found a gap in his unlaced chest armor, and sank the point of her rapier through his arm pit into his heart. Before he could fall she stabbed the man behind him. As allies closed in on either side, she used their protection to dance to a new area.

To her left an enemy soldier cut down a villager. He used his sword well, and kept his shield up. Two other dying invaders already lay at his feet. She bolted forward before more victims fell. He lasted through three exchanges, more than she liked, before she pinked him on the arm, and, with the opening created, drove a follow-up thrust into his chest.

They had already pushed the defenders half the distance to the barracks. She dared a glance at the battlements. They were secure, though an archer was causing grief from one of the keep windows. She dived back into the fray, praying that there were few guards of the mettle she had just encountered.

Beside her a companion took a battle ax in the side of his head, spraying her with blood. She killed the wielder, even as she blocked a thrust from another opponent with the ward around her gauntlet. Iregg came to her rescue, though she was not in great difficulty, and together they surged forward another few steps. They stepped over a body—another fallen ally. Too many dead, Elenya cursed to herself. So far Puriel's men had taken the worst of it, but the men of the garrison were professionals. They would recover if given enough time.

"*Elandri tu!*" she cried, dodging a pike. The hilt of her weapon burned like a hot coal, sliding in her grip as if greased. She feinted, thrust, twisted, blocked, letting her sword lead and adapting her body as needed. In one of those brief, clear moments that sometimes occur in the midst of battle, she saw a young soldier, third in line to confront her, freeze at the sight of her skill, as she dealt with the intervening foes. He was unable to raise his shield or blade; she harvested him like wheat.

Only then did she realize she stood at the threshold of one of the entrances to the barracks. A sudden rush of guards propelled her backwards, but she grinned. The tide was shifting. The barracks would be theirs, and after it, the keep.

Outside the castle, at a safe distance, waited the women, juveniles, and elders of Old Stump and the surrounding estates, ready to support the invasion as best they could. Owl the tavernmaster sat on a wagon, trying to calm his jittery pair of oeikani. The trees hid the castle, but the sounds of armed conflict rang clear, violating the ears of the assemblage.

Owl felt a drop of sweat trickle down his face and into his collar, to be absorbed by his drenched inner shirt. His nephew was among those who had scaled the walls. He had not even known the boy was a rebel until a few hours earlier, when he, like so many other residents, had suddenly swarmed to the support of the Elandri twins.

The signal came. Owl cracked the whip lightly, guiding his vehicle into its place in the line. A total of ten wagons rolled down the road to the castle, clattering across the drawbridge with the women and youths jogging along beside them. Most were empty, their beds covered with straw, intended for transporting the wounded out of the battle zone. Owl's own was loaded with tarps and sacks of sand with which to snuff fires, for the battle would surely see many lamps shattered and candles knocked from their sconces. An unchecked blaze in the main part of the fortress would create havoc for both sides.

The clamor of shouting men and the dull thump of a battering ram pounding somewhere in the bowels of the keep swept over Owl. He strove to keep his composure as he guided his team between the bodies of the fallen to an open space by the outer wall, away from the fighting. He climbed down immediately and freed his animals, for the latter could help in the effort to evacuate the injured. Some of his companions loaded stricken combatants onto the other wagons, in order to rush them back to the aid stations that had been set up beneath the trees. Others tended men still lying where they had fallen.

The courtyard was clear of Puriel's men, except the dead. A small fire snapped and spat in the barracks. Several men and women rushed to Owl's wagon and grabbed material. Those not occupied with saving the living were dragging the slain out of the way, stripping Puriel's guards of armor and weapons which might be used inside by those still fighting. Owl swallowed hard and told himself to relax. The battle was finished here. He was safe.

A cadre of townsmen emerged from the main keep, urging a group of a dozen women along ahead of them. They collected the captives in a corner of the yard and put them under guard. The women's nightgowns showed no soil or rents to indicate that they had been touched. Owl nodded in satisfaction. Battle or no battle, the rebels and villagers of Old Stump would not stoop to the sort of abuses indulged in by the governor and his soldiers.

Owl surrendered his oeikani and went to the assistance of two women who were moving the bodies. One was his neighbor, Nalicia, with whom he had grown up. The sight of her, shaking and pale, momentarily quieted his own faint heart. He met her eyes, and his own relative calm bolstered her courage. Together the three of them hauled the burden to the side of the yard.

Nalicia sighed, bit back tears, straightened her spine, and started toward the next one. Only then did Owl realize that the corpse was that of Yenni, the silversmith's son. They both knew his father well. But then, most of the casualties would be people with whom they were acquainted. The next, in fact, was a man who had swept the floor of his tavern as a boy. Fearing that the next victim might be his nephew or a close friend, he diverted Nalicia toward a fallen castle guard.

As he and Nalicia each grabbed an arm and lifted, the supposedly dead man awoke, despite the evil-looking gash across his pate, and with a sudden jerk of his elbow sent the unprepared Owl tumbling into the dirt. The latter inhaled a mouthful of grit, coughed, and scrambled to his feet. Too late. The guard plunged his knife into Nalicia's chest.

Owl cried out.

The guard let Nalicia fall, and stared about, dazed and unsteady on his feet. At Owl's outburst, he turned, widened his eyes, and charged. Owl gasped and, without consciously meaning to, kicked his attacker's knee. The man crashed forward, knocking the wind out of the tavernmaster, taking them both down. The knife spun away, kicking up dust an arm's length from their heads. Owl, for lack of a better strategy, seized the guard in a bear hug.

Had the guard not been disoriented and weakened from blood loss, he would have broken free in short order, but as it was, Owl held him just long enough that a teenage boy reached them and, using a mace salvaged from another fallen member of the garrison, caved in the man's head.

"Are you hurt, sir?" asked the boy, as he stared dumbfounded at the man he had just killed.

Owl wiped a fleck of blood from his eyelid. "No. My thanks." His stomach heaved. Next to him, Nalicia stared sightlessly up at the stars.

Hiephora took wing, abandoning the security of the forest. Once more, she endured the jolt as she broached the aura around the castle. This time she cried out, stabbed to the core. The energies roiled and snapped, fed by the fear of the dying, the cold dispassion of the dead, and the hatred of foe for foe. She flew high, where the impact was less severe, and hovered over the great courtyard. She could not bring herself to look downward.

"Cyfee!" she called out.

No response. She quailed to think that her protégée lay embroiled in the carnage, yet Cyfee and three other rythni had not returned to the woods. They could not be dead. Her prophecy had been clear in that regard; no rythni would die in this fight. Otherwise she could not have asked a single one of her subjects to participate. She called again, flying a circuit of the fortress walls.

Over the governor's keep, away from the worst of the din, she heard a faint, urgent, keening cry, unmistakably a rythni song of distress. Yet, strangely, she thought she could detect an alluring whisper beneath it. Both emanated from the northwest tower of the keep.

The wizard's sanctum.

She circled warily before she dared land on the balcony. The room within was dim, foreboding, tinged with the mephitis of sorcery. The distress cry flowed from it clearly, mournfully. She ventured nearer the opening. A strange music, very unlike the harmonics of the forest, reached out and murmured to her.

"My queen!" cried a familiar voice.

Hiephora peered inside. Four rythni lay on the table in the center of the room, under a faintly luminescent net, beside a crystal vase containing a sprig of herb thick with white flowers.

"Cyfee!" At last Hiephora identified the odd undertone that she had heard above the castle. It came from the herb—a whisper promising love, dancing, dreams, and song, the perfect lure for a rythni. It was subtle, almost subliminal at first, drawing in the unsuspecting listener until the trap was woven too tightly for escape. She herself wanted desperately to venture inside, though clearly she, like her subjects, would be snagged like a fly in a web.

"Are you hurt?" Hiephora called.

"No," Cyfee replied. "But it won't let us go." She lifted an arm. The strands kept her from extending it. The other three companions, though awake, seemed unable to move at all.

"Stay still, then. I will bring help as soon as I can."

The wind over the lake licked at Alemar's hair, twisting it into his face. He blew it clear, since his arms, like the rest of him, were propped up by dozens of rythni. They were getting tired, these little ones. They had carried him non-stop from the site where he had been maintaining the camouflage spell around Claric until Omril's arrival. Their strength was fading rapidly, or perhaps it was the essence of the castle, sapping them of their resolve as they drew near.

"Just a little farther," he murmured. "You've done well."

A flutter of movement ahead of them pulled his gaze away from the battlements. "Prince Alemar!" called a small voice.

"My queen?" Alemar frowned at the sight of Hiephora. "What's wrong?"

"Treachery from the wizard," she declared. "Fly with me to his tower."

Following their monarch's lead, the weary carriers deposited Alemar on the balcony. "Stay," she commanded. "The prince will need you to take him off; the stairs are not safe." They gathered obediently upon the balustrade, though they shivered, stared nervously to either side, and occasionally flitted an inch or two into the air.

Alemar stared into the wizard's den, a furrow gathering in his forehead. He glanced back at the serene waters of Rock Lake, watching the ripples gleam from the light of Serpent Moon. Omril and his men would scarcely have reached the shore. It would take them until dawn to return to the fortress. His fingers abstractly stroked the pommel of his sword, unaccustomed to the weapon's presence on his belt.

From down in the guts of the keep came the sound of furniture breaking and doors being rammed open, and the shriek of metal on metal. Alemar disregarded it, focussing on the threshold between the balcony and the room. He saw a glow, hanging like a veil across the opening.

"There is a guard spell here," he told the queen, and suddenly thrust his gauntlet forward. The veil parted, falling into shreds on the floor and slipping like water into the cracks of the masonry. "Not a potent one. Just one to put strangers asleep should they intrude. Rythni must be too small to activate it."

He entered, found an oil lamp, and gingerly set it on the table.

"Touch nothing," he warned as he lit it. The yellow glow spilled across shelves of thaumaturgical volumes, bottles of rare minerals, and complex equipment. The cage of pigeons caught his attention. The birds cooed, bobbing their heads, as graceless as only pigeons could be.

Cyfee and the three rythni waited quietly, their eyes full of doelike apprehension. Alemar examined the vase, the herb, and the net that confined them. "It's a moly—see the black roots? You'll have to warn your people. Omril may have planted others in the forest in order to snare you."

He plucked at the net with his gauntlet hand. The fibers clung to the gold mail like cobweb, and would not let go. It did nothing to free the rythni, merely mired himself.

"Hmmm," he muttered. He traced the strands to their source, a series of minuscule holes in the stems, just beneath the seductively fragrant blooms. He moved the flame of the lamp beneath the latter. The petals shrivelled and blackened, giving off an acrid smoke. A portion of the web loosened, allowing one of Cyfee's companions to sit up.

"It's working," Hiephora said.

Alemar nodded, and moved the lamp to the next stem. Suddenly the flame leaped sideways, igniting the entire net, enveloping the captives in a conflagration. Alemar gasped, flinging aside the lamp. The rythni shrieked.

He dived for the curtains, tore one from its rod and cast it over the table, snuffing the flame. At the same time, in the far corner, a new fire sprang from the spilled oil and licked its way up a bookcase. He ignored it, pulling back the fabric.

The four rythni writhed in agony, coughing, their skin baked deep red. Seared stumps twitched where their delicate, membrane-thin wings had been. Alemar choked.

It was instinct alone that made him duck. A massive tome on alchemy sailed through the space where his head had been. From another direction, a bottle launched itself from a rack. He twisted sideways. The glass shattered against the wall, releasing an acid that sizzled and ate into the marble floor. A drop struck his wrist, dissolving a patch of his skin the size of a small coin.

Hiephora landed on the table, wilting over Cyfee as if unable to believe what had just occurred. "Out!" Alemar cried. He raised his gauntlet to fend off more books. The queen acted as if she did not hear.

Alemar's sword tried to draw itself from its scabbard. He slammed it back into place. Then, with a flash of insight, he drew it on purpose and whirled toward the cage of pigeons.

One of the birds was staring straight at him, unperturbed by the fire, the moans of the little people, or the cyclone of flying objects.

Alemar lunged, thrusting, and drilled his sword through its avian chest. It died without a flutter.

Immediately one of the two remaining birds ceased its panicked squawking and beating of wings, and settled onto a perch. Alemar's weapon twisted in his grip, the tip slicing toward his throat. He seized the blade with his gauntlet, immobilizing it.

Before the barrage of objects, or some other magical attack, could begin again, he kicked the cage from its table. As soon as it struck the floor, he kicked it twice more. It bounced into the fire raging in the corner. The lacquered wooden bars sizzled and burst into flame.

"You're mine, Omril," Alemar snarled. "Beware the hour we meet!"

He jabbed his steel between the bars. The pigeon danced to the side, barely dodging the point. The blaze ignited its feathers. The spark of intelligence left its eyes, and like its companion, it whirled madly around its confines, screeching in desperation.

Alemar kept hacking at the cage, until he had decapitated one bird, and skewered the other three times. His boots smoldered as he retreated. He stamped his feet.

Except for the fire, the room was at last still, with no sorcerer looking on to guide an attack. Consumed with black anger, Alemar only gradually became aware that Hiephora was staring at him, horrified. She shrank back as he approached.

"Don't!" he pleaded, but even as he spoke, she darted out the archway and into the night sky, screaming a note he had never heard a rythni make before.

A cold hand clasped Alemar's heart. He steadied himself, keeping the shock in check. Cyfee and the three other injured rythni still moaned on the table, tucked into fetal positions.

He tugged off his gauntlet, held it under an armpit, and picked up the diminutive creatures as gently as he could. He carried them from the heat and the smoke, out to the balcony. The rythni who had transported him across the lake had vacated the balustrade, abandoning their comrades, abandoning him. He clenched his teeth, blaming himself. One could not make the little people into something they were not. They could not have stayed to watch the fight, any more than he could take these wingless ones down into the castle, into the battle. The atmosphere of combat would kill all four, just as surely as would the burning of the tower.

He laid the tiny bodies on the balustrade. They flopped into limp piles, unconscious, save for Cyfee, who opened her mouth as if to speak, but fainted before she could. They all still breathed.

Come back, Hiephora, he prayed.

He heard the clatter of boots on the staircase. The door appeared to be locked, but it would not hold against desperate men, as these must be to have climbed the tower in search of escape. He glanced down. From this height, a leap into the waters of the lake was foolhardy, even assuming he missed the rocks hidden just below the surface. The fire was reaching the main mass of scrolls, books, wood, and cloth; in a few moments Omril's sanctum would become an inferno. He slipped the gauntlet back on his hand.

Heavy blows landed against the door, making it vibrate. Men cursed. Abruptly Alemar plunged across the room, sleeve in front of his face to ward off cinders. Smoke stung his eyes, stealing breath. The door groaned on its hinges. Wood cracked. He drew his blade.

He released the latch. The door slammed open. The foremost of the men on the other side stumbled into the room. Alemar tripped him, propelling him into the worst of the blaze. The prince spitted the second man before the latter realized there was an enemy present.

There were four others crowded on the landing beyond the threshold, one of them holding a thick coil of climbing rope. Once they saw Alemar's expression, they stepped back.

The prince had not wielded a sword in actual combat since his sojourn in the Eastern Deserts, but at that moment nothing felt more natural in his palm than the hilt of his weapon. Even his former swordmaster, Troy of Calinin South, could not have intimidated him. As the burning man rolled out of the fire, screaming, Alemar dealt him a deathblow of almost casual expertise.

Alemar gathered his rage about him in a pulsating, almost tangible shroud. "Come in," he told the others.

Two of the soldiers were armed only with knives, including the one holding the rope, and all of them drooped, battle-worn. Only one, at the rear, wore enough armor to pose a problem. Alemar feinted and jabbed his point into the lead man's gut. As the man groaned and bent forward, clutching his wound, Alemar kicked him into the armored man. With two swift thrusts he mortally wounded the two knife men. He danced back, letting them fall.

Only the armored man was left. He gawked at the swift disposal of his comrades, but the blossoming conflagration seemed to worry him even more. In another few moments it would not be possible to cross the room. He charged forward, swinging his broadsword.

Alemar ducked and leaped sideways, narrowly avoiding the steel. The fire and the tangle of dying men on the floor left little room to dodge. The prince jabbed, but the point hit the mesh of his attacker's hauberk and bounced away ineffectually. Fortunately the man's haste made him clumsy. Alemar stepped into the next swing and grabbed the blade with his gauntlet, immobilizing it. The gauntlet's ward saved his palm. He kicked the man's knee. It gave way.

The man screamed and fell to the floor. Alemar bounded through the bodies of the wounded men at the threshold. One of them, snarling in pain, tried to grab his ankle, but he was too fast. Back in the room the heat reached an amphora of oil. It ignited with a sinister hiss.

A man howled in agony. The one who could still move crawled frantically after the prince, leaving bloodstains as he went.

Alemar whispered a plea once more for the rythni on the balustrade and sped down the stone steps, his jacket hot against his shoulders, the cloth reeking with smoke. He coughed, unable to clear the sooty pungency from his breath.

He heard the sound of footsteps coming to meet him.

Around the curve of the wall came another guard, so worried about what was behind him that he was oblivious to the situation above. He turned just in time to see his death arriving.

Alemar pushed the body aside and continued on. At the bottom of the stairs he emerged into a corridor. To right and left he heard muffled sounds of clashing metal and screaming men. A tendril of smoke, from still another fire, undulated against the high ceiling.

Two of Puriel's soldiers, fleeing for their lives, rounded a corner and bore down on him. They spotted him and halted in their tracks.

He lifted his gauntlet, showing them a blazing jewel on the middle knuckle. Their expressions changed as they recognized him. One man stepped back, eyes wide. The other advanced, smiling.

"He's alone," he told his companion.

Alemar charged, his thrust bursting out the closest man's back. He abandoned the weapon without breaking stride, and took out the second man with a straight punch to the face with his gauntlet fist. It was not so much that he was as fast as Elenya, but that, once moving, he could not be deflected. He returned to the first man, set his boot against the man's chest, and freed his sword on the third pull.

Footsteps.

He whirled. Three more men rounded the corner, stopped, and stared at the dead men.

"Well met, m'lord," one of them said. It was Tregay and two villagers.

Alemar inclined his head in solemn acknowledgment. "My sister?" he rasped.

"The audience chamber. That's where most of the garrison made their stand. We've won, my prince. They've surrendered. We've only to ferret out pockets of resistance."

"Carry on, then," he said gruffly. "Don't bother with the wizard's tower." As they passed him, he set out in the direction from which they had come.

He found the first body lying in an archway, blood congealing on its neck. He soon encountered more, both castle troops and villagers, often in contorted poses, some of them still managing a few final ragged breaths. With the heightened senses provided by the gauntlet, he saw their auras flicker and fade out of existence. The tragedy of their deaths made no inroad into the hard, frozen place inside him.

Hiephora had been right to flee.

He entered a foyer where the fighting had been especially intense. Blood pooled under five bodies. One man was still alive. As Alemar drew nearer, he saw that it was Iregg. The rebel's jerkin was crimson across the entire front, and his aura was faint. He held up a mangled hand, opening his mouth. He produced no words, but the entreaty was plain.

"I can't help you," Alemar said.

The tremulous quiver of hope disappeared from Iregg's eyes. He lowered his hand. Alemar winced as if pierced by a lance. "I'm sorry."

The prince heard a noise to his left, and spun. A soldier jumped out of a doorway, battle ax high. Alemar ducked the swipe, but was bowled over by the man's charge. They tumbled. Chain mail pressed against the prince's face. They both rolled

125

free and reached their feet at the same time. The attacker had lost his ax. Alemar had lost his sword.

The man was fully armored. Perhaps he thought himself invulnerable to an unarmed opponent, since he waited, as if he expected Alemar to try to pick up his weapon. Instead, the prince stepped in and punched. The gauntlet augmented his power, driving the mesh of chain mail into the soldier's sternum. The latter wheezed, red flecks flying from his lips. Alemar pounded again, and a third time. Ribs splintered with both blows.

He hit the man in the face, bending in the chin guards of his helmet, splitting lips, knocking teeth loose. The man choked. He had died with the first terrible blow. Now at last he wobbled, and, no longer supported by the pounding, slammed heavily to the flagstones.

Alemar stared at the gore on his gauntlet, transfixed. He turned back to Iregg. His comrade had lost consciousness. His aura waned. Alemar bent down, cradled Iregg's limp, broken hand inside his.

The prince could not help himself. Though certain that he would fail, he nevertheless tried to summon his healing power. A dull throb, a shadow of former vigor, thrummed along his bones, but nothing flowed out.

Impotent, he waited until the end. It came swiftly.

His muscles had grown painfully stiff; it was a struggle to straighten up. He retrieved his sword and walked on.

He met no more enemies. Instead, allies grew thick about him. They hailed him raucously, but he acknowledged them only with a raised hand. They directed him to Puriel's great audience chamber.

The shattered table, scattered braziers, dropped weapons, and fallen men gave evidence of the viciousness of the fight here. Elenya stood at the hearth. She issued orders to three of her lieutenants and the men hurried away.

One could hardly tell that Elenya's tunic had once been white. Alemar stared at her matted, crusted hair.

"None of it's mine," she said, gesturing at the blood. "Except this." She displayed a superficial slice along her forearm.

"Puriel?" Alemar asked.

"Not found. He wasn't in his chambers." She frowned at the sight of his red gauntlet and drawn sword. Without realizing it, she slipped into mindspeech. *"What happened?"*

"I was just up in the wizard's tower."

She nodded slowly. *"I'm told it's burning."*

He did not answer with words, but merely sent an image of the four rythni losing their wings, the death of the pigeons, and the abandonment of the little people on the balustrade.

She wiped some of the gore off her cheek. "Not much you can do for them now," she said gently. "There are people in the courtyard who need your help."

He raised his sword. The blood on it had dried and would harm the metal if he left the blade uncleaned. He shoved it back in the scabbard without wiping it. "I pity them," he said, and stalked out between the shattered doors.

Omril knelt at the lake's edge, cupping water in his palms and running it over his face until his fine vest was soaked. He stared morosely across the water. His tower, tiny in the distance, burned like a commoner's candle. His scrolls, his talismans, his birds—all gone.

"My lord?" asked his senior lieutenant. "Are you well?"

Omril's cohort waited expectantly, still shocked that their citadel was under attack. Many chafed to ride on. When the wizard had first called a halt in order to send his eyes to his pigeons, the junior lieutenant had begged to split the group and ride ahead. Omril had refused.

The wizard stood. He would not play a losing game. By the time he returned to the keep, the rebels might be in control, if they were not already. He might still win the day, but it would be a struggle, perhaps even a risk of his life. Time to regroup. He would save his counterattack for a better day, when he had more men behind him, when he could shape the situation to his advantage.

The garrison at Yent was the nearest source of reinforcements. That was where he would go. He gave the order.

The lieutenant was startled. "What of Lord Puriel?"

"Time for a new governor," Omril replied.

Owl lifted a blanket from a villager who had just died of his wounds, and carried it a short distance to another who still could make use of it. The wool weighed heavily in his grip. How could he be so tired that a single blanket would seem like such a burden? The man he tended shivered violently; the added covering seemed not to help. Owl had little doubt that soon he would be free to move the blanket again, as well as the one beneath it.

The tavernmaster stretched, popping his spine. The crowded barracks, where most of the wounded had been moved from the courtyard in the past few hours, had grown lighter. One of the nurses extinguished a lantern. Dawn.

The Elandri prince still worked, as he had done ever since he had emerged from the keep. He seemed to know which of the injured had a chance, and which did not, and concentrated on the former. He set bones, stanched bleeding that had thwarted the ministrations of others, relieved pain with powders, potions, and even the pressure of his fingers on certain places. Whenever not busy with their own efforts, Owl and the others watched in awe. And yet, for all his skill, Alemar did not seem to be using his legendary magic. The rumors must be true, Owl thought. The prince had lost his power. Fortunately, he was a fine physician even without it.

As if the new day were the cue he had been waiting for, Alemar abruptly left the barracks. Owl, seeing that there was nothing to be done for the patients at that moment, followed.

Alemar walked to the center of the courtyard, stopped, and gazed up at the wizard's tower. A faint wisp of smoke still spiraled from the gutted upper chamber. No one had tried to put the fire out, as it had not threatened the rest of the structure. Only now had it spent itself.

The castle had been secured, the drawbridge raised. The stronghold of the Dragon's forces had now become the stronghold of the rebels. Even those villagers who had not participated in any part of the battle now crowded within its walls. Anticipation and worry hovered in the air, palpitating Owl's skin with bony fingers. He followed Alemar up the stairs to the battlement to join the horde who waited above, nervously scanning the landscape outside the main walls. The princess stood there also, straight and intimidating in spite of her small stature.

"No sign yet?" Alemar asked his sister.

"None. Some of the scouts should be returning soon."

Owl was puzzled. What had happened to the little people, who had helped so much early in the fight? Surely they would keep track of Omril's position for the twins. Suddenly afraid, Owl realized that the wizard, with a full cohort, could be out there in complete concealment, waiting for the best moment to strike, able to raze the village while the residents hid behind the fortress walls.

Achird rose two handbreadths above the treeline. A scout jogged up to the moat and gave the password. In response the drawbridge lowered, and the man climbed up to report to the prince and princess.

"The wizard has taken the road to Yent!" the scout announced triumphantly. "He's running away!"

Owl expelled a breath he had not realized he had been holding. Wood spirits be blessed; they had won! A shout ran through the assemblage, down the stairs, into the keep. It took some time for the tavernmaster to notice that the twins, though relieved, were far from elated.

"He's going to rendezvous with the garrison there," Elenya said ominously.

Owl's smile faded. They could have held off a cohort of men, given the protection of the castle, but if the wizard gathered reinforcements . . .

"It will be a few days before he can mount an attack," Alemar said, to everyone within hearing range. "Spread the word to abandon the castle."

"My lord?" asked the man nearest him.

"The forest is a better hiding place."

The news spread, and suddenly the grounds crawled with movement. Those who had been repairing the damaged fortress defenses abandoned their work, and began systematic looting. They piled armor, weapons, gold, iron, and food in the central courtyard. Anything that could be moved was moved, until only bare stone walls and thick beams were left.

Owl started as the prince approached him and said, "These spoils will need to be distributed among the villagers. I propose an equal share for every man, woman, and child. Will you help see that this is done?"

Owl widened his eyes and stammered, "Of course, my lord. The elders and I will see to it. Aren't you taking any?"

"A little. But only what can be carried with us on the run. More would only hinder us. Better to let it go to the many, especially the armor, where it can be hidden until future need."

The tavernmaster nodded vigorously, but before he could engage the prince in further conversation, the latter marched off toward the keep.

The climb up Omril's tower seemed unusually long, at least three times as many steps as it had been coming down. Some of the men Alemar had killed still lay curled in postures of death. The stench of cooked flesh choked him as he reached the landing.

Little was left of Omril's sanctum save piles of charred wood and hardened pools of molten metal. His boot dislodged a piece of smoldering bone. He tested the floor, and tiptoed gingerly out to the balcony.

Cinders and fine soot coated the balustrade. He ran a finger across the stone, and held up the blackened tip. No trace remained of the four rythni, only ash, smoothly laid down.

At mid-morning, Owl was helping load a cart with sacks of goodroot from the castle larder when a pair of burly rebels dragged a gaunt, greybearded man into the courtyard. "Let me go!" the man growled imperiously, but his captors merely laughed. They led him before the twins.

"We found this hiding in the dungeons."

"My lord governor," Elenya said, affecting a bow. Puriel bit back another outburst. Elenya, though she had cleaned away some of the vestiges of the battle, was still a sight to stop hearts cold. His mouth fell into a palsy. Several people next to Owl called out for the governor's death.

"I don't think they like you," Elenya said.

"The Dragon will have your heads for this," he promised.

"Perhaps," Alemar replied. "But not in time to save you."

Puriel started to reply, then swallowed it.

Elenya drew her rapier. "Shall I be quick?" she asked her brother.

Alemar pursed his lips. "No, I think slow would be better. Like Milec."

Puriel sagged and would have hit the ground had his captors not held him by the scruff of his nightgown. Even Owl, who had nothing to fear, shuddered.

"I have just the thing for you," Elenya said, sheathing her blade. As if according to plan, one of her compatriots produced a harness, which she fitted around Puriel's torso. She tied a rope to it and fastened the other end to her saddle.

"Stay there a while," she told him. "Later this morning we'll go for a ride."

Puriel stood, surrounded by the hostile gazes of the villagers, until at length he began to moan. He stared at the ground, flinching whenever anyone stepped close. Alemar and Elenya ignored him. Owl was not sure what the twins had in mind, but he smiled to see Puriel so uncomfortable.

The looters divided the spoils and loaded it onto carts and pack animals. Several hefty villagers tethered the main group of prisoners together and led them away. Squads of men piled broken wood and straw against the structures and doused them with oil. Only then did the twins return to the governor.

Elenya climbed into the saddle. "Mind you keep up, now," she said, as if offering Puriel a dollop of sincere, friendly advice. She shook the reins.

Her mount trotted across the bridge at a pace that made Puriel run, fast enough to wind him, but not so fast that he would fall. The crowd surged behind, shooting, laughing, encouraging him to step lively, making jokes about his bony ankles.

They stopped at the edge of the forest, and waited there while the castle was evacuated. The men who brought out the last load lit fires as they departed. Puriel watched the flames lick at the bowels of his sanctuary. "The heat will weaken the mortar. Then we'll pull down the walls as well," Alemar told him. The governor licked his lips, wide-eyed and incredulous, clearly shocked, as Owl had been earlier, that the rebels were not keeping the castle as their own. But even the tavernmaster had quickly seen the logic: They did not have the strength to defend it against a concerted attack. It would only provide the Dragon with a target, and his retribution would be terrible enough without making it simple for him. Far better to dissolve into the forest and the towns, where they could not be easily found and/or identified. For the Dragon to reestablish his presence, his minions would have to spend long hours rebuilding the fortifications.

But much of that work would wait until the next day, when the bonfires had burnt out. Meanwhile, Elenya led the procession into Old Stump. Puriel jogged behind on unsteady legs. When she got too far ahead of the crowd, she turned and came back, starting again at the tail end. The governor began to pant, clutching his side, holding the rope with a death grip. She slackened the pace just enough that he could keep his feet, her toying glances always hinting that maybe, around the next bend, she would spur her mount and drag him. Puriel's eyes bulged. Spittle dotted his slate grey beard. Once, as he passed the line of prisoners, he called out to his men to aid him, but every one of them pretended he did not exist.

She rode him three times around the center of the town, gradually drawing the circle tighter around the remnant of the great father tree, where Milec had been pinioned. The people gathered around, jockeying for the best view. Small children, lacking the patience of their elders, pelted the governor with pebbles. One boy ran up close and flung a stone that struck Puriel hard on the bridge of his nose. Puriel snarled and kicked out at the child.

Only then did Elenya jerk him forward, yanking him face first into the dust.

Three rebels picked him up, stripped him, and tied him to the tall stump. He panted so hard that Owl felt sure the man would faint. Once again the observers began to chant for his death.

"Be done with it," he moaned.

She rode back and forth, scanning him as a goat breeder would examine a prize buck. "I think not," she said.

His brows crept closer together. "Eh?"

"I think the folk of this town will be able to determine what sort of justice you deserve." As Puriel grew pallid, she, Alemar, and thirty or forty of the core group of rebels turned and rode away, leaving the governor in the care of the locals.

Owl solemnly watched them go. He had expected the sudden turn of events; the twins had told him and some of the other elders that the fate of the prisoners would be given into their hands. But he was surprised to see his own daughter, twelve years old with figure still delicate and uncurved, dance over to Alemar's oeikani and lift a flower to him. He took it. She smiled at her audacity, caught her father's eye, and scampered back into the throng.

Owl recognized the gift as a bough lily, the flower of Cilendrodel, a pale lavender, trumpet-shaped bloom with a faint, comforting aroma. The traditional victory flower.

Victory, thought Owl. It finally struck him just what the prince and princess had accomplished. For the first time since Gloroc had sent his minions out of the boundaries of the Dragon Sea, he had suffered a clear defeat. He had lost his single greatest weapon in Cilendrodel—the fear of the general population that no one could defeat his forces. If he had lost once, he might do so again. The people would not soon forget Alemar and Elenya's vengeance. Nor would Gloroc.

Owl and his companions turned to the former governor. Let them worry about reprisals another day. For the moment they would have satisfaction.

The twins and their party did not ride free of their audience until far past the outskirts of the hamlet. Alemar held up his hand in salute, but the motion was perfunctory, unconscious. As the trees closed over their heads, he stared up into the branches, looking for some hint of movement, for the sweet, melodic call of tiny voices. The wood mocked him with its silence.

Never in his life had rythni shunned him. Throughout boy-

132

hood, this fact had set him apart, given him one of the greatest joys of his life. He had never conceived of losing their trust.

The cost of victory had been too high.

"Come back," he sang in bittersweet rythni. Elenya, the only one of his companions who could understand him, closed her eyes in pain.

He gradually became aware of the object tickling his hand, and for the first time saw the bough lily. He let it fall into the dust.

PART TWO
SCHEMING DRAGONS

Hidden dragon. Do not act.

—*I Ching*, First Hexagram, First Line

≈ XVIII ≈

Janna did not stay in her sea chamber, but took Toren to a reception room near the pool decorated with rugs, tapestries, overstuffed pillows, and curtained alcoves. He sat down, the tortoise cupped carefully in his palms.

The high priestess took an ornate glass bottle and a snifter from a cabinet and poured him one swallow of a scarlet liquid. He took it, sniffed it mistrustingly.

"It will ease the shock when your totem is restored," she said.

The concoction smelled similar to that used by his own Fhali shaman for the totem ceremony. He drank. It coated his gullet with a hot, medicinal film.

"It is very strong," he said, suspicious.

"It needs to be," she explained. "This procedure is not going to be the pleasure you have imagined."

His fingers knotted around the stem of the glass. "My ancestors," he said anxiously. "They were harmed inside the gem?"

"No," she answered quickly. "They are intact. It is you who have changed." She rubbed her cheek, looking guilty. "Except for the potion, there's not much I or Struth can do to prepare you. When you awaken, I will be gone. This is something you will have to deal with by yourself."

His eagerness dribbled away, but nevertheless he longed for the reintegration. She replaced the snifter in the cabinet and ordered him to lie down on the divan. The potion melted into him, grasping at his consciousness. The tortoise shimmered.

Janna's incantation built from soft, crooning tones to full-voiced song. His tortoise lifted its head, blinked its eyes, and crawled forward. Its pads left brief, smoky tingles along his chest and throat. It slipped into his mouth like a bird into its nest, dissolving as it passed his tongue, following the path smoothed by the potion. It merged with him.

The room dimmed. Janna's shadowy form hovered nearby. A kind of drowsy half-sleep overtook him, and dreams filled the empty place in his mind, dreams of his father, his grandfather, and all his ancestors along the male line back to the founder of the village. He was no longer a cheli.

The peace and joy of reacquaintance lasted an instant, then he fell into a chasm of screams.

Deena draped her feet in a pool in the garden of Struth and kicked. Spray danced to the tiles on the far side. The sun sparkled and beamed off the ripples. The water kissed her aching, road-weary soles.

She jumped as a shadow fell across her.

Janna stood beside her, though Deena had not heard her approach. The high priestess reached down with her intimidatingly beautiful hands and caressed the top of Deena's head with long, carefully polished nails.

"I thought I'd find you here, though I expected you'd be bathing more than your feet." Her eyes flicked toward the dusty riding clothes on Deena's body.

"I was planning to," Deena replied. Heat rushed to her cheeks. Must she constantly feel unfeminine in Janna's presence. "It's been so long, I wanted to savor it."

"Not to mention that you were lost in thought," Janna said, laughing.

Janna always treated Deena like a favorite niece. The role never hung easily on the latter's shoulders. "Well, yes. As I told you, it's been an eventful journey."

"Yes." Janna picked up the barrette that Deena had left on the tile. "It's just as well you haven't changed clothes. Tie your hair back up, too," she said, handing her the clasp. "I want you to look like you did the last time Toren saw you."

"Why?"

"I want you to visit him."

Deena's heartbeat quickened. "Why?"

Janna lowered her head, frowning. "I've just given him back his totem. It may be important to his adjustment to see you. You . . . will remind him of what he's been through in the last few weeks. At least, that's what Struth hopes."

Deena sprang to her feet, and hurriedly rolled up her hair. "Child," Janna said, setting her palm firmly on Deena's shoulder, "I doubt that he will *want* to see you right now. He will probably shun you. If so, let him be. What matters is that you confront him just long enough for his ancestors to take note of you."

Subdued, Deena nodded, and reached for her socks. "He's in

137

the Soft Room," Janna said. The priestess smiled and glided away into the fronds that surrounded the pool and isolated it from casual view.

Deena tugged on her boots and threaded her way down a flag-stone path. She strained to remember exactly where to find the Soft Room; she had seldom been there because the chamber served mainly as one of the hospitality rooms.

She wavered outside the closed door, poised her knuckles to rap on the wood. A groan and a muffled impact filtered through the barrier. She caught her breath and threw open the door.

Toren rolled across the floor, clutching his head, digging his heels so sharply into the finely woven carpets that he bunched the fabric into dramatic folds and mounds. He tumbled toward her, forcing her to leap over him. He came to a stop against a tapes-tried wall.

"Toren?" she murmured.

He jerked his gaze toward her. She quailed, frightened by the feral glow in his pupils. A string of clipped, foreign words streamed from his mouth.

"I don't understand," she said soothingly. "Use Mirienese."

He jerked with each syllable, as if physically struck. He shook his head, focussed on her once more, and snorted in disgust. She swallowed a lump so big it bruised her throat.

"Toren, what's wrong? It's me, Deena."

He shouted a brief, stern phrase, and jabbed his finger toward the doorway. Stung, she ventured half a step toward the opening. Janna's warning rang in her mind: *He may shun you.* Indeed he had. The rejection stabbed her deeper than she could have imag-ined.

She was not quick enough for him. He seized her by the waist and tossed her. She flew like a sack of grain out of the room. His strength awed her. She was lean, but she was not *that* small.

She scampered down the corridor, getting herself out of range. Toren slammed the door closed. She stopped and looked back, wincing at the pinched spots on her waist. Tears trickled down her cheeks. She cursed the bitch who had sent her to him.

She kicked the floor like a cast-off toddler and walked stiffly away. Behind her, the door shot open. To her horror, Toren came charging down the tile after her. She whimpered, ducked down, and buried her head under her arms. No. What had she done to deserve this?

He ignored her, barreling past as if she did not exist. He

138

sprinted out of the archway, through marble columns, and plunged into the dense shrubbery of the garden.

Deena flopped back on her rump, panting. Her weeping gradually dissipated. As her pride recovered from the shock, she fretted anew for Toren. What were his ancestors doing to him?

Toren crawled to the base of a tree and hugged it. His breathing slowed until, at last, he no longer had to inhale through his mouth. The bark against his cheek eased the storms in his head. Though the tree's size compared poorly to those of the Wood, it and the foliage around him blocked off all view of the temple. Dirt lay under his body, not strange, flat stones or impossibly colored fabric. His ancestors ceased clamoring to be released from the square walls of the room where they had reawakened. His own mind fought its way to the top, and began to function.

Deena. That had been Deena in the room, and in the corridor, cowering from him. Deena, his friend.

No, his great-great-grandfather's specter rambled. *A woman cannot be your friend. A modhiv makes friends among his fellow scouts; he has no time for females, save to beget sons on them. If a modhiv fails to return from a foray, his comrades will understand; a woman will not. And that one was a foreigner. A Fhali should not even speak to females of other tribes.*

Nearby a flower bloomed. His ancestors could not name it, but Toren had encountered it in the mountains the day before. *"Liris,"* he said, repeating the name Deena had taught him. "It means Beauty."

No, his forebears protested. *Flowers have names like shadebloom, whiteroot, blossom-that-opens-in-autumn. Beauty is a name for a pet animal.*

Toren shook and curled into a fetal huddle. One after the other, his ancestors condemned him. *Why have you left the Wood? Why have you eaten sacrilegious food? What is this talent springing from you, that should belong only to a shaman? The sun lies nearly overhead, when it should ride the sky to the north.*

It's not my fault, Toren cried.

Where are we? Why are we here? If not your fault, whose is it?

He explained with imagined images of a dragon and armies marching over battlefields. He gave them firsthand memories of the Frog God and a wizard whose blood smoked and dissolved steel. But all these things—even the steel—stunned them with queerness, sent them cringing away to things familiar and secure.

139

Finding none, they accused him again of betrayal.

I had no choice, he moaned. *They took you away from me, sealed you in a talisman.*

His ancestors recoiled. *You let them strip you of your totem? Cheli! Non-human!*

I am a cheli no longer, Toren protested. *You are restored.* But the revelation had overwhelmed them. Dizzy with their silent yells, Toren crawled over to a tiny pool and dunked his head in and out. The shock of cold water on his face gave him back his wind, kept him from retching. A cloud of fish darted away from the impact point.

The activity caught his eye. Desperate to occupy his mind with anything but his ancestors' voices, he counted the number of species in the pool. There were four. At the bottom, a few scum-suckers browsed. Tiny minnows clung to the protection of roots and water lilies. A broad, puffy type dominated the open water, challenged only by a long, streamlined, rainbow-hued sort.

His ancestors recognized none of them, which gave them all the more reason to wail. Toren gritted his teeth and kept his glance on a specimen of the fourth species. A memory struggled to coalesce, battered by the hurricane within him.

The day before, in the mountains, he, Geim, and Deena caught five such fish in an alpine stream, and roasted them for dinner. A good meal. The pure white flesh tasted light and flavorful.

"*Aumeris,*" he murmured. That was the name Geim had used. It meant streaker. "*Aumeris.*"

He barely heard himself. Twenty-five generations insisted that they knew all the fishes of the Wood. There was no need to know the names of fishes elsewhere. What if their meat was poisonous?

His ancestors did not know this world, did not want to know this world. Then let them keep theirs, and leave him to deal with the one he was living in.

The voice that shouted most loudly was that of his great-great-grandfather, who had also been a modhiv. He called for his descendant to remember the code of a warrior, to hold to the ways that had served the tribe generation after generation, to purge himself of foreign tongues, ideas, and loyalties.

Toren reoriented a small connection in his mind. His great-great-grandfather's voice vanished from the din. Toren choked back a sob. Quickly he searched, and found that every part of that ancestor's experiences remained, accessible to his call. But now, the information came only *if* he called it. The dead man's spirit lived on, but was bound, forbidden to speak without permission.

What had Geim said? *"Things change when one has no ancestors to tell the living how things should be."* For Toren, at that time and in that place, things needed to change. He stilled his father's voice, and his grandfather's. He wept, but the pain of separation was less excruciating than the condemnation, confusion, and disquiet of the active totem. He had heard legends of Vanihr who had silenced the speakers within, but he had judged the tales to be myth. That they might be authentic occurrences had been inconceivable.

He repeated the adjustment until he had muzzled every ancestor. "Forgive me," he whispered as he shut out the founder of the Fhali nation.

All at once, the tiny grove into which he had fled seemed disturbingly vacant. A small frog splashed noisily into the pool, startling him. Birds fluttered in the upper reaches of the trees, suddenly very loud. He accessed the recollections of his father, just to be sure he could. His sire, a stern believer in the value of tradition, chastised him because he had let his hair come loose. The manner in which it was fastened was one of the ways Fhali denoted their tribal identity. Toren cut off the admonishment.

He rose unsteadily to his feet. Like most of his ancestors, his father had been angry that Toren had been abused, livid that the totem had been violated. Strangely, Toren could not summon one breath of rage.

He stumbled out of the grove, uncertain of his destination. The Soft Room did not beckon, nor did he wish to see Struth or the high priestess. He did not wish to see anyone. In time he would seek out Deena, at the very least to apologize, but not yet. He turned away from the wing of hospitality rooms, discovered a path through the garden, and headed for the front of the temple complex.

No one challenged him, though he passed a pair of priestesses, and sentries gazed down at him from their posts on the outer walls. The drelb, to his surprise, courteously opened the exit for him. He meandered into the amphitheater via the main entrance, tucked himself into a corner, and observed the petitioners at the Oracle of the Frog God.

The supplicants cast their offerings and uttered their questions. Struth declined to answer. As the afternoon wore on, Toren huddled farther and farther back toward the wall. Though the people at the dais represented many nationalities, none spoke

Mirienese, and certainly none used Vanihr. Toren ached for the turn of a familiar phrase. He caught barely a word here and there, trivial terms whose meaning he had picked up listening to Geim and Deena converse during the journey.

He missed his ancestors. He needed them. He clenched his fists. Why could they not have *whispered*? Why did they have to shout?

He rose and left the temple. Walking down the avenue of temples, the fire of anger flickered at last. The irony struck him. That morning, he had projected his fury at Struth because she had stolen his totem; now he resented his ancestors and had to wonder if the Frog God had done him a service by muting them.

He nearly bumped into a fat acolyte of one god or another, who cursed him. Gibberish, more gibberish. Other passersby mumbled their unintelligible gossip. What was he to do with himself? The confrontation with his totem had proven that he had, after all, somewhat adapted to this northern world, but that did not mean he belonged here yet.

How could he get back to the Wood? Only there, in familiar lands, could he possibly let his totem live as it had before. No, he was deluding himself—he could never let his ancestors speak freely again. They would always remind him of what he had done. But the Wood was still the only place he could call home, and Rhi waited for him there.

To leave the continent, he would have to cross the ocean. He would need to know the speech of the sailors to find passage, work off debts, and avoid opportunists. The only scheme that tempted him was to return to Irigion. He knew the route, and once there, some of those who spoke Mirienese could teach him the tongue that most of the northern principalities seemed to share. A year or two might be consumed before he reached the Wood, but that would still return him home long before his son came of age.

He threw the dream up at the wisps of clouds gathering in front of the setting sun. Struth had snared him well.

His warrior instincts told him that one of the people walking behind him was making straight for him. He turned.

Geim joined him. For an instant, the sight of another Vanihr reawakened his totem. His ancestors strained at their bonds. Toren winced, but kept them in check.

"You are well?" Geim asked.

Toren laughed wryly. "I am healthy, if that's what you mean."

"Not exactly," Geim stated, but let the matter drop. The bracelet on his wrist, the talisman of pursuit, drew Toren's glance. Geim shrugged. "You know you're too valuable to us to let you wander far. Struth felt you needed the time alone, but now it's best that you return to the temple."

"Why not?" Toren said, and reversed direction. "Thank you for reminding me of my imprisonment. I was just reflecting on what a clever cage it is." Under the sarcasm, it astonished him how good it felt to be able to discourse with ease and subtlety.

"The precautions are for your own safety. Gloroc's spies and assassins have a formidable reputation, and even Struth's eyes cannot be everywhere."

"The concern of the goddess touches me," Toren said.

"You really *are* free to go, if you wish."

"I may do that—later." The language matter refused to settle down and leave Toren be. "Tell me," he asked as they turned down the alley toward the side entrance, "why did Deena teach me her native tongue, and not the one that you and she shared? Was that deliberate?"

"You mean, why did we keep you from learning the main language of the north?" Geim asked bluntly.

The forthrightness pleased Toren. "Yes."

"It was not to handicap you, if that's what you're thinking. Just the opposite. Struth wants you to learn the High Speech immediately. Deena and I were prohibited from teaching it to you, in part because it is not a native tongue to either of us. We each speak it with an accent. Would you like to start now?"

Toren blinked. "As a matter of fact, yes."

The drelb admitted them to the temple. "Very well," Geim said. "We had planned to wait a day or two, but I think tonight will do. Come. There's someone you need to meet."

≈ XIX ≈

Dusk hallowed the corridors of the main edifice of the temple complex as Geim led Toren up spiraling stairs to the third floor. They stopped before a door in the northeast corner of the building. Geim knocked. A thin, warbling voice responded.

They entered a small, hexagonal chamber whose walls overflowed with books, scrolls, and tablets. A high, arched window provided a view over the wall of the temple grounds—the city

143

climbed into the heights of the gorge, and the final traces of sunlight scintillated off the snow banks of the high peaks. Sweet herb incense burned in a freestanding brazier. A narrow bed took up space along one wall; otherwise the only furniture consisted of a small round table and a broad, soft chair.

A man sat in the chair. As they entered he touched the lamp on the table and the wick caught, staving off twilight's impending gloom. The illumination flickered over a flowing white beard and glistened on a bald, age-mottled scalp. Toren stared at his host's hand, but the fingers held no match or striker.

Geim uttered a sentence. The old man nodded. Geim turned back to Toren and said, "This is Obo, former counsellor of Keron, King of Elandris."

The name jogged Toren's memory.

Obo inclined his head. "I see you've heard of me," he said. Though his voice quavered, each word seemed to echo.

"You were Ivayer's teacher. The wizard who made Geim's net," Toren replied. "You speak Mirienese?"

At the mention of Ivayer, Obo's eyes clouded. "Yes. My apprentice was with the party sent to capture you," he stated sadly. "And I made the talisman, though Struth had to teach me a few tricks to do it. As for the last, I was born in Mirien."

"Ivayer died well," Toren said. It was the highest compliment a modhiv could pay, but he could tell that Obo was not consoled.

"Yes. Geim told me." He ran his fingers through his beard. "Such a promising lad. I had hoped to finish training one last apprentice before my days came to an end."

"The men who killed him did not escape unscathed," Toren said.

"I care nothing about that," Obo said, ending the matter. "Geim tells me you're in a hurry to learn the High Speech. Did he mention what's involved?"

"No. The topic came up by accident."

"It's a dramatic technique. I've had to prepare for several weeks. But the result will be worth it. I would be happy to get it over with early. Have you eaten?"

The question took Toren by surprise. As if in response, his stomach growled. "Not since dawn, before entering the city."

"Excellent. That's best for this type of spell."

Toren's eyes narrowed. "Another spell? I am getting worn down by all this sorcery in my life."

"Young man," Obo said flatly, "if you could see your own

aura, you would know that you were born to have sorcery in your life."

Geim shuffled. "I need to report to the high priestess that I found you, Toren. Are you staying?"

The modhiv shrugged. "Yes. I suppose so."

Geim made his excuses to Obo and departed.

"Very well," Toren told the wizard, "another spellcasting probably won't bruise me more than what I've been through today."

"It won't," Obo said reassuringly, as if he knew all about the totem's restoration. Toren had no doubt that he did. The modhiv had never met a person who projected such a sense of wisdom and knowledge. "Though I suspect you gained something, however uncomfortable the experience may have been."

"That remains to be seen," Toren said. It bothered him to think the sorcerer could guess that.

"Indeed." Obo lifted a tiny flask off a shelf and uncorked it. "Drink this. Be forewarned it will make you sleepy."

Another potion. Toren sighed and sniffed the concoction, catching a hint of licorice. He sipped carefully, no more than a drop, and a few moments later was surprised to discover that he had eagerly swallowed it all. He stared dumbfounded at the flask.

"More?"

"That's plenty," Obo said quickly.

The potion left a warmth like wine. His stomach stopped complaining. The promised effect was immediate. Drowsy and calm, he let Obo lead him to the bed. The modhiv tugged off his moccasins and stretched out on his back.

"Relax," Obo said. "Clear your mind. All is well." The words made an extraordinary amount of sense. The wizard pulled the chair close to the bed, sat, and placed a palm on Toren's forehead. The room faded, leaving only a faint afterimage of a cobweb high in the rafters.

He saw a cliff two thousand feet high, rising sheer above a plain, cut with deep erosion scars and banded with brilliant strata. His vantage point was a window of a farm house down on the plain. The setting left him with vague sensations of security, curiosity, and awe—childlike emotions.

Next came images of an island, and Toren, who had visited an ocean only on two brief occasions, realized that the vast expanse of water before him felt familiar. The island was Acalon, the center of the Calinin Empire, once the home of the wizard-kings, and still the best place for a sorcerer to get his training. He saw the columns and gardens of an ancient, distinguished academy. The people walking through the halls and along the paths spoke words that clung to his memory—not the content of their conversations, but the words themselves, the usage, the vocabulary, the grammar.

Next he saw another ocean; but this time, his view was from within it, looking through a glasslike dome at the waves above. The city within the dome was spectacular, exotic, beautiful, and the people in its streets spoke to him in the same language as that used in Acalon, but with a more pure, precise flavor. They called the city Firsthold, capital of the nation of Elandris.

And finally Toren saw a forest, one of trees that dwarfed those of the Wood itself. The people there called the place Cilendrodel, and at times they spoke a tongue almost identical to the people beneath the sea, and at other times the words mutated into alternate forms, their metaphors calling up visions of wood and shade rather than sea and salt air, their dialects losing the uniformity of the city speech.

Toren knew what was happening to him. The experience was similar to that he had endured during his coming of age ceremony, when he had first received his totem. It differed in that the lives and personalities of his ancestors had come to him full-blown, whereas he was receiving only specific aspects of Obo's life—the general milieu, the cultures, languages, and scenery of the northern lands. Unlike his shaman, the sorcerer could control what was transferred.

Toren roused briefly. Obo stooped over him. Moons' light streamed through the window, supplementing that of the lamp.

"Don't try to hold it all," the mage cautioned. "Take in only what reaches for you."

Toren obeyed. He felt safe. The surroundings were becoming familiar. He was only slightly disconcerted to hear his own voice whispering passages of classic tomes. Neither he nor any of his tribe knew how to read or write. This spellweaving was quite the opposite of Struth and Janna's earlier in the day; the irony made him chuckle drunkenly. Obo was making himself Toren's ancestor.

He awoke with a ravenous appetite. Obo had obviously anticipated the need, for a stack of roast fowl and other tantalizing foodstuffs waited on the table. A small kettle of carrots boiled above the brazier.

Toren paused. Before going to sleep, he would have been unable to identify the carrots. Now he could name everything in the room.

Bright daylight streamed in, setting a cheerful mood. Obo strolled in, dragging a stool. "I don't often have visitors up here," he said amiably. "One chair is usually enough."

The magician spoke in the language that had haunted Toren's dreams. Toren paused, disoriented.

"What's the matter? Did your tongue fall off?"

"Good morning," Toren blurted. Yes, he had said it right. He grinned with almost childlike glee.

Obo smiled. "Excellent. No accent. It will become easier very soon. You'll have to practice, though. Transplanted speech patterns pale compared to those you actually use. That's why Deena and Geim couldn't teach you the High Speech. You might have continued to speak with their accents and other faults even after learning correct usage from me."

"You said you were born in Mirien. Have you no accent?" The image of the Great Cliff of Mirien spontaneously returned to Toren's mind.

"I left my home ninety years ago, and have used the speech of the Calinin ever since in one form or another. I have a good ear, and I had started to learn it as a child. I have my quirks, of course, but they'll not handicap you. Convenient, is it not, to learn a language in only three days?"

"Three days?"

"Well, three nights, to be precise. It's now the third morning since you went to sleep."

Toren nodded. Some part of him had kept track. "My tribe's shaman took a week to put my ancestors' spirits into me."

"That doesn't surprise me. It would have taken Struth and Janna that long to put them back had the pathways not been forged already. The part that took me so long was sorting out the information. No need to transmit the tale of my life—you've enough going on in your head as it is. The language, the cultural referents, were all that were necessary. I shielded the rest. It's a technique you can use, by the way; it will help you keep your ancestors cooperative. Search within and you will find you already know how to summon that ability, a fringe benefit I thought you might appreciate."

For the first time, Toren realized he was not having to strain to muzzle the voices of his totem. "Thank you. I do appreciate it."

Toren trusted Obo. He remembered enough of the wizard's

life to know that a good man sat across from him. This security, even more than the cultural transferral, mitigated the shock of being in an alien land. In all his life, the only "person" he had trusted at such a level was the collective voice of his totem, and with the latter disrupted, he valued the chance to talk with the old man.

Obo yawned. His lids drooped. In the full light of day, his pallor stood out all too clearly. His hand wavered unsteadily as he lifted the kettle lid.

"Are you well? Have you slept?" Toren asked.

"The spell did not exhaust me, if that's what you're concerned about. My part took only a few hours each evening. The rest of the time you were sorting the information, tucking it away. I am simply very old. *Breathing* tires me."

Suddenly he shrugged off his somber tone. His eyes regained their spark. "Enough of this serious talk. The food's ready. Let's not waste it. You've an audience with Struth today."

Starting gradually, Toren began to make up for his long fast. Either the potion had sharpened his taste buds, or the fruit and bread he ate were exceptionally flavorful. The meal almost banished the dread of confronting the Frog God again.

≈≈ XX ≈≈

In Janna's audience chamber, Toren sat across from the high priestess, the fingers of their left hands interlaced, knees touching knees. Her gentle lecture carried softly over the hushed murmurs of the "sea" outside the dome. Her perfume wafted lightly up his nose, mixed with the scent of the perspiration brought on by her spellcasting—a pheromone that inspired Toren to vivid reminiscences of his lovemaking with the mother of his son. But his arousal was a side effect, not the intent of either participant. Toren put the memory aside, taking small notice of his body's craving. A deeper sort of lust preoccupied him.

"Like we did yesterday," Janna said, her whisper crystal clear and penetrating. "Remember what Struth told you. Yes. You're getting close. Can you tell?"

"Yes." Toren strove to channel his excitement; it would aid the sorcery. He concentrated, eyes closed. The room faded. The divan on which he sat dissolved into empty air. The only sensations that remained were the sound of Janna's voice, the pressure of her fingers and knees, and her scent. He floated, free of constraints, anchored only by the high priestess's presence.

"Keep your mind calm, and open your eyes," Janna said.

He did so. The first glimpse of the scene before him nearly jostled him out of his trance, but unlike the previous day, he kept his attention steady. Only one week after his arrival in Headwater, he already had the confidence vital to successful spell-weaving.

He viewed the temple amphitheater, the Oracle of the Frog God, as if he were sitting on top of the great statue's head. His back rested against the ridge of one of the frog's eyes; Janna leaned against the other. Below, petitioners shuffled forward in their line. A crone dropped two copper errons in the pool and asked whether she would live to see another spring. The oracle did not reply. The woman spat in the water and stalked away. From the vigor of her angry steps, Toren guessed she would survive twenty more cycles of the seasons.

They watched for a few minutes. The wandering glances of the people in the line proved they could not see Toren and Janna. Yet Toren felt as if he were actually there. He moved normally, except that he made certain not to break contact with the priestess. The stone on which he sat resounded with cold substantiality. When he peered too far over the nose of the frog, vertigo teased him.

Gradually he noticed that the entire top of the statue glowed with a faint network of bright lines. The tendrils emitted a fragrance of thaumaturgy. On a hunch, he tried to thrust his hand beyond their perimeter. His fingers encountered a soft but definite barrier. He strained, pushing an inch or two further, until the resistance grew so firm that it hurt his hand.

Janna smiled at him. "Good. I was hoping you'd notice that without my help." She resumed the position she had occupied when they had first materialized. "Time to go back. Your control is slipping."

Her words rang true. Toren shook unsteadily as he sat back. He closed his eyes.

An instant later he opened them, and saw Janna's dome. An octopus and a pair of sea snails clung to the transparent wall, presenting a dramatic perspective of their suckered appendages. The divan cradled him. Across from him, the glazed look left Janna's pupils.

"Good!" she cried. "Much better! How do you feel?"

"Light-headed," Toren replied.

"You should be. That was a great deal of progress for one session. You'd better rest for the remainder of the day. Tomorrow Struth will adjust your energies a bit more, and you and I shall try the same journey with your eyes open. And after you've become used to that; you can work on projecting all by yourself. Now, any questions?"

"Yes. Were we there, at the oracle, or not?"

"No. Our bodies were here the whole time. Only our awareness travelled. It's the same technique Struth uses to listen to the supplicants."

"She sends her voice, too?"

"Yes. An adept can even send a visible image. If you continue at your present rate of advancement, I'll teach you that next week. Struth uses the technique not only at this oracle, but to visit her temples in other cities."

"Is there no limit on distance?"

"Not really, though it's a little harder to project oneself to the other side of the world. The handicap is that you must have visited your destinations at least once in the flesh, otherwise you won't know where you're going. And, of course, there must be a reception zone ready to catch your projection."

"Like the net on the statue's head?" he asked.

"Exactly. It took sophisticated sorcery, and a great many days, to create that. There was no choice, however. I know of no person or being so powerful as to be able to project himself to a random location. At least the zones are permanent once woven; they last until the weaver dies."

Janna slid her hand from his. His skin tingled where she had touched it. Hints of his earlier arousal returned.

"More questions?" Janna asked, blowing the sweat between her fingers dry.

"No," Toren said, startled. At her gesture, he excused himself. He found the door using his magical senses—a test Janna had foisted on him earlier in the week—and took his leave.

Deena found Obo sitting in a gazebo inside the garden of Struth, one of the many small hideaways to be found within the temple grounds. On the table before him steeped a pot of tea, and next to it sat three empty cups. A chunk of honeycomb oozed on a small plate. The wizard put away the scroll he had been reading and filled two of the cups.

She smiled as she sat down. She had missed the ritual of her

150

quiet conversations with him. How many times had they shared tea in this spot during the months before she had left for the Wood? Ten? Twenty?

"You're losing the look of the traveller," Obo said, giving her a glance that, in a younger man, might have been called admiring.

"Thank you," she said, self-consciously picking a piece of lint from the smocking of her dress. She folded her arms so that they concealed the scar on her forearm.

"You've kept out of sight a great deal since you arrived. Any particular reason?"

His fatherly eyes saw too much, she thought. "I just needed some time alone. The quest proved to be quite a strain."

"Yes," he said, nodding. He blew over his cup to cool the contents. "You conducted yourself well, from all accounts."

"The mission was important to me," she said. "But you compliment me too much. My only real accomplishment was to have survived."

"That's no mean feat," he countered, and briefly his glance focussed on some distant place. Remembering Ivayer, she guessed. "Toren has been asking about you," he added abruptly.

"Oh?" she said, feigning calm.

"I told him you had stopped by while he was asleep, learning the High Speech. It's been five days since he woke up. Are you avoiding him?"

"No," she answered instantly. "He's just been very busy. I understand Struth and Janna have started teaching him how to use his abilities. I've not wished to disturb him." She carefully steadied her hand, and added a dollop of honey to her tea. She licked a drop off her thumb. "How is he doing?"

"He's progressing even faster than we had hoped. It's now easy to understand why Struth was so adamant that we locate him in spite of the incredible distance. Had we found him as a child and nurtured that talent as he grew . . . well, let's just say he's doing the best that can be hoped for in spite of the lack of proper shaping, distinctly better than the previous candidates. He may not be quite right for the gauntlets, but he's close. Very close."

"How long before he's ready?"

"That's not the question. We only have about two months, whether he's ready in that time or not. The Dragon's army is becoming too entrenched in the East. The situation in Cilendrodel is deteriorating. We have to set our strategies in motion and hope for the best. The uncertainty at this point is Toren's motivation."

"What more incentive does he need?" Deena remarked sarcastically. "We stole him from his land, ripped out his ancestors' spirits and then alienated him from them. Surely he is hopping with eagerness to help our cause."

Obo chuckled humorlessly. "Geim said much the same thing only yesterday. But it's not entirely hopeless. Though Toren believed in his tribe, his life in the South was not happy. I glimpsed pieces of his life, just as he did of mine, when I gave him my ability to use the High Speech. His shaman was jealous of him, and I have no doubt the man worked behind Toren's back to eat away at the tribe's opinion of him. Toren was a fabulous scout, and yet he was given the least desired missions and was seldom acknowledged for his successes. At the very least, his shaman kept him from developing his sorcerous talents. A man of Toren's abilities could never have prospered among the Fhali. I think the boy is beginning to realize that, beginning to see that his culture was so tradition-bound by the weight of all those generations of ancestors living inside every adult that an aberration such as he could only be stifled and shunned. And wasted. I am not guilty for what we have done. I know how I would have felt if my family had denied me the chance to study with the master wizards of Acalon."

Deena felt a burden lift from her shoulders. Thank the gods for wise old men.

"We will see what happens," Obo continued. "The transformation I am hoping for is not one that all the high sorcery in the world can manage. It's up to Toren himself." Obo slurped a quick, bracing sip of tea. "I've invited him to join us, by the way. He's done with his tests early today."

"You did?" Deena blurted. Her pulse quickened.

"Yes," he replied smugly. "In fact, here he comes now." He lowered his voice. "Keep in mind what I've said, young woman. And keep blushing. It becomes you."

Damn him, she thought. The heat in her cheeks increased. The conniving old trickster must have known his comment would have that effect.

The modhiv ambling toward was not the same man she had journeyed with across long reaches of two continents. The aura of disorientation had left his posture, replaced by determination, interest, and alertness.

He stared at Deena a long time. "You look different," he said. Was that approval she detected in his tone?

"I don't have to wear such, um, *sturdy* clothing now that I'm

152

not on the road," she replied, adjusting the laces of her bodice.

"You've let down your hair."

"That, too."

"She's also had a bath recently," Obo said dryly. "Have some tea, boy, or it will get cold while you catalog all the changes in her appearance. I get the feeling you didn't know you were in the company of a woman on your trek."

"We were busy fighting cannibals and wizards," Toren said. "She was my comrade-in-arms."

"You'll be reassured to know I've been keeping up my archery practice this week," she informed him pointedly.

He chuckled. "That's good. But to be frank, I rather like the change." His speech pattern did sound remarkably like Obo's, she reflected. "Women shouldn't be warriors."

Obo guffawed. "There's a woman I know in Cilendrodel who would have a few words to say about that."

Deena smiled. "No, Toren's right." She nodded toward the modhiv. "By the way, your High Speech is excellent."

"It *should* be," Obo quipped.

Toren shrugged. "It is a very . . . round-about tongue. When a Vanihr needs to say something, he says it. I prefer Mirienese. It's more direct."

"We can speak it if you'd like," Deena offered in the afore-mentioned language.

"No," Toren replied in the High Speech. He dipped honey in his cup. "You know I still speak it in a fractured way. I like not having to search for the right word."

"I suppose I could have taught you Mirienese as well," Obo mused. "You could have slept another couple of days . . ."

"That's all right," Toren said quickly. "I'm content."

There was a short, pregnant gap in the conversation. Each of them sipped from their cups.

Obo cleared his throat. "I have a matter to attend to. If you'll excuse me."

Deena almost stepped on the hem of his robes to keep him in place, but the sorcerer slipped out of his seat with the elusiveness of a child, and sauntered away across the flagstones, his gait barely betraying his feebleness.

Deena turned, and found Toren staring into the pattern of the tea leaves at the bottom of the pot. He looked up, met her glance.

"I was not myself when I last saw you. I'm sorry."

She sucked in her lips. "Yes. Well. I knew that. Don't worry about it. I trust you and your ancestors have . . . come to an arrangement?"

"They are there, should I call them," Toren said wistfully. "But not in the way they used to be."

She nodded sympathetically. "Aside from that, how has it been for you? The tests?"

A sly smile crept over his features. He set two fingers on her cup. His eyes glazed. Steam began to rise from what had been lukewarm tea. When he was done, she picked up the cup, darted her tongue in it, and nearly burned the tip.

"Clever," she muttered. "You could be handy in the winter."

"I feel like an eagle whose wings have been bound all its life, freed. I can't ride the thermals yet, have yet to make my first kill, but I have learned to glide from nest to ground. True flight is only a matter of time."

"And has Janna been a good teacher?" she asked, pretending nonchalance.

"Yes, though it's difficult at times to think of her as a teacher."

"Oh?" Deena's eyebrows rose. "And what else would you think of her as?"

"A female."

"I see." She smoothed her skirts, was annoyed at the knobbiness of the knees under them.

"But I keep my attention on her lessons. The alternative is to study with Struth. I do enough of that. Something about learning from a big frog raises the hair on the nape of my neck."

"I didn't know you had any," she snapped, referring to the relative hairlessness of his body.

He blinked at her tone. "Janna has a gift for clear explanations. Hasn't she ever instructed you?"

"Not about sorcery. I have no gift."

"Of course," he said quickly. "So much goes on in this temple, it seems that everyone is a magician."

"No," Deena said. "Some of us must settle for less."

He frowned. "I didn't mean to imply you were a nettle among flowers."

"Sometimes I feel that way."

He regarded her carefully. "You are a mystery, Deena. How did you come here? How long have you lived at the temple?"

"Not long. Early winter before last, the Dragon's troops invaded Mirien, sacked my home, killed all my family. I fled to Serthe. One day I happened by the Oracle of the Frog God. I threw in a coin and asked what I could do to hurt Gloroc. Struth liked that. She gave me a home. I was not suited to be a priestess, so I helped in small matters of business. The goddess found it handy to have a woman around who had had some martial training—that happened because my father was a career soldier who had no sons. I escorted the last candidate from her home in Aleoth, and then I was chosen to help fetch you."

"What happened to that candidate?"

Deena paused. "She failed the tests. She died."

Toren scratched his chin.

"So you see," Deena continued, "why I have reason to favor the Elandri resistance against the Dragon."

"Yes. Did you lose children in the invasion?"

"No. I've never been married."

He refilled his cup. "I've never been married either. That did not keep me from having a son."

Her cup slipped from her grip and landed noisily on the table top, nearly tipping over. She sucked spilled tea from her fingers. "No wife? When you mentioned your child, I assumed . . ."

"A natural mistake, I suppose. Modhiv are not permitted to marry. Their lives are constantly at risk; it would not be fair to a wife. In addition, a warrior must be able to go to a skirmish without worrying about a spouse left behind."

"But your son."

"A Vanihr must have offspring to carry the totem. I made an arrangement with a woman. She bore Rhi, and cares for him when I cannot. But she is not my wife. In fact, three years ago she married my cousin."

Deena traced patterns in the spilled tea. "Yes, it would be important, to have a recipient for your totem. Your immortality, as you said last week. I almost expected you to leave as soon as Struth restored your ancestors, to go back and be with Rhi."

"I long to," Toren replied. "But what would be the point of dying on the way? Until I pass on my totem for the first time, I must survive at all costs. I don't know what my final decision will be, but for now staying at the temple and developing my talents seems more sensible than running for the Wood with the Dragon's assassins at my heels."

"I hope you will choose to aid us," she said. "It is a good cause. And good people stand to die if the Dragon has his way. Like my family."

"I've thought of that. Self-preservation is not my only emotion." Suddenly he reached out and tenderly brushed the tip of her chin. "I'm well aware of the goodness of some of the people here."

She coughed, and to her dismay, the action caused him to remove his touch. "Whichever you decide—to go back to the Wood or to take up the gauntlets—I pray you do survive," she said emphatically.

She interlaced the fingers of her right hand with his. He did not pull away.

 XXI

The sun burst out from behind a thin, solitary wisp of cloud as Wynneth climbed the hill. She trod carefully due to the extra weight in her belly, but vigorously, no longer burdened by the sleepiness of the second and third month, no longer weakened by morning sickness. This was the good part, her female relatives told her. She had started to swell; she could feel the baby move. It was becoming real.

She clambered to an outcropping, joining Solint the Minstrel at his lookout station. To the south stretched yellow prairie. A dark line denoted the edge of the great forest, nearly lost in the shimmer of the warm, midday air. A hundred leagues farther, separated by tracts of pristine, barely explored timberland, lay the coast of Cilendrodel and the town of Old Stump.

"Do you think we've lost them?" she asked. No telltale smoke or cloud of dust rose into the sky.

Solint strummed his lute; he was not one to allow guard duty to prevent him from composing. "For the moment."

Eight weeks after the sack of Puriel's fortress, Omril still pursued the rebel band, accompanied by two cohorts from the garrison at Yent. He had left the punishment of Old Stump's citizens to the acting governor and had singlemindedly chased Alemar and Elenya into the wilderness. Nothing dissuaded him, not the difficulties of supplying such a large group of men over such a distance, not the tediousness of cutting their way through tracks of untamed forest, not the attrition of the company by wild animals, booby traps, or nighttime rebel harassment. Three times the twins had tried to establish camps and enjoy some much needed recuperation; three times Omril had located them.

In their latest effort, they had waded along a river for a day to conceal their tracks, while a few members of the band created a false trail. Wynneth hoped they had finally bought themselves some time. The wizard would think it unlikely that they had ventured into open terrain. He would assume that the rythni were still helping Alemar's band, and rythni would not leave the forest.

Thus far it had worked. For the first time, the rebels looked less haggard, and had caught up on sleep. But Wynneth still fretted. Alemar needed more than a few days respite.

"I brought some sour cakes," Wynneth told Solint. "We've got the oven working." She waved at the crude construction down in the camp. A faint trace of smoke rose from the stack: a risk. However, the plains were often dotted with the campfires of the indigenous nomads. It had been too long since the rebels had tasted fresh bread and other baked goods. The presence of the oven had already boosted morale.

Solint smiled, stuffed his mouth full, and kissed her. She brushed the crumbs off her lips and laughed, recalling the sweetness of his kisses during the years before Alemar returned from the Eastern Deserts and married her. If music and sex had been enough to fulfill her, she might have lived a very different life.

She descended the hill. Elenya was still drilling a half dozen of the company in unarmed combat. At the moment they were performing an endurance exercise, kicking by her count. They paused for one deep breath between each set of ten. They were up to three hundred, and had the other leg yet to go. Elenya still kicked high and strong. All but one of the others had withered. Two barely raised their feet higher than shin level.

Wynneth kept her face averted, sparing them the embarrassment of an extra observer. They grimaced in frustration. They had exercised continuously for over three hours. She might soon have to interrupt. She could use the freshly baked treats as an excuse.

Elenya was a hard taskmaster; she demanded performance close to her own level. Even those with the youth, strength, and stamina to match her normal pace were being taxed to their limits lately. Wynneth winced as the princess yelled for everyone to kick higher.

They needed Alemar's tempering influence. She glanced nervously up the hill to the north, to the cave where her husband had secluded himself. She should not interrupt him. Still, he might appreciate some of the sour cakes. She had not bothered him for an entire day.

Before she could talk herself out of it, she loaded a small basket and started up the path. She felt Elenya's glance follow her all the way up.

Alemar lay at the mouth of the cave, staring up at the sky. The crescent of Serpent Moon hung there, a pale imitation of the brilliant blue and white half-circlet displayed at night. He heard Wynneth approach, but did not react.

She set the basket down near his head. "Your son and I have come to visit you," she said cheerfully.

He gradually turned and met her gaze. He glanced at the basket. "Just leave it. I'll eat later."

Wynneth sucked her lips inward, then puckered them, then sighed. She moved the cakes next to his other supplies and left, chin hung low.

Guilt settled on him like gnats at a lakeside. But he did not call her back. The visions in his head killed his involvement in the current moment. His relationship with his wife, his sister, and his comrades paled against the misery of those internal images. Rythni wings burned like oiled torches. Iregg's hand, crippled in battle, turned blue and lifeless as he held it. Memories of power now lost haunted him. The gentleness that caused the little people to be enamored of him eluded his grasp. He knew Wynneth had only been expressing concern, but all he wanted was to shut out the world.

Retreat. He waited for the ritual that he had learned in Zyraii to heal the healer. He clung to the belief that it would. Until it did, he could not face the challenges before him, could not forgive himself, could not care if he lived or died.

What had his teacher said? "The sorcery within is a fragile gift. When nothing is left but embers, it must be banked and nurtured, or it will expire."

Perhaps the embers had gone out.

Elenya's group paused. As Wynneth went to splash some water on her face at the spring, the princess walked over, limping slightly. "Well?" she asked, obviously trying to keep the tone conversational.

"No change," Wynneth said. The chill of the water made her shudder.

"They have a saying in Zyraii. 'There is nothing so distant as a Hab-no-ken on Retreat.'"

"I know why they say that," Wynneth murmured.

"In fact, if he were to follow the tradition of Zyraii healers, he would have sequestered himself in a spot where no one could have found him."

"Then I suppose I should be grateful." Her sarcasm dripped off her tongue like acid.

Elenya gently laid a hand on her sister-in-law's shoulder.

"I'm sorry," Wynneth said, sighing. "I just didn't expect him to cut himself off from *me*."

"Why don't you show me some of those things you've been creating in that oven? I was wondering when someone was going to make use of all these sourberry vines," Elenya said, waving at the brambles near the camp.

Wynneth tried to smile. Elenya took her by the arm and they walked together toward the rich, enticing scent. One of the other camp women withdrew a fresh batch of the tiny cakes. Elenya and Wynneth each snagged one. They blew on them to help them cool.

They had just swallowed them when Solint let out a cry. Instantly the entire camp was in motion. Elenya sprinted toward the lookout point, rapier drawn, followed by four others. Men rushed to put on their armor and saddle the oeikani. Wynneth and the women gathered supplies. She cast a quick glance toward Alemar's position, but could not see him.

The band paused while Elenya, Solint, and the others on the hilltop stared southward. A rabbit bounded across the grass, startling Wynneth; she had inadvertently stepped on its burrow. Elenya came down the slope at a less hectic pace than when she had ascended. Wynneth released a pent-up breath. Whatever Solint had spotted was apparently not cause for panic.

Elenya dispatched men to the flanks of the southern approach to the camp, ordering them to conceal themselves. She told the others to wait to break camp. "It's one rider. He's making straight for us. Let's see what he has to say for himself."

Archers lined up on one side of the path, arrows ready. The rider continued without slackening his pace, between the hidden ambushers, over the concealing rise to where the bowmen and the rest of the rebel camp waited. Only when he was well within range of the arrows did he rein up.

Elenya stepped to the front, a hundred paces away from him,

159

rapier out. Her gauntlet glowed even in the daylight.

Thick dust, broken by sweat tracks, coated the rider's swarthy face, his raven hair tufted and scattered by the wind. A young man, he wore a loose-fitting violet robe, embroidered in the intricate whorls and geometric patterns common to the Eastern Deserts, very similar to that decorating the white Zyraii garb Elenya, by coincidence, wore that day. He carried a scimitar on his belt, as well as a demonblade, and a small recurved bow projected from the rear of his saddle.

He raised his hands to show his lack of drawn weapons, inclined his head toward the archers, and called out to Elenya in a voice rendered hoarse from long, dry travelling. Wynneth did not understand the language.

Elenya frowned, and haltingly responded in the same tongue. "Let him approach," she told her band.

The rider dismounted, left his weary mount to nibble at the nearest clump of grass, and walked forward. *He moves with the grace of a dancer*, thought Wynneth. It was remarkable considering how stiff he should have been from the ride. The grime quite possibly hid a handsome face. As he neared, he unhooked a scroll canister from his belt, which he held out to Elenya. He kept a respectful three paces distant.

Elenya hesitated. Wynneth guessed why and stepped closer. Finally the princess slipped the parchment from the container and unrolled it. Glyphs that Wynneth recognized as Zyraii characters appeared, the brown ink rendered almost black against the wheat-colored surface.

Elenya's eyes went wide. Wynneth could no longer stand it. "Is it from Lonal?" she blurted.

Elenya chuckled wistfully. "No. This man is a Surudainese. But the message is from Zyraii."

Wynneth blinked. "How did he find us?"

"The scroll led him." Elenya held it out, and translated: *I can feel his pain even at this distance. Retreat will not cure him. But there is a way. Ask him to heal you. If he questions you, mention the name Ilyrra. He will understand what he must do. —Gast.*

"Gast?" Wynneth whispered. "Alemar's teacher?"

"Yes."

"What does it mean?"

"Alemar will have to answer that." Elenya called over to the camp women. "This man has ridden hard. Feed him, give him wash water and shade to rest under. Someone should groom his

160

oekani." She spoke to the man. He nodded and went to enjoy the hospitality.

"Coming?" Elenya asked as she started for the cave.

Wynneth nearly stumbled over her sister-in-law's heels in her haste.

≈≈ XXII ≈≈

Elenya felt healthy. The wounds from the ambush and the attack on Puriel's fortress no longer troubled her. It seemed odd to ask her brother to heal her.

"I can't," he said. "What brought you up here to ask that?"

"Word from an old friend. He said to mention the name Ilyrra."

Alemar stood up suddenly. "You've word from Gast? How?"

"I don't know how the messenger crossed the sea, but he found us." She handed him the scroll.

Alemar poured over it. "It's definitely his calligraphy. A Zee-no-ken could have helped him charm the parchment, so that it was drawn to me. Yes. Look. There's a strand of hair woven into the fringe—mine, no doubt. We kept samples of each other's hair and blood for use in certain healing spells."

Elenya was encouraged to see Alemar so alert and involved. "What did he mean? Why do I need to be healed?"

"You don't, exactly," Alemar said. "But we all suffer the affliction of being who we are. Most of us muddle through as best we can, even though we could benefit from care. Gast is suggesting that I perform a very special type of healing, like that I did for Ilyrra, a Sholi slave girl."

Elenya frowned. "How are you going to do it? Your power is drained."

"So I believe. But if Gast says that Retreat will not help me, I believe him. Shall we try his way?"

Elenya shrugged. "It seems little enough to endure."

Alemar smoothed his long hair back. "That's where you're wrong."

They erected a tent at the far end of the valley, under the shade of two old oaks, in view of the rest of the encampment, but secluded by the distance. They stocked it with a three-day supply of water and food, and Alemar left strict orders that no one was to approach the site unless an emergency arose, such as the arrival of Omril and his army. By dusk, only Wynneth remained with them, until, giving her a hearty embrace, he asked her to leave as well.

"No matter what sounds you hear through the cloth, no one is to disturb us. If I need help, I'll step outside to call for it."

She nodded, kissed him, and left, though Elenya could tell she wanted to stay.

Alemar closed the flap, shutting out the sunset. In the light of the single lamp, his eyes seemed fathoms deep. Elenya involuntarily stepped back.

"What's next?" she asked a little faster than she meant to.

"Clothes off," he said, doffing his shoes.

Elenya undressed more slowly than usual, feeling inhibited, which was strange, because she and her brother had never been shy about being naked together. They had bathed together only an hour before, and she had given the nudity no notice whatsoever. Perhaps it was his gaze, which seemed to penetrate more deeply than ever before, even into regions not shared during their mind-speech.

"Lie down on the blanket," he said, his voice soft and soothing. "On your stomach."

She lowered herself, wrapping her hair, still damp from the bath, into a tail and placing it so that it would not be in her face. The blanket, and the mat beneath it, gave her just the right combination of firm support and cushioning.

Alemar began massaging her. He cupped her toes to warm them, wiggled and slid a finger between each digit. He pressed the side of his thumb firmly into the calluses on her soles, working out the kinks. He alternated with a light, finger-tip stroke. As he reached her ankles, she sighed with pleasure.

He continued up each leg, over tissue sore from the kicking exercises. She hovered at the delicate point between pain and relief. He kneaded her leg muscles until they turned to jelly. She had not realized until now how stiff she had been. He was finding layers of aches, drumming out the stress of the long flight northward, and the battle before that.

By the time he reached her torso, she was almost crying. He gathered small areas of her skin and released, he pressed gently on her lower vertebrae until they shifted, he pounded lightly until the broad muscles of her back let go of their tension. He used fingertips, palms, elbows, forearms, forehead—even his hair, with which he brushed her backside with broad, feathery strokes.

"Where did you learn this?" she murmured.

"No talk. Relax."

She eagerly obeyed. Presently she realized that his movements followed the rhythm of her breathing, first in obvious ways, then with increasing subtlety. Something else was happening, too. Something in the touch itself, the human to human contact. She had never been so aware of the healing nature of hands upon her. It ceased to matter if he were her brother, or a lover, or a stranger—the rightness flowing from his body to hers was palpable, deep-seated, and intense.

Alemar, she bespoke.

No questions. It is happening. Feel it. Where his hands pressed, she could feel an electrical tug; she could almost hear the crackle in the air. Her ears began to ring, a steady note from deep inside her skull.

She let him in.

They had bespoken many times, but those conversations, though intimate, had always been between distinct entities. This time they shared the same place. She could sense him delving deep, rooting out a source of wrongness that, until that moment, she had not realized existed. She felt him hesitate, evaluate, and decide. Then he took her there, to show her what he had discovered.

The lawns of Garthmorron Hold were stiff and itchy, and hot now that the sun had angled past the trees. Her bare feet danced back and forth across the sward, finding purchase, digging in, jumping, until the soles were completely green. The aroma of crushed grass filled her nose. Side-step. Thrust. Twist. The area sang with the rasp of steel on steel.

Her opponent was Alemar. She circled, keeping outside his range. She had the length advantage, thanks to the growth spurt of adolescence that had not yet occurred for him. Though still lean in the hips and completely flat-chested, she towered half a head over him. She strove to maintain control over her breathing, but it was difficult. The practice blade weighed heavily in her hand.

Alemar plunged forward, thrusting. She turned away, but not in time. The tip of his sword jabbed her sharply in the ribs, almost on top of the bruise from his previous thrust. He had taken her twice with the same technique.

They returned to their starting points. Alemar seemed sympathetic, but it was hard to see much of his expression behind the grid of his face mask. He dipped the blunt at the end of his weapon into the paint pot to restore the red coating. She frowned at the marks on her tunic. The garment looked like it had measles. Alemar's displayed only one stain, and that had been made by a different opponent.

She glanced at Troy, but she dared not meet his flinty gaze. She would not whimper or ask for a rest, no matter how tired she was.

"Begin," Troy ordered, though they had not paused any longer than normal.

Alemar moved in, confidently, aggressively. Elenya parried and retreated. She clenched her teeth in frustration. She was better than he. She won well over half their matches. But she was exhausted, and he was fresh.

He "wounded" her in the heart, ending the match.

She sighed and returned to the starting point. At Troy's command, they bowed to each other.

"Alemar may retire."

As her brother returned to the small knot of other young noblemen waiting at the side, Elenya suppressed her tears. Again. Troy was making her spar *again*. She had fenced all six of the boys twice without resting. She longed to be excused.

Troy stared at her impassively. "Enns, take your place," he commanded.

Enns strutted forward like a peacock, resplendent in his fine beige tunic, already tall and imposing despite being only a year older than Elenya. Her heart sank. Enns was the best of all of Troy's junior pupils, in part because of his age and size, but also because, since early childhood, his rich father had hired none but the best fencing instructors to train him. The best instructors, that is, until Lord Dran had enticed Troy from Calinin South to become the tutor at Garthmorron Hold.

Enns grinned. He had bested her twice that day. The first time she had scored two marks to his three. The second time, none at all. She licked her lips, chapped from panting. Her arms felt as if she wore lead bracelets.

"Begin," Troy said.

Enns rushed in, creating openings for his thrusts by the sheer intimidation of his charge, taking full advantage of her winded condition. She lasted for the space of ten quick heartbeats, until he landed his point in the center of her belly.

She gasped from the violence of the impact. Her tunic was

well padded, and the blunts discouraged serious injury, but the precautions assumed a certain amount of consideration on the part of the attacker. As they walked back to their places, the pain next to her naval proved that Enns had been too harsh.

They faced each other once more. He smirked behind the mask. He, the nephew of a duke, had shown her, a mere game-keeper's granddaughter, a noble only by adoption, her place.

"Stand up straight, *girl*." Troy's shout made her jump. How many times had she heard that tone in the months since he had arrived, always with the same bite placed on words that referred to her gender? Out went her small hope that Troy might repri-mand Enns, as he had yesterday when Enns had been unnecessar-ily rough against another boy.

She felt cold, deliberate fury exude from her pores, drenching her body, banishing her weariness.

At the command, Enns drove in as before. This time she held her ground. He was caught completely off guard, had to attempt his thrust early. She easily twisted aside and let him run into her jab. A thick glob of pigment stained the left breast of his hand-some tunic.

She smiled impishly at him. The mask could not disguise his anger.

Troy made no reaction other than to utter the next starting command.

Enns charged again, this time in a less headlong fashion, aim-ing a good, strong thrust to her upper chest. She dropped to her knees, extending her sword. His tip split empty air over her head. Hers landed squarely in his groin.

Enns stopped abruptly, emitting a deep, sudden grunt. Elenya twirled to the side, out of counterstrike range, not because she feared a response—Enns did not look likely to mount one soon —but simply because it was proper fencing strategy, which Troy would notice.

For the first time that day, she stared directly into her instruc-tor's eyes. He met her gaze with an equally firm one of his own. That only fueled her state of mind, keeping the flow of energy open to her tortured limbs.

She faced Enns, smiling. It was his turn to have difficulty standing up straight. As he had not done with her, Troy gave the boy a moment to recover. She thought Enns looked ridiculous with a red crotch, and recalled the rude, typically boyish joke he had made one day when she had been "wounded" there. The memory kept her at peak in spite of the delay.

Troy gave the command. Enns assumed an *en garde* position, preparing to move in, this time with full caution, but she did not wait. She leaped in, aimed low, then high, then middle. He parried frantically. Knowing how good he was at defense, she did not let up, did not give in to her protesting arms, until she scored with a high cut.

At first, Enns did not acknowledge that the contest was over. "Stop!" Troy called harshly, and the youth froze.

Enns walked stiffly back to his place. Elenya took hers, her limbs shaking uncontrollably. Her body felt light, almost ethereal, like a rythni in flight. At last she had driven a response out of Troy. *She* was responsible for his raised voice, for Enns's loss of favor, and, best of all, for the undisguised respect in the eyes of the other boys.

She bent low at the waist, mocking Enns for his virtually nonexistent bow.

"Enns may retire," Troy said curtly. He paused, just long enough to dissolve Elenya's sense of victory. "Sit down and rest," he told her.

She sat, knees forward, buttocks resting on her heels, and felt her stomach grow heavy and the parched sensation in her throat become fierce. Once again she had incorrectly assumed that she had fought her last match.

She glanced at Alemar. He scowled in protest. But what could either of them do? They were twelve years old. Lord Dran did not tolerate children defying their tutors. "Noble blood should have a proper dose of humility," said he, adding that the only time to learn to be modest was before coming of age.

When her breathing had slowed to a relatively normal rate, Troy fitted his mask over his head and picked up his practice blade.

"Once more, girl. Try your best."

He did not advance. Furthermore he left her a wide, obvious opening. She hesitated, suspicious. Avoiding the bait, she aimed elsewhere. He shifted so little that her sword blunt missed by only a finger-width, but it was enough.

He planted a mark on her chest with a plain, almost casual gesture.

"You should have taken the opening," he said. "I won't give you another."

He was true to his word. The second time he tagged her in the belly almost before she realized he was charging. His head and shoulders did not shift when he moved, his spine stayed straight, his body upright. Only his legs, and at the end, his sword arm, gave away his intent. She could not anticipate his tactics.

The third time, as if mocking her, he performed exactly the same technique. The only difference was that her sword nicked his as it was withdrawn, a reflex rather than a conscious reaction.

Tears welled in her eyes. She stared at the crushed, pungent grass, avoiding Alemar's sympathetic frown and Enns's smug sneer.

"You've got a way to go, girl," Troy said. He pulled out his polishing cloth and rubbed the paint off his blade. "You're excused. Get a drink of water. You look like you need one."

She stalked off, jaws clenched. *Someday*, she vowed, *I will be the best*.

Without opening her eyes, she became aware of her surroundings: Alemar's scent, the wind batting the tent cloth, the woven texture of the blanket underneath her. She shuddered violently, tears squeezing out between tightly shut lids. Her throat ached.

She did not understand how the memory of a single incident could evoke such agony. *Look*, Alemar insisted, and in her mind's eye she saw a network of bright lines, each one a filament of pain, each one ultimately stemming from a single junction— the embarrassment and humiliation she had felt on that day at the age of twelve. The filaments ran through the years, bits of suffering piled onto the old, until the aggregate formed a wound too raw to be faced. Therefore, she had buried it.

Alemar guided her vision toward other, lesser junctions. She withdrew, trying to cover them up again, but with firm, compassionate maneuvering, Alemar made her look.

The barn smelled of fresh hay. Streamers of light blazed in through knot holes and around the edges of the wide double doors, illuminating the dust and hay particles in the atmosphere. Around the opening of the loft Alemar and four of the keep boys hung like vultures. The dim, striated interior of the barn made it a challenge to follow the movements of the two combatants on the ground.

Elenya vaulted a bale of hay and slashed. Troy sidestepped, putting another bale between them. She hopped back to outdistance his counterthrust. The spectators bit back their exclamations; the only sounds in the barn consisted of the loud breathing of the participants, the impact of their feet, and from time to time, the rasp of sword contact.

Troy darted down a corridor between two high stacks, out of sight of Elenya and the boys in the loft. She circled to the left, stepping carefully through a patch of loose straw. Troy chose that moment to reappear, charging, forcing an instant response. She kept her footing, parrying three times, countering once. He retreated. She backed out of the straw, waited for him to follow. He declined, vanishing around the stacks once again.

She glided to the center of the open area, listening carefully for signs of Troy's movements behind the hay. She counted silently to five. As they were supposed to do any time either combatant paused under the loft opening, the boys shoved armloads of straw at her. She danced away from the downpour, and was ready when Troy sprang out of concealment.

They fought their way around the low bales. Elenya paid close attention to her breathing. Troy understood far better than she how to conserve energy. Though she was fifteen and he nearly forty, stamina was his advantage. After half an hour of sparring, she was at the edge of losing her wind.

Yet, as they continued, the edge receded. Though using obstacles to simulate true battle conditions was one of the most difficult types of fencing, she had matched Troy blow for blow, strategy for strategy. She had two red marks on her tunic, and so did he. For the first time in four years of instruction, she stood within one point of winning against him.

Sweat dripped from Troy's eyebrows. He blew out a sharp breath between pursed lips. Elenya concentrated on his expression, as he had taught her to do whenever they fenced without masks. He glanced down. She thrust.

A sudden pain flared in her wrist. Her rapier careened through the air, landed with a hush against a loose bale, and slid to the ground. She gawked, not comprehending how he could have disarmed her. The boys above murmured in awe.

Troy calmly touched the tip of his weapon to her tunic. The paint was so dry from their long battle that it barely marked her. As she gathered her thoughts, she realized Troy suddenly seemed only slightly winded. He smoothly sheathed his blade, the corner of his lips curling upward in a familiar, self-satisfied smile.

He had tricked her. He had been far from his limit. He could have stepped up the pace and defeated her at almost any point. All the long months in which her confidence had grown, her plans been laid, her hopes constructed, had been rendered meaningless with one quick gesture.

"Another time," he said. "Maybe your luck will change." He

chuckled as he opened the barn doors. The brightness of the day stabbed her eyes.

Her throat was dry from her weeping. Alemar poured water into her mouth. She choked, swallowed some, inhaled a bit, and lost the largest part down her neck. She was tired. She wanted to stop. The pain, however, had lessened. The tendrils had unravelled from the first junction, and were doing the same with the second, leaving the areas cool, green, and untainted.

She was in a sitting position, with Alemar wrapped closely around her. Wherever their skin touched, energy passed back and forth. She trusted him utterly, knew that he would guide her tenderly and well through the rest of it, but she doubted her own ability to continue. She felt like a cripple. But the more he touched her, the more her breathing calmed, the more her muscles relaxed. She drifted back into sleep as he drew her to the next junction.

The clop of her oeikani's hooves was crisp and sharp, like her mood. Ahead the great, green canopy of the forest yielded to blue sky, a sign that she was nearing Garthmorron Hold. Alemar rode at her side, engrossed in his own thoughts of homecoming.

"Look. There's the tree where we talked with father," he said, pointing to a trunk heavy with creeping vines. Keron had visited them only once in their memory, staying only two days. One afternoon he had walked along this road with his twins to have a private moment with them.

She nodded absently, still playing out in her mind what she would do after their arrival, once the homecoming celebration began and she could arrange an encounter with Troy. She imagined the scene:

"Learn anything in your year in the Old Kingdoms, my lady?" he would ask, politely but patronizingly, lifting a goblet of wine to his lips.

"The men of Numaron like their women fat," she would respond, sipping from her own goblet, "and the folk of Sirithrea are astonishingly rude."

"True, true."

"And," she would add casually, "the wizards of Acalon make fine rapiers."

Troy would pause, meet her eyes, remember he had wine in his mouth, and swallow. "That they do. But they don't let go of them easily."

"I know." Her eyes would sparkle. "Nevertheless, I happened to obtain one. Would you like to see it?"

Troy would try to seem nonchalant, mildly interested. Perhaps he would even decline her initial invitation, but eventually she would open the polished hardwood case, revealing her prize. He would hold it reverently up to the light, check its balance, examine the swordmaker's signature on the pommel. "Seth of Tsiris. They say no one has ever broken one of his blades." He would betray a hint of envy, for though he had two Acalon swords, neither had been made by such a famous craftsman. "How did you get it?"

"He made it especially for me, for a price no higher than a common smith would charge. He was impressed by my fencing." And she would smile.

Perhaps she would mention the training she had received from other swordmasters, hinting at the new tricks she had learned, or perhaps she would surprise him. Sooner or later he would want to discover for himself why his pupil, still a mere eighteen years old, had merited such a trophy. Perhaps she would even use her Acalon rapier, for they were both at such a level that they could dispense with the precaution of practice blades.

Then they would see who was the best.

She and Alemar rode through the flowered archway that led to the main hold, and saw an animated gathering of people on the broad stone steps. Their mother, Lerina, and the rest of the party with whom they had toured the capitals of the Calinin Empire had preceded them by half an hour, and by now most of the residents had turned out to welcome the travellers. The twins eased through the crowd of servants and friends, touching hands, smiling, offering greetings. Elenya was surprised to see her mother leave Lord Dran's company and thread her way through the celebrants. Elenya had to lean over in the saddle to hear her somber words.

"Swordmaster Troy caught the ague and died two months ago," Lerina said.

All at once, the grounds and the people around her became shadowy and unreal. So deep was her shock that she did not hear her mother's next words.

"It's so sad. He was so proud of you."

This time, as Alemar focussed the memory, she heard the comment, and finally understood that over the years, Troy *had* come to respect her. She had been so anxious for overt acceptance that she had missed the small, subtle signs that he had given, indications that a perceptive observer like Lerina had recognized. Elenya had pushed for total acknowledgment, not seeing that Troy's pride would never let himself stand revealed so openly. His death had meant to her that she could never prove herself, never resolve the matter between them, not knowing that it had already been resolved.

She no longer resisted the journey along the filaments. The suffering was tolerable now. She stalled at only two places. The first was when she looked back at her life in Zyraii, and realized how much her unhappiness there had been exacerbated by her own character. Another woman would not have had as great a problem with the sexual inequality of the desert society. The second was when she remembered Milec, and realized that part of the reason she had failed to fall in love with him was that he, in turn, could not measure up to the other men she had known, from Alemar to Troy to Lonal.

The strands unravelled, releasing the pain. Alemar had been right; she had never suspected the ills hidden within. Though she had never concealed the memories from herself, she had forgotten and denied the depth of the emotions associated with them.

She opened her eyes. She could see almost nothing, only the dark backdrop of the ceiling, the dim shape of Alemar asleep beside her, and the murky glow of Motherworld leaking in at the edge of the tent flap. Her throat smarted, dry as dust. Caked perspiration clung to her like a shroud, moist only at her waist, where Alemar's arm was draped. She lifted his limb away and set it gently on the blanket. He did not stir. In fact, he was so lifeless it frightened her, until she made out the steady rise and fall of his chest.

She swayed as she sat up, and decided not to stand. She crawled to the water bags and, ignoring the cups, put the spout to her lips and did not remove it until her stomach felt like it would burst. The dizziness faded. She tore off a tiny hunk of bread, put it in her mouth, and held it, her tongue and cheeks pressed against it, finding more comfort in the possession of the food than in the actual consumption. When she trusted herself not to fall, she crawled outside, closed the flap, and stood up.

The cold breath of night greeted her, stiffening her nipples and raising the hair on her legs. The valley was still with the promise of dawn; she saw no sign of activity across the meadow, in the camp. She considered fetching a shawl, but decided against it.

The cold felt good. Her nudity felt good. The world would not harm her this night.

The dew brushed her ankles as she walked. She scooped her hand across the grass and wiped her forehead, delighting in the wet caress. Warm in spite of the air, she was strong, contented, free.

It felt good to be herself.

She stretched, vigor increasing by the second. She was ready to stalk the grass like a great cat. She felt a victory more profound than that at Old Stump, or in the Eastern Deserts.

The horizon paled to violet before she thought of Alemar. She had been healed, but what of him? She could not guide him through the corridors of his inner being as he had her. She had neither the training nor the innate talent. What had Gast meant?

Alemar would know.

She smiled. Concerned though she was, nothing could spoil her mood. The answers would come. In the meantime, she would need to sleep, as would he. She started back toward the tent.

≈≈≈ XXIII ≈≈≈

The oeikani's withers stood nearly as high as Toren's chin. He and Geim watched the buck canter across the corral. Despite his lack of experience with the animals, Toren knew what a fine specimen he viewed. Its legs were sleek and sturdy from its thighs to its cloven feet. It wielded the knot of hair at the tip of its tail as if it were a mace, slapping the flies off its hindquarters. Toren had never seen such massive antlers; he was relieved that their shape was blunt and knobby, rather than pointed as was the case in the south.

In spite of the buck's intimidating size and grace, Toren felt completely unthreatened. When the trainer brought the animal over to them, it nuzzled Toren's cheek, accepted a sweet, and stood contentedly while the Vanihr stroked its mane.

"The perfect temperament for a new rider," the trainer stated. The oeikani seemed to incline its head at the compliment. "He'll never throw you."

"He's big," Toren said.

"You'll want a sturdy beast like this on the trip to Cilendrodel," Geim declared.

"If I go," Toren said absently, putting off thoughts of the actual journey until he had made his decision. "In any event, this is a fine animal." He could not believe he had mistrusted the breed as recently as his arrival at the temple of Struth only two months earlier.

"I thought you'd agree with the choice," Geim said. "Would you like to ride him back to the temple?"

"I can try."

Geim paid the owner and the two Vanihr mounted up, Toren on his new prize and Geim on an equally handsome, though strong-willed, individual. As they rode off, Toren marvelled at the ease with which his animal responded to his commands, anticipating turns and changes in speed. Toren knew only the bare rudiments of riding, yet the oeikani tolerated his hesitant guidance with no sign of nervousness. The modhiv commented on this as they rode past the stables and pens that filled this section of Headwater.

"He's a smart buck, that's true, but give yourself credit. You must have picked up something during those riding lessons Deena's been giving you." Geim grinned suddenly. "Or do you mean to say that you and she did something else with all that time?"

Toren restrained his smile. "Nothing you and Yari wouldn't do."

"That covers a wide range."

Toren chuckled. "I'm sure it does."

They let the mounts go at their own pace, and took advantage of the chance to view the city's hubbub of activity from a height. "You didn't seem tempted by Deena's interest during the journey from the Wood," Geim added as they approached a public fountain. Girls walked to and from it with incredibly large urns balanced on their heads.

"Was she interested then?" Toren asked.

"I think so. I'm not the best judge, and she's not the type to say much. Did she ever tell you why she alone, of all her family, survived the Dragon's pillage of eastern Mirien?"

"No."

"Thought not. She killed two of the Dragon's mercenaries. Hand to hand. There's a great deal hiding under that quiet demeanor of hers."

"Yes, there is," Toren said firmly. "I suppose during the trip I was too preoccupied with other concerns to notice."

"Obviously you're feeling better about yourself now."

Toren shrugged. "I can do things that my shaman could not have imagined. I can't deny I'm proud of that, and the training has been invigorating, in spite of the demands. Certainly I wasn't as happy in the Wood, not even as a child. I was a fourth son." He scarcely noticed that he had slipped out of the High Speech into the Vanihr tongue.

Geim smiled ironically. "So was I."

They reached the broad avenue that would take them to the temple district. Toren deliberately stepped up his mount's pace, just to see if he could do it correctly. The oeikani snorted happily as it obeyed. Geim's animal trotted along with matching strides.

As the two Vanihr threaded their way through the temple grounds, walking their mounts to the Frog God's stable, Toren noticed a pair of men in the shadow of a trellised walkway next to the main building. One was Obo. The wizard conversed with a short, lithe man in riding garments. The latter's dark hair showed strands of grey, though he seemed no more than forty years old. Heavy dust and flecks of dried mud covered the surface of his very plain cloak, but beneath, visible between the unbuttoned lapels, a tunic of freshly laundered fine brocade peeked out. An aura of sorcery hovered about him, nearly as strong as that emitted by Obo. Something about the man's features haunted Toren.

"Who is that with Obo?" he asked Geim.

Geim studied the stranger's features. "I saw him once last year. That is Keron, the king of Elandris."

A jolt of nostalgia darted out of the recesses of Toren's mind. Obo had served Keron many years; though most of the memories of the wizard's life had long since drained out of Toren's conscious recall, feelings lingered. Toren experienced a sense of *déjà vu* each time he visited a place that Obo frequented, or read a piece of literature the old man favored.

Obo turned and saw the Vanihr. He motioned for them to wait, and with Keron, walked into the sunlight to meet them.

"May I present his royal Highness, Keron the First of Elandris," Obo said.

"So this is the candidate," Keron said, acknowledging their bows. "I've waited three long years for Struth to find you, while the Dragon swallowed my kingdom and chased me across three nations."

"Sorry to inconvenience you, Your Majesty."

Keron chuckled wryly. "It was mutual, so I understand. Obo

was right. You have the impudence of the Dragonslayer. A good sign."

Toren smiled. "I seem to remember bantering with you in decades past," he said, glancing meaningfully at Obo. "Perhaps your wizard afflicted me with impolite habits."

"I did nothing of the sort," Obo quipped. "I simple taught you the language of the Calinin."

Probably true, Toren thought. He certainly could not remember details of any such conversations; only a faint impression had led to his comment. He had probably been testing Keron, to see what kind of person led the resistance against Gloroc, whether he had a sense of humor.

"I was not told you would be coming," Toren said, deliberately redirecting the topic.

"The fewer who know I'm here, the better," the king said. "I have just come from Xais, where I petitioned the emperor of the Calinin Empire to lend me his army. If your mission is successful, the Dragon will be dead, but his human minions may seize power in the wake of his death. As soon as Gloroc dies, I must march in great force. Or did you think you were going to save Elandris single-handedly?"

"At times I've had that impression."

"I would be happy to leave it all to you if it were possible," Keron said blithely. "But it is not that easy. Rather the opposite, in fact. If you take up the gauntlets and succeed in killing Gloroc, your part will be done. You can rest, reap whatever rewards we can provide, return to your home. My work will just be starting." He turned back toward the walkway. "I am due for an audience with Struth. I leave in the morning for Tazh Tah, in Simorilia, where my son and my army are camped, but perhaps we can talk this evening."

The larger picture of the war against Gloroc, though it had been explained to Toren several times, had, at least until that moment, remained remote. Lost in contemplation, the Vanihr answered belatedly, "Of course, Your Majesty. I would be honored."

"Good," Keron said. "In the meantime, there is something I would like you to do." He unbuckled his belt, a strap of dragon hide embroidered with gold, set with rubies in the shape of a dragon in flight. He handed it to Toren. The smell of magic exuded from it.

"That is the belt of Alemar Dragonslayer," the king said. "It multiples the strength of the wearer. My son and I are the only living men who can activate it. If you are all that Struth hopes, it will work for you. You may give it back to me tonight."

King and wizard walked away, resuming their conversation. The belt, lying in Toren's palm, already tickled. He strapped it on. It rode on his waist like air—no weight at all—but otherwise he felt nothing out of the ordinary. He waited for the energies to stir within him.

"Well," Geim said, "Try something."

"Like what?"

Geim scratched his head. "Perhaps you could lift your oeikani."

"Don't be foolish," Toren said. Obviously the belt did not work. And even if it did, the oeikani weighed far too much. But for the sake of the experiment, he braced himself under his mount and lifted.

The animal, much to its surprise, rose completely off the ground. Toren set it down quickly, huffing. Geim stroked the buck's neck to soothe it. True to its nature, it regained its composure immediately.

Vigor, hot and pounding, coursed through Toren's body. His muscles shuddered uncontrollably. After a bit of trial and error, he managed to adjust the talisman's output. The power faded. The belt waited quiescently on his hips for the next demand.

The modhiv grinned from ear to ear. He slapped Geim on the back—not too hard—and they headed for the stable.

Keron tried to calm all the thoughts bubbling in his head as he and Obo strolled together toward the dome of the high priestess, but concerns only sprang forth with renewed vitality. "Toren shows a spirit I found lacking in the other candidates," the king said. "What do you think of him?"

"He is a good person. He loves to succeed, becomes morose when he fails. All the pride of the Dragonslayer, tempered by an occasional lapse of confidence that serves to keep him humble. I like him, my liege."

"But will he be able to use the gauntlets?"

The wizard glanced at his toes. The furrows of his forehead deepened. "In my judgment, he is well beyond the level of the earlier candidates. Struth and Janna concur. But no matter how closely his powers seem to echo those of Alemar the Great, he is a different person. I doubt that anyone alive now or yet to be born will ever be able to activate the talismans as completely as the sorcerer himself. And if Toren *is* that gifted, that poses a whole new set of questions."

"What do you mean?"

"Think of what might happen to the world if an adept as powerful as Alemar Dragonslayer were set loose in it. Your ancestor changed the face of the civilized world."

Keron whistled softly. "That's true. But Alemar had the help of his sister, who by all accounts was nearly as powerful as he. And the two of them lived an incredible number of years. They had already lived more than a normal lifetime before they killed Faroc and Triss. To build Elandris required centuries more. No sorcerer since that time has learned how to stretch his years over such a long span."

"Don't remind me," Obo said.

Keron frowned. The skin on the back of Obo's hands and on his temple had thinned almost to translucence. Dark purple veins showed through. His gait wobbled. The last three years had not been kind to the wizard. It pained the king, after losing so many comrades to the war, to have to lose one to nature.

"There is a master in Acalon known to be almost two hundred years old," Obo mused. "But he has dedicated his career to longevity spells and elixirs. You have a point. Toren has limits, if for no other reason than that his talent was stunted in childhood. And this speculation may be moot. He may die fighting Gloroc."

"And will he be willing to fight for us?"

They came to the portal of the dome. Obo paused. "Yes. I think he will. Not that he will be eager, but at this point he has little to gain by refusing. I pray we are not leading him to suicide."

They crossed the threshold. Janna waited in one of her divans. She stood.

"Welcome, son of Alemar," the high priestess called. "The goddess awaits you." She gestured at the opening in the floor. The stairs beckoned him.

Keron sighed. Even after three years of alliance and a half dozen visits, an audience with Struth intimidated him. Obo hung back. "Aren't you coming?" the king asked.

"No. I need to rest." The wizard turned and waddled away, spine bent. A little dagger of melancholy nicked Keron in the chest. He stroked his waist, but the belt was not there to comfort him.

Janna waited calmly, as alluring as he had always found her to be. The sea vista outside the dome's walls reminded him of his home. He wished he could linger, but he sighed again and descended into the blue werelight of the passageway.

"What word from the emperor?" Struth boomed.

Keron waited near the base of the stairs, where the speaker's great bulk did not seem to loom quite so high. "He has agreed to send his army. He has recognized that Gloroc poses a threat to the commonwealth. The muster has already begun. The battalions will be led by the emperor's second son, Fanhar."

"An excellent choice."

"Yes. A level-headed young man. He seems willing to put himself completely at my disposal, and stay out of the way when necessary. I couldn't have asked for a better field commander. He is very unlike his father."

"The prince is a bastard," Struth said. *"The emperor is sterile. All his children are the result of his wife's infidelity."*

Keron did not ask how Struth knew, but he had no doubt it was the truth. "Then I admire the lady's taste. She chose the right stud," he commented dryly.

"The queen is a remarkable woman. I went to some lengths to maneuver her into the emperor's bed, some thirty years ago. It is no accident that the weight of the Calinin Empire has tipped in our favor."

"I did not assume that it was. The emperor acted like a man under certain . . . pressures. Though it did not strike me as coming from the queen."

"It came from all quarters. My temples have been busy. How soon will you be ready to march?"

"I'll begin the offensive as soon as Fanhar and his army arrive in Tazh Tah. We have the strength to push Gloroc's forces back to the coast. If Toren succeeds, I'll seize ships and take the fight back to Elandris."

"Good. Once the usurper is dead, the dynasty of Alemar must show its fitness to rule. Gloroc's generals and sorcerers are an ambitious lot."

"I'll gladly fight his men. Without a dragon to bolster their confidence, they can be daunted." Keron wiped sweat from his eyebrows, though the cold and clammy chamber provided little reason to perspire.

"Indeed. I will be happy to let you. Gloroc is all I care about. Once he is dead my duty will be fulfilled. I promised the Dragonslayer only that I would help destroy the children of Faroc and Triss."

"But you will continue to aid us?" Keron asked quickly.

"Of course. I may decide to erect a temple in Elandris. But my support will not be on the level of finding candidates for the gauntlets, and hiding them from skilled searchers. I am weary. It is time for the game to end. I have searched the surface of Tanagaran and there are no more people alive with the qualities we need. Toren must succeed."

"And do you think he will?"

For the first time in his life, Keron thought he detected a shrug out of Struth. *"He must."*

Keron's joints ached. His muscles protested each time he did as little as trade his weight from one foot to the other. An end to the game? That seemed an incredible luxury. Keron could not see an end, only the part he must play, and that burdened him like a cloak laced with gold and lead.

"How soon will Toren be ready, assuming he agrees to the mission?" the king asked.

"Janna will give him his final test in three days. By the time you have rejoined Prince Val and your subjects, my messenger will have caught up with you with the news."

Keron sighed. Not the end of the game, but perhaps the conclusion of endless preparations. In a few weeks, successful candidate or not, the campaign would begin. Keron's shoulders drooped.

"Do you have more questions of me?" Struth asked after a silence.

"Not now," Keron said. "Perhaps I will think of more later today. A request, however. I would like to see my ancestors."

"Certainly." Struth's giant eyes blinked, and suddenly a narrow doorway appeared in the wall behind Keron. The king turned and without a word strode across the threshold.

The doorway opened out into a sepulcher. The cerulean tones of the werelight shifted to emerald. The greenish glow reflected off two sarcophagi in the center of the chamber. Pale fungus streaked the stone surface of the coffins. A body lay in each, visible through transparent vartham covers.

Embalming and the sorceries within the sarcophagi preserved the corpses in an almost lifelike state. Only a waxy stiffness in the skin betrayed that they were dead, not merely asleep. On the left rested a woman. She was slender, short, girlishly figured, attired in an exquisite satin gown. A thick sprawl of jet black hair pillowed her head. The first crinkle of age showed in the corners of her closed eyes and the creases of her lips. *The wilting of a*

179

flower, Keron thought. By rights the body should have resembled that of a crone, since she had died of old age.

In the other coffin lay a short, spare man. His hair matched his companion's, except for a dusting of white at both temples. Again, only slight signs of age marred otherwise youthful features. Plush silk upholstery lined both sarcophagi, cradling the occupants in finery as rich as their garments, beds fit for the highest royalty.

Both resembled Keron as if they were his parents.

The king tried to swallow, but his parched throat refused. He had had the same reaction the first time that he had viewed these remains of Alemar Dragonslayer and his sister Miranda. The latter particularly affected him, since he could not help but recall the phantom of her he had seen at her oracle in Firsthold, when she had told him of the existence of the talismans of Setan, and he had sent his twin children to the Eastern Deserts in search of them. She had seemed so alive then.

How much easier his burden would be now, had the sorcerers been able to cheat time another millennia. How long had they lived? Seven centuries at least, before the years bore them down at last and they hid here, with Struth, where Gloroc could not find their bodies and violate their repose as he had that of the line of Elandri kings housed in the royal crypts in Firsthold. Alemar the Great could have taken up the gauntlets and defeated Gloroc upon his first appearance, before the Dragon could conquer as much as one city.

Keron sighed bitterly. "You left it all to me, you bilge drinkers." *Me and my children and cousins, all exiles now, clinging to a desperate hope. We didn't even know where this sepulcher lay until three years ago.*

The king reached out and set his hand on the lid of the Dragonslayer's coffin. "Better for us all if you had never taken a wife," he murmured.

But the wizard had. And from the son of that union had ultimately come dozens of branches of descendants, though the attrition of the war had devastated the current generation. *At least*, Keron thought, *your greatest ally survives in this temple.*

The king of Elandris turned and stalked back out. He felt the need to spend a few quiet hours with Obo, before his old friend likewise passed out of human ken.

≈≈ XXIV ≈≈

Three days after Keron's visit, Janna summoned Toren to her chamber. "Time to decide," she declared. "Struth and I have done what we could to train you. We'll teach you no more unless you agree to help us kill Gloroc. Will you do so, or will you leave for home?"

Toren paced back and forth, staring out at the crustaceans and kelp "outside" the dome. He took a deep breath. "Yes. I will wear the gauntlets, if I can."

The high priestess nodded, losing none of her solemnity. "Then it is time for one more test." She strolled back to the table between her divans, where a kettle of water heated above a small brazier. "Only one candidate before you reached this point. I must warn you that this test killed her."

"I know. Deena told me."

Janna folded her hands. "It was unintentional, of course. The spell is both powerful and delicate. When I sensed that she was failing, I tried to halt it, but I was too late. The same may happen to you. If Struth and I were convinced that you would fail, we would not have you attempt it. But we have reason to think you will overcome."

Toren continued pacing. "Then let's be done with it." His mind filled with thoughts of Rhi, and then with thoughts of Deena.

Janna blew out the brazier flame and sprinkled tea leaves into the steaming water. The liquid darkened. She let it steep for the count of five, then she hurriedly poured two cups, as if the timing were critical. She handed one to Toren. "Drink this when I tell you. It will be as hot as you can stand it, but you must get it down quickly."

A pungent fragrance smote his nostrils. "What is this called?"

"The Tea of Dreams. A bit like the potion you took when Obo taught you the High Speech, or when your shaman created your totem, but its effects are more short-lived. It will last just long enough for the test."

"You have to drink it as well?"

"Yes. That's one of the reasons I couldn't save the former candidate. To push you to your limit, I must tread a fine line of

181

equilibrium myself. There is danger for me as well as you."

The porcelain warmed in his hands. Finally she gestured. He followed her example and drank the tea by sucking it in very quickly, almost inhaling it, letting the air cool it. His tongue and inner cheeks tingled from the heat, and from the spicy flavor.

Janna moved the table from between the divans and they sat across from each other in their customary arrangement: knees touching knees, left hands clasped. Their gazes locked. Gradually the background noises grew unusually loud. Toren's pulse murmured in his temples. A faint echo of ocean currents beat at the walls. A whale sang somewhere in the distance. Janna's pupils became black pools, drawing him within.

He heard a sudden buzz, followed by the by-now-familiar sensation of being elsewhere. The high priestess's dome vanished. He waited to be taken to whatever place she intended, but no visions came. Blackness surrounded him, neither warm nor cold. The only sound was a rhythmic beat, like that of his heart.

The place was old.

He could not say how he knew this when he did not even know where he was, or how a dark, featureless location could have an age to begin with, but he felt the centuries weigh down upon him. Weariness took him. There was nothing interesting here. He wanted just to sleep, just to shut off his awareness.

No.

Alarm overwhelmed him. He tried to break through the dark walls, and they squeezed more tightly. He started to inhale, but a veil coated his face, smothering him. He tried to retreat, but there was nowhere to go. He had no limbs, he had no eyes. He was caught like a gnat in honey.

Sleep, said a voice. *Be mine. I am your one and only true guide.*

An inner conviction told him he had to break free now, or not at all. But his limbs refused to move, and the direction out of the blackness eluded him. He desperately stanched waves of panic and screamed, "*Geim! Stop her!*"

He had last seen Geim helping repair the mortar around one of the pools in the garden. Toren despaired. There was no time for his fellow Vanihr to run here from the site. Toren saw pinpoints of light flicker chaotically in front of his eyes. The veil of suffocation clenched more tightly. Oblivion reached up for him. Not enough time . . .

But time flowed strangely here. Suddenly his head rang.

Janna's audience chamber splashed into view. All his senses returned.

Janna lay sprawled across her divan. Geim stood over her, his open hand upraised. He shook his head, slightly glassy-eyed. A red welt was rising on the priestess's cheek.

Toren stared, dumbfounded. Geim recovered his wits and grunted in astonishment. The woman on the divan, though nearly identical in height, complexion, and hair color with Janna, was not the same person. Her body was narrower, her breasts smaller, her chin more angular, her fingers slightly longer. As she groaned and lifted her head into full view, Toren noticed faint lines at the corners of her mouth and eyes, the first traces of lost youth.

She blinked. "I'm sorry, my lady," Geim blurted, helping her to sit up. "I didn't mean to hurt you. I don't even know why I burst in here."

"You were compelled," she said evenly, gently pressing her cheek. She winced. "That was an excellent maneuver, Toren. Struth and I thought of a number of ways you might break out of the trap. Bringing help from outside didn't occur to us. But it was legitimate—and most important of all, it worked. You passed the test."

Toren heard her words, but their full impact did not sink in. He continued to stare at her in puzzlement. "But your appearance?"

Janna smoothed the delicate lines in her neck. "A gift from Struth—an illusion, like the ocean you see through these walls. I was so wrapped up in the spellcasting that I couldn't do my part to maintain it."

"But why hide your features?"

"Many things are hidden in the temple of Struth. Call this one a woman's vanity." She waved a hand over her face. As it passed, her familiar countenance returned. "You see? Isn't this more attractive?"

"You were lovely the other way, too," Toren said.

Janna smiled. "You are a flatterer. Think of my junior priestesses. They are all stunning. How would it seem if their teacher were less than exquisite?"

"The illusion is perfect," he said, still confused. "After all this training, why I can't detect the magic that maintains it? All this time, I've never suspected you were masked."

"That's because of Struth," Janna said, and rose. "Speaking of whom, if Geim will excuse us, it is time to visit her."

Geim, rubbing his pate, nodded and walked somewhat drunkenly toward the door. When he was gone, Janna opened the entrance to the Frog God's sanctum. She and Toren descended into the strange blue depths.

Struth's chamber already blazed with the werelight, boldly displaying her gigantic amphibian contours. *"Welcome,"* the goddess rumbled, broadcasting directly to his mind. *"How does it feel to be alive?"*

"It is much better than being dead," Toren said. He frowned. It did not seem natural to exchange jokes with a goddess. He blinked several times. Something was odd. The image of the giant frog was blurry, almost smoky. Struth winked. Instantly her outlines sharpened. Their clarity then matched the walls and columns surrounding her.

Toren's jaw dropped.

"Can you sense her spellcasting?" Janna asked.

"No." He described what he had noticed.

"She allowed you to see that," the high priestess explained.

"Magic has many levels," Struth declared. *"Though you are an adept considerably beyond the talents of most wizards, there is a great deal you cannot do. Enough. I'll tease you no more. You've passed the test. You have earned the right to see me as I am, and learn my story. First, let me show you how I weave my illusions."*

Struth winked again. Immediately an itch flared in Toren's head. No, that was not correct. The itch had been there previously, but he had not felt it. Thin tendrils of sorcery, almost undetectable even now, held a part of his perceptive apparatus bound. He growled and pushed at them. They clung like spiderweb. At first, for each one that he eliminated, three took its place, but he counselled himself to patience and methodically dealt with them. At last he checked the invasion, and after more effort, forced the last of them out. He shuddered, relieved. He looked at Struth.

There was no giant frog in the room. What replaced the illusion was just as big, but the new shape had a serpentlike torso, massive talons, and deep indigo eyes.

Struth was a dragon.

And a very old, crippled one. The flesh of one of her wings hung in scarred shreds, incapable of sustaining flight. Great bags ringed her eyes. The tips of her fingers, at the base of the talons, were dry and deeply fissured. Unlike the brilliant tones of the dragons of legend, her skin was uniformly grey, showing no scales. But even decrepit, Struth was an intimidating sight. Age

184

had not dimmed the incredible depth of her eyes. And Obo had once told Toren that the older a dragon was, the greater its power.

"How?" Toren whispered. "Why?"

"You are ready for my story?" Struth asked.

"Yes."

"At one time I was like other dragons. I lived apart from humans and others of my kind. I ruled an island in the strait between the Dragon Sea and Sea of Luck. More than three thousand years ago I fought a battle with another dragon, named Triss. As you can see, I lost. I was in estrus, a thing that happens to a female dragon only two, or perhaps three, times in her entire life. I needed a male, and unfortunately the closest available was Faroc, the mate of Triss. Dragons do not usually mate for life. When I seduced Faroc, I did not expect his jealous spouse to attack me. My condition made me weak, and Triss, though young, was powerful. She left me for dead."

"But you lived."

"Yes. Triss did not stay to kill me herself. She had ruined my wings, which eliminated the threat to her sexual territory— dragons mate only in the air—so she decided to nurse her wounds while I bled to death from mine." Struth lifted a great, taloned leg, and Toren could see massive scars across her underbelly. *"She rather enjoyed the thought of me taking many days to expire.*

"But luck was with me. As I lay, unable to move, growing weaker, a man appeared. This was unusual, since Faroc, Triss, and I did not tolerate humans in our region, and few ever came there. But come he did, and even in my desperate condition, I had the ability to capture his mind. I made him sew and bind my injuries. He found me food and water. It took weeks, but I was eventually able to move, and in time I returned to health, save for my wings.

"Naturally, I could not live as I had. Originally, I tried to reestablish my domain. But this was impractical without flight. Furthermore, Triss discovered my survival. Now that I was recovered, I was able to protect myself from her by retreating within a ward, but eventually she succeeded in driving me away from my lands. It was only then I thought back to the circumstances of my rescue. I had eaten the man when I no longer needed his services, but I realized there were others like him, and through them, I had the means to create a new domain.

"I made one mistake. At first, I did not conceal the fact that I was a dragon. I soon found that humans avoided me. They would

185

run away unless I kept them constantly under my mental control, which grew quite tedious. Thus, over the centuries I created the Frog God. Now my temples attract men of influence from far and wide, willingly yielding useful information to my priestesses. In various indirect ways I am able to pull the strings in all the countries of the Calinin Empire, and several beyond. It is not a path I would have ever dreamed of in my youth, but all in all, it has been a comfortable and amusing existence these past millennia."

"And you've managed to hide even from Gloroc?"

"Yes, though as I told you when you first arrived at the temple, he knows there is a being of great power somewhere in or near Headwater, because of the spell I cast to find candidates such as you. Perhaps he suspects another dragon. And perhaps not. Dragons are creatures of the sea. We absorb most of the energy for our sorcery from water. Unless there is a large body of it nearby, our magical strength is greatly reduced. That is precisely why I chose to locate my main temple so far inland—no one would suspect a dragon to be here."

"But how do you maintain your power?"

"There is a vast underground reservoir beneath this city, fed by the Slip River. There is no rule that a dragon needs salt water. In fact, thick storm clouds will do, as Gloroc's enemies in Tamisan learned this winter. With luck, my ruses have defeated Gloroc and his spies. Only those who live at the temple know that Struth is more than a great statue with an oracular voice, and until this moment only Janna, Obo, and the royal family knew that a dragon hid beneath the guise of the goddess."

Struth stretched her body, and Toren took a step back. "I see now why you're allied with the dynasty of Alemar," he said.

Struth seemed to chuckle, if the light trumpeting could be called that. *"Let us say that I was pleased when the wizard destroyed Faroc and Triss. In time Alemar sensed my existence, and I made myself known to him. We understood each other, kept our spheres of influence from encroaching on one another. And when the wizard's time grew short and he came to my temple to die, I gladly promised him that when the offspring of Faroc and Triss at last appeared, I would aid his descendants in their fight should they ask it."*

"Your gratitude has lasted a thousand years?" Toren asked.

"It is more than that. Gloroc is an impulsive, feral child. He has never been educated in the proper limits of behavior. He wants to rule everything—the entire world. If there were a portal

back to Serpent Moon, he would go through it and try to rule there, too. He threatens my realm. Even if I didn't hate him for his mother's actions, I don't need an upstart disrupting my handiwork. Kill him, Toren. The gauntlets will give you the power to negate his powers of illusion—all his powers if you can get near him. Touch him with them and even his physical strength will fail him."

"That powerful? It sounds as though they could stop you as well."

"Why do you think I've insisted they be kept in Cilendrodel? I would not take kindly to their presence within the borders of Serthe. Had it been otherwise, Alemar would not have had to hide them in the Eastern Deserts."

For a moment, Toren pictured himself as a giant, with his hands around the neck of a pitifully small dragon. Suddenly the tiny creature spat flame. The bolt struck Toren in the eye and killed him. Somehow Struth made the prospect of Gloroc's assassination seem overly simple. "You're sure I am properly attuned to use the talismans?"

"As certain as I can be. Only the actual use of them will prove it. The Dragonslayer wasn't absolutely sure they would work even for him."

Toren glanced at Janna, seeking the reassurance of a familiar face, but without the sorcery affecting his perceptions, he saw only her older aspect. He sighed. If one dragon could trick him so thoroughly, what might Gloroc do? "Let's not waste time, then," he told Struth. "How am I supposed to do this thing?"

"First, of course, you must journey to Cilendrodel, to obtain the gauntlets from Alemar and Elenya, the children of King Keron. From there you'll travel to Gloroc's capital, Dragonsdeep. It will be a hazardous mission, but I have high hopes. Thanks to a trap the Dragonslayer laid long ago, Gloroc has unwittingly left himself vulnerable."

Deena tightened her belt and checked her reflection in the burnished urn on her vanity table. "I'm ready," she told Toren.

The modhiv scanned her riding garments, a sentimental gleam in his eye. "Now you look like the woman I walked beside through the long leagues of the Wood." He gently brushed the underside of her chin, his habitual gesture of affection. "Though I was getting used to the accommodating temple girl."

She stroked his wrist. "I may be friendlier on this road than on the last." They grinned knowingly at each other.

"Come, then," he said, smile fading. "The rest of the party should be there by now."

Pinpricks of nervousness danced along the soles of Deena's feet as they walked toward Janna's dome. No safe haven at the end of this journey. But she could not have stayed, as Toren had suggested, not when she had a chance for revenge. The ghosts of her family clung to the hem of her cloak.

Three guards nodded gruffly at the entrance to the dome. An empty chamber greeted Toren and Deena as they stepped in. The opening to the stairs yawned. They descended without pause.

Deena heard the shuffle of feet and hooves and the murmur of voices even before they reached the bottom. The great frog, as motionless as the statue in the amphitheater above, waited at the far side of the audience chamber. To the left stood Janna. To the right Geim and a group of five temple guards clustered near the wall, holding a dozen oeikani—eight handsome saddle animals and four sturdy pack beasts with heavy loads.

Deena wondered how the oeikani had been brought underground, but was not surprised to see them. One became accustomed to the incredible at the temple of Struth.

The men seemed glad to see Toren and Deena. Their glances darted nervously in the direction of the Frog God. Deena, who had only seen the goddess twice face to face, empathized with them.

"*The party is assembled,*" Struth boomed. "*Tarry no longer. I have waited more than a thousand years to see Gloroc fall. Remember what I have shown you, Toren.*"

Toren nodded. Of all those present, he alone faced Struth squarely.

The modhiv patted Deena on the shoulder and strode alone to the wall near the assembled travellers. "Cover your eyes," he said loudly.

Deena did as she was told. Daylight blazed into the chamber, banishing the werelight, shining red between the gaps of her fingers. The oeikani cried in confusion, dancing on their cloven hooves. Blinking, Deena faced the other way. She saw Struth towering toward the ceiling, ugly and horrific in the full illumination. She gulped and turned back to the wall.

Where dank stone had been, now the view showed a mountain valley, deep in shadow, thick with trees. A meadow spread out before them, lush green, dotted with wildflowers, waterlogged from the midsummer run-off from the glaciers much higher up.

Toren lowered his hand. Deena noticed that he lacked a lens or other talisman. It seemed to be no strain to him to keep the portal open without one. Perhaps it was as Obo had once hinted to her: A portal *was* a talisman, for those who could use it that way.

It was at times such as these that Toren was a stranger to her. The scope of his sorcery chilled her.

Toren smiled ironically at Geim. "Your turn to go first, my friend." To the whole party he said, "Remember to keep your mouths open as you pass through. There will be a slight change in air pressure."

Geim gathered the reins of his animal and one of the pack beasts and stepped through. The other men followed in disciplined order. Toren gave Deena both of their mounts. "You showed me how to do this once," he said, and chuckled.

She smiled, knotted the reins tightly around her hand, and pulled her charges through. The usual slight tingle flitted across her skin as she crossed the line. Abruptly her ears felt as if they had been skewered with needles. She worked her jaw. Her eardrums popped five times in a row.

The oeikani did not appreciate the change in altitude, either. She pulled them forward across the spongy grass, momentarily awed by the magnificence of the snowcapped peaks. The ranges just north of Serthe were foothills by comparison.

"The Syril," Geim said. "I wandered through these mountains once, a year before I came to Headwater."

Deena began to fret. Toren had not come through, and she could see only a black rectangle behind her. Finally he appeared. He winced at the pressure shift and waved his hand, closing the portal.

"Problems?" she asked.

"A farewell kiss from Janna," he said, straight-faced. Her eyes flashed. He grinned. She slapped him good-naturedly. Perhaps she had misjudged his composure in the face of Struth; he seemed tremendously relieved to be out of her sight.

"The Frog God seems to have a portal for every occasion," she commented. The annoying ring in her ears was fading.

"Far from it," Toren replied. "Portals are rare. Struth chose to build her temple there partly because of the presence of that one. For escape."

"Struth needing escape? That's a frightening thought."

"I don't think she's ever had cause to use it," he replied. "In any event, it's mostly luck that we had a short cut north. As it is, we still have a long journey out of these mountains and across the western half of Cilendrodel."

The sun blossomed into incandescent glory along the ridgeline to the east. Toren stepped forward, reconnoitering. To either side rose towering cordilleras. The terrain would force them to ride due north for many leagues, even though their destination lay eastward. The meadow loam sucked noisily at his heels. Thickets of aspen and birch shivered in a brisk alpine wind. A falcon skimmed above a barren, scree-ridden slope. A partridge suddenly bolted from concealment.

"No settlers, plenty of game," he said. "For once may we travel with no incident." Deena could tell he was pleased to be moving, gratified to be in command.

"Let's ride," Toren said, and helped Deena into her saddle.

XXV

The sound of rustling cloth pulled Elenya gently out of slumber. She opened her eyes. A beam of light shone down through a pinhole in the fabric, announcing the presence of full day. Alemar was sitting cross-legged with one of the water bags in his lap. From time to time he would sip.

She raised up on one elbow. The euphoric feeling of the night before had dimmed, but she still felt wonderful—alive, rested, tranquil. She smiled. He nodded calmly.

"Thank you," she said.

"You're welcome."

"How are you feeling?"

He sipped again, held the water in his mouth, and swallowed. "What's important now is how *you* feel."

"But what about your powers?" she insisted. "Does this mean that they've come back?"

Alemar smiled wistfully, and played with the pattern of the blanket like a boy lost in a dream. His eyelids hung half-closed. "I'm not ready to talk about that just yet. I have some . . . things to do, things to think about."

After the events of the preceding night, Elenya felt closer to her brother than she would have thought possible. It was a shock to be suddenly outside of him, cut off from his thoughts. She rose into a kneeling position, wearing a small frown.

"I would like you to fetch my wife," Alemar said.

She did not want to be put off, but she would not argue, not when she was feeling so peaceful. She crawled over to Alemar and kissed him. He hugged her, and his firm fingers pressing into her back told her that she was not being banished—she was still loved. She, who had been worrying that he had seen too much in the journey into her past, sighed and held him close.

"I'll join you soon," he whispered.

She nodded, climbed into her clothes, and left the tent.

A breeze stroked her, taking the edge off the hot sunshine. It was a clear, warm day, the perfect complement to her mood. She walked with long, easy strides, and even the sight of the ever-vigilant sentries and the fugitive demeanor of the camp could not bring her down. The rebels greeted her appearance with interest, though they were too polite to intrude.

She found Wynneth helping the camp women to sort chaff from their dwindling supply of grain. "Alemar wants to see you," she said, and chuckled out loud at her sister-in-law's bright smile. Wynneth immediately dropped her task, straightened her hair clip, and hurried toward the far side of the valley.

Elenya turned to one of the other women. "Is that porridge I smell?"

It was, still hot from the midday meal. She took a bowl to a shady spot and began to assuage the fierce hunger left by the healing. Again, the rebel company left her alone, letting her decide when to mingle. She waved at Tregay, Solint, and one or two others, but for the moment enjoyed the solitude.

As she licked the last dollop from her spoon, she noticed that the stranger from the south was putting his mount through a few paces. He was a superior rider. He ran the animal only briefly, just enough to bring a faint glisten of sweat to its deerlike coat; then he made a thorough check of its joints and hooves and wiped it down. The oeikani had clearly done some hard riding. In lesser hands such a journey might have broken a leg. She waited until he had tethered the beast to let it graze before she approached him.

"That's a Zyraii steed," she stated in Surudainese.

He patted the animal's flank and smiled. His face was smooth and open, with glittering, large-pupiled eyes. "Yes. We can speak Zyraii, if it pleases you." His accent was distinct, but he obviously understood the nomad language far better than she knew his tongue. She accepted his offer.

"You've lived among the sons of Cadra," she said.

"For the past three years and more," he replied. "Since shortly after you left."

She raised an eyebrow. "And what else do you know about me?"

"I apologize," he said quickly. "We didn't have the opportunity to be introduced earlier. My name is Dalih. I am from a small oasis near the great city of Surudain. I know you because I have lived among the T'lil and studied swordsmanship under the opsha."

"Lonal?" she said, her heart quickening to utter the name aloud after such a long time.

"The same. I sought him out because I had heard of his reputation with the blade. To my great joy he decided to tutor me himself. In the past few seasons we have fought side by side in the battles against the Dragon's armies."

"He is well?"

"Yes. He has more lives than a oeikani has fleas. He is an awesome war-leader," Dalih said with undisguised respect. "He is the reason the Dragon has not conquered the Eastern Deserts."

"So I have heard," she said, lost in memories.

"He speaks well of you. He has named a son in your honor. His first wife gave birth a summer past, though the midwives insisted she would never bear another child after the difficulty with the last one."

"I remember," Elenya said. "This is his first son by her, true?"

"His heir. He says that he will teach him the High Speech, so that you may speak it with him should you ever visit the desert."

An image came to Elenya's mind's eye of dunes, eroded buttes, and goatskin tents. "Who knows?" she said. "Tell me, he didn't name his son Elenya, did he?"

Dalih seemed startled. "No. He used Yetem."

"That's wise. Some things do not change."

"No. Nor should they."

Elenya smiled at Dalih's seriousness. "How is it that you came to be here?"

"Your brother's former teacher, the Hab-no-ken Gast, came to the T'lil camp more than fifty days ago. He requested a warrior to carry the message you saw. Lonal chose me."

"Why? You seem as if you were valuable to him."

"For one thing, he wanted someone he could depend on to reach this destination."

"How *did* you get to Cilendrodel?"

"I followed the Ahloorm to its source and over the mountains north of Zyraii. Gloroc's men control that land, but it is sparsely inhabited. There are still smugglers who cross the strait, knowing that the Dragon's attention is directed toward the southwest. I hired one to bring me over."

Though his summary was perfunctory, Elenya had the impression the mission had not been so simple an accomplishment. "You did well," she said. "You should be proud."

He inclined his head. "I had my own reason for coming."

"Oh?"

"Yes. Lonal thought I would benefit from it."

"How so?"

"He told me that he had taught me as much as I could learn from him. It was time to send me to someone who could teach me more. He said you were the only person he knew who could do that. I hope that you will accept me."

Elenya's evaluation of Dalih, which had already been high, moved up another notch. "How well did you do in your matches with Lonal?"

"In the past few months, I have beaten him as many as two times out of five."

Elenya watched carefully, but saw no sign of guile or boastfulness. Two out of five. No one had ever beaten Lonal that often. "Suppose I agree to teach you, does that mean you would not go back to the Eastern Deserts?"

"No, indeed," he said firmly. "This is a strange land—more trees than I knew could grow on one world—but I will adjust. My sword is my life."

She tapped her toe into the dirt, testing the spring of her feet. The porridge lay lightly in her stomach, just enough there to give her energy without weighing her down. Her body was ready for some vigorous exercise.

"Well," she said. "First things first. Let's see how good you are."

The entire rebel camp turned out for the match, with the exception of Alemar, Wynneth, and the individuals on sentry duty. Elenya enlisted Tregay as judge. They had no practice blades, so they improvised. Both players tied a thin sack of corn around their midsections, outside of light mail shirts. The match would not be the best test of skill, since it was one thing to defend a small area from attack, and quite another to protect the entire body, but it would give Elenya an approximation of Dalih's ability. To make it more realistic, they agreed to allow pinking on the forearms, though such strikes would earn no points. She left off her gauntlet; defeating him while wearing it would prove nothing. They would spar until five total points had been scored.

They faced one another. Tregay gave the signal. Elenya plunged forward, thrusting, and sneaked the tip of her blade into the burlap just before Dalih could twist away.

"First point, Elenya," Tregay announced.

Dalih blinked. She nearly always used the tactic with an opponent who had never seen her fence before. Her lightness, speed, and the committedness of the movement nearly always caught them by surprise. It had failed only with Troy and Lonal.

Dahih bowed, and they assumed their starting positions once more. Elenya readied herself to repeat the maneuver, though she knew a masterful player would not give her a second chance.

Dalih did not. He changed his stance immediately, eliminating the opening, and danced in with a series of short jabs designed to draw her counter. She did not take the bait. Instead she backed away, leading him into a trap of her own. He abandoned his drive, and they stared at each other from a distance.

He had tried an attack known to Elenya as the Northern Opening. She doubted Dalih had studied classical fencing, but he had the moves. He used them naturally, instinctively, not as would a man who had been taught them by rote.

She tested him with the Southern Feint. He was not fooled, as the technique was intended to create an opening to the lower gut, which was off-limits in this contest. His counterthrust made her scamper backwards.

While she pondered what to try next, he charged. She sidestepped, leaned in, and scored. Damn, he'd been fast. Almost too fast. They backed away.

"Second point, Dalih," Tregay said, a hint of surprise in his tone.

Elenya hesitated, then looked down. A kernel of corn was jutting through a tiny rent in her sack.

He *had* been too fast. Her counter had come too late. He had used the same strategy that had given her the first point. Perhaps the lack of her gauntlet had caused her to misjudge, but she thought not. Dalih was simply quicker than she had given him credit for.

She acknowledged him with a nod. It would be interesting to see what happened now that they each had a measure of the other's speed.

Their next exchange was furious. They travelled all across the sward, forcing observers to back-pedal out of the way. They clashed until sweat broke out on their brows and they began to draw deep breaths. In a sport where points are typically determined with a single exchange, they continued a long time indeed. Part of it was the small target area, but mostly, Elenya knew, it was that they were closely matched.

Finally she pinked him near an elbow. Though he covered himself and prevented a follow-through, her success seemed to break his concentration. During her next charge she scored.

They rested for a few moments, while one of the camp women tied a strip of cloth around Dalih's cut.

The fourth round began as intensely as the third, but Elenya sensed a subtle difference. Dalih was pushing harder than before, and not being as careful. She stayed on the defensive, pacing herself, letting him tire.

He began to pant. His drives, though they made her retreat, did not score, though once Tregay stopped the round in order to see if there was a second hole in Elenya's sack. A crease appeared in the Surudainese's forehead.

Finally he slowed his pace, to gather his stamina. She chose that moment to press, and narrowly managed to score. Dalih stared down at the burlap as if he could not believe the new slice existed. His lips drew into a thin line as he bowed to Elenya.

The sight of his frustration nearly made Elenya smile. She had nurtured that reaction, in order to take advantage of the effect. She caught herself. She was doing as she had done in every match for the past ten years—making sure she won.

But that was not the point of this contest. How well did she know Dalih? What sort of good could come from humiliating him? As Tregay gave the word to begin the fifth and final round, she decided to change tactics.

Dalih came in aggressively, but cautiously, intent on avoiding his earlier mistake. He was a quick learner, she noted, able more than ever to evaluate him since she was no longer as intent on her own performance. Her concern over his feeling humiliated had been unfounded. They engaged five times to stalemate. Both came close.

The next time she pressed, Elenya deliberately left a small, momentary opening.

Dalih took it so fast that she could not have countered even if she had tried. His sword punctured the exact center of the sack, deep, almost to her mail shirt. Her eyes went wide.

"Point five, Dalih," Tregay said instantly, excited by the clarity of the technique.

The contestants sheathed their blades and reached out to clasp hands.

"Excellent swordplay," Elenya said.

"The last round was a little easier than the others," Dalih said meaningfully, though he did not seem displeased.

"To tell you the truth, I wasn't sure you would see that opening, much less take advantage of it. Lonal taught you well."

"You will accept me as a student, then?" he asked humbly.

"If you will accept me as a teacher."

"I would be honored."

She untied the burlap sack and dropped it on the sod. The audience waited with interested gazes, reminding her that she and Dalih had been speaking in a language that none of them could understand. She placed a hand on the southerner's shoulder and said, "Dalih is going to stay in Cilendrodel, and be a member of our company."

They cheered. She introduced the rebels to Dalih one by one. He, of course, had no words with which to respond to his welcome, but he rose to the occasion with a warm smile and a firm grip on the hands that were offered to him.

Elenya guessed he was perhaps twenty—more than five years her junior. Still coming into the prime of his physical abilities, while she was perched at the pinnacle. As good as he was now, he would get stronger and faster. She might not. Greater experience and a keen sense of strategy might keep her on top for many years, but sooner or later, the student might surpass the teacher.

The thought, much to her satisfaction, did not alarm her. In fact, it was like a saddle being lifted off her back. She was drawn back into the warm, soothing frame of mind she had felt that dawn, just after the healing. What better way to step down, than to shape one's own successor? She finally understood some of Troy's motives, saw why he had used her stubbornness and anger to make her a better fencer. Fortunately, Dalih, with his quiet confidence and genuine modesty, seemed the type who would not need to be tricked into excellence.

The final person in the line to be introduced proved to be Wynneth. Elenya was startled. Her sister-in-law smiled and tilted her head toward a nearby tree. Alemar was leaning against the trunk.

"He's ready to see you now," Wynneth said. Elenya could not help but notice the satisfied glow on her face.

The princess excused herself, letting Dalih get to know his new friends as best as he could manage. Even before she stepped into the shade, she knew that Alemar had seen the end of the match.

"You walk with a lighter step, sister," he bespoke, grinning.

"I have you to thank."

"Thank Gast. Tell me, does this mean you will let me win if we spar?"

"If it will help your technique. But you don't practice much these days."

"I will now."

Her shock threw her back into mindspeech. *"What? Why?"*

"It has to do with my power," he replied calmly. "It was never gone, though it was temporarily drained healing the wounds Enns gave you. It's as Gast once told me—I have more of it than any man since Umar, the legendary Zyraii healer. It's long since been reaccumulated, but now it's blocked, except for certain specific channels such as the one I used with you yesterday. You could say that I am hoarding it."

"I don't understand. Why didn't you know?"

"I could ask why you didn't know the things you learned about yourself yesterday. I am not consciously blocking it. It is being held back by an inner reflex, something I suppose must be called self-preservation. That reservoir of energy can be used for other purposes. My inner guide knows that, and it is forcing me to save it. It knows I may need it."

Suddenly Elenya understood. "For the fight against Gloroc."

"Yes. Until that is resolved, I will not be able to heal others, except in mundane ways. Gast was right. No amount of Retreat would have restored me, because the fundamental conflict would have still been there. I will get my power back when the threat of the Dragon no longer hangs over me and my family."

She pinched a bit of bark off the tree. "I'm sorry. I wish I could help you."

He shrugged. "I'm content. Disappointed, yes, but now, for the first time in many months, or maybe years, I have no doubt of which direction my life will go. I was wrong to have taken us all into hiding for so many weeks. We need to consolidate our gains before the Dragon sends serious reinforcements. As soon as I meet our new ally, I'll give the order to break camp. We're heading south."

The announcement was met with grateful sighs, animated murmurs, and the particular glint in the eyes of warriors who have been held in check for too long. That night they held a celebration—a carefully inconspicuous one—and at sunrise the next morning every man and woman stood ready to ride and march.

They hugged a small tributary of the Thank River, using its trees, thick stands of marsh grass, and brambles as cover. As twilight neared, with a pair of moons promising a bright night, they reached the edge of the great forest. They had not gone far when they heard a subtle, pleasant song. It seemed to glance off every leaf.

The column halted. "Do you recognize it?" Alemar asked Elenya.

"The rythni canticle of well-being."

Alemar nodded, a small tear hovering at the tip of an eyelash. "Wait here," he told the company. He rode just out of speaking range.

Hiephora stood on a limb at his eye-level. When he drew near she stopped singing, but other, unseen voices carried on, spreading tidings of welcome through the foliage.

"Greetings, Prince Alemar," the queen said.

"Well met, Your Highness," he murmured. "I am very glad to find you here."

"And how could I stay away? You have the aura of a man who believes in himself." She laughed merrily. "I brought someone to see you."

"Who?"

Another rythni crawled out from behind a leaf. It was Cyfee.

"Greetings, my lord."

Alemar stroked the young rythni's body. She was real.

"It is truly me," she said cheerfully, and spun a slow pirouette. Her flesh was white and vibrant. The only trace of damage was where her wings had been anchored, where there were two long scars. "My queen returned in time to save the four of us who were injured."

"My prophecy was true after all," Hiephora stated. "Not a single rythni was lost in the battle."

"But your wings," Alemar said solemnly, leaning over Cyfee. "They won't grow back, will they?"

"No, they won't," Cyfee replied. "But that is not so great a thing compared to my life and health. Our menfolk have no wings. I had none when I was a child, and I would have lost them when my childbearing years were over. It is not so bad. Now I look old and wise a millennia early."

"Alas that she could not *be* wise as quickly," Hiephora added impishly.

Alemar chuckled.

"We came to warn you," Cyfee said, turning serious. "Omril's troops are only three leagues to the west. He has lost your physical trail, but he seems able to track you without it, given sufficient time."

Alemar made a sour face. "It's the gauntlets. It's hard to dampen their energies, and the wizard knows their pattern. We'll ride east, then, and camp only briefly tonight."

"That is best, my prince."

"And will you watch over us?" he asked.

"Yes. Sleep safely and well."

The rebels slept in a thicket without benefit of a campfire, their bedrolls scattered over a wide area where they could not easily be surrounded, sheltered by loosely hung tarps and shawls that could be taken down and packed within moments, should the alarm be sounded. Four of the company hid within the brush, keeping sentry duty. And, of course, from their vantage points on limbs or in their cleverly constructed bowers, the rythni held vigil.

The moons' light filtered only weakly through the canopy of leaves, leaving deep shadows, turning the clumps of trunk fungus into ghost-white specters. Crickets and nocturnal rodents made their discordant music. A male rythni, dozing in the grass near the camp, awoke suddenly, feeling a vibration in the ground on which he lay, as from the tread of a man or large animal. But he could see nothing on the path, nor did he hear any suspicious sounds. He closed his eyes and nodded off.

Had he been lying three paces to one side, he might have seen a bootprint form in the soft forest loam, then another and another, leading into the rebel camp. Perhaps he would have noticed a fern bend out of the way or a strand of spider web snap. But he still would not have seen the owner of the boots, nor heard any sound as twigs broke under foot.

The intruder stopped near one of the sentries, who glanced up at a moonbeam, oblivious to the surveillance. The stalker continued into the center of the area, weaving through unsuspecting sleepers. He did not harm them, because even if they died silently, their auras would change and the rythni would be disturbed.

Slowly but with few detours, the bootprints created a path to the fallen broadleaf tree where the twins had fashioned their shelters. The stalker approached Elenya first, but as he did, the amulet on her throat gave off a bright green flicker. She stirred. The intruder backed away, so quickly that for the first time, his tread was audible.

The flicker was not repeated. None of the sentries or rythni seemed to have noticed it. The stalker stood still for many moments, then inched toward the den where Alemar and Wynneth huddled.

On the prince's throat, another amulet glowed in warning. This time the trespasser backed up immediately, cancelling the effect before anyone had a reasonable chance to see it. Alemar slept on.

The intruder stayed where he was for a very long time, all the way through the changing of the guard. The last watch of the night began. A daylark roused briefly and serenaded the grove.

Finally Wynneth opened her eyes, crossed and recrossed her legs, and sat up, grumbling softly about the curses of pregnancy. She crawled out of the shelter without waking her husband, and found a convenient spot several paces down the length of the fallen tree, where she raised her skirt and, using a spur of the trunk to brace her awkward body, relieved herself.

She emitted a small sigh of refreshment, stood, and took one step toward her bedroll. Abruptly her eyes glazed, and she slumped. Something caught her under the arms, and then she vanished.

A few moments later one of the guards, who had noticed her rise, turned and, finding her gone, assumed she had already crawled back into the shelter. The rythni, who had glanced away to give privacy, whispered among themselves, but seeing no sign of violence, reached the same conclusion. However, more than one increased the vigilance with which they watched the area around the fallen log.

Meanwhile, the bootprints, concealed by the dimness of the night, formed one by one along the trail where they had first appeared, except that now they pointed the other direction and sank deeper into the soil. They continued out of the camp, beyond the many watchful eyes. A hundred paces from the perimeter, the sound of strained breathing and the scuffing of soled feet arrived out of nowhere, frightening the shrews in the underbrush and launching an owl into sudden flight. A pair of rythni scouts heard, and worked their way through the plant life toward the source, but, finding nothing there, were mystified.

Crossing a small creek, the stalker and his prize came upon a sturdy battle oeikani well-concealed within a thicket. The beast, with the aplomb of a fine breed meticulously trained, was unperturbed at the sudden appearance of its master beside it, remaining just as silent as it had been all night.

Omril groaned and lowered Wynneth to the ground. He straightened up, grimaced, and rubbed his back. He swayed, as if fighting off an attack of dizziness, and held onto the saddle while he regained his breath. As soon as he had, he gathered his strength one more time, picked up his prisoner, and draped her over the oeikani's withers. He climbed up behind her, settled her into a position from which she would not fall, and rode off toward the west.

≋ XXVI ≋

Omril collared Wynneth and chained her to a post in the middle of a clearing. He permitted a canopy to be erected in order to screen her from the sun, but he forbade walls, so that she would remain under open surveillance at all times. One of his cohorts surrounded her, filling the clearing and much of the adjacent forest, a ring of nearly five hundred armed men through which even the wind could not have infiltrated unannounced.

He sent the other cohort to attack the rebel camp. He did not expect they would find anyone there, but the trail would be fresh. At the very least, it would keep the rebels occupied, and give his men the blood scent.

He gulped down a restorative potion and slept, his pavilion tightly guarded by his personal retinue, while the rest of the small army watched for some sign of the enemy. He did not awaken until late in the afternoon. His concoction banished the debilitation caused by his long maintenance of the invisibility spell. The bags under his eyes shrank away, the shakiness left his limbs; he felt strong. The muscles of his back still ached from the challenge of carrying a grown woman many hundreds of paces, but that was the only lasting evidence of the strain of his feat.

He ate a hearty meal, groomed himself, and listened to the captain of his company render a status report. When perfectly ready he strolled over to visit his captive.

"Your companions have fled. It must be convenient, having

thousands of small allies to keep watch for you. I used to have pigeons to help me with such tasks," he said pointedly.

Wynneth avoided eye contact. Her glance wandered toward the sacks of food and the deer carcasses strung up on nearby limbs. She paused as if calculating how far a bit of venison and a dwindling pile of flour would go among so many men. Omril was impressed. No common trull, this one. Another woman would be fretting at her bonds; she was judging how much the pursuit had cost him.

She stared at her feet. "Must I have all these men watching me all the time?" she asked.

"Indeed, yes. And tonight there will be lanterns on every side of you. One never knows when an invisible man may slink inside the camp and steal you away."

"What are you going to do with me?"

"If you prove to be insufficient bait, I will take you south with me. There is a great deal I can learn from your mind. If I take my time I'm sure I can pull it out of you, no matter how well your husband may have schooled you to resist. If I cannot, perhaps I'll send you to Gloroc."

She glared and tugged her hem further down over her knees. Omril chuckled.

"My lord," exclaimed his page an hour later. "The rebel prince is at the perimeter."

Omril put away the crystal into which he had been gazing. "And what is he doing there?" he demanded.

"He is . . . walking forward."

The wizard nodded, strode past the messenger, and emerged from his pavilion. A great knot of his soldiers had gathered on the eastern edge of the clearing. Omril summoned his captain.

"This may be a diversion. See to it that the other directions are carefully watched."

"Yes, my lord."

Omril watched the jumble of men gradually separate. Alemar walked down the corridor between them, pace slow and deliberate, gaze unfocussed. Three of his gauntlet's jewels scintillated, each with its own deep, pure color.

"Kill him!" Omril shouted.

The soldiers paused, as if to say they had just tried that, then set about their task. They thrust and swung their swords, axes, pikes, and knives at the rebel prince. Every point was turned. None came closer than an arm-length away. A deflected ax gashed one of the soldiers in his thigh. Alemar continued on, though he slowed to a turtlelike shuffle. The group paused.

Omril smiled. "Keep attacking until I tell you to stop," he ordered. His cohort hastily obeyed. Meanwhile, the wizard turned to his page. "Go to my tent. Find the small chest with the ruby clasp. Bring me the coil of twine you find within."

The page, eager to please, took a step, but Omril seized him sternly by the shoulder. The boy winced.

"*Do not touch the clasp with your fingers*. Flip it open with your boot, or the tip of your knife, but do not set living tissue against it."

The boy paled, swallowed a lump, and ran to the pavilion. Omril turned back toward the commotion. A grin tugged at the corners of his lips. His men flailed, as ineffectual as ever, but on the other hand, Alemar now hesitated between each step, checking his balance before putting the next foot forward.

He was good, Omril had to admit, or he was able to use the gauntlet more fully than anticipated. The wizard himself would have been challenged to maintain a ward in the face of such an onslaught, though he was certain he would have been able to continue walking normally. But as a rescue attempt, it left much to be desired. More than ever, Omril took this to be the diversion. The princess would be making an appearance at some point.

Pace by pace, Alemar progressed through the ranks of men and steel. Omril's page returned with the twine, which the sorcerer tucked out of sight in his sleeve. When the prince had only twenty strides to go, Omril ordered a halt to the attack.

"Back away," he told his men. "Leave us room."

The soldiers virtually stumbled over themselves doing as he asked, though Omril's tone had been mild. Within moments, only he stood between Alemar and his wife.

"I am disappointed," the sorcerer said. "A good strategist knows when a person is expendable."

Alemar did not respond. Omril doubted that he could without losing the ward. If he dropped it for an instant, he would die. Omril glanced at Wynneth, who had risen to her feet and now waited, biting her lip, for the tableau to be played out. The wizard considered slaying her, now that Alemar was so close, but she was still valuable as a hindrance.

Alemar did not hesitate. He kept walking straight toward Wynneth.

Omril stepped aside.

As soon as the prince passed, the wizard anchored one end of his twine to a root and began running in a circle, unravelling the cord behind him. Alemar reached Wynneth. She embraced him —lightly so as not to disturb his concentration. Omril completed a circle around them and tied the ends together. He laughed as he dropped the knot.

"I have you now, son of Alemar. Forget any plans you have to walk out of here."

Alemar turned and faced him. "I'm in no hurry."

Omril was taken aback. The prince was surely enough of a mage to recognize that, ward or no ward, he was locked inside the circle. Perhaps he thought he could remain where he was, protecting himself and the woman, until his sister launched the second half of the rescue. But Omril would not allow that.

He spoke to the twine, muttering in a sibilant, repetitious language, one that had not sprouted from a human culture. The twine suddenly convulsed. The ring shrank a few inches in diameter. He kept talking.

Alemar regarded the shrinking without apparent alarm, though the flickers from the gauntlet increased in frequency and brilliance. Omril sauntered along the outer perimeter, confident and smiling.

The sixth contraction, however, was not as complete as the first five. Omril raised his voice. Once again, the twine twisted and danced over the ground.

This time the circle was the same size as before.

"Your talisman is useless," Alemar said. "I have made an Ultimate Ward."

Omril scoffed. "There is no such thing as an Ultimate Ward. It's a myth. Even if it were true, you couldn't move it from this site. And sooner or later, no matter how good you are, you'll have to sleep."

Omril decided the prince was stalling for time, and redoubled his efforts. His men watched intently. Several of them whispered among themselves. The twine danced to eye level and down again, snapping like reins in a oeikani race.

Through it all Alemar stood unshaken. Sweat beaded on Omril's brow, but the prince's stayed dry. For the first time, the wizard noticed a strange, high-pitched hum, almost like a song. It seemed to come from the trees on every side of the clearing.

"You're mine now," Alemar said.

Omril gasped. Suddenly his twine sprang outward, over his head, capturing him within the boundary. He fought a tremendous compulsion to walk forward. Alemar held out his hands.

"No!" the wizard cried.

"Come to me," Alemar demanded.

Omril took a step. He locked his muscles, refusing to take another. He stroked one of the rings on his fingers, trying to focus, trying to set up a ward of his own. The blood in his temples pounded, making him dizzy. How? He was a wizard of the Ril. He was more than a match for this healer prince. He screamed, but the sound from his throat seemed drowned by the chanting from the trees.

The rythni! Somehow the prince had collected the energies of the little people, and had channeled them through himself. He had the strength of the entire forest to draw from—enough for an Ultimate Ward, enough to spin a trap. Omril choked, and took another step forward. He heard his servitors beat uselessly against the ward. Their frantic yells tortured him. Worthless soldiers.

He should have killed the woman while he had the chance.

Alemar's hands loomed. The sorcerer tried to raise his own to brush them away, but he could only get them as high as his waist. With tender, uncompromising finality, the palms closed around his jaws.

Wynneth struggled not to be frightened, as Alemar stood next to her, frozen eye to eye with the wizard, hands holding the latter's face. The sun dropped under the horizon, leaving the clearing brightly lit by Motherworld. Still the two combatants did not move. The Dragon's soldiers pounded against the ward, the cacophonous din driving her to tears. Would they never stop?

They had slowed down, she told herself, trying to be objective. They thrust their swords and pikes steadily but half-heartedly. The cohort that had been chasing the rebel band returned empty-handed, and they joined the ranks of awed observers. She hated those eyes, never giving her a moment to herself. That was almost worse than the fear that Alemar, in spite of his performance thus far, would fail.

Suddenly the wizard groaned. His eyelids fluttered like a man in a seizure. His knees sagged, and he sank out of Alemar's grip, hands clawing ineffectually at the prince's clothing. He curled up in a fetal position on the ground and whimpered.

Alemar sucked in air. His pupils contracted, and he gazed out at the armed throng surrounding them. They put up their weapons and gaped in shock. Finally he met Wynneth's worried stare.

"What did you do to him?" she asked, scooting away from Omril.

"I...showed him himself. It was more than he cared to know." Suddenly the prince sighed, and two great teardrops welled at the corners of his eyes. "He was not an evil man. He was just...unfeeling."

Then Alemar seemed to draw a veil over his expression, and when he turned to face Omril's army, he bore himself like a monarch. "You've seen a sample of my power. I give you a choice: fight me, fight my sister who waits in the forest, or leave. If you return straight to Yent, we will leave you unmolested. Refuse now and not a single one of you will live to see the coast."

They did not even murmur among themselves. They turned their eyes toward their captain, who stood just outside the circle of twine, scowling down at what had become of the Dragon's sorcerer.

"What of him?" the captain asked.

"He is mine."

The captain gnawed his lower lip. To return to the garrison without such an important figure would mean heavy discipline. He was a grizzled, barrel-chested man of advancing years, a veteran with the scars to prove it. He tapped his foot in the dust.

"The woods are thick between here and the settled provinces," Alemar commented mildly.

"We keep our arms?" he asked.

"If you wish."

He turned to his men. "Break camp. We're leaving tonight."

Alemar accepted the surrender with outward nonchalance, standing within the battle circle as if it were the site of his throne. Wynneth, on the other hand, knew that this was a façade intended to intimidate his audience, and she leaned against him and cried. The soldiers acted on their decision with dispatch. Except for the occasional wide-eyed stares, they pretended the rebel prince, his wife, and the defeated wizard no longer existed, as if nothing mattered, in fact, but beginning the march homeward.

A tiny figure buzzed over the clearing and settled on Alemar's shoulder. The latter echoed its song of greeting.

"Half my people fell unconscious from the effort," Hiephora announced.

"He was stronger than I realized," Alemar said, his composure not quite masking his relief. "I'm not sure any single man could have defeated him."

"But you were not alone, beloved," said the rythni queen. "Nor will you be as long as you stay within the forests of Cilendrodel. Rejoice. You have won."

He laughed. Wynneth smiled to see him so triumphant.

"Very well," he said. "The wizard is mine. Let's be off to the south, where the real battle lies."

XXVII

Toren woke suddenly, but like a warrior, gave no outward sign. He opened his eyes to slits. The forest whispered with the echoes of falling dew. He saw a single leaf, high above, caught by the morning sun. Two young wrens were practicing flight, darting from branch to branch. Deena's back pressed warmly against his. Geim and the rest of the party still slumbered, curled on either side of the ashes of last night's campfire. All was serene.

But he was being watched.

He scanned across a log that lay beyond his companions. A beetle clambered through the crevices in the bark toward a knot. It paused, waved its antennae, and abruptly changed direction.

A tiny man squatted behind the knot, peering out at the three humans.

Toren had never seen a rythni before, but Obo had, and the sight of one sparked a warm rush of nostalgia. He was mesmerized by the clean, slim lines of the little man's body—hairless, like a Vanihr, except for the thick blue mop on his head. Without rising Toren called out softly.

"Greetings."

The rythni jumped, stared at Toren for an instant, then ducked around the log faster than a hummingbird could fly.

Toren had expected nothing less, considering the timidity of the race. Even if he had known their language, he knew he could not have convinced the rythni to stay.

Geim, Deena, and the others lifted their heads and peered about with sleep-encrusted eyes.

"We had a visitor," Toren said, and told them what had just happened. "It's good news. Obo told me that rythni are seldom reported in western Cilendrodel. We must be getting close to our destination."

"Good," Geim grumbled. His mood had soured as soon as they had descended out of the Syril Mountains, out of the cool mountain air into the muggy climate of Cilendrodel in summer. "Maybe we can find a place that serves a decent meal soon."

Geim's hopes materialized by midday. They found an inn, a tiny establishment in an equally tiny community nestled at the edge of a grove of silk trees.

Toren and his group were dressed in the manner of the traders of the foothills of the Syril, who often arrived during the season to barter for silk. The innkeeper regarded the tall, blond, beardless visages of the two Vanihr with a quizzical frown, but he seemed satisfied with the others. His expression softened even more when Deena acted as the spokesperson. She gave him the standard story, that they were on their way to trade with quarn merchants near Garthmorron.

The innkeeper called to his wife, who hefted her massive body out of a chair and began clattering about in the kitchen. Her husband wiped down one of the common room's two tables and gestured for his guests to sit.

"That's bad country to be making for right now," he said.

"Oh? Why?"

"There was a rebel uprising at the governor's fortress near Old Stump three months back. They killed Lord Puriel, and tore down his castle. The Dragon sent troops to burn down the village, and now the whole province is in open revolt. And now some incredible news has come from the north."

"Which is?"

"Alemar, the Elandri prince, defeated Gloroc's sorcerer in single combat, and kept two cohorts of men at bay while he did it. The cohorts, when they returned south and saw that the countryside had risen up, joined the revolt."

"Are you sure?" Deena asked. She and the others masked their reactions, not knowing where the loyalties of the innkeeper lay.

"Am I sure?" he said animatedly. "I wish I weren't. I can just see the Dragon's armies storming through our forests, once they can be pulled from the New Kingdoms or the Eastern Deserts. The prince will need all the power he can get." He spat in a porcelain spittoon. "Isn't it be something, though?" he said in a more subdued tone. "Imagine, a wizard of the Ril, whipped like a baby. That Alemar, he was born and raised in Cilendrodel. It's

208

time one of our own kicked the Dragon in his hind end."

"Indeed it is," Deena replied in a firm but noncommital tone. "Tell me, what would be the best way to reach Garthmorron?"

He stepped on a wood ant and swept the insect out with the side of his boot. "Stay here, is what I'd say. We're too far from anywhere for rebels or Dragon's men to worry about. But if you must go, keep off the roads once you get to Yent."

"Many thanks."

The innkeeper shook his head and ambled toward the kitchen, frowning in the manner of a man who has no patience or love for political events. The group waited until he vanished behind the curtain before they exchanged worried glances.

"We're arriving just in time," Toren murmured. "Our host is right. If the Dragon has lost a wizard of the Ril, he'll send serious reinforcements, and soon. We'd better step up our pace."

The fare was simple but sustaining. After weeks of camp food, it went down with a satisfying evenness. Toren especially liked it. It was different from the cuisine of his home, but it was forest food, and for all its newness there was something familiar about it.

"Aren't you going to throw up?" Deena teased. Toren rapped her knuckles lightly with his spoon.

They resumed their trek before noon. The innkeeper muttered to himself and cautioned them not to make light of the conditions ahead. Deena thanked him.

"We'll keep to the open road," Toren announced. "It's faster. But we'll have to start camping out of sight."

An herb growing at the base of a giant tree caught the modhiv's eye—as did the rich, black soil in which it grew, and the unusual striations of color on the bark above it.

"Something wrong?" Deena queried.

"No," he replied. "The countryside just seems familiar." And well it should, he thought. Obo had lived in this land for almost nineteen years. The impressions reminded Toren of those he used to receive from his ancestors. In a gesture of sentimentality, he awakened his father's spirit. His sire murmured that it was good to have found forest again, but then berated him about the colorful native garb he wore. He restored the totem fragment to its niche and closed the lid.

On the second day, they encountered a squad of three armed men who glared at them but passed by without comment. From then on they kept off the main highway. On the third night after their meal at the inn, Toren's hands began to tickle, as if coated with strands of cobweb. The sensation intensified when he faced east.

"What does it mean?" Deena asked.

"Alemar and Elenya are closer than Garthmorron," Toren said.

The next day the tickle became an itch. It felt as if he were wearing something on his hands. It guided him slightly south of east, nearer to the coast. As the afternoon wore on he grew annoyed by the effect, so he dismissed it. From then on he summoned it at will, normally only when they came to forks in their path and had to choose a direction. At each such time it pulsed more strongly.

They passed a gutted estate. In the shade of the trees at the edge of a corn field they found freshly turned graves, one of them marked with a shattered sword. Unharvested corn lay knocked to the ground, stalks broken, the grain denied its chance to mature. A league farther east, as they searched for a way to cross a major stream, they found a destroyed bridge.

A middle-aged woman sat on a boulder just upstream from the broken structure, fishing. Startled, she pulled in her line and watched the travellers intently as they approached. Toren, senses keen to any premonition of ambush, felt no danger.

"How close is Yent?" he asked the woman.

"Ye stand within the province," she responded. "The town be five leagues east by northeast." Her reply fell oddly on his ears. She spoke in the local vernacular, the Low Speech of the Cilendri.

Toren thanked her and they rode on, obviously much to her relief. They soon found a ford and crossed the stream.

They detoured toward the south, avoiding the provincial capital. The deep patches of uninhabited forest vanished, replaced by groves of silk trees, corralled thickets, and even cleared fields. They saw prevalent signs of recent conflict—burned buildings, despoiled crops, and a distinct absence of normal traffic on the highways.

They concealed themselves in a brush-filled gully while a patrol of twenty armored men galloped past, the Dragon's insignia emblazoned on their jupons. Many of their helms were dented, and links had been shattered in their chain mail hauberks. Two of the soldiers wore bandages.

Toren called a halt when they found an abandoned barn. "A good place to hide for the night," he declared. The scent of goat and pig and dog still hung strongly in the air, as if the animals resided there still, but they shared their slumber with only mice and bats.

As dawn beamed in through open knotholes in the walls, Toren let his hands feel the pull once more. He sat up in surprise. The sensation was definitely stronger than it had been when they bedded down. He roused the others.

"They're close, and they're moving. Let's go. We can eat breakfast as we ride."

The barn was not far from a thin road scarred with wagon ruts and choked with weeds. They had avoided it the evening before, but now Toren announced they would follow it.

His hands itched so furiously it was hard to hold the reins.

"Stop there!" cried a voice from the trees.

Toren and the others halted. The canopy of leaves above their heads glowed beneath a noonday sun. Ten archers stepped out of the thick growth on either side of the road, arrows nocked and drawn. The speaker was a tall man dressed in doeskin.

"What is your business here?" the man demanded.

The temple guards stiffened. Geim's fingers inched toward his throwing net. "Be at peace," Toren told them. He considered what he would tell the stranger. Given the intensity of the itch, the choice came easily. "We seek Alemar, Prince of Elandris, and his sister, Elenya," he said loudly.

The leader regarded them calmly. "Why?" he said finally, and Toren knew he had chosen well.

"I will share that with the prince or princess. Tell them that I come from the temple of Struth."

The tall man smoothed his hair back. "The prince has told us that a man may come from the South. He is to be asked three questions."

"Go ahead," Toren replied.

"What is the capital of Serthe?"

"Headwater."

"Where do statues speak?"

"At the Oracle of the Frog God."

"Where were you born?"

"In the village of Ten Trees, in the Land of the Fhali, in the Wood."

The tall man smiled. "'In the Wood' was sufficient. Well met," he said, and at his gesture the archers eased their bowstrings. "My name is Tregay. And you?"

Toren gave his name.

"You truly are from the Wood," Tregay mused. "I thought that was just part of the code. You've come a long way to meet my lord and lady. I am happy to announce that your journey is at an end. They're less than a quarter of a league away. I'll take you to them."

≈≈ XXVIII ≈≈

Alemar knelt over Omril. The Dragon's sorcerer lay limp on his pallet, drooling and uttering weak, piping noises. His silk robes reeked from a month without laundering. Alemar's men had repeatedly tried to remove the soiled garments during the month since the fight in the north, but Omril clung to them with hysterical vigor. Attempting to take them was the only thing that could provoke the magician to action; otherwise he did nothing more than whisper to himself or stare at beetles and grubs on the ground. He had to be reminded to eat and take care of bodily functions.

Alemar closed the flap of the one-person tent and placed his left palm on the wizard's forehead. On his right hand, the gauntlet warbled, Omril ceased fidgeting.

"Good," the prince murmured. "Now remember where we were yesterday. You were showing me your quarters in Dragonsdeep."

Alemar probed. And cringed. The damage worsened every day. The wizard, in his confusion, was exaggerating what Alemar had begun, consuming his own sense of identity, warping his inner being in frightening and irreparable ways. But Omril responded to Alemar's entry. He calmed, and gradually the twisting corridors of his mind straightened. The times when the prince looked within were the wizard's only moments of respite from himself.

The memories welled up. Alemar trod down a by-now-familiar path from Omril's well-appointed room deep in the Dragon's palace, through the wing where most of the sorcerers of the Ril lived, and into the audience chamber of Gloroc himself. In this particular recollection, the wizard stood in front of the Dragon and received his orders to come to Cilendrodel and ferret out information concerning the gauntlets, which Gloroc had determined were indeed the talismans that had been taken from Setan. Alemar switched the memory to others he had explored less often, such as the locations of guard stations, secret exits from the palace, or even the nature of some of the tomes of necromancy lying in Omril's private library. The wizard was a wellspring of lore. He had been second in rank of all the Ril wizards.

Fatigue called the healer back. Satisfied that he had gleaned a few more bits of information useful to the rebel cause, Alemar sighed and lifted away his hand. A forlorn squeak escaped Omril's lips, then he fainted.

Alemar shuddered. Even enemies did not deserve such torment. But as long as Omril could provide strategic knowledge, the prince could not afford to put him to rest. Thanks to Gloroc's mind-reading powers, no spies had ever penetrated the central reaches of his palace; Omril was therefore especially valuable.

The prince left the tent. The fresh forest air blessed his lungs. He wiped Omril's sweat from his palm and checked the camp. Recently wounded men lay in hammocks or still in the travois on which they had been dragged to the site. A brief look at their auras showed that they were in stable condition, except for the one who could not be saved. Sentries kept an alert watch, as did rythni hidden in the treetops. Wynneth approached, having seen that he had finished his session with Omril.

"The roast boar is ready," she said. "Eat before you think of something else to do."

He nodded wearily. Good advice. Since the band had come south, it seemed there was always too much to do. He slipped his arm around his wife's waist and joined the knot of twenty or thirty individuals gathered near the base of a gigantic broadleaf tree. Solint the Minstrel handed him a steaming strip of meat. The aroma stirred the ache in his stomach. How long had it been since he had eaten a real meal? He wolfed down several bites.

Suddenly his gauntlet whistled. All five of its major gems blazed. A few feet away, Elenya's did the same. The twins stared at each other. The pulse coming from the talismans resembled nothing they had ever experienced.

Rythni chirped, announcing the arrival of strangers. The rebels tensed and reached for their weapons, but Alemar gestured for calm. The rythni indicated no cause for alarm. In another few moments, the sentries confirmed the little people's report. Boughs and shrubbery parted. Tregay's patrol strode into the glade, leading seven men and a woman.

Alemar knew instantly who it was. At the head of the newcomers walked two tall, yellow-haired, golden-skinned individuals. The lead man's aura gleamed like a bonfire on Dark Night. The gauntlet tugged Alemar's wrist, as if trying to slip off his hand. A cold tingle spread goose pimples all across his chest and back.

"At last," Elenya murmured.

The stranger stared at the talismans, and at the twins, with wide-eyed, almost childlike fascination. He swallowed deeply.

Tregay led him forward. "Struth's candidate is here, my lord," the rebel announced excitedly.

"So I see," Alemar said, remembering how to speak. He introduced himself and his sister. "You are Toren?"

"Yes," the stranger said. Finally he glanced up, away from the gauntlet. He seemed to notice the glade, the camp, and the crowd around him for the first time. He gestured belatedly at his companions. "This is Geim. And that is Deena." He named the five temple guards. "All servants of Struth."

"The first two names are known to me," Alemar said. "You were on the mission to the Far South." He smiled at Geim and Deena.

The gauntlets hummed. Even those without magical talents sensed the pull between the talismans and the newcomer. "Well," Alemar said, holding up his right hand, partially closing his eyes against the glare from the gems. "I intended to offer you the hospitality of camp, meager as that may be. As you can see, we've just been through a battle." He waved at the wounded men. "A successful one, I'm happy to say. We've driven the Dragon's garrison back into its stronghold in Yent. After today's defeat, I think they'll stay there, waiting for reinforcements from Elandris. We've earned a respite, if only a lull before the storm." He realized he was rambling, chuckled, and slid the gauntlet off his hand. "But food and rest can wait. You've come here for a reason. Let's be sure you haven't wasted your time." He thrust out the talisman.

Toren regarded the proffered object with a dry mouth and a flush of heat around the neck, acutely aware of the eyes upon him, particularly Deena's. The itch was gone, but bands of energy flowed from his palms to the gauntlets, creating an unbearable tug deep in the bones of his arms and shoulders. He reached forward, hand trembling, and hesitantly wrapped his fingers around Alemar's gift.

Toren inserted his right hand and pulled the finely meshed

214

mail snug over his fingers. Suddenly the talisman grew heavy. He grunted and tensed his arm in order to keep it from plunging to the ground. The twins seemed impressed that he succeeded. Within moments the gauntlet grew light.

And the world changed.

First, and most fundamentally, he felt strong. Each breath pumped vigor into him. The weariness of the long journey dissipated. Secondly, the auras of the people around him sharpened, achieving a clarity that he had previously enjoyed only at night, away from the interference of background light. That belonging to one of the wounded men was sputtering. Toren guessed the rebel would die before nightfall. Complex and eye-pleasing filaments of energy shone around the twins, brightest of all except for the hearty glow streaming from the abdomen of the pregnant woman near Alemar.

Like the auras, sources of magic stood out like the solitary trees in the pasture lands of Irigion. In addition to the riot of tendrils blazing around the gauntlets, Toren saw the bursts coming from the amulets on the twins' chests, though the talismans were hidden beneath their collars. The throwing net draped over Geim's saddle horn flickered prominently. But far more intriguing was the forest itself. Before donning the gauntlet, he had been completely blind to a deep-seated, primal force contained in the foliage. A tiny bit radiated from each living leaf and twig, a virtually inexhaustible supply of energy should one know how to tap it. Someone could, for he sensed infinitesimal fractions of that power being drawn upon and guided in conscious ways. *Of course*, he thought. *It's the rythni.*

He laughed. He smiled at Deena. The anxious frown left her face. He turned and reached out his hand toward Elenya. "May I have the other gauntlet?"

The princess gazed at the talisman as if she had never seen it quite as she saw it then, slipped it off with a precision that betrayed a reluctance to part with it. She held it out to Toren.

"Be sure of yourself," Elenya said. "My brother and I each tried to put on the whole pair soon after we left the desert. We were both knocked unconscious. They might have killed us had we been slightly less attuned." Toren heard a hint of challenge in her tone, along with a note of concern.

Toren felt the compelling force in his right hand and said with confidence, "Struth knew what she was doing when she sent me."

The Vanihr took the second talisman and cradled it, examining

215

the inset stones and the delicate, yet virtually indestructible gold filigree. He licked his lips, nodded, and inserted his left hand.

A ward automatically swelled around him, but other than that he felt little change. The most distinct difference was that he could sense what the rythni were doing with the forest energies he had detected earlier. They were weaving spells of concealment. Toren had only to adjust his inner vision a slight degree and the little people stood revealed, as visible to him now as if they had stepped from shadows into full sunlight. He was reminded of the moment when Struth had dropped the illusion on her countenance, except that in this case, the rythni were still actively trying to cloak themselves. The talismans utterly nullified their attempts. He hoped they were equally effective against Gloroc's illusions.

The relatively minor improvement in his senses worried Toren. Surely this was not all. Then he remembered how Keron's belt had acted when he had first put it on. The way to test the gauntlets was to do something with them.

One of the spells that Janna had taught him came to mind. He had been unable to master it at the temple. He recalled the technique and concentrated.

Jaws dropped and eyes widened on every side of him. Deena cried out.

"Where did he go?" Tregay blurted.

Toren had not moved. Smiling, he slipped to the side just as Elenya, less disoriented than the others, reached into the spot where he had been standing. She waved her hands over the area.

A voice carried over the hubbub of the rebels. "He's invisible." It was the pregnant woman who spoke. Toren noted a certain wryness in her tone.

The modhiv continued to wend his way through the assemblage, testing his spellweaving. No one heard his footfalls, no one felt the wind of his passage. As he ducked under a frond of bracken, careful not to brush against it, he noticed a queer pattern of magic, quite powerful but chaotic, emanating from a small tent just ahead. Leaving his confused audience behind, he ventured forward and lifted the flap.

A man in dirty silk robes came into view. He drooled and spun away from the light as if stung. Toren identified the strange energy pattern, and grunted in surprise. He dropped his invisibility just as a rebel noticed the open flap. The man called out, and moments later Alemar and Elenya led the observers to the tent.

"A wizard of the Ril," Toren said. "The one you defeated in the north?"

"I see you've heard about that," Alemar said. "Yes, this is Omril, a short time ago one of Gloroc's most favored pupils."

"What is wrong with him?"

"He has been dragon-touched," Alemar said.

Toren frowned. "Something you picked up from Struth?"

"No. I've only seen Struth once. It was actually a variation of a healing technique. Dragon-touching, a battle of minds—it's all the same sort of magic in the end." He dismissed the topic with a peremptory wave of his hand. "I take it that the talismans work for you?"

The query sank in. For a moment, Toren recalled the simple scout he had been less than a year before. On impulse, he freed the voices of his ancestors, and they simply waited, silent, absorbing the difference in their descendant, finding comfort that they were once again in a forest. It was his turn to shape the day. He clenched his fists, joyful at the power in them. Struth had stolen him from his home, but she had repaid the debt. He had come full circle—he was a warrior again, with a battle ahead as big as any modhiv of the Fhali had ever dreamed of. He could dream of better circumstances, perhaps, but with these talismans he had what he needed: a fighting chance.

"Yes, I am able to use them," he said. "It remains to be seen whether they are strong enough for Gloroc, but Struth has made a good plan. I'll accept that hospitality now, and I'll tell you about it."

≈≈ XXIX ≈≈

Alemar leaned back against the broadleaf tree, Wynneth nestled in the crook of his arm. His right hand, bereft of the gauntlet, slid back and forth over his wife's rotund belly. The baby kicked. Alemar and Wynneth exchanged a smile.

The couple were part of a ring of people that surrounded Toren and received an account of his travels. Alemar listened with mute detachment, saving his questions. He felt warm and relaxed, able for once to be himself and enjoy his wife's company and his comrades' excitement. One of the burdens of his life had shifted to other shoulders.

Toren spoke clearly and well. The rebels insisted on lengthy descriptions of the Wood, which amazed them both by its resemblance to and difference from Cilendrodel's great forest. They listened raptly to the account of life at the temple of Struth, eager to know more of their strange ally. Fond memories welled up inside Alemar when the modhiv mentioned that Obo was the source of his skill with the High Speech. The prince approved of the candidate's open, guileless countenance and the patience with which he answered questions. He had not known what to expect from a man sent by a dragon. He also liked the tender glances the Vanihr shared with his woman companion. Could it be true that, after all these years, their designs to reconquer Elandris were coming to fruition?

All too soon, the preliminaries were done. Toren related the plan that Struth had given him.

"As long as the Dragon lives, Elandris will not be taken by force of arms. The emperor of the Calinin has committed his forces, and King Keron will soon be leading an offensive through Tamisan and Thiagra, but effort will be doomed unless we succeed in assassinating Gloroc. I will lead a group of five or six men in secret to Dragonsdeep. Gloroc resides in the palace there. If we can surprise him in his chambers, we can kill him."

The audience listened in total silence. Alemar's pulse quickened. There. It was said. And even though Toren had faltered before pushing out the last four words, the hope had been made solid and immediate.

"Catching him there is crucial," Toren continued. "But there is good reason to think we can do it. Alemar the Great prepared the trap when he built Dragonsdeep—called Wizardsdeep then—over a millennia ago. As the last of his undersea cities, he made it more grandiose than any of the others, made it the capital of the empire. Its reception hall is one of the few indoor locations in the nation vast enough for a dragon's comfort. For those reasons alone it was natural that Gloroc choose the room as his lair, but that is only part of the story.

"The reception hall contains a portal. Alemar knew that dragons have a penchant for portals. They and the Shagas came to this world through a portal from Serpent Moon. They can sense these passageways from great distances and make use of them whenever they can. Just after Alemar slew Faroc, Triss arrived on the scene by means of one."

Alemar raised his eyebrows. He had heard the account of the slaying many times, and had always wondered how the female

218

dragon could have responded so quickly to her dying mate's summons.

"Most portals that men know of are useless," Toren continued, "because they lead into solid rock, or ocean bottom, or the mouths of volcanoes, or to places . . . elsewhere. But dragons, as flying creatures, can make use of the relatively large number that exist between points in midair. They prefer to live near one. The reception chamber at Dragonsdeep contains a portal that leads to a corresponding hall in the palace of the nearby city of Seacliff. Alemar deliberately built around both those sites, partly for his own convenience, and partly because the lure would prove irresistible to Gloroc."

"But that's not a trap," Elenya interjected. "That's an escape."

"True. That is one of the reasons Struth hopes Gloroc does not suspect his vulnerability. The portal *is* an escape route. When we surprise him, we must do it so suddenly and completely that he cannot slip out through it. Or if he does, we must be prepared to follow."

"And how are you going to manage that?" Elenya asked skeptically. "How can you even get into the city without being discovered, much less get inside the palace?"

"There is a tunnel under Dragonsdeep, again built by the Dragonslayer. His own escape route, you might say, though he never had cause to use it. It runs from the art gallery adjoining the reception hall to a spot two leagues outside the great dome. We'll come up inside his guards, inside his gates. We've only a few dozen yards of gallery and a long foyer to traverse to get to him."

"It seems too easy," Elenya countered.

"With luck, getting there *will* be easy. The assassination itself will be the hard part." Toren splayed his fingers, holding the gauntlets up to the sunshine filtering through the forest canopy. "That's when these play their part. If I am indeed able to use them to full potential—and if the Dragonslayer designed them correctly in the first place—then Gloroc will be powerless. There is a deposit of thrijish coral under Dragonsdeep, though not as much as under other Elandri cities. As you know, thrijish disrupts dragonmagic. Gloroc thinks he has insulated himself from it, but with the gauntlets, I can heighten the effect of the coral many times over. I can immobilize him while my companions stab him with knives coated with dragonsbane. The uncertainty is that we really don't know just how powerful Gloroc is, or whether I have the needed resources. If he breaks free, if I lose my concentration, if human guards appear at the wrong moment . . . I think you

219

see the challenge. In particular, if he slips through the portal, my capture spell will be shattered. I can follow, but I would have to cast it anew on the other side. Without the element of surprise, Gloroc would surely roast me to a cinder before I could succeed."

Elenya pursed her lips and said nothing.

"Those who accompany me may die," Toren said solemnly. "Even if we succeed, Gloroc's guards or sorcerers could find us before we make it back to the tunnel. I have no choice but to go, but I will demand it of no one else. Geim has volunteered, but I will need others who know the ocean."

"I will go," Tregay announced. "I was born in Elandris." Several others echoed his cry.

"I'll make no choices today," Toren said. "I want all of you to think about it. Tomorrow is soon enough, or the day after. Come to me one by one, when the presence of your comrades is not there to goad you to impulsive decisions."

Alemar felt Wynneth's gaze boring into him. He turned and met it. Her expression intensified.

"Oh, no," she murmured. "I know that look."

"I have to go," he said as they lay in their tent that night, naked bodies pressed against each other for warmth.

"Why?" she hissed. "Alemar. The *baby*."

"I'll be back before the birth."

"Let Elenya go. She wants to see Gloroc dead. She won't believe it unless she's there when it happens."

"Elenya hasn't looked into Omril's mind as I have. I know the layout of the palace, of the city. If something goes wrong, we may need that information."

"But you're needed here," Wynneth insisted. "The Dragon's ships could arrive any day with the reinforcements. The people need their prince."

"They'll accept Elenya. In pitched battle, she's a better leader than I."

She tugged at an errant lock of hair. "I'm sorry. I know you have your duty. I know we have to use every resource. But I just can't be stoic about this."

He stroked her cheek. "You've survived before, when I was gone to the Eastern Deserts."

She sat up abruptly. "Don't try to console me with that! You were supposed to be gone a few months. It turned out to be two and a half years. Besides, we had scarcely become lovers when you left. We had no obligations to each other."

"This obligation can't be transferred."

He hated having to argue his side. Wynneth's every word stung, because he could not deny her right to feel as she did. It irked him to have to put Elandris first. Though he could name every island in the Dragon Sea, and every city beneath it, he had never been to his father's kingdom. Cilendrodel was his home, a frontier province free of the whimsies and affectations of the ancient kingdoms, a place where he could disappear into the groves and sing with the rythni. Except for a brief months during his apprenticeship with Gast in the Eastern Deserts, he had never been happy anywhere else.

"I don't *want* to go," he said hoarsely.

She opened her mouth to say something more, but her shoulders drooped in defeat. "Of *course* not, you wood maggot," she cursed, but the spite was gone from her tone. Suddenly she leaned down and pressed her lips against his. They lingered that way, and when she at last pulled away, a different kind of fire smoldered in her eyes. She cupped her hand around his groin, and squeezed gently until she obtained the response she wanted.

"You're here now," she sighed. She shifted her round belly out of the way with an experienced air and pulled him toward her.

Toren and Deena snuggled together, savoring the afterglow. She wiped a light beading of sweat from her cleavage and wiped it impishly over his nose. He jumped in surprise.

"Thoughts elsewhere already?" she asked.

He ran his fingertips along the side of her body and down her leg from the knob of her pelvis to her knee. "I'm afraid so," he admitted.

Her light-hearted gleam dimmed. She turned his head away from the gauntlets, which lay quiescent beside them. "Are you sure you won't let me come with you?"

He shook his head. "It's as I said before. I would worry about your safety. I need as few distractions as possible."

"And the revolt here could use an archer of my caliber," she said, finishing his speech for him.

"Yes."

She rolled over and shook a twig from her short brown locks. "To be truthful, in some ways it is easy to part ways now. I will lose sleep over your safety, of course, but if fortune favors us, we'll be reunited. Much better for me than to see you depart for the Wood, never to return." Even in the dim illumination, Toren could read her posture. She was not reconciled to either course.

"I haven't decided what I will do once this task is over," he said. He stroked her spine. "If I went back to the land of the Fhali, would you come with me?"

"I've been there," she said in Vanihr.

"Your accent is terrible," he said, realizing as he spoke that she had deliberately exaggerated it.

"That's my point. I don't belong there. But if you asked me to go, I would."

She lifted her head to peer at him. He stared back, lips poised to respond, but he thought of nothing to say. She nestled up against him and they began a long and largely unsuccessful attempt to sleep.

The surface of the sea loomed just above Elenya's head, thick with foam. The breakers boomed, loud despite being muffled by the water. She adjusted her airmaker and glanced back at her team. They rose in perfect formation. The dive had wasted away most of the morning, but it was time well spent. Her students had shown how well they had absorbed their lessons.

Behind her swam Toren, Geim, and the three men chosen to fill out the raiding party. The latter included Tregay and a pair of Elandri refugees named Match and Ebben. All were longtime rebels of unquestioned loyalty. They scarcely needed to hone their underwater skills. The trio knew the sea better than Elenya, and had proved it during the week of training with their suggestions and demonstrations. But they participated in every dive, to adjust to working as a team.

Dalih accompanied them, though he was not going to Elandris. Elenya had simply felt it efficient to teach him to use airmakers and vests as well.

Her head broke the surface. Hot, invigorating sunshine pummeled her back as she waded into the shallows, doffing her airmaker. She sighed gratefully at the warm rays; Achird had finally burned back the persistent layer of fog rolling in from the Dragon Sea.

Alemar stood on the bluff, high above the crashing surf, shading his eyes against the glare. She waved a signal of all's well.

The others joined her on the beach, clambering onto a pitted outcropping of rock to rescue their feet from the scorching white sand. Dalih helped her remove her vest and weights.

"Well? Do you like it better yet?" she asked the Surudainese.

"The sands I know are dry," he declared, "and water is meant for drinking."

She chuckled. "Perhaps I should show you how to fence underwater."

"Then it might be worth it," he stated.

She stepped over to a nearby tidepool to stow her gear in the net that waited there, so that the dry air would not hurt the devices. Toren and Geim passed theirs to her as well. She nodded approvingly to them.

"You're quick learners. One can never know too much, of course, but you've grasped the basics. You've a hundred leagues during which to become proficient. There's no need to delay the mission any longer."

Toren glanced down at the gauntlets. Wet and cleansed by the swim, the mail cast scintillations of gold and spectra toward the sky. "Good," he said simply.

The two Vanihr rejoined the others in order to hear Ebben and Match's critique. Elenya, body dried by the ocean winds, slid into the tunic she had left on the beach and started up the switchbacks and ledges to Alemar's vantage point. As she left she heard Dalih ask Ebben a question in High Speech. She smiled at his butchery of Calinin syntax.

Her face was solemn by the time she reached her brother. "That's it," she said. "You can leave in the morning."

Alemar stared into the fog bank hovering offshore. She knew it was not the fog he saw, but Elandris far beyond. How ironic that she, who relished new sights and sea travel, should be the one to stay. At the same time, she was not complaining.

"I imagined I saw the Dragon's fleet out there," he said. "But it was only the mists."

She bowed her head, thinking of the work ahead of her while he was gone. "It won't be long until they really do appear," she said. And when they did, she would struggle to keep the resistance alive. For the moment the populace dreamed they could shake off the Dragon's yoke, but an invasion in force could dampen their enthusiasm very quickly. "Gods, I wish you weren't leaving."

"Nor I," Alemar muttered. He raised his right hand and stretched his fingers. The hand was still not as tan as the left, but its color had deepened in the week since Toren had arrived. He glanced down at the beach.

"What do you think of him?" he asked, indicating Toren.

"Sometimes he speaks of his abilities as if they were facts. Other times he doubts himself. Let's hope you reach Dragonsdeep on one of his good days."

"The rythni like him."

She tapped him meaningfully on the top of his head. "You're wasting energy. It's not as if we have a choice about who to send."

Alemar sighed. "I wish I had Treynaf's globe here now. Toren could probably use it, you know, if he's that closely matched with the Dragonslayer."

"The globe works when *it* wants to. Ask what will happen on this quest and it will show you your great-grandson climbing a tree."

"At least that would be something," he said. "I would know that either I will survive, or my unborn child will, and that my descendant will live where there are trees."

A cold gust curled up off the ocean. Alemar took her hand and led her away from the bluff, into the edge of the great forest. "If I don't come back, try to get Wynneth and my son out of Cilendrodel," he said pensively. "Send them to Lord Dran in Aleoth."

"You'll come back," she said firmly. They both knew she had no reason to sound so confident.

They embraced, arms wrapped tight, chins draped over each other's shoulders. He shook in her grip. Their mindlink opened, but all Elenya received was a gush of fear, no words.

She held him until the salt of his tears dried on her collar. Finally she drifted out of his grip. She readjusted her tunic. A sore, bruised spot ached inside her chest, just behind the heart.

"I'll let you deal with the final preparations," he said. "I'll be with Wynneth tonight."

≋ XXX ≋

Pre-dawn. Alemar, Toren, Geim, and the rest of the raiding party shuffled through a dense bank of fog to a tiny private dock. Their transport, a small fishing vessel, did not loom out of the mist until they were almost on top of it. The craft's owner, his beard prematurely grey at the edges from years of exposure to the weather, waited at the tiller while his two grown sons readied the oars. The tide beckoned them to be outward bound.

Tregay, Match, Ebben, and Geim boarded. Alemar and Toren paused on the creaking planks. Elenya, Wynneth, and Deena stood solemnly at the juncture of dock and shore, wan figures in the lantern glow. All others had given their farewells the night before.

Toren kissed Deena. She smiled, tears welling. "Your totem is not yet passed," she said, barely managing not to choke. "Don't you dare die yet."

"I don't plan to," Toren said, and parted with a lingering brush of fingers on fingers. He stepped awkwardly into the boat and sat down on a pile of netting.

Alemar sighed, glad that the mists concealed the forest. He imagined he heard a mournful rythni song coming from the trees. A minuscule crab scuttled over his foot and into a crack between the planks.

"Hold your head up," Elenya said, chiding him. "Gloroc would laugh if he could see you now."

He met her gaze. To his surprise, tears trickled down her cheeks, too. She had changed a great deal in the past month. Their amulets flashed, and suddenly they were speaking mind to mind.

"I want one of the Dragon's teeth to put above my hearth," she bespoke. *"Think you can get one without skewering yourself on it?"*

"I'll bring you two," he answered with a buoyancy he did not feel. *"Just find a hearth to hold them, and keep it safe until I return."*

"A bargain," she said aloud, and turned away, fading quickly into the murk, leaving Wynneth alone with him.

His wife said nothing, nor did she come forward. Finally he stepped over to her. He held her, and slowly, she returned the embrace, as if she wanted to withhold it but could not bring herself to retreat completely.

"I'll return," he promised her. "And when I do, I'll never leave you again."

She frowned, skepticism blatant. Then she kissed him fiercely and virtually ran after her sister-in-law. Her lantern's glow lingered on the edge of visibility for the count of three heartbeats.

Alemar bowed his head again and hopped into the boat. The fisherman grunted and ordered his sons to cast off. They cleared the dock and as soon as the fisherman's brawny offspring gave three heaves on the oars, the dock and the coast vanished behind them.

Morning came. The mist brightened from shades of charcoal dust to light ash. A breeze awakened, died, and awakened again.

The crew set aside the oars and hoisted their sail. Heavily loaded, the craft rode low. Occasional gusts drenched the occupants. The swells drove bile into throats.

Alemar hunkered near the prow, ignoring the salty spray, thinking of Wynneth.

Toren looked ill. Geim seemed better off, but of all the party, only Match and Ebben, veterans of the sea, seemed comfortable, if anyone could be in such weather.

They cleared the fog bank two hours after sunrise, emerging into bright, late summer heat and light as suddenly as if a curtain had been drawn back. Behind them the grey mass brooded, daring the sun to burn it off the coast.

The fisherman cast an apprehensive eye at the horizon, as did Alemar. The Dragon's ships patrolled this coast with diligence. They saw no masts or sails.

"Time to go," the fisherman said.

Alemar nodded, slipped a pearl ring off his finger and whistled through it. He repeated it at intervals. Achird rose toward zenith and dried them out. Alemar did not realize until then how chill the splashes and the fog had made him. He indulged in the change. It would be many days before he would be this dry again.

The dorsal fins of dolphins broke the surface in the distance, and Ebben cried out. Alemar lifted the ring again and whistled the tune that Obo had taught him years before. The princes of the sea heard and six of them surrounded the fishing boat.

The fisherman's son released the sheets, and their father pointed the boat directly into the wind. Sails fluttering uselessly, they coasted to a stop, then began slowly drifting backward.

"My thanks," Alemar told the old sea man.

The fisherman doffed his wool cap. "Gut that dragon like a salmon, that's gratitude enough."

"We'll try," Alemar replied. He and the other five stripped off their fisherman's garb, revealing diving skins and vests. They took airmakers, weapons, and flasks of drinking water from a niche hidden beneath one of the benches. Alemar checked both Vanihr to be sure they were appropriately prepared, then slid rump first into the waves.

One by one the others followed. The bubbles cleared. They swam out of the path of the vessel's keel. The dolphins dutifully offered their fins. Each man grasped one and they were off, propelled by the creatures' powerful flukes. A thrill ran down Alemar's spine, recalling the first time he had travelled this way at the age of eight. The hull of the fishing boat disappeared behind them almost before the prince secured his grip. Elandris beckoned them southward.

The first night, Alemar remained awake for hours, though bone weary from the swim. Bright moonlight filtered through the waters of the Dragon Sea, all the way to the bottom. Even here, in the deeper northern region, the sea floor seldom dipped lower than a few dozen fathoms. A ridge poked up to one side, supporting a coral reef that stretched almost to the surface. Dim shapes of fish and squid darted past. Spectral limbs of kelp rose all around them, shifting in the current; the men had tied themselves to them to avoid drifting apart.

It had been too long since Alemar had slept at sea. It was the gentlest bed he could imagine, but he preferred firm support beneath him and blankets above, not steady, even pressure on every side. He resisted the urge to tie himself in a horizontal position. Though his vest grew more or less buoyant as needed, keeping him at a consistent depth without the need to move his limbs, he still felt the urge to tread water. Nearby Toren and Geim shifted restlessly, even less accustomed to the arrangement than he.

The one thing that Alemar did not suffer from was the common fear of Elandri divers that somehow he was breathing water and would suffocate. On the contrary, he relished the air filtering through the membrane of the airmaker. It was sweeter than the salty, fish-tainted atmosphere above the waves.

He reminisced about the Eastern Deserts, thinking of the nights when he would lay, bedroll pressed firmly against the sands, and ache for the touch of water around his body. At last he drifted into sleep, dreaming of cacti and scorched salt plains.

At noon on the third day, they found a tiny islet. Alemar called a halt to take advantage of the chance to eat a meal on solid ground. The dolphins—the fifth set to haul them—splashed off in search of their own dinner, cavorting in their characteristic way. Ebben and Match found a variety of shellfish clinging to the coral in the tidewaters and showed Geim and Toren how to harvest them. Meanwhile, Alemar assembled his watermaker and began transmuting salt water into fresh, in order to refill their flasks.

As they ate, Toren came over and examined Alemar's apparatus. He stroked its rubbery membrane, fascinated.

"Another legacy of the Dragonslayer," Alemar said. "Like the airmakers and the vests."

"But not a talisman," the modhiv said in admiration. He waved his hands over it. "It needs no conscious guidance for its magic to work."

"No. But try making one without high sorcery and you'll face quite a challenge."

"I think I shall make one," Toren murmured.

Alemar raised an eyebrow. Why not? Far better that Toren use his power for such things than to kill dragons all the time. There were perhaps two living magicians who could successfully manufacture the devices. The prince wondered what sort of life the Vanihr would have once the mission ended, assuming its success. He buried the thought. It was not the time to look so far ahead.

Toren stared down at the raw flesh of the small clam he had just broken open.

"Don't like it raw?" Alemar asked. "We usually marinate them."

Toren shrugged and slid the meat down in one gulp. "I can eat anything," he bragged. Nearby, Geim guffawed.

Gigantic dolphin sharks wandered near on the fifth day, delighted to find six of their favorite prey slowed down by passengers. Match and Ebben released capsules of effluvium. As soon as the great fish smelled the oily substance they vanished into the murk.

As the sea bottom rose, marking the borders of Elandris, Alemar worried less about such natural perils and more about human enemies. He consulted the map often, steering their course away from undersea cities. They replaced their steeds four times a day instead of two, to be sure those with them were always fresh. Their luck lasted until they passed between the last two cities still between them and their destination, through a narrow gap of only a few leagues.

Ebben brought his dolphins close to Alemar and signalled to the prince. *Sea dogs*.

Alemar saw a forest of kelp to the right and pointed. The men abandoned their transport, slipping into the concealing growth as fast as possible. The dolphins streaked away.

Four sea dogs—sinuous creatures with bodies like giant eels and whiskers like catfish—glided slowly their way, in a formation that no wild denizens of the sea would adopt. Their whiskers twitched, ferreting out scents that did not belong—especially those of men. Their gift of smell was as acute as their eyes were poor. Small chance existed that they would fail to detect the traces left by Alemar and his party. If they did, they would hurry to the nearest city and guide one of the Dragon's patrols back with them.

Alemar signed to Toren. They focussed their sorcery on their trail, gathering the residue left behind and increasing the weight of each infinitesimal particle until they sank into the silt. Alemar's head rang with the strain of such subtle manipulation, but it was worth the pain. The sea dogs cruised past without the slightest deviation from their course. The other four men smiled at the magicworkers with relief.

After coming this far, nothing so ordinary as ocean bloodhounds were going to keep him from reaching his great enemy. They waited an hour, then Alemar summoned a fresh set of dolphins.

Dragonsdeep came into view quite suddenly, dome sprouting dramatically above the crest of the ridge ahead of them. It was leagues in the distance, but it was already difficult to take in in one glance. Alemar stared, momentarily awestruck. He had never seen any of the cities of Alemar Dragonslayer, much less this, his masterwork. He had thought Omril's memories would prepare him for the sight, but experience shared secondhand did not convey the full impact.

Thousands of people lived under the glasslike ceiling, cultivating and harvesting the surrounding sea, creating crafts and handiworks prized throughout the civilized lands. The palace sprawled in the center, a lavish, architectural wonder—a small city in itself. It spread from a central nexus into eight twining wings, like the limbs of an octopus. The dynasty of Alemar had ruled from the site for many hundreds of years.

The city had not changed its configuration much in all that time. The secret of manufacturing vartham—the hard, transparent substance that made up the domes—had been lost with the great wizard and his sister. Rumors claimed that Gloroc was trying to rediscover the process. If so, he had failed, as Alemar spied no additions to the main enclosure.

The dome peaked less than two fathoms below the surface. Huge ventilation towers sprouted upward, reaching far above the waves. Next to the west, north, and south gates were massive watermakers capable of processing enough drinking water to supply the entire city. Despite the briny sea in every direction, the inhabitants of communities built by Alemar and Miranda never needed to worry about importing water. The younger Alemar shivered to think of the power his ancestor must have had to create such wonders.

Between their locations and the perimeter of the city were broad tracts of cultivated sea bed, and small underwater outposts. The traffic between the city and the surrounding ocean was constant. There was no way to approach the walls without being seen. For a moment, Alemar worried that they might have to get closer, but Toren led them in a wide semicircle that carried them farther away. They forsook the dolphins, hugged the bottom, and kept in the shadows of reefs and stands of kelp, keenly aware of the proximity of the city. They encountered no patrols, though once a spearfisherman passed by in the near distance. They successfully hid from him.

They arrived at a crevice in a reef. Barnacles and coral made the opening too small to accommodate the men. Toren began tearing loose the growth. The others tried to help, but the task required the strength of the gauntlets. Silt clouded the water. As currents carried it upward, Alemar grew worried that, like smoke on a horizon, it would reveal their position. But shortly thereafter, Toren pulled away the last piece.

The Vanihr removed his vest and supplies, except for the airmaker, and squeezed through the opening. Alemar followed, slipping down a cramped tunnel and into a manmade chamber lit by a dim, cerulean glow. Match, Ebben, and Tregay came next. Geim relayed down the cast-off gear and joined them. Once everyone was inside, Toren closed a hatch across the entryway and spun the lock wheel.

Three of the walls were featureless—fused, bare stone or coral. The fourth contained another hatch and spindle similar to that in the ceiling, but larger. Not far from it was a lever. Toren swam to the latter and yanked it downward.

Four small ports opened in the floor and began sucking the water out of the chamber. Another pair of ports appeared in the ceiling, out of which came air. Within a quarter of an hour the group stood with their heads and shoulders out of the water.

They peeled off their airmakers. The atmosphere was stale, but breathable.

"Obviously no one's been here for a very long time. That's a good sign," Toren told Alemar. "By the way, I had to neutralize a guard spell on the way in. Otherwise we would have been squeezed to death in the tunnel."

"That sounds like my ancestor's touch," Alemar said.

"Does it? Well, it's repairing itself. Keep that in mind on the way out."

The water receded to knee level, below the bottom of the hatch in the wall. They found a niche in a corner of the floor into which they placed their airmakers, suits, weights, and vests. Toren opened the side hatch, revealing a tile-walled tunnel. Geim reached in, rubbed his fingers across the smooth floor, and blew on them, producing a cloud of dust.

"Not exactly a well-travelled route," he commented. He lifted his foot as if to cross the threshold.

"Don't," Toren said firmly. He ducked, reached an arm's length into the tunnel, and pressed a tile that Geim might have stepped on had he entered.

A pair of crossbow bolts suddenly shot out of the walls to either side, whisking over Toren's head and impacting so hard they chipped the masonry.

Geim whistled. Ebben cursed.

"The Dragonslayer really didn't want strangers to use this route," Toren explained. "There's a booby trap like this at the other end. I'll have to lead, so I can trip it."

"Be my guest," Geim said.

The drains sucked up the last of the water with loud, indelicate sounds. The men sorted through their gear selecting the bare essentials. In particular, they each broke into carefully wrapped, identical packages and withdrew long, tapered daggers. Each ceramic sheath was sealed with wax. They made sure the seals were intact. The blades were coated with fellit—dragonsbane—a substance which could kill a man with the slightest contact.

They ate a somber, quiet meal and set out down the tunnel.

 **XXXI**

The tendons in the back of Toren's heels ached, unaccustomed, after so much swimming, to a normal, dry tread. He welcomed the discomfort; it proved he was a man, not a fish. But he did not like the low ceiling. His lower back rebelled from the constant stooping. Of all the party, only Alemar was able to walk upright.

Geim cursed as he bumped his head again. "Let me guess.

The Dragonslayer was a short man, and this is his revenge on the rest of us."

"Is this tunnel ever going to end?" Tregay asked.

Toren felt sorry for his companions. To them, the dim illumination and featureless walls must have made them feel as if the tube were constantly squeezing in on them. It was not that way for him. As they had approached the city, and eventually passed under its foundations, he sensed more and finer details about the place they were breaching. He detected several routine magical spells in progress. He estimated that several dozen sorcerers lived in the city, including fourteen adepts worthy of a king's court. Three were as powerful as Omril. He felt one particularly potent miasma of power.

"The Dragon is in residence," he told Alemar. "I smell him."

"Good," the prince said flatly. Toren caught a certain ambivalence in his tone.

The palms of Toren's hands broke out in a sweat inside the gauntlets. Another league and his journey would be over. He tried to focus on the center of the energies, learn what he could about the exact strength of Gloroc's magic. His probing yielded unexpected results.

"Strange," he muttered.

"What?" Alemar inquired.

"The Dragon's emanations are diffused. I can't pinpoint them. What could be causing that? I can locate every other source of magic with complete clarity."

"I don't know. You'd think such a powerful nexus would stand out like a beacon."

"Yes." Distracted, Toren bumped his head again.

When his forehead stopped throbbing, he probed once more. The source refused to resolve itself sharper than a wide, vaguely defined sphere. He estimated the zone to be about a hundred feet in diameter. He would need greater precision than that once they reached the great hall and he tried to snare his prey.

The tunnel angled upward. Belly cramps plagued Toren as they climbed. He murmured prayers to his ancestors. What had he gotten himself into? Surely, if he was right for the gauntlets, he would be able to pinpoint his enemy. A bitter, adrenaline tang filled the back of his throat.

"Geim?" Toren called.

"Yes?" the other Vanihr called from the back of the group.

"I just want you to know that whatever happens to you up ahead, it's your own fault for capturing me back in the Wood."

"I've been thinking what a stupid thing that was to do," Geim replied dryly.

Toren tried to laugh, but he coughed instead. An image of his and Deena's farewell lovemaking welled up, but the memory of her musk drowned in the stale sea reek of the passageway. Maybe he did not need to know if the gauntlets worked. If he hid well enough in the Wood, Gloroc might never find him until long after he had died of old age.

And Rhi and his descendants would bear the totem of a coward.

He sighed, trudging on, arms trembling from the anticipation. The Dragon's radiations grew in intensity, all without resolving to a proper locus.

The tunnel ended almost before he expected it. "Stop," he told the others, and triggered the second crossbow trap. Three paces farther he found a hatch like that at the other end. The gauntlets dealt with the lock.

He stepped out into a small, empty room lit with the same bluish phosphorescence as the tunnel. The werelight bothered him. It was powered by a subtle, pervasive spell. Who was this Dragonslayer, to cast spells that lingered centuries after his death? Struth illuminated her subterranean chamber the same way. He would have to ask her how he might reproduce the light.

The aura of dragonmagic was overriding, no longer muffled by layers of sea bottom. Toren rubbed the palms of his gauntlets together. They cracked with static. Near, so near. He wished his knees would quit shaking.

Alemar smelled the Dragon's presence as well, even without a gauntlet to augment his senses. The inner lining of his cheeks turned to cotton. He hesitated at the mouth of the tunnel until, realizing that he was blocking the progress of the others, he shuffled forward. Match, Ebben, and Geim all sighed gratefully as they emerged, able at last to straighten their spines.

Toren waited in the center of the room, eyes closed, gauntlets still pressed together. Beyond him stood an apparently open archway. Alemar approached it, alert for signs of sorcery. Beyond the threshold lay a gallery filled with statues and sculptures, paintings and tapestries. By stark contrast, the room they were in was empty. Dust puffed with each footstep. The light in the gallery was bright, artfully balanced to best display the collection of masterpieces, but none of it came within the dusty alcove. Alemar could see his companions strictly because of the werelight.

He reached into the archway. His hand flattened against a solid wall. Tregay, equally intrigued, tapped his knuckles lightly against an adjacent spot. "Hard as rock," he muttered.

"An astounding bit of thaumaturgy."

Toren's voice made Alemar jump. "Don't worry about making noise," the modhiv added, noticing the prince's reaction. He joined them at the threshold. "No one in the palace can see or hear us. To them this archway is just another section of the wall. Even Gloroc would never suspect our presence, even if he coiled up ten paces away." Toren leaned nearer the invisible wall, admiration sparkling in his eyes. "It must have taken weeks to cast the spell that made this illusion."

Alemar, equally amazed, lifted his amulet out of his collar and placed the gem against the surface. Not so much as a flicker came from the talisman. The mirage was so well-wrought that it swallowed its own telltale emanations.

"How do we get through it?"

"It's keyed to the gauntlets. As long as I hold my hand in the opening, a person can pass through."

Alemar recognized the gallery from Omril's memories. "The Dragon's chambers are scarcely two hundred yards away." He licked his excruciatingly dry lips. His hand settled uneasily on the hilt of his poisoned dagger.

"Once we step through, Gloroc will sense the talismans," Toren stated. "I'll have to weave a cloaking spell. That will take me at least two hours. It should hold long enough for us to run to the hall. Let's rest first. It's only early evening."

Alemar wondered how Toren could tell the precise time of day when they had been in the tunnel so long, but it matched his own gut feeling. He sighed. The delay would wreak havoc on their nerves, but the strategy was wise. They would attack in the dead of night when the palace activity was at its nadir.

The prince settled stiffly against one of the walls. Tregay offered him a strip of dried fish, but he declined. Who could eat now?

An hour dragged by. Ebben chewed short seven of his fingernails and started on the eighth. A drudge entered the gallery, swept up a few motes of dust and wiped down several sculptures, including the one immediately in front of the alcove, a remarkably lifelike rendering of a kelp shark. Alemar instinctively shrank up against the wall, but the woman departed without once glancing in their direction.

Geim continued to scowl at one of the statues across the room long after the servant had cleaned it. He nudged Toren. "Take a look at that," he said.

Alemar also glanced where Geim indicated. He saw a full-size figurine of a slim, petite woman in a flowing gown, a delicate scepter in her grip. The prince recognized it immediately; small versions existed throughout Elandris and Cilendrodel. His father had given one to his mother.

As Toren stared at it, his jaw slowly fell open. He uttered something in Vanihr that could only have been an expletive.

"Is something wrong?" Alemar asked.

"Do you know whom that statue is modelled after?"

"Of course. That's Miranda, sister of Alemar Dragonslayer."

Toren exhaled suddenly. He and Geim exchanged a meaningful glance. The modhiv rubbed his head so firmly he creased his scalp.

"Does that mean something to you?" Alemar asked.

"Yes. But I'm afraid this isn't the time or place to discuss the matter."

Alemar frowned. Toren's tone closed the subject. The prince let it rest. Too many other thoughts and memories crowded his mind. Once Toren began weaving the spell of concealment, it was all Alemar could do to sit in one place.

The strands of the spell fell into place one by one and became a seamless fabric. Toren would have grinned if he had not been so frightened. With the gauntlets, his magic flowed like the waterfall of Headwater, straight and unstoppable. He stoked his internal fires. Once he and his companions passed out of the room, no time would remain for slow, careful spellweaving.

I am coming, Gloroc.

Just short of two hours after he had begun, he tied the final ethereal knot, and the cloaking spell shrouded them. "I'm ready," he announced.

The others stood and, fingers shaking with nervousness, untied the bindings around their knife hilts. One good yank and each blade would rush free of its sheath.

Toren thrust his hand into the gap of the archway. "Your lead, my prince."

Alemar stepped through. The others quickly followed. Toren thrust aside all distractions and moved forward. A silky feeling enveloped him, like cobwebs being drawn across his entire body, then melted away. Behind him stood a bare marble wall. His companions stared at him oddly. It must have seemed to them as if he had sprouted directly out of the stone.

"Let's go," he whispered, and walked briskly toward the exit, as fast as he could go without disturbing his concentration. The gauntlets moaned. Alemar and the others cleaved to him, so that he would not have to extend his sorcery too far. They left the gallery and entered a short, vaulted corridor leading to the foyer of the great hall.

A wave of force tore at his cloaking screen. He bolstered it, stifling a wave of panic. He was certain he had woven it correctly. Nevertheless, it began breaking up. "Run!" he shouted as they crossed into the foyer. "The Dragon knows we are here!"

He abandoned the deteriorating spell, casting all his energies into the real challenge. He gathered the feeble emanations coming from the thrijish coral beneath the city and condensed them, intensified them, and focussed them on the great hallway. The snare closed. Only moments had passed since Gloroc had sensed them. If the gauntlets worked, the Dragon was immobilized.

The talismans throbbed. He shuddered and trebled his effort. An inarticulate cry of pain escaped his lips.

"Hold on!" Alemar cried.

Toren clenched his teeth. The gauntlets blazed, their golden beams overwhelming the great candles in their wall sconces.

A wave of retaliatory magic struck like a hammer against his skull. Lightning sprang from every corner of the room. It hissed and snapped inches from his skin. He landed on his side. Alemar and the others were slammed back down the hallway.

Toren staggered to his knees, ignoring the lacerations on his cheek. The stench of sulphur and singed clothing smote him. He clenched the gauntlets together, hanging desperately to his spell. His snare held, barely. He crawled forward. He had to get nearer. The spell was weaker than it should have been. But the closer he got to the Dragon, the tighter he could focus his strength.

Another counterattack rocked him to the floor. Suddenly everything vanished. Fog surrounded him, a grey mist so thick he could not see his own hands. He wormed his way forward, refusing to be stopped.

"Which way?" Alemar demanded, voice weak and distant. Toren snarled, finally realizing the nature of the counterattack. He was crawling the wrong way. Alemar cast energy toward him. He seized it, supplemented it, and blocked the counterattack. The mist evaporated. He and his fellow assassins lay sprawled in the center of the foyer.

236

Match stared sightlessly upward, hands around his throat, face purple from suffocation. The aura of life fizzled out before Toren could attempt to break the spell.

The modhiv shuddered. The snare snapped. Crying in fear, he wove a new one, felt it settle once more on its victim.

You won't get away, he vowed. Spittle dotted his lips. He gasped and climbed to his feet, skin crawling with minuscule, flea-bite pinpricks of terror. How could Gloroc be so powerful?

Within three steps, the marble floor disappeared. He fell. Slick, cavelike walls whisked by beside him. Below loomed a floor strewn with spearlike stalagmites. He twisted, but the points were too closely placed. One of them was aimed straight for his heart.

Toren cast a screen of interference. The illusion shattered. He was once again on the floor of the corridor. He was not falling, but he was holding the tip of his drawn dagger in front of his own chest. The blade gleamed with a coating of whitish unguent. The potent odor of the dragonsbane nearly emptied his stomach.

Alemar and the others cried out. They were safe, but barely; Tregay's knife point lay only a finger width from his skin.

Sweat streamed down Toren's neck. With Alemar hot on his heels, he bolted to his feet and charged toward the great doors.

Just ahead the floor opened, and a chasm much like the previous one appeared. This time Toren could tell it was real. It was too late for him or Alemar to stop. "Jump!" Toren ordered, and leaped into the air. As their feet came down, circular disks of energy flew out from the gauntlets, providing pads to land on. Four steps took them across. Geim and Tregay loped just behind. Ebben hovered at the edge, trembling, not willing to bridge the gap.

Toren abandoned the rebel. The Dragon's maneuvers had weakened. No time to hesitate. He jammed the gauntlets against the entrance. The doors flew open.

"Look out!" Toren shouted. He dived to the side, as did the three men just behind him. A purple bolt of dragonflame shot past them. It caught Ebben standing in the foyer. He exploded.

Momentarily blinded by the brilliance, Toren instinctively brought the gauntlets up and bolstered the snare for all he was worth. A keening scream deafened them. Toren opened his eyes.

The hall stretched before him, incredibly high and long. In the center of the room a dragon writhed, caught in the center of Toren's phantom net. It beat its wings furiously against the stone floor, screeching in agony and outrage.

And on the right side, close to one of the walls, loomed a *second* dragon, jaws outstretched in feral hatred, eyes glittering. The edges of the snare barely contained its massive body.

"By my grandfather!" Toren cried, just as the second dragon spat. A bolt raced straight toward Toren, who threw power desperately into his ward, spreading it out to shield his surviving companions. The flame thundered off, corona dancing to the vaulted ceiling. Char rained down.

Toren's snare, despite his best efforts, collapsed to half its size. The second dragon spun. A portal suddenly popped into existence. The great serpent dived through it. An instant later the window snapped out of existence.

At long last, the power flowing through the gauntlets focussed into a single, irrepressible beam. Toren, blinking, strands of his long hair curled into wisps from the heat of the dragonflame, nearly fainted from the force of the energies. He tightened his snare. The remaining dragon screamed and sagged to the floor, pinned, thrashing weakly.

Toren stumbled forward. "Knives!" he shouted.

Alemar, Geim, and Tregay brushed past, brandishing their daggers. They hovered just out of the dragon's range. Feeble as the creature's movements were, one sweep of its tail or wings could crush them.

Toren, barely able to lift his feet off the floor, continued on until he felt the wind of the dragon's panting. It raised its forward claw a few inches and dropped it. Toren reached out and buried his fingers in the flesh of its neck. It stiffened and with a final whimper ceased all movement, save for the fluttering of its eyelids.

"Now!" Toren shouted.

Alemar plunged forward and sank his dagger to the hilt in the dragon's belly. Tregay and Geim followed through on the other side. They abandoned the weapons and darted back out of the way.

Their haste was unnecessary. The Dragon did not shift. Finally it sank into a limp pile. Its head glanced off Toren's ward and came to rest at his feet.

Toren opened his hands. The web of energy coalesced and disappeared into the gauntlets. He swayed. Alemar and Geim caught him as he fell and dragged him away from his dead opponent.

Tears rolled down the modhiv's face. He had done it. He had been the correct candidate. Had there been only one dragon,

238

Match and Ebben need not have died. He brushed the gauntlets against his bruised face. His cheeks were numb. All of him was numb.

"Two dragons," Alemar whispered.

The pounding of many boots rang in the foyer. Geim and Tregay sprinted to the great doors and slammed them shut. Toren cast a lock spell.

"That will hold them," he said, and coughed up a slug of vile phlegm. "At least until a wizard arrives."

"We've got to get out of here!" Geim said.

"Not yet," Toren said grimly. He turned to the side wall and concentrated. The portal opened.

Through the opening they saw a room much like the one in which they stood. Over a hundred men-at-arms crowded up to the opening. Four finely robed figures waited behind them, auras bright with the power of high wizards, one of them no doubt of the Ril. The escaped dragon towered at the rear of the room. One arrow-quick shake of its snout told Toren that it had completely recovered from the attack.

As soon as the window opened, the guards rushed forward. The lead row simply disappeared, out of view. The one-way nature of the portal prevented their entry. The second row halted, shaking their pikes and swords, shouting in anger.

Toren locked eyes with his giant enemy. "Gloroc," he said.

"Foul little creatures!" the Dragon hissed. *"My parents were not enough for the likes of you! You have killed my sister as well! Escape if you can, but I shall find you!"*

Tregay and Geim staggered backwards, caught unprepared by the waves of hate accompanying the words, which penetrated where physical substance could not. Toren let it wash over him without effect.

"I've been a fool," the modhiv murmured under his breath. Alemar stared at him quizzically.

Toren smiled wryly, realizing how artfully he had been duped. Of course Struth would want a candidate to use the gauntlets. Since Faroc and Triss had had more than one offspring, Toren's enlistment was simply a means of evening the odds.

Gloroc snapped his jaws. His indigo eyes flashed. *"Tell the Dragonslayer he won't be so lucky next time! I know now that he lives, and I shall find him, also!"*

Alemar let out an astonished squeak. He stared up at Gloroc. The Dragon leaned forward.

"A spawn of the wizard in the flesh! Come to me, little one. Wouldn't you like to throttle me?"

Alemar lunged forward, hands outstretched.

"No," Toren yelled. He waved his hand. The portal shut just before the prince reached it. Alemar tumbled forward, checked his momentum, and sagged against the wall. He shook, realizing that he had been hypnotized, sobered to see how willingly he had been rushing toward his doom.

Men battered loudly at the doors. Toren pictured an entire city of enemy soldiers, sorcerers, and magical creatures chasing them and tried not to be sick.

"Now can we leave?" Geim demanded.

"We'll head for the tunnel," Toren said authoritatively. "Gather inside my ward. We might make it if we don't run into a sorcerer of the Ril."

"What did Gloroc mean?" Alemar asked as they collected in a tight diamond-formation. "The Dragonslayer lives? How can that be?"

"That's what I couldn't tell you earlier," Toren said as he dispelled the lock on the doors. "Struth is an illusion."

≈≈ EPILOGUE ≈≈

Keron sat stiffly on his cushioned divan, high in the ambassador's minaret in the city of Tazh Tah, overlooking the once fertile plains of Simorilia. He saw a battlefield. The Dragon's army camped where crops should be growing, held at bay by local forces desperate to keep their capital out of enemy hands. Yet, morale was high in the city. Boisterous, drunken sounds of revelry wafted up the masonry of the minaret from the streets. The shah had broken the siege, partly as a result of Keron's strategies, and the army of the Calinin Empire was on its way. According to the latest reports, the first contingent of troops was halfway through Numaron, and would reach them in a fortnight.

Keron stood abruptly and paced, oblivious to the celebration. In his alcove, Treynaf stared into his globe equally aloof. The king glanced once more at the battlefield. The first campfires of evening sparkled in the dusk, and their number confirmed the report that Val had just given him. The king turned and faced his son, who stood dutifully at attention, boots still dusty from his reconnaissance.

"I don't like it," Keron said. "It doesn't feel right."

"Do you think it's a trick?" Val asked.

"I don't know." He picked up his mug of hot wine and sipped. He scowled; the liquid had gone tepid. "It's not the time for the Dragon to withdraw a third of his troops. You say they're on a forced march back to the coast?"

"It seems that way. Perhaps he's worried about the emperor's army."

Keron set down his mug. "All the more reason to increase his strength. I expected him to try to take Tazh Tah before our allies arrive."

Val shrugged. Keron considered dismissing him, letting the boy share in the festivity. Whatever else, the Dragon's retreat meant a lull in the fighting, and Val had earned some relaxation.

"Perhaps this has something to do with the situation in Cilendrodel," the king mused. Word had recently come of Alemar's victory over the Dragon's sorcerer, and of the subsequent revolt. Keron pictured the withdrawn troops heading north.

Cilendrodel was a backwoods province. It did not have the means for a sustained fight against the Dragon's empire.

Toren would have arrived there by now. Keron's grandson would be born soon.

Disquieting energies thrummed down the haft of his scepter.

"Dragons!"

Treynaf stood up, knocking over his small table. The globe struck the flagstones and glanced off a wall so hard that, had it been ordinary crystal as opposed to a talisman, it would have shattered. Keron and Val jumped.

"Two dragons!" Treynaf cried. "To arms, cousin! March to Elandris! Do not wait for the dawn!"

Keron felt a cold, hard, satisfying knot in his gut. The scepter warbled. Two dragons? Time to sort the meaning later. For once, he knew unequivocally that his relative had seen with true Sight. Enough waiting. The time for action had come.

"Pass the order," he told Val. "We attack tonight."

GLOSSARY & CAST OF MINOR CHARACTERS

Achird The sun. The star around which Motherworld revolves.

Alemar Dragonslayer Founder of Elandris; slayer of the dragons Faroc and Triss. Also Alemar the Great, Alemar I.

Alahihr A union of tribes of the same race as the Vanihr, living in the Flat. The Alahihr practice of clearing land directly opposes the religious tenets of the Vanihr. The two peoples are bitter enemies.

Amane A Vanihr tribe of cannibals.

amethery An herb of the Cilendri forests, often used to prompt abortion.

burrost Dried tree serpent, a Vanihr staple.

Cadra Progenitor of the Zyraii.

Calinin 1. An ancient nation in the far west of the southern continent. 2. The empire which originated in Calinin, composed, at various times, of the countries Calinin South, Aleoth, Cotan, Acalon, Tanjand, Agon, Neith, Tiandria, Serthe, Riannehn, Sirithrea, Numaron, Irigion, Rhida, Rhada, and Moin, as well as the motherland. 3. Those lands culturally and linguistically tied to the empire, including the countries above as well as Ranagara, Elandris, and Cilendrodel. 4. A commonwealth of the old kingdoms of the empire. Calinin, Calinin South, Cotan, Aleoth, Tanjand, and Acalon continue to be governed by the emperor in Xais; Riannehn, Serthe, Neith, Sirithrea, Tiandria, and Numaron are independent countries tied by treaties.

cheli Among the southern Vanihr tribes, a person who is not capable of housing the memories of his ancestors, normally because of brain damage or mental retardation. Such persons are considered to be less than human and are not permitted to breed.

collberry A low-lying tree of the Wood whose fruit is often eaten or fermented.

Dark Night A holiday, celebrated on those occasions when

Achird, the Sister, Motherworld, and all the major moons are below the horizon. Most cultures observe it annually, though due to orbital dynamics, there is sometimes more than one dark night in a year. Likewise, many Dark Nights are not dark at all; total lack of suns, moons, and mother planet is never common, and in some years happens not at all, or for only a few minutes. One of the major preoccupations of early Tanagaranese astronomers was the calculation of when dark nights would occur.

Dragonsdeep Capital city of Elandris under Gloroc's rule. Originally called Wizardsdeep, it was the last city built by Alemar Dragonslayer, and served as capital of his empire for many centuries.

eret-Zyraii The western fringe of Zyraii territory, uninhabitable because of its extremely arid climate.

erron Small copper coin, smallest monetary unit of some of the Old Kingdoms.

Faroc The male of the pair of dragons that once ruled the Dragon Sea, slain by Alemar the Great.

Fhali A Vanihr tribe of the southern Wood, to which Toren belongs.

Firsthold Original capital of Elandris.

the Flat An unforested region in the center of the Wood, home of the Alahihr.

forest stalker A very large, highly venomous spider indigenous to the Wood, known for stalking and killing large mammals.

Garthmorron A large barony in central Cilendrodel, birthplace of Alemar and Elenya.

Hab-no-ken Healing sect of the Zyraii priesthood, distinguished by their green clothing.

hai-Zyraii A state conferred upon an individual through blood ritual, in recognition of deeds that greatly benefit the Zyraii nation.

hayeri A small, deerlike animal of the Wood.

High Speech Originally the formal court language of the Calinin Empire, now the *lingua franca* of the civilized lands.

Ijitia 1. A nation along the east bank of the River Sha. 2. The ancient empire originating along the Sha, spreading over the Mountains of the Gods into Agon, Tanjand, and Aleoth. Also included Tunaets and Fornaets.

Lerina Mother of Alemar and Elenya.

Miranda Sister of Alemar Dragonslayer; inventor of the airmaker; co-founder of Elandris.

modhiv The warrior caste within the southern and central Vanihr tribes of the Wood. Plural: modhiv.

mong A huge, maneating fish indigenous to the River Sha.

Motherworld The gas giant planet around which Tanagaran revolves.

New Kingdoms The countries which were part of the Calinin frontier at the time of its greatest expansion, including Irigion, Numaron, Rhada, Rhida, and Moin.

oeikani (wah-kah-nee) A large, herbivorous mammal found throughout Tanagaran, used as a saddle and pack beast, and occasionally as a source of food. Plural: oeikani.

Ogshiel A Vanihr tribe of the northern Wood, bordering the River Sha. Legendary enemies of the Shagas.

Old Kingdoms The northern continent monarchies conquered early by the Calinin, consisting of Riannehn, Neith, Sirithrea, Tiandria, and Serthe.

opsha The military leader of the Zyraii nation. Until Lonal's ascendancy, it was considered a mythical title, because of internecine rivalry among the various tribes.

Po-no-pha (Po-no-fa) The warrior class among the Zyraii, distinguished by their white clothing.

Retreat A ritual hermitage observed by Hab-no-ken in order to recuperate from overuse of their powers.

the Ril Gloroc's elite cadre of sorcerers.

Serpent Moon A moon of Motherworld, original home of dragons and shagas.

Shaga A race of lesser dragons, roughly man-size, that came from Serpent Moon. They built a great civilization along the River Sha, which thrived until overrun by Ijitians from the north and Vanihr from the south. The refugees relocated in the Valley of Serpents.

Shahera A prophet who lived at the height of the Calinin Empire, a century before the founding of Elandris. Considered the greatest master of the Sight ever to have lived, her auguries often dealt with the fate of nations and entire peoples. Her declaration that the Calinin Empire had already reached its maximum extent earned her the wrath of the emperor, who had her executed.

the Sister Achird's orange companion star, visible from Tanagaran even in daylight.

Tanagaran The world. Fifth moon of Motherworld.

thrijish A type of coral whose proximity negates a dragon's ability to absorb sorcerous power from water.

T'lil The second largest tribe of modern Zyraii, descended from Cadra's seventh son, Lil. Lonal's tribe.

Triss Female of the pair of dragons that once ruled the Dragon Sea.

Urthey Smallest major moon of Motherworld.

Vanihr A golden-skinned, blond-haired race inhabiting the Wood, the archipelagoes, and much of the Far Western Lands. Disdaining large-scale agriculture and deeply devoted to traditional ways of life, the Vanihr have remained a Stone Age culture, separated into many small tribes. Plural: Vanihr.

vartham A transparent, incredibly strong substance created by Miranda and Alemar the Great, used to form the domes that enclose the underwater cities. Like the airmakers, the secret of its creation was lost with the two great sorcerers.

Xais 1. Capital of the Calinin Empire. 2. Ancient capital of Aleoth. 3. Former northern capital of the Ijitian Empire; its conquest by the Calinin drastically altered the balance of power in the regions surrounding the inner sea.

Yent A province in central Cilendrodel.

Yetem A false name used by Elenya during her years in the Eastern Deserts.

Zee-no-ken Monastic sect of the Zyraii priesthood, uninvolved in political and social life, often hermits. Many are skilled sorcerers.

Zyraii 1. A nomad nation of the Eastern Deserts. 2. The people or language of the Zyraii nation.